I0663843

# SUMMARY

## Book XI in the Vampire Queen Series

*What she wants is what he needs...*

Ranch owner Quinn Pedraza has to find someone to run the bar he won in a bet, but more than that, he wants a woman who can handle his alpha personality...and closet submissive sexual cravings.

When vampire Selene Torres arrives on the scene, he gets everything he wants—and learns what he really needs.

*Publisher's Note:* When Desiree Holt's cowboys meet up with Joey W. Hill's vampires, sparks are sure to fly. See the end matter of this book to find more great reads from Desiree!

# NIGHTFALL

*A Vampire Queen Crossover Novel*

## JOEY W. HILL
## DESIREE HOLT

**Nightfall**

A Vampire Queen Series Novel - Book #11

Copyright © 2014-2019 Joey W. Hill & Desiree Holt

ALL RIGHTS RESERVED

Edited by Briana St. James

Cover design by W. Scott Hill

Original publication September 2014 by Ellora's Cave Publishing, Inc.

SWP Digital & Print Edition publication January 2016 by Story Witch Press, 452 Mattamushkeet Dr., Little River, South Carolina 29566, USA

Digital ISBN: 978-1-942122-24-1

Print ISBN: 978-1-942122-25-8

# CHAPTER ONE

*Q*uinn Pedraza stared at the stack of bills and swore colorfully to himself. He didn't need this aggravation. The After Hours Saloon had become nothing but a pain in the ass to him. Vendors wanted payment right now and, even though it was crowded every night, the place wasn't generating the cash he'd hoped.

*What did you expect out of a place you won in a poker game?* He'd thought it would give him an extra source of income. What a laugh that was.

The office, its tiny space filled with the desk, a filing cabinet and two chairs, was a symptom of everything that was wrong. The floor and furniture were scarred and scuffed, paint was peeling on the walls and it seemed every day he accumulated more trash. He'd even stopped changing from his work clothes before heading out here. What difference did it make if the smell of horses and cattle and everything else still clung to him? The saloon wasn't much better.

The inside of the building needed work and the bar setup needed a good overhaul, but with the end of summer and work ramping up at the ranch he didn't have any time to get to it. He'd shut the damn place down, except in Nightfall there wasn't

1

another spot for people to hang out. That included men and women, ranchers and hands, good people and bums. If he shut down, they'd probably lynch him.

On the plus side, bad as things were going, he was lucky there was no competitor within miles of the place. But working the ranch all day then spending hours here at night was draining him, and not just financially. He'd spent too many years on the rodeo circuit, living out of trailers and tents, crowded into places with mobs of people. Privacy was important to him now. So why did he hang onto this place where he was thrust in the middle of people every night?

His Comanche grandfather, his mother's father, would have berated him for even having a place that sold alcohol. Which was ironic, because Quinn had kept the place thanks to the advice of another Comanche—Sam Red Elk.

The Indian who looked as if he was a baked part of the Texas landscape had been in and out of Quinn's life since his teens, the kind of steady mentor his volatile father never had been. He had an odd way of showing up at unexpected times, giving Quinn counsel that, while sometimes cryptic, usually steered him onto the right path.

The night Quinn had won the saloon, Sam had pulled one of his unexpected appearances at the game. He hadn't wanted to play. Instead he propped himself in a chair in the corner, whittling on a stick. Didn't say a word until Quinn won the saloon. Then Sam looked up, dark eyes meeting Quinn's. He nodded and rose, leaving the game as if his task was done. When Quinn caught up to him in the parking lot, he mused aloud about selling it, but the Indian shook his head.

"You'll want to keep this, Quinn. It will bring something good into your life."

Quinn knew Sam was considered a shaman among his own people. He himself had seen enough in Sam's company to accept it without a doubt. Though when it came to the saloon, he was starting to wonder if the man had been in a snake-bite delirium.

Not that he'd ever say that where Sam could hear him. The shaman might be able to turn him into a coyote or something. Though if he had to deal with this mess much longer, that might start to look pretty appealing.

Leaning back in his chair, his booted feet up on the scarred old desk, Quinn closed his eyes and rubbed his temples, trying to ease the headache that wouldn't quit. Beyond the closed door he could hear the usual noises of a rowdy crowd, warming up as the evening wore on. He needed to check on Artie. Make sure he was taking care of business out there.

He'd thought hiring a manager and a couple cute local girls to help him bartend and bus tables would keep him from putting in all these hours at the saloon at night. But he'd quickly found out he couldn't afford a good bar manager, not when the bigger cities had more to offer one. Hiring Artie Sampson had truly been a last resort. The man had been fired from every job he'd ever had, but Quinn was desperate and told himself he was giving the man a second chance. Apparently, some people didn't deserve second chances. The girls seemed too busy flirting most of the time to be any help at all.

A loud crash jerked him out of the chair. Rolling up his sleeves, he yanked open the office door and stomped out to the saloon, his boots striking the boards loud enough they should have been heard over the noise. The scene he walked into made him want to shoot someone. Or himself.

The blast of the old-fashioned jukebox overrode the hooting cheers of the beer-guzzling crowd, egging on the two men pummeling each other in the middle of the room. As Quinn watched, they rammed into a table, overturning it and shattering the wealth of uncollected empty glasses it had been holding. A chair splintered under the men's weight as they rolled over it.

*Fucking shit.* Drawing a breath, Quinn prepared to wade in and yank the two drunks apart by the front of their shirts. But then *she* beat him to it.

He was sure no one like her had ever walked into After Hours, or any other local bar or saloon he'd experienced. She couldn't have been more than five feet tall, but the high heels of the fancy dress boots she wore beneath a pair of snug jeans gave her at least another four inches. Hair like spun gold fell in waves to her shoulders, shimmering as she moved. A thin blue short-sleeved top with a light spray of sparkles across a New Orleans bar logo hugged breasts that would be a nice handful, and Quinn had large hands. A silver pendant that looked like a tiny dagger through a heart pointed right down at the tempting hint of cleavage, a warning and invitation together.

When he pushed himself past the usual focal points to get to her face, he found features like blown glass, perfect and delicate. At first glance, he thought she wasn't much older than the pair of twenty-one-year-old girls he'd hired for low wages to pour drinks. But a second look said this was a fully mature, sexy woman. Ethereal yet earthy. Her eyes matched the blue of her shirt, the smoky color of an early dawn sky.

When she stepped between the two men without hesitation, he bit back an oath. He was ten paces away, too far to keep her from getting mashed like Spam between two slapped-together pieces of Merita.

Instead, one slim hand landed on the barrel chest of Howie Gold, a regular, the other on the arm of a drugstore cowboy who'd probably said something stupid to set off Howie. They both had clenched fists and alcohol-induced stupid written all over their faces, but then she leveled that blue gaze on them. "You're interfering with my getting a drink. And that pisses me off."

She didn't raise her voice, but she didn't need to do so. The impact of her expression turned them into deer frozen in the headlights, waiting for a truck to hit. Those blue eyes held something... Well, he knew how crazy it sounded, given he could have picked her up under one arm, but the word that came to mind was *dangerous.*

*Mesmerizing* was a close second, and he meant it literally. Something about her quieted the crowd and held both men in place, those fists loosening into uncertain curls.

In contrast, that sense of danger made Quinn want to keep coming toward her. His cock had hardened, pressing against the denim of his fly and demanding release. No, demanding to be plunged into the tight wetness of her body.

There was no way she could sense his reaction. A handful of occupied tables were between him and her, plus a bunch of people on their feet to corral the fight. He was just one in the crowd. Yet when his cock stiffened, her gaze flicked away from the two men and lasered right to him.

He had a voracious sexual appetite and liked a dozen different kinds of kink. All the women he'd chosen in the past fifteen years —and the rodeo circuit had provided a lot of those—had seemed to enjoy sex with him. He tried to be a generous lover and, without ego, he knew he had the kind of alpha male personality women liked, strong and demanding in the right ways. Their willing compliance should have been enough for him.

Yet sometimes, lying awake in the hours before dawn, a sleeping woman next to him, he wondered if they were too obedient. Too acquiescing. And damn it all, that didn't make any sense. It wasn't as if they just lay there and waited for him to give them orders. Most of those relationships had had some substance to them, such that a couple became more than just casual sex. Annie had been the last of those, some time ago.

Since then, he'd had the occasional casual fuck, but it was half-hearted. He'd told himself it was because of how hard he was working, but he knew that was a lie. Every relationship had lacked some intangible thing he couldn't put his finger on.

Something that he had the oddest feeling had just put its finger on *him*.

In her eyes, he saw a deep, reciprocal interest. Deep as in dark and mysterious, a cavern that held unknown hazards. But almost as soon as he registered it, her attention went back to the two would-be combatants. "You can take this outside," she said. "Beat the shit out of each other in the parking lot. I don't care. It's not happening in here. But whether you do that or you stay inside and behave, you'll go give the bartender an extra twenty for the glasses you broke. That's only fair, right?"

She wasn't patronizing or sarcastic, which might set them off again. If anything, her no-nonsense tone reminded Quinn of the way his own mother used to handle problems between him and his brothers. She had a quiet firmness that convinced them of two things—she loved them, and she would beat the hide off them without remorse when they deserved it. Even when they reached the ages that they towered over her, they respected her the same way. She also stood between them and their loud, domineering father, the only one he seemed to listen to.

This woman gave Howie's chest a light tap, her fingers tightening on the drugstore cowboy's arm. "I'm not in the habit of repeating myself, boys. Do we have an understanding?"

"Yes ma'am," Howie mumbled as the other man dragged his hat off his head.

"Good." She gave them a tight smile and glanced over her shoulder at Maria, the goggle-eyed waitress and barmaid on shift tonight. "Charge my tab for one of those pizzas with all the fixings and bring half to each of them with a pitcher of ice water. That'll soak up some of the alcohol interfering with their better judgment."

Releasing them, she stepped back. With only a brief shift in expression, she made it clear they were dismissed to do her bidding. Quinn watched in amused disbelief as the stubborn cowhand and dumbass kid both moved to the bar, reaching for their wallets.

Then he had bigger concerns. As the crowd started to wander back to their tables and own conversations again, her gaze came right back to him.

He knew he had features that most women found pleasing—a rugged physique, thick brown hair and brown eyes. One woman had told him when he looked her way it was like falling into a vat of melting chocolate. However, this woman considered him from head to toe as if she was watching molasses meander down his naked body. It was the first time a woman had looked at him like he was something she was literally considering eating.

That disturbing thought should have given him pause, but his dick was doing the compass pointing as he drew closer. Since he'd been getting worried about its lack of interest in anything lately, he was kind of glad for the proof otherwise. But now it was time he took hold of himself. Mentally, that is. This was *his* bar and she'd just handled something that was his job to do. Or his worthless, nowhere-to-be-seen bar manager.

"Thanks, I could have taken care of that. You shouldn't get in between two cowboys in a tussle."

She shifted to one hip. The men at the table behind her glazed, suggesting they had an enviable view of her ass working that denim. "You're such a little thing," Quinn added, clearing his throat. "You could have been hurt."

"I'm in more danger from alcohol poisoning from the drinks your poorly trained bartender is over pouring. Or the old cooking grease in your food."

She had the voice of a black-and-white movie starlet, the words mulled on her tongue like they tasted sweet. She'd taste sweet, for sure. Thank God he'd pulled his shirt out of his jeans while doing paperwork, but as she criticized his bar, he had to resist the urge to tuck it in, try to look more professional. *Yeah, that adolescent hard-on I'm sporting would be real professional.* Best to leave the shirt out.

What the hell? He'd worked a full day and didn't have time for this shit. "Thanks for the customer feedback," he said coolly. "We'll cover the pizza. Tell Maria the house owes you a free drink. Watered down so you can handle it."

She arched a brow, blue eyes sparking. Taking a side step, she picked up a full shot of whiskey off one of the tables. The patron sitting there, a gruff ranch hand from the Bar Q, began to protest, but she merely laid a hand on his lean shoulder, stilling his protest as she tossed it back in one swallow. No cough, no eye watering.

When she put the glass down with a decided thunk, a wave of whistles and catcalls came from the other three men at the table and those around them, but her face remained impassive. She never took her eyes off Quinn.

"Put that one on my tab," she said.

As the men guffawed, Quinn shot them a quelling look. By the time he brought his gaze back to her, she'd stepped in front of him, close enough their conversation was just between them.

"Your biggest problem is your bar manager is a drunk," she continued as if the interruption hadn't happened. "I can smell the alcohol coming out of his pores from across the room, and he eyes the bar like a kid who can't wait for the candy store to close so he can take his fill. He's also not ringing up a good percentage of your sales, so he's stealing from you, during and after hours."

Quinn's brow creased, his eyes flicking up to find Artie. He still didn't see him. Yeah, the bar manager was a screw-up, but stealing? He'd given the asshole the only chance at employment in town. She had to be yanking his chain.

"But let me guess," she tapped a well-manicured short nail against her full bottom lip, "he was the best the area had to offer, and you figure anything he screwed up, you could step in and fix, because you're the kind who thinks he can handle anything."

Quinn set his jaw. He wasn't going to respond to any of this. He should just walk away before he said something regrettable. But even as she was tearing down his place, he wanted to keep watching her, being near her. His exhaustion was obviously affecting his better judgment.

Her gaze slid over him. "Your attire—and smell—says ranch to me, so you're trying to run both places." Stepping even closer, she laid her palm fully on his chest. Not the simple finger tap she'd given Howie. While Quinn was absorbing the impact of the intimate touch, she went from a discreet murmur to a low purr. "Sometimes a man has to learn how to give up control."

Then she pivoted on her booted heel and left him standing there.

Quinn let out the breath he'd been holding. Aware of people staring at him, he scowled. "Show's over, folks. Anyone else who thinks about brawling in here better think twice. She asked them nicely. I won't. Next asshole who tries to break up my place will get his ass kicked into the parking lot, right into the sheriff's car. You can spend the night in his little hotel for drunk and disorderly."

There were some half-chuckles, rueful looks and raised hands of acknowledgement, then the noise level started to rise again. They knew he meant it. He'd fought damn bulls and roped stock for years. Tossing out a couple drunks was as easy as pitching hay.

Forcing himself not to look where his intriguing female had gone, he turned his attention to getting up the glass that had been broken, because it hadn't occurred to Maria to do it. He'd have told her to get her ass out from behind the bar, but Artie still wasn't around and she was serving drinks. Plus, Quinn found himself too disgusted with all of it to even bother. He was tired and needed a drink himself, one he wasn't going to be getting anytime soon.

Righting the table, he went to find the broom and dustpan. Despite his irritation, he realized the past few minutes were the longest and most interesting interaction he'd had with a woman in quite a while. How pathetic was that? Ever since he sent Annie, his last real relationship, packing, his life had been unremitting work and more work. He was all too aware a great deal of that had been his choice, because he'd just plain lost interest. Every woman seemed the same. Wrong.

"I don't understand," she'd said, tears in her eyes. "We're good together, Quinn. Really good. And I love the ranch."

Yeah, she loved the ranch as much as she loved rattlesnakes. What she really loved was all the money she thought he had. She'd always been nattering about redecorating the house. Making changes. They hadn't been good together, no matter what Annie thought.

At forty-two, he ought to be thinking about settling down. What good was building up this ranch, doing everything he was doing, without a wife to share that life with him, and children to pass it along to?

Quinn filled the dustpan as full as he could and carried it over behind the bar to dump it. As he wove his way through the tables, he noted none of them had been bussed in quite a while. Every surface was filled with empty bottles, glasses and mugs. The overturned one probably hadn't been an isolated incident. Didn't Artie or Maria ever think to clean the damn tables until the end of the night?

Probably not. Quinn had cleared tables at closing many times, believing Artie when he said they were overworked. But in reality, the people he hired were just lazy. Artie was nowhere to be seen, and he was supposed to be managing the bar when Maria was handling the tables. Whereas Maria had brought some drinks to a table but now just stood there, arms crossed beneath her breasts to show them off and one hip twitched out in a jaunty manner. All while she carried on with the cowboys. Quinn thought bitterly she probably figured flirting was her reward for having to do two jobs.

Sweeping the broken glass into a pile, he got it up and banged the dustpan against the inside of the trash can to get all the glass debris from it. When he straightened, he made himself think past his ego about what his five-foot-tall unlikely bouncer had said about his bar. Though it had riled him, she hadn't been shooting off her mouth. She'd sounded like a woman who knew exactly what she was talking about.

He glanced up, toward the bar. Just in time to see two of his so-called customers leaning over the service station, helping themselves from the beer taps. *Shit.*

Putting the dustpan and broom aside, he strode behind the bar, sending those customers skedaddling with a fierce look before he stomped back into the kitchen area. "Damn it, Artie. Where the hell are you?"

He was practically shouting, at the end of his rope. Then he noticed the cracked back door and smelled tobacco. Taking an hour-long smoke. Of course.

Artie slid in, crushing the butt out in the door frame. "Yeah, boss?"

Quinn pinned him with every bit of pissed-off he could level on him. "We've got customers out there serving themselves while Maria is flirting like she's turning tricks. Get your ass in gear."

Had the man always been such a disgrace? As Artie hurried past, Quinn noticed how the man's T-shirt was covered with unidentifiable stains and his jeans had spots worn through. Quinn paid the man enough he could buy himself some decent clothes. But she'd been right. He smelled like an alcohol-soaked sponge.

He knew Artie had a drinking problem, but...aw shit. He could keep telling himself the barn was clean enough, but every day the manure was rising higher and higher. Eventually he wouldn't be able to avoid having it right in his face.

Quinn took a deep breath, calming himself down. He'd get through tonight, then maybe he'd do some hard thinking after closing. Sam's wisdom aside, it might be time to call it quits on this.

For now, he returned to the floor and made one more pass at the shattered glass on the floor. Grabbing the big serving tray from behind the bar, he started bussing the closest tables. But as he carried the empties to the bigger trash bin, his attention was caught by a customer coming up to pay his tab. Narrowing his eyes, Quinn gripped the dustpan hard as he watched Artie open the drawer—without ringing up a sale. He gave the man waiting with beer bottle and cash in hand whatever change he was expecting.

She was right. The motherfucker was stealing from him.

Maybe it had been happening for a while and her pointing it out had taken off the blinders. Either way, he saw red. He considered himself a civilized man, but at the end of the day there was a code for dealing with this kind of shit. It didn't involve lawyers or calling the cops.

In the time it took to blink, he'd crossed the floor, slammed the dustpan and tray on the end of the bar and lifted Artie from the spot where he was standing. He shoved him against the wall.

"Not only are you lazy and a slob," Quinn spat, "but you're a goddamn thief. How much of my drawer goes into your pocket every night, Artie? How the fuck much?"

"B-B-But, Quinn," the man blubbered.

"But nothing, you ass. I should—"

Quinn broke off. He realized he was honestly mad enough to do the man real harm, his hands just itching with the need to break and bludgeon. It was then he found out where the delicate-looking woman with steel blue eyes was sitting. At the table right next to where he had Artie pinned.

She'd picked the spot that had a full view of the floor and the door, and was backed up to a corner. It was the table the sheriff preferred when he came to drink, and any of the active military guys on leave.

When Quinn glanced down and to the left, she was less than two feet away. Even so, she hadn't vacated her seat. She didn't seem flustered by him slamming Artie against the wall hard enough to make it vibrate right behind her head. She had her gaze on Quinn, and what he saw in those eyes steadied him.

Cool understanding.

Reaching out, she hooked her slim fingers in Quinn's jeans pocket, giving his hip bone an intimate stroke. She tilted her head, a subtle shift toward the door that said volumes.

*He's not worth it. Kick him to the curb and be done with it.*

Unbelievably, his cock had sprung right back into a hard jam against his fly, just from that brief contact. But his reaction to her was more than physical. Though the touch aroused him, it also settled that enraged core that was about to do something he couldn't undo. She held him until he steadied, gave her an answering nod. Then she leaned back, letting him go.

Looking at the sniveling mess he was holding, Quinn dropped

the man from his grip. "You're fired. Don't ever let me see your miserable face again."

He made sure of it, marching Artie to the door amid applause and grating comments like "about damn time". In the parking lot, Quinn stood there, arms akimbo and legs braced, watching Artie climb into his junker truck, grind the engine into gear and trundle out onto the road. As the dust settled, Quinn tilted his head back, stared up at the night sky. What a fucking mess. Pinching the bridge of his nose, he massaged, closed his eyes.

*Okay. Get through tonight.*

But when he turned to face the double doors that would take him back into After Dark, Quinn realized the only thing that made him want to go through them ever again was the woman sitting in that back corner.

Yep, he wanted to go right back to her, but there was no time for that. He didn't think Maria could handle the rest of the night on her own. Hell, Quinn wasn't sure he could trust her to close out the cash register properly.

But what if the woman disappeared during that time? She was definitely not a local. Probably on her way to one of the big cities, someone he'd never see come this way again. He didn't like the idea of that. But he couldn't think of a single thing to say to keep her sitting at that table until closing time. Nothing that wouldn't come off crazy and drive her away faster.

When he came back in, he found it wasn't an issue. She wasn't at the table. Feeling a spurt of panic, he looked around, gaze darting here and there, feet itching to run him back to the parking lot before she drove away. Then he saw her.

Working.

She was acting as if he'd left her in charge, instructing Maria to bus the tables with the tray he'd dropped while she took point behind the bar. She was in the middle of mixing what appeared to be three different drinks, her head cocked to listen to other orders coming in. With a professional warm smile, she responded to one of the patrons, popping the top of a couple beers and sliding them his way. Then she rang up two sales, a cash and a credit transaction.

Anyone else, he would have been over that bar, demanding an explanation for what the fuck she was doing, but her competence was as obvious as a veteran cowhand working stock. He was looking at a woman who'd worked in a bar for a long time. Or a lot of different bars.

Fine. Yeah, she might present herself better than Artie, but that didn't mean he was going to just let her take over without knowing what she was about. It didn't take a rocket scientist to know his cock was interfering with his judgment. He needed to engage his other brain, the supposedly higher-functioning one, and take a good hard look at this situation.

How he wished he hadn't used the word "hard", because that just made it more difficult to keep that part of him in check.

Libido aside, he had to admit it was difficult to argue with the proof in front of him. He'd only been out in the lot ten minutes or so, yet everyone sitting at the bar had drinks and Maria was quickly finishing up the table bussing, Quinn's sexy sprite giving her the direction Artie never had. It made Quinn rethink whether the barmaid was truly lazy. She and Carol, the other one he'd hired, were barely kids, after all. Maybe they just needed more supervision, like what he was witnessing.

The woman was ringing up another sale when his muscles finally unfroze.

"Hey, Quinn," someone called as he strode behind the bar. "Nice to see you finally got some class in this place."

Quinn forced a smile and nodded. "Just for you, Mike."

The register rang again and she handed back change, but before she could reach for another empty to refill, he clamped his hand around her wrist, turning away from the patrons so they couldn't hear him. He jerked his head at Maria to take over as he drew the woman toward the back wall. The position brushed her shoulder against his chest, and put her close enough he could inhale the scent of her hair. The scent of her, period.

She smelled like cool things. Freshly turned earth in the shade of an old oak, churned butter pulled from his grandfather's icebox, and rain in the fall. All things he liked. "No offense, but I just tossed one guy taking advantage of me, so what are you doing behind my bar? Where the hell did you come from? Do you have a name?"

He'd intended to sound gruff and demanding, but as she lifted long-lashed eyes to study his face, her head barely reaching his shoulder, he knew he was more curious than anything. She wore a light covering of lipstick, a coral pink that looked good against her fair skin. That glossy sheen suggested moist invitation. When she spoke, he smelled mint and the faint flavor of the Jack. It really was uncanny, how young and old she seemed. If he was only going on her looks, he'd guess she was at least ten to fifteen years younger than him. But her eyes said she was quite a bit older.

"Selene Torres," she said. "I came in from the road for a drink. And I didn't say it was okay for you to touch me yet. Let go."

*Yet?* It was funny how a man could latch on to one word like a steer's horns and let the beast drag him right off the cliff. But she wasn't being coy. She had the same set to her mouth she'd had when she'd dealt with Howie and his potential punching bag. She wasn't intimidated by the difference in their sizes or Quinn's tone of voice. Appearances certainly were deceiving.

Selene. A beautiful name to go with a fascinating woman. She affected him, no question. Though he loosened his hold, he didn't let go, wanting to see what she'd do about it. He craved her response to a challenge, enough that his need for it made him uneasy.

A blink later, he discovered she could call enough fire in her eyes for someone twice her size, but the heat of it was something he'd willingly embrace.

"Don't test me right now," she said. "We can discuss that later."

She removed her hand from his grasp with a deft twist that surprised him with the subtle torque. Almost as much as how she reversed it, her fingers now resting on his forearm, her index finger making a light pass over his wrist bones before she took that distracting touch away.

"Your skin is sun drenched," she observed, gaze sliding over the tanned expanse of his face, his throat, back down to his arms, revealed by his rolled-up shirt sleeves. "But..." She wet a finger, giving him a quick glimpse of the tip of her tongue before she rubbed the pad of that forefinger over his wrist. "You have an ink mark there."

Quinn stared down at the crown of her head. He wanted her. Not like a buckle bunny, a quick fuck against the wall, though he could easily see that happening. He wanted her in so many ways it was like a crazy film reel shooting images through his head so fast he couldn't list all the things she was making him want.

"Hey, Quinn." One of the men seated at the bar called down to him. "Don't take her head off. In ten minutes, she's run this place better than that asshole you just threw out ever did. And she's a damn sight better to look at."

Agreement traveled down the bar like the wave at a sporting event, but Quinn's attention remained glued to her. When she lifted her gaze again, she didn't break eye contact. Out of all the captivating things about this woman, that was what he kept noticing the most. No blinking, no wavering. It was the most direct stare he'd ever experienced, as if she could do it for hours without twitching. There was an odd stillness to her. Funny how he'd never noticed how much people moved even when they didn't seem to move. But she didn't.

Her thumb stayed pressed over the small spot of his skin tingling from her moist care while the rest of her fingers wrapped around his wrist, holding him. As she tightened that grip, he had a sudden vision of himself on his knees, lifting both hands to her as she ran a rope in figure eights around his wrists, over and over.

The thought startled him so much, he almost pulled away from her. He'd never had a single woman in his bed he would have let tie him up. He thought of his earlier discontent with former lovers, how they'd almost seemed too compliant. In this woman's eyes, he saw so many fantasies he'd never pursued, but which had drifted in his subconscious, permeating early morning erotic dreams he pushed away at dawn. With her, he wanted to bring them to life, and it scared the shit out of him.

Fuck, he was in a bunch of trouble here. *Focus on the bar, asshole. Stay away from anything else.*

"We should talk," he said. "Will you stay until closing?"

During the bated moment before she answered, he found himself trying to understand why he anticipated her answer so much. Leaning in, she braced herself on his chest once more, lifting up onto her toes so she could put her nose close to the pocket of his throat. The current between them was electric as she inhaled, her breath caressing his skin through the open collar of his shirt.

"Sun drenched," she murmured again. "Yes, Quinn. I'll stay until closing."

Sliding down his body as she put her heels back on solid ground, she turned away and left him.

# CHAPTER TWO

*H*e helped out, ostensibly to watch her like a hawk for the remaining couple of hours until closing. But he would have watched her anyway, and he wasn't alone. Male and female patrons alike seemed awestruck by Selene. She took over the mixed drinks and had Maria running the beer tap, bussing tables and ferrying the drinks to the floor. Selene also stayed on top of the food orders, keeping the tickets organized and clear for Manuel, the cook in back.

She was so efficient she even worked in a little entertainment, putting together a new drink that she finished with the flame flourish of an atomizer Quinn didn't know they had. "Gives it a woodsmoke taste," she told the fascinated patrons, offering them a provocative wink. "Who wants one? Show of hands. Ten bucks each."

Hands shot in the air, and she lined up her glasses, serving out nearly a dozen of them in a handful of minutes, complete with the deft bottle spins most of them had only seen in the snazzy city theme bars or that old Tom Cruise movie. She was graceful and swift, no wasted motion.

Everything about her said there was no way in hell he could afford her.

But she'd agreed to meet with him at the end of the night, and he wouldn't let go of that, no matter how pointless it might be, or that he couldn't explain to himself why he needed to hold onto her as long as he could. All he knew was it was the first time in a while he'd felt something real when he looked at a woman. And she'd looked back.

Though on the surface she never seemed out of control, he had a good bit of time while watching her to rewind, go back over everything he'd noticed about her. She might have knocked him off his axis, but he was rallying, taking her measure the way she'd obviously taken his. Earlier she'd seemed more tightly wound and watchful. As she interacted with the bar patrons, he got the sense she genuinely enjoyed this, that it eased up things inside her. It gave her eyes a sparkle, her smile more relaxed. She went from flat-out beautiful to something even more approachable, something a man wanted to be near.

Earlier what he saw had been something he'd want to fuck, and that was dangerous enough. What he saw now was even more perilous. The kind of woman he wanted to be curled around at night, whose scent he wanted in his bed, on his skin. He'd cherish the small sounds as she shifted and murmured, the grazing touch of her fingers as she curled her hand over his forearm, pressed under her breasts as he spooned with her.

She'd probably consider that quaint, the dumb cowboy in the middle of nowhere with his apple pie and grow-old-with-me ideas of marriage and a relationship. It wasn't like he was going to share such nonsense with her though. No matter the vibe she gave off, he knew she wasn't that type. He might give the idea of fucking her a really good shot though.

Of course, he might crap out and turn into a pumpkin before then. When it was clear she and Maria had things in hand, he'd taken a seat at the table she'd vacated earlier. He'd put one booted foot up on the opposite chair, bracing the other on the floor as he crossed his arms over his chest, and just enjoyed the show. While it was the first time he'd been able to do that since he'd taken over the saloon, the day's ranch demands had apparently caught up with him.

He roused at a hand on his shoulder. Lifting his head, he blinked blearily at Maria, who gave him an uncertain smile. "Mr. Pedraza, it's past closing time. Selene said Manuel can walk me out to my car if you don't have anything else for us tonight. She split all the bar tips with us. Said we deserved it."

Well, look at Maria, practically glowing with a sense of self-accomplishment, not a shallow, care-about-nothing-but-herself kid after all. He was too used to dealing with the more straightforward temperament of ranch hands, obviously.

"Yeah." Clearing his throat, he straightened, rubbing at his face. "You all did a hell of a job tonight. Good job."

She glowed like a firefly. Manuel, standing behind her, nodded and smiled as well. He looked far less frazzled than Quinn had ever seen him. Guilt tinged his gut as he realized the kind of firefight being between him and Artie these past few months had probably been. "I hope she can stay," the cook said in a low voice, tilting his head to the bar. "She's good, Mr. Pedraza."

"Yeah she is." Probably way too good for After Dark. Maybe for Quinn too.

It wasn't like him to feel unsure about himself around women, off balance. But wasn't that part of the problem he'd been having with women lately? Always feeling like there were no surprises? That they were just too accepting of everything he was and wanted, letting him set all the terms? But wasn't that what a man was supposed to do, women wanting the whole take-charge, alpha thing?

Maria and Manuel left, carrying the last bags of trash with them, something Quinn had been having to do himself at the end of the night. As he got his ass off the chair, Selene was coming out of the kitchen, clean bar rag in hand, which she folded and placed on the counter. Everything might be beat up, run down, but it was all cleaner than he'd seen it left at closing since he'd taken owner-ship. Hell, how long had he been asleep?

NIGHTFALL

A glance at the clock showed him two hours past closing time. Fucking hell. He really was worn out.

She came around the bar, leaned against it, the cling of her shirt outlining her breasts nicely as she propped an elbow on the counter and laced her fingers beneath them. "So, Quinn Pedraza. Owner of this saloon and the Last Chance Ranch. Good name. Your choice?"

"No. But I liked it." So she'd been finding out things about him while he'd been visiting the sandman. He didn't know if that was good or bad. She excelled at being unreadable, as if she'd spent a long time practicing a poker face. It was a trait of card players, con artists and people who knew the wrong expression could cost them more than they could afford to lose. It was also something people learned to do to cope with the deeper emotions beneath the surface, as if the expression was a dam on emotions too strong to let bust loose.

He knew about strong emotions like that. So much of his childhood and teen years had been chaos. Though he'd been raised on a ranch, he actually hadn't been able to get past the noise to appreciate it, to realize there was a quiet to be found there, in the land. When he finally had figured that out—thanks in large part to Sam's first appearance in his life—he'd decided he wanted to own his own ranch more than anything.

It had taken his years on the rodeo circuit to secure the Last Chance at a bargain price. In the five years since he'd taken it over, he'd worked his ass off building it up, making it a profitable operation again. Only about fifteen hundred of the five thousand acres were actually useable, but the rest of it gave him the privacy he craved, that he hadn't been able to experience during his childhood or on the frenzied rodeo circuit.

From how much of his time was spent in the middle of this disaster, no one would guess how much he wanted that solitude. But here after closing, just her and him, he embraced that sense of being the only folks around. It was the first time he'd had that experience here. Usually he felt a huge weight bearing down on him the minute he crossed the threshold.

The quiet wasn't at odds with the strong sexual heat he felt for her. Not at all.

"Perhaps you should think of selling this place," she said.

"I would if I had a buyer. Believe me. If I just close it up, all these people won't have a place to hang out. We're the only game in town."

"Well." As she studied him, he had the uncomfortable feeling she saw through the partial lie. "It seems to me you have to make some kind of decision or it will be made for you."

"I suppose you think you're the answer to fixing my problems here?"

"I know I am. The question is whether you're the answer to what I'm seeking."

It was a strange way to put it. But he rose. "Why don't we go to my office and talk about that?"

When she nodded, he gestured to her to precede him toward the office hallway. She pushed off the bar and came toward him, filling his nose with her essence again, that aroma of soothing coolness and primitive earth. He had to restrain himself from pouncing on her right then and there. He bet her taste would be delicious and her body would be—

*Stop it, you jackass. What in the world is going on here?*

When she brushed past him, his body jerked at the contact. He hadn't done that before, but they hadn't been alone before. He slid a glance at her but she didn't seem to notice his reaction. Or have one of her own.

"Sit down," he said brusquely when they reached his office, more order than request. That appeared to be the only way he could keep control of the situation.

"Please," she told him.

"Excuse me?"

"Sit down, *please*," she repeated with exaggerated patience.

"Please." He gritted out the word. Why did she seem to think she could give *him* orders? Or rather, why did it feel like he was waiting for her to do just that?

Seating herself in the small chair beside the desk, she crossed her legs. Then she released the tie she'd put on her hair while she was working the bar. Shaking out the golden shimmer of locks brought him a wave of her provocative scent. His gaze latched on to the curve of her hip, the way her buttock pressed into the chair. He could scoop one hand under that firm cheek, put the other hand at her waist and lift her right off her feet. Let her hook her legs around him, slide her down inch by inch along his bare body. She'd feel so damn good against him, all that cool pale skin.

Tease. That was the word that came to mind. Not the only one, but he was going to have to shut down his mind and put his cock in a coma if he wanted to get through this conversation. Looking at her conjured up all kinds of images. Her naked on his bed. Her golden hair spread out around her. Perfect round breasts with rosy nipples begging for his mouth. Legs spread wide so he could feast on her pussy. Would she be shaved or have golden down between her legs? He didn't care as long as slick pink lips tasting of her honey waited.

If he didn't stop this soon he'd have to step outside and take himself in hand.

"Listen." He shifted in front of the desk, allowing his big body to take up most of the small space. It was a tactic he'd used to good advantage in dealing with anyone trying to intimidate him. "I don't know who the hell you are, but my trust isn't the best anymore. You came here, took over my bar—"

She rose right up in front of him. "I didn't take it over." Putting that same finger against his chest, he was surprised to find the pressure strong enough to back him into his desk so he had to sit his ass down on the edge of it or let the digit shish-ke-bob a vital organ. That put her standing solidly between his spread thighs, and put them close to eye level, though he still had some height on her. He caught her wrist in self-defense, though he didn't remove the finger from his chest.

Leaving her wrist in his grasp, she let her gaze course over him in that intimate way, like she was already seeing him sprawled in her bed. That ride was going two ways, for sure.

"I simply kept it from imploding tonight," she said conversationally. "You want me to take it over, I can make you money and give you time to sleep. You're running the ranch during the day and working this place at night. You're plowing yourself into the ground and doing a half-assed job at both."

"Thanks for the news flash. I have a mother already."

"I hope you don't look at your mother the way you're looking at me now."

He surged up off the desk. She gave way gracefully but stayed close. Way too close. "Quit showing off your body. That won't work with me."

The look in her eyes told him she didn't believe a word of what he said. "I think you have bigger problems than my body."

Still in control. She'd been holding the reins from the first, and it didn't annoy him the way it should. Instead, it gave him an odd mix of panic and arousal. He needed to act like a boss. The guy in charge.

"You think being a wiseass is the best way to prove to me how good a bar manager you'd be?"

"If the past few hours didn't prove that, you're not as smart as I assumed you are."

He stared at her then shook his head. His chuckle seemed to surprise her. "Ah, fuck me. Whatever. Let's try this again." He gestured her back into the guest chair. "Sorry, I should have dusted that off first. I don't know the last time it was used. Okay, Miss Know-It-All. Tell me what else you saw tonight that will help me run my place better. Impress me."

She already had, but apparently that was a gift that was about to keep giving. She reclaimed her seat with that sensual flow of motion, crossed her legs again. "As I said earlier, your bartenders are over-pouring, probably costing you about fifty percent of your potential drink profits a night, above and beyond what Artie was stealing. Yes, you only offer bar food so that you don't compete with the two restaurants in town, but there's no reason for it to be drowning in old grease and coming out with no presentation. I can help with that.

"You have presentation problems at the bar too. Your good-quality spirits are hiding in the well instead of placed on the shelving behind it. There's no lighting to really draw people that way either. You could add a fresh coat of paint and some regional decorations that would give the place an inexpensive facelift until you can afford something snazzier. You're nearly out of basics like bar napkins and vodka, and that can be fixed by proper supply management."

She lifted a brow. "Shall I keep going?"

"Why not?"

Her eyes narrowed, but she complied. "Your demographic may be small, but they have a good median income and you have the potential of attracting the business of other nearby small towns if you have something better to offer them than their current watering holes.

"Your dance floor is run by an ancient jukebox. It's quaint, but you could keep the façade and install a computerized system with far more selections. As you said, you're the only game in town, and where else are they going to go, but the current setup makes locals reluctant to spend entertainment dollars here. You give them a quality place, they'll drop money, and I bet you might just attract people coming through town as well. Offer better food, occasional live entertainment and a fun drink list that's more than just whiskey and Coke, and warm draft beer—by the way, your cooling lines need to be checked—you'll do better on your bottom line.

"Your bartender and cook are hard workers," she said. "They're just slow and need training. Your other girl can be taught how to pour a decent drink, if she's as eager to please as Maria. Once they realize a good bartender can get better tips than a bad one, no matter the size of her rack, that will be a good incentive, though

Maria's not lazy. She's just young and has lacked proper supervision."

Pretty much what he'd realized tonight, thanks to her temporary management. She stopped, leveled those killer blue eyes on him. "That's plenty. You already know I'm an experienced bar manager who knows what I'm doing. I need a job and you need me."

"Correction. I know you can handle being a bar manager. But I don't know dick about you as a human being yet, and that's part of this job too."

A surprising yet very appealing twinkle passed through her gaze. "I might not qualify in that regard."

"Let me be the judge of that. What's your full name?"

"Selene Torres."

"But you're not from around here."

"Not recently. I was working up north, in New York." She lifted her chin, gave him an imperious look. "Does that disqualify me?"

Quinn had to swallow a grin. "Only if you talked like you were from there, which you don't. Do you have references?"

"Did the man you just threw out?"

As she did the leg crossing thing again, he had to restrain himself from throwing her on the desk and yanking down her jeans to fuck her senseless. But she did have a point. "How about this?" she suggested. "Try me for a month. If I haven't whipped this place into shape you can toss me back out on the highway."

"A month, huh? You think you can turn this place around in that time?"

She nodded. "I know I can."

Quinn studied her with shrewd eyes. "I may prefer to work with cattle, but I don't have manure between my ears, Selene. You have the skills of a big-city bar manager. Why would you want to work here?"

"I'm tired of the north, big cities and lots of attention."

"You running? Abusive boyfriend, something like that?" Though he couldn't see this one being slapped around unless it was the last thing the poor bastard ever did, for some reason the flicker in her eyes raised something protective in him. That really made him a dumbass. *Don't get into trouble you don't want to invite, Quinn.*

"I needed a change of scenery. Beginning and end of story." The set to Selene's jaw said that was all he was getting out of her on that point. For now.

He let his eyes roam over her again. *Pedraza, you've been without a woman too long.* This could be a worse mistake than Artie. Anyone could see there was more of a story here than she was telling.

"A month," he said at last. Scribbling on a sheet of paper, he shoved it across the desk to her. "That's the salary. That suit you?"

He expected her to laugh, ball it up and toss it in his face as she sashayed out. Instead, she scanned it with serious eyes, then nodded, folded it neatly and reached behind her to push it into her rear jeans pocket, making him wish he could slide his fingers into the same snug place. Maybe a couple other snug places too.

"We're open from seven at night until two in the morning," he said. "You can clean everything up when you close and set up for the next day or come in early and do it."

"After we close. I like to leave the bar ready to open. But you don't need to micromanage. It will just annoy me. You have a problem with how I'm doing something, tell me. But otherwise, let me run it the way I want. Bitch at me if the bottom line isn't what you want it to be."

God, the combination of her wraithlike appearance and her go-to-hell attitude turned him on like a six-burner stove.

"We're not open on Monday. Otherwise it's a six-day work week." He narrowed his gaze. "Think you can handle it?"

"Yes." She didn't blink. "But I have three conditions."

Okay, the other shoe was about to drop. He braced himself. "Let's hear them."

"One, I don't work before sundown. Ever. I'll do extra hours from two a.m. to dawn if needed, but every daylight hour is my own time. I'll make sure I coordinate with deliveries and suppliers so that doesn't cause you any hassles."

He'd been ready to point that issue out. Still, he pursed his lips, unwilling to show her how quickly she'd anticipated his concern. "Not sure how well that will work, but we'll see how that goes. Do you have a problem with daylight?"

"I have a condition that requires me to sleep during a lot of daylight hours and stay out of sunlight. You can call it vampirism, since that's what most people do."

He gave her an odd look. "Does your doctor have a longer name for it?"

"That's my business and not yours, long as it doesn't interfere with how I do my job. It won't. Condition number two. In your storage cellar, you have a backroom filled with old junk. I want it for a place to crash. I'll handle cleaning and reorganizing what's in it, and furnishing it."

"I can do better than that." He hoped he wasn't going to regret this. "There's a two-room apartment above the saloon that you can have as part of the job. It probably needs a good scrubbing, but if you can manage for one night I can get a couple of the hands to come out and help with the worst of it."

"Fine. I'd like both rooms. If I'm working late nights, I want to sleep somewhere dark and quiet during daylight hours. Having a cot in that backroom will give me that. I'll take care of the cleaning. No need to pull hands from your ranch. Sounds like you have plenty for them to do out there."

"You know, you haven't told me dick about your experience," he said bluntly.

"I watch a lot of *Bar Rescue*," she said without missing a beat. "That Jon Taffe, he's the bomb."

"Yeah, reality shows definitely set you up with the skills I saw tonight." He didn't smile, but neither did she. "You're sending me one of two messages, honey. Either 'hands off, my past is off limits' or 'I've already proven I can do this job, unless you're too much of a dumbass to see it'."

"I think we already covered the latter," she responded, then flicked a glance over him. "But the hands-off part is my final condition of employment."

That look said she wasn't just talking about her past. His brow creased. Was she suggesting he needed to keep his hands to himself? Hell, except for him holding her wrist a couple times, she'd been the one doing the most touching. Though the chemistry was undeniable. Maybe she'd noticed he'd been nursing a perpetual hard-on since she'd walked into the bar.

*Hell, honey, there isn't a man alive who could control that around you, and you know it.* Maybe that was why she felt she had to reinforce the hands off. Maybe there were guys who'd had trouble with the word *no.* Well, he wasn't one of those dickheads.

"You don't have to worry about that," he said, meeting her gaze head on. "I don't go where I'm not invited. Ever."

"Your behavior behind the bar earlier tonight suggests you're not that well-behaved." Her tongue slid out between her full lips, the tip of it touching the lower one. Her gaze was a lick of flame along his skin.

*Oh sweet Jesus.* His balls already ached from her proximity, enough he knew he'd be jerking off tonight when he finally hit a bed.

"You misunderstood me," she said. Her blue eyes did that laser thing that speared him right down into his scrotum. "Condition number three. *You're* one of my employment benefits. And that starts right now."

# CHAPTER THREE

*S*elene knew this was a mistake. She was hungry, and she knew better than to make decisions when she was hungry. For a young vampire, hunger was more than a quick carb-protein snack. It was an all-consuming, all-encompassing need for nourishment. For the body, soul and libido. Particularly the libido.

She'd actually detected Quinn Pedraza when she first entered the bar. Amid the moderate-sized crowd of about seventy people, she'd looked around, seeking the source of that wonderful smell. Red blooded, male, strong. A powerful man, and not just physically. She'd drawn him in through her all her senses, the potential nourishment tailored to her specific requirements like a chef catering her favorite meal.

It was hard to explain how she could pick that out. It was a skill that wasn't usual, even for vampires, so she kept it low key in her shadowy world. But this had been too appealing to resist. She'd targeted that hallway to the office area and, though she couldn't see him, she'd known he was there. He was the only blood in the building she wanted.

She'd always been a picky eater.

God, she was in Texas, of all places. Since most vampires weren't attracted to places where the sun could fry an egg on a rock, it was a good choice. She wanted to be away from where other vampires were, particularly one vampire. Texas was as far from New York City and Laurent's normal milieu as she could imagine without leaving the country. That had been her primary concern, until she'd seen Quinn and realized the last time she'd really fed had been three days and eight states ago.

He was the quintessential alpha male, stepping right from the pages of a Marlboro Man ad. He wouldn't expect her to know what that was, any more than he would expect her to be sixty-two years old. But he'd picked up on the different maturity level pretty quick, as well as some other things she hadn't expected.

Though he was attracted to her, he hadn't let his wits drain all into his cock. Bad as Artie was, Quinn understood something was off about her. But, intriguingly enough, he gave off the vibe of a man who had the courage to find out if that was good or bad...and how he could help. Which meant she should be leaving tonight, not applying for a job. But she was just too damn hungry.

He was tall, broad-shouldered, lean-hipped. She'd been told he was a rodeo cowboy, a rancher, and the rugged face and intimidating physique were silent proof he was the real thing. His misery being in the midst of all these people was as clear to her enhanced senses as a man with a flu virus. She'd already seen enough to know his sloppy hiring practices and the state of the bar had to do with an overworked, exhausted owner too used to having to take care of others. If he had a blind spot, it was that he didn't know when he needed help.

There was a solid core to him like the stillness of a mountain. He didn't look at home here. She suspected if she saw him at his ranch, she'd see him where he was meant to be. She could help him with that.

She wanted to see him looking a little more relaxed. Almost as much as she wanted to see the flip side of that. Him bound and stripped, all those muscles straining against restraints she'd put on him, so she could bite, suck and lick every inch of skin, tease every scar with her nails, impale herself on that impressive cock straining beneath worn denim. She'd made it test the limits of those fibers more than once tonight. He thought his untucked shirt concealed it, but arousal was as detectable to her senses as blood.

Blood pulsing in his throat, beating strong through his heart in that wide chest. When she'd leaned close to him at the bar, her fangs had started to elongate. She wasn't one to deny herself long, not when it came to a human she wanted. A male like this.

His warm brown eyes were framed by dark lashes, and his sable hair tempted touch. When Maria had woken him, Selene had been watching from the kitchen access. She'd imagined waking him by stroking her fingers through that hair, tugging lightly. Once those eyes opened, she'd tighten her grip. Yank. Make fire spark in that gaze the way it had behind the bar when he decided not to obey her command to release her wrist. Yeah, he wanted a woman's strong hand, but he was all male animal. He'd want to fight over it. He was itching for that fight, and so was she.

When the meaning of her "third condition" sank in, she saw that spark again. His lips pressed together and he shifted on the chair, probably to give some relief to that erection that just wouldn't quit. *You'll need my permission getting relief with that, baby,* she thought. *After I enjoy tormenting you a good, long time.*

Her fingers curled in on themselves where they rested with deceptive ease on the chair arm and her thigh. His gaze kept returning to her crossed legs, the way she was resting on one hip, the closer one turned up enough his gaze could trace the curve of the buttock.

She rose. "Does the upstairs have a bed? One we can use right now to seal the deal?"

His gaze snapped up to her. While New York didn't have a lot of rodeos, she'd picked up enough stories tonight to know about eager-to-please buckle bunnies. He'd be making a grave error if he lumped her in with those. She wasn't flirting, simpering or giggling. She was more than an alpha bitch. She was going to be the alpha, period.

As that unspoken message registered, his expression said he

was warring with uncomfortable feelings about it. He hadn't yet said yes, but this wasn't exactly a verbal kind of contract. Blood, sweat and some satisfying, sticky sex were going to be the signature on the dotted line. She was all too aware his unease was coming primarily from how she was turning him on. It was part of what she'd sensed, what had attracted her to him. This was a man who'd been required to be in control in all ways from the time he'd reached sexual maturity. His true power, all that delicious strength and sexual drive, would come to glorious, raging life with a different tactic.

"As I said earlier," she said, "I'm not in the habit of repeating myself."

She turned away and almost made it to the door. Because she could move far faster than a human, she was ready for him when he swiftly closed the distance between them. When he pushed her back against the wall, she ducked beneath his hold, reversed it, and put him against the wood paneling, holding him there with a hand curved around the base of his corded throat.

His eyes widened. He'd put a defensive hand on her forearm, but his touch was gentle. He was gentle with women, even when he was demanding. He clearly knew how much stronger he was, and she expected he'd never hurt a girl. Well, not unless she enjoyed it. She saw that in him too, and wondered how many playful spankings he'd given. But had he ever had his own ass caned? Had a woman run her lips over every throbbing welt, her slim fingers gripping his ass cheeks, spreading them so she could play with his rim with her tongue? She bet he'd buck against the mattress, come, make a mess against his belly and the bedding.

His touch became a little less gentle, testing her grip when he couldn't dislodge her. She constricted it enough to make him feel his breath labor in his windpipe. Though he didn't yet realize it, she had at least three times his strength. For a normal human male, the multiple might be more, but the man was tough as leather and powerful. She liked that.

"I'm like a rodeo bull," she said, holding his gaze. "I can be ridden, but only if you respect how much stronger I am. And how easy it would be for me to crush you."

He swallowed beneath her grip, but it wasn't nervousness. Not that kind. A different awareness came into his eyes. He had questions, yes, maybe, but something else took precedence. While she'd expected that reaction, seeing it come out the way it did was a lovely surprise.

Reaching out, he hooked a finger in the vee of her shirt. Tugged lightly, encouraging her to come closer. She gave him a step, laying her other hand on his chest. That large finger caressed the valley between her breasts, found the edge of her lacy bra. He ran his knuckle over the rise of one curve, then down between again. The man had a nice, seductive touch, and she saw that awareness in his eyes, but he wasn't manipulating her. He just needed to touch her. He was hungry too.

So she closed the last step, letting her hand slide from around his throat to behind his neck, finally indulging in a nice dive into those thick brown locks that curled over her knuckles. As she lifted up on her toes, he anticipated her mouth, but she nudged against his jaw, making him turn his head away. She traced his carotid with her tongue, her lips.

He had his hands on her hips, gripping her belt loops, then he slid into her pockets, making the paper she'd put in there crinkle. His fingers curved, gripping toned flesh. She made an approving noise as she reached his ear, cruised across his cheek. He had his eyes closed. Her hand was tight in his hair, keeping his head still, a message that she was setting the pace.

"I want to fuck you," she breathed. "I want to hear you beg for my cunt. Hear you say *please* in a rough voice. That's new for you, isn't it, Quinn? You were taught to demand, not beg. That's what women usually want, don't they? For you just to take. But sometimes you'd like her to be the one to do the taking. It feels good to get lost in someone else's demands. And I have a lot of demands. You can get lost with me for a good...long...time."

"Two-way street, honey."

She was impressed that he'd managed the response, even as she heard the gruff tone she'd wanted to hear. "We'll see." Then she took her first taste of his mouth.

*Oh yes.* This was going to work out just fine. His lips parted, and the heat of him was welcome, sending a searing liquid rush between her legs. She'd be welcoming his clever mouth down there too. Eventually. She pressed harder against him and he accommodated her unspoken need wonderfully, hands sliding out of her jeans pockets and down to cup her ass and hike her up his body. He reversed their positions so he had her against the wall, his hard cock pushing between her legs, rubbing even with the frustration of two layers of denim between them. When he broke the kiss between them to curve his muscular back and take a nip at her throat, tangling one big hand in her hair to tug her head back, heat shot through her. Yes, he wanted her to take control, but he'd push the boundaries, do some taking of his own. She liked that mix.

Wrapping her legs around him, she tightened her thighs, watching his eyes darken at the noticeable constriction around his hips, the press of her boot heels against the base of his very fine ass. Watching him deal with Artie, those haunches tight and biceps bunched, had been a display that only whetted her appetite for more. She wanted to take a nice healthy grab of that ass and squeeze until he'd show finger-shaped bruises.

"Upstairs," she said. "Now."

"Not against the wall?" His eyes glinted with mischief, and she gave him an arch look in return, digging a nail into his collarbone.

"I like to eat in bed."

"Yes ma'am."

The address stilled her, and she saw his gaze flicker, noticing her reaction, but she let it pass. Too much, too soon. A strong man who'd denied his true desires, thinking they didn't fit with his image of himself, could be easily spooked by them, at least at first. She wanted the stallion who would come looking for the bridle while still occasionally fighting it for her pleasure. She wasn't interested in the horse she had to break to accept restraint.

He hitched her more securely against him, having no problem carrying her out of the office despite the fact she knew she was heavier than she appeared. He went down to the end of the hall, to the access stairway. As he clomped up the two flights of stairs, she indulged herself by sliding her arms around his wide shoulders, tightening her hold over them. She ran lips and tongue along his jaw, rubbing herself against him, enjoying the feel of her breasts pressed firmly against his chest.

He groaned, stopped to push her against the wall again, bracing one boot on the next stair up so she was sitting on that leg as he gripped her hair once more to force a kiss between them. She permitted it. Frankly, she was getting lost in his passion. She wondered how long it had been for him. Beyond that, how long had it been since he'd had a woman who'd truly satisfied him?

The possessiveness that surged through her was unexpected, setting off some warning bells, but she wasn't going to get bogged down in the possibility of complications. All that mattered was right now.

"Gotta let you down, sweetheart. Gotta unlock the door." He let her slide down his body, but she straddled his thigh as he did, dipping her fingers into his front pocket. It was right above where her pubic mound pressed against hard muscle. When he braced himself against the door frame, pleasure rippled between her legs. He watched her with a half-amused, half violently aroused expression as she fished out the keys, including a nice tease against the bulge of his ball sac before she pulled the keys loose, dangled them in front of his eyes.

"Here you are."

He managed to unlock the door without fumbling, which impressed her, then he banded an arm around her waist, lifting her off her feet to carry her through the door and kick it closed. He didn't let her feet touch the floor until they reached the bedroom. "It's dusty in here," he said, glancing around. "Probably a few spiders."

"I'll protect you from them."

36

He snorted, but she could see the concern about what she'd think of their surroundings. He might be hot and horny as a rutting bull, but he was a gentleman. She liked that. The bed was draped in a sheet, which he tugged off to reveal a decent but worn coverlet, a couple pillows with cases that looked clean enough. Serviceable for a ranch hand or as an army barracks.

"This isn't really the greatest place to take a lady," he began. "We can—"

"All I want is you, right now, right here. And shut up." Even though she liked the masculine rumble of his voice, she wanted to hear it strained by harsh groans, punctuated with fierce, fervent oaths as she did everything she wanted to him. She moved to the bed, lifting a hand to stop him when he followed right behind her, hands reaching for her.

"I know you're a cowboy, so you probably come with your own whip. But now I'm in charge. Take off your clothes. Slow. I want to savor."

His lips twisted at that. She could tell he knew women found him pleasing in all the right ways, a matter-of-fact thing helpful to get between their legs but sometimes maybe a pain in the ass to him when he wanted something more. She stretched out on the bed, leaning back on her elbows. Though she was conscious of the heat of his gaze on her, she lifted a brow expectantly.

He slid open the buttons of his shirt, keeping to a gradual pace to suit her demands. Maybe he didn't do it in a striptease fashion, but he wasn't that type of man. She didn't mind that about him.

He had a gorgeous upper body, layered with a working man's musculature, marked with some scars. He'd worked shirtless enough that there wasn't much of a tan line between his exposed neck and forearms and the rest of him. She loved the look of a shirtless man in jeans and boots. When he sat down on the end of the bed to pull his boots off, she shifted and closed the distance between them, kneeling up behind him on her knees to slide her palms over his shoulders and back, feeling the way the muscles rolled as he performed the simple action. As he stood to slip the button of the jeans, he turned to face her, and she sat back on her heels, watching attentively.

"I'm used to girls talking when I do this. You don't talk."

"Why would I talk when that takes attention away from what matters?" She met his gaze, then lowered it pointedly, a nonverbal message. *Get on with it.*

An attractive quirk of his lips, and he pulled the jeans open, the zipper making its pleasing *tick-tick* noise. He wore basic cotton boxers, nothing fancy, and he took them down with the jeans, removing socks so the whole man stood before her.

He was tough and lean from head to toe, and sporting a cock stand that made her pussy even wetter just to look at it. Sliding off the other side of the bed, she gestured to the mattress. "On your back, cowboy. Legs shoulder length apart. I want to be able to see everything I intend to touch, lick, suck and taste."

"Jesus." He paused, giving her a once-over. "You're a little over-dressed."

"That'll change when I'm ready. I gave you an order."

She was testing him. If she'd put a little flirt into it, she knew it would give him an out. He could laugh it off and rationalize that it was silly sex games, nothing serious, but she wasn't in the mood to give him that much mental lubrication. She was going to be honest with this man from the very beginning and all the way through. Maybe because she sensed the yearning in him to cut through a world of bullshit and find something real, something solid, that she'd always needed herself.

*Selene, this really might be a mistake.*

Their gazes held. "Trust me, Quinn," she said. "If only for this."

Another weighted moment and then he moved to the bed. She wished she could be inside his mind, hearing every turn in the decision wheel that brought him to the mattress, but pleasure surged through her at the end result. He stretched out that long, powerful body, linking his fingers behind his head in a pose of deceptive casualness, even as his brown gaze stayed locked on her expectantly.

Moving to the end of the bed where he'd dropped his jeans, she picked them up. Sliding her hand inside the seat, she enjoyed the warmth of where his ass had been. Then she stripped the belt out of the loops. It still carried the heat of his body as well. She came to the head of the bed, leaned over him. He watched her as she curled fingers around his wrist, tugging so she guided his hand to the iron rails of the headboard. She brought the other there too, making him cross his wrists before she looped the belt in a figure eight around them, cinching and doing a tie that would hold them unless he gave serious effort to getting loose. He didn't look as if he had that plan.

Instead, his breath had stilled, then become a little shallow, even as the pulse in his throat jumped, increasing her blood hunger. His lips parted, tongue wetting them, an unconscious act of anticipation or anxiety.

"Feels good, doesn't it?" she said.

He swallowed, eyes staying on her, jaw tight. "Don't know."

"What a strong man says when the answer is yes, but he doesn't know how that reflects upon his masculinity. Grip the rails of the headboard," she said. "Don't let go."

Keeping an eye to the lower latitudes, she saw his cock surge again as she gave the order, as she cinched the belt and did a loose loop around the rails to reinforce the hold of his fingers. She heard the expulsion of breath, saw the glitter in his eyes. Yeah, he liked this, even as she saw him continue the internal war over it. "Big, tough cowboy," she said quietly, running a nail over his sternum, circling his nipple, biting into it with the edge. "Always in control. In control of your men, your ranch, this place, with women. But there's a different kind of male power, Quinn. One that you've always known is waiting for you, waiting to serve a woman if she knows where to look for that treasure."

He swallowed again, but he didn't speak. Didn't deny it. He was listening, learning about himself. About her. She could see all the wheels going in his head. He didn't know what to say. He'd think about all of it later and they'd probably hit a few bumps as a result when he tried to backpedal. That was part of the pleasure. For now, it was all reaction, and she was fine with that. Very fine.

She stepped away, stood by the bed as she began to lift the hem of her knit shirt. "Close your eyes."

"No." His voice was hoarse. "Hell no."

She stopped, gave him a leisurely once-over. "You can look at me, or you can feel me. Which would you prefer?"

"You get both. Why can't I?"

"Because you get what I give you. No more and no less."

"What if I'm not willing to give you...everything you want?"

A smart question, and one he didn't realize had gone beyond his control the minute a vampire walked into his bar and decided she wanted him. Correction. It was beyond his control if she embraced the whole humans-are-inferior-and-ours-to-use-however-we-want vampire credo. And if she decided she wanted everything from him.

No. Forty years ago, she'd been human herself. Albeit sometimes she felt like she was clinging to a mortal conscience by her fingernails, she still made the effort. Beyond that, she couldn't want everything from him. She wouldn't be able to stay here that long.

Wanting everything meant making him her fully marked human servant, and she'd not yet taken that step with any human. Female vampires were choosier, usually taking that step as they drew closer to the century mark, whereas male vampires might do it before hitting fifty. But looking at him, restrained by his belt and their mutual desires, she felt a clenching in her lower belly that was part sex, part need, part longing.

*God, Selene. Shut up and fuck him already.*

She hadn't answered his question, too busy wrestling with her own, but now she summoned a smile. "If you close your eyes, you'll find out if you're willing to give me everything I want."

He sighed, hard, but shut his eyes, probably not realizing his fingers clenched as he did it, a quiver running through all those impressive muscles. His cock just got thicker, standing up tall and eager. She removed the shirt, shimmied out of boots and jeans, leaving on the dark-blue silky bra and matching lace panties. Then she leaned over him, sliding a hand over his biceps on the far side, pressing her breasts to his chest. She blew on his lashes, making him frown and then smile.

"You *want* to give me everything I want, Quinn, but you think you need to fight about it. I like a fight, for the right reasons. This is not that moment. Let yourself feel. Let me enjoy you."

She straddled him then, and he groaned as she rubbed her lace-clad pussy, the crotch already soaked through, against the length of his cock. Reaching behind her, she cupped his ball sac, a nice weight in her hand, as she rotated her hips on him. "Feel how wet I am?"

"Yeah. Fuck yes. Want your panties off. Want to feel your cunt."

"Then ask me for that. Nicely. Remember 'please'?"

"Please."

"Please what?"

"I want to feel your cunt against my cock. Please."

"Very nice." She stood up, removed her bra and dropped it on the floor. Then she shimmied out of the panties. When she sat back down upon him, she draped them over his face, pushing the crotch against his lips. "Taste, Quinn."

He licked, then his lips closed over the fabric, giving it a gentle suck. She took her hand away, leaving the sheer garment spread over his face like a veil. His nostrils flared beneath thin lace.

"That's all for you, Quinn. When you had Artie shoved against the wall, and I reached out and touched you, I wanted your cock right then. I wanted us to fuck right up against that worthless piece of shit like he didn't matter at all."

She also wanted to rip into Artie's throat, make him howl in pain and gush blood for stealing from Quinn, for feeling like he had a right to take advantage of her cowboy. But she'd save that vicious tidbit. The sex side of being a vampire was overwhelming enough to humans.

"God..." His hips twitched, pressing his cock up against her labia.

"Easy there, bronc," she said breathlessly, tightening her thighs on him. "Keep it in the chute right now."

She reached between them, gripped him. Yeah, he was thick as a tree branch, and when she squeezed and stroked, his thigh and biceps muscles bunched, body straining to stay still. She let him go, stroked her pussy along his length, working him with the moisture between her slick lips as she leaned down and began to taste his chest, his nipples, his shoulders, moving back toward his throat. His fingers stayed clenched around the headboard. He was fighting the restraint, but the arousal was also intensifying because of it.

As she reached the carotid, her fangs lengthened, not to be denied this time. So hungry. She turned her head, lifted it enough to see his eyes open beneath the lace, staring at her through that hazy barrier. His lips parted, seeking air, seeking her. She rose up over him, let him see her body arch as she gripped him once more, guided him into her, controlling the pace, the descent.

"Condom..." He had the presence of mind to protect them both, but she shook her head.

"Not needed, cowboy. Promise. That's the one way you're totally safe with me."

*Maybe the only way.*

She was sure he wasn't naïve enough to let that pass, not normally, but this wasn't normal. That was obvious from how she could feel his passion unfolding beneath her, reckless, uncertain, wild. It was what she'd meant when she'd said if he ever unleashed it for the right woman, his response would overwhelm them both in a way he wouldn't anticipate.

But he wasn't the only one taken unawares by that. As she descended, inch by inch, feeling his cock stretch her, slide in deep, her eyes were caught by his behind that barrier. She should tell him to close his eyes again, but it was as if that lock held them over a chasm. Neither one looking away, knowing to do so would be to fall. The worst part wouldn't be the tumble, but falling alone.

"Free yourself," she whispered.

It took him a couple minutes. He twisted his hands in his bonds, pushed and pulled, strained, while she rode him like she might a cantering horse, enjoying the unexpected thrusts, slides and angles of his cock inside her. He was a good-sized man, filling her in a way that had her pussy spasming, clutching him hard. When he finally got one hand free, that took care of the other. He surged up from the bed, banding his arms around her to drive her down hard and snug on his loins, ripping a cry from her. She bowed back in his hold, gasping as his lips clamped over her right nipple. Gripping his hair, she worked her hips on him in a circular rhythm as he sucked, drawing deep.

"So fucking good," he muttered. "Want to taste your cunt. Taste all of you."

He thrust with the skill of a man who knew how to bring a woman's body to pleasure, and the first orgasm took her fast and quick. Her clit swelled and hardened, pussy gushing over him. She cried out again, digging her nails into his back. It had been too long since she'd gone this route to feed and she didn't know her own strength. She raked hard enough to draw four furrows of blood.

*Blood.* The scent filled her nose, and she brought her fingers to her lips, tasting what she'd taken from him. He flipped them then, all effortless strength. She was always an on-top girl, so it surprised her how much she welcomed the feel of him on her like this. She gazed up at him as he pressed her into the quilt, kept thrusting, giving her searing aftershocks that had her moaning, holding onto him, taking full pleasure in the ride. Since she stared into his face as he stared into hers, she saw that rigid state that took over right before climax, knew when his body was gathering. She reared up, slid her arms around him. When he thought he couldn't hold out any longer, she spoke against his ear.

JOEY W. HILL & DESIREE HOLT

"Hold out for me, Quinn. Not until I say. Ssshh, cowboy. Hold..."

He groaned against her temple, kept thrusting, but she felt his body taut as a bowstring, obeying her. It was a drug all its own, none like it.

"Come for me, Quinn," she commanded at last. Then she bit him.

She could release a rush of pheromones with her bite, and she did so now, propelling his orgasm to a much higher intensity, though if his was anything like hers, it was already more intense than expected. His blood flooded her mouth, and she'd never tasted a man who was so every-kind-of-taste she wanted. Bittersweet chocolate, just like the color of his eyes. Leather and sweat, open prairie, the heat of a horse's flanks, sunsets over open land, the terrain she'd driven in darkness since she entered Texas. All of it was in him.

Oh God, she was so hungry. She really had waited too long to feed. A couple of his more thoughtful looks in the bar had suggested he'd picked up on some sense of vulnerability in her, and maybe it was the weakness that came with hunger. That wasn't acceptable in normal circumstances, but all she could think of right now was that he would nourish her, help restore her in so many ways.

She knew how much to drink without endangering him. He'd be a little lethargic tomorrow, but he'd be fine, no worse than an aggressive blood donation. If she gave him the first mark, she could figure out where he was, imagine what he was doing...

It was good she was on the downhill side of her climax when she had that thought, because the shock of it might have stopped her mid-peak. She'd never been tempted to give a man *any* one of the three marks that were the steps toward making a human a vampire's full servant. She was too young, right? Or maybe it was because she'd been dealing with too much shit from Laurent to have time to focus on it.

Quinn might just be wrong time, wrong place. But it didn't feel that way.

The geographical locater, the first mark, wouldn't be too bad. She'd always know where he was, would be able to tell when he was coming to the bar. Of course she'd scented him over a room full of people, so that was a weak justification.

Nevertheless, she did it, releasing the serum as she drank. It tingled through his blood in a way that made him shudder once more, but it also had the least side effects of any of them. It was okay to know where he was. She wanted to know where he was. Always, even when she had to leave him behind as a fond memory. Part of her history.

He groaned out the last of his release, her holding him close. She didn't want to let him go, and he gave a half chuckle against her temple when he tried to shift off her and she merely tightened her grip.

"I'm too heavy."

He wasn't. He was like the shelter in a storm, his heat, his scent, the steady thump of his heart. What was wrong with her? He couldn't protect her. No one could.

"Hey." His hand slid up to cup her skull, to hold her face pressed to his throat and shoulder as she held him even tighter. "You're shaking, honey. You okay?"

"Yeah." She cleared her throat, forced herself to smile before she laid her head back on the pillow. "You're right. You're heavy. Get off."

He gave her a searching look even as he smiled and slid to the side. When he gathered her up against him, it was no hardship to drape over his chest, put her cheek down over that reassuring heartbeat, feel his fingertips stroke through her hair, down her bare back.

She threaded her fingers through his light mat of chest hair, followed the arrow of it to his ridged abdomen, stroked his hip bone and studied his cock, now replete but so obviously capable of giving a woman pleasure. He turned his head, pressed his lips and nose into her hair. It was an intimate position, one that unfurled things inside her. Unexpected things.

"Selene." He paused, and she liked how her name sounded on his lips. "Who are you hiding from?"

She propped herself up on an elbow. He gave her a searching look, reached up to slide a finger along her cheek, her jaw. In return, she settled her fingers on the bite mark on his neck. She knew he hadn't really registered it too much. The euphoria the released pheromones caused could do that, but now he put his hand there as well. She moved her hand so he could touch the bites, but put her fingers back over his and pressed down, let him feel those two punctures, understand they were a bit more extreme than the usual love bite.

"No one who is part of your world, Quinn." If she did everything the way she should, that world would never be part of his. Yeah, she'd given him the geographical locater mark, but that was a minor infraction, not a big deal. It actually protected him a little bit.

"So you're really strong. You don't like daylight. And…"

She saw his fingers slide across his throat again. He wouldn't say it aloud, but she could hear him thinking it. She'd drunk his blood.

"Yes, I'm a vampire."

He wouldn't believe her. That was the point. The powerful vampires on the top of the food chain who called the shots for all of them mostly lived in their mansions, cloaked in a veil of mystery. As such, they could harp all they wanted about never breathing a word about being a vampire to the human world and make that work.

In contrast, she was an average-income working girl with fangs and no permanent home. So in the twenty-first century, full of zealots and freaks in the news, she'd found the opposite tactic worked. Instead of hiding all the obvious vampire peculiarities, she put them out in the open, claimed she was a vampire, and people just shrugged and expected she was an escapee from the Discovery

Channel Taboo series. It was the best century *ever* for a non-human to blend.

That strategy worked best when she worked and stayed in large cities, which Nightfall was decidedly not. But Quinn had seemed desperate enough to be worth the risk. If she proved she could run his bar and give him a good time in bed, he'd probably roll with it for a while. Guys tended to accept a crazy chick if the sex was worth it. And if she didn't cause him any hassles with running After Dark.

"A vampire, hmm?" He had that measuring look in his eye, already weighing her potential crazy-chick factor against Artie's many shortcomings. After her performance this evening, she expected she still had Artie by a mile.

"Yeah, but if you don't mind, I'd ask that you keep that information to yourself. And not just so people won't think your new bar manager is a freak."

As he mulled that, Selene watched him with a frown. The way he was processing the information seemed different from most humans. Almost as if it wasn't his first encounter with something otherworldly, something more significant than the typical every-one-has-a-ghost-story-to-tell imaginings.

There was no scent of magic on him, yet the look in his eyes, while not total acceptance, was...wait and see. She didn't know if that made things more or less dangerous for her here.

Though she was curious, she couldn't grill him on it right now. The timing wasn't right and this might not work out at all. She could be back on the road tomorrow, for all she knew.

Turning on his side, he touched the pendant lying on her breast bone. "Odd necklace for a vampire. Looks like a dagger through a heart." His gaze flicked up to her. "Or a stake."

"It's a reminder that none of us are as invincible as we think we are."

"Hmm. What if you can't trust me? What if I tell the local paper? Call Van Helsing?"

"If he looks like Hugh Jackman, go right ahead. But technically,

I'm supposed to kill you if you tell anyone. I'd prefer not to do that. I need the job."

She lay back down in his arms, nestled her head under his chin. Once he went home, got up in the morning to do his normal ranch day, he'd probably rethink hiring a woman who acted like a vampire, who'd drunk his blood.

But that was later. For now, she'd lie here and imagine that maybe, for at least a little while, she'd found a place to be. Planting a distracting suggestion might help. Not that she needed a reason. She'd much rather play sensual games with him than talk about things that sent off alarm bells in his world.

"Quinn?" She whispered it against his ear, pleased at the strength of the arm that tightened around her, the heat of his body, the sleepy male grunt of acknowledgement. "Do you own a whip? Chaps?"

She actually felt him go more still, and hid a smile in his shoulder.

"Yeah."

"Next time you come to me, I want you to bring them." She drew back, put a finger on his lips before he could ask. "I'm not going to tell you why. Your job is just to obey. Understand, cowboy?"

He tilted his head down to look at her, those brown eyes that were so deliciously conflicted, the firm mouth she wanted to spend a lot more time tasting...and make taste her. Thinking of curling her hand in that thick hair, pushing his lips against her pussy, she shivered with pleasure. He felt it, his eyes darkening. She'd ride him again tonight. Maybe a couple more times.

Cowboys had stamina, after all.

"Yes ma'am," he drawled, with a glint in his eye.

# CHAPTER FOUR

"*D*on't move, cowboy."

*How could a voice like a whisper over the skin be so dominating at the same time? It held him in place on his knees, hands behind his back, even as he craved to reach out and touch the creamiest skin he had ever seen. Quinn gritted his teeth, chafing at the tone of command even as his body responded to it. His cock throbbed with urgent need and his mouth watered to taste again every inch of the petite woman standing before him.*

"*Do you want to lick my cunt?*"

"*Yes.*" *He ground out the word. He wanted to lap her incredible essence more than he wanted his next breath. What stunned him was the desire—no, need—to wait for her to give him permission. As if his body was chained with invisible restraints that could only be released by a word from her. A nod. Perhaps even a touch.*

*Her tongue slid over her plump lips before they curved into a knowing smile.*

"*No touching me except with your tongue.*"

*He tightened his fists at the small of his back until his nails dug into his skin. Shockingly, the pain sent lust spiraling through him and the throbbing in his cock increased.*

"*Well?*" *she prompted.*

*"You're tough."*

*"Oh cowboy." Her eyes glinted with hunger. "You have no idea."*

*While his brain couldn't reconcile the ethereal vision before him with her whipstrike authority, his body was having no trouble telling him to get right on with it before he imploded. His pulse pounded in his veins as Selene moved forward until barely a sheet of paper would have fit between them. Widening her stance, she spread the lips of her pussy with slim fingers, presenting him with all that slick pink flesh.*

*His tongue snaked from his mouth, the tip gliding down from the top of her slit. He paused briefly to circle her clit, stimulating the knot of flesh, then following the path back up to the top. Her sigh of pleasure spurred him on, and he did it again. And again. And—*

Quinn woke. He'd neglected to close the blinds last night and the morning sun poured over him, burning his eyes. The quilt was crumpled at the foot of the bed and the sheet was draped haphazardly from his waist, his aching shaft tenting it enough to make room for an army.

*Shit. Holy shit.*

The dream had been so vivid that he thought it was real, leaving him looking around the room for Selene. But of course she wasn't there. She was sleeping, either in the dark cellar or in that little apartment above After Hours. Recharging her energy, she'd told him when she sent him on his way.

In every relationship he'd been the one in control. The one to call the shots. To demand. Oh he always paid attention to his partner's needs, making sure she was completely satisfied. Tested and teased to find out the things that turned her on. Excited her. But it was his rodeo. He'd been in charge all his life, first with his competitions, then with the ranch, now with the bar.

But last night Selene had taken command. When she wound his belt around his wrists, restraining him, he'd been harder than he ever remembered. When at last she permitted him to come— *permitted!*—his release nearly blasted the top of his head off.

What was it she'd said? *There's a different kind of male power,*

*Quinn. One that you've always known is waiting for you, waiting to serve a woman if she knows where to look for that treasure.*

It would have to be on her terms. Could he accept that?

Maybe.

Maybe that was why he'd had the dream. A message that she was unlocking a side to him he'd never acknowledged but sensed, particularly in his growing dissatisfaction with his existing relationships. He saw it as a battle of wills, himself the animal craving to be both goaded and tamed. While one part of his brain said *fuck, no* the other part said *more, more, more.*

Forcibly shutting down his internal dialogue, he shoved himself out of bed and padded into the bathroom. In the shower he realized he couldn't possibly get dressed with his penis so heavy and hard. As he leaned against the tile wall of the shower, hot water beating down on him, he stroked himself roughly to completion.

Closing his eyes, he imagined standing before her. His mouth grew dry at the vision of her spun-gold hair drifting around her face, the pale tracery of veins beneath her delicate skin, the faint beat of her pulse at the sweet hollow of her throat, blue eyes gleaming with hunger as she watched him come for her. Maybe when he was finished she'd lift his hand and lick it clean before wrapping those moist lips around his cock.

*Stop!*

He had to get dressed. Get outside. The hands were moving part of the herd from one pasture to another today and everyone was needed, including him. His hand was shaking as he turned off the stream of water and stepped out to dry himself. He managed to pull on his clothes and his boots without passing out, but his body was so weak it took a supreme effort of concentration.

By the time he reached the kitchen he had thankfully managed to pull himself together.

"Everyone else ate and headed out," Annette scolded.

The woman had come with the ranch, so to speak, having served as housekeeper for the previous owner. She lived in a tiny house just past the barn that looked as if it had been built one year before God, but she always assured him that it suited her just fine. No, she didn't need him to make any improvements, thank you very much, so quit pestering her about it. Quinn wasn't sure of her exact age. Somewhere between forty and sixty, he guessed, with a solid body. She wore her graying dark hair in a long braid down her back and he'd never seen her with makeup. Or clad in anything except jeans and shirts, come to think of it. She dispensed the law of man according to Annette along with the most delicious meals he'd ever eaten, and kept the hands under tight control. Every morning he prayed she hadn't decided to pull up stakes and move on.

"Late night?" she prodded.

"Hard night at the bar," he mumbled.

That had been the damn truth. Only it wasn't the bar that had been hard.

Annette poured coffee into a mug for him and took two egg and sausage biscuit sandwiches out of the oven. She studied his face. "You'll kill yourself running the ranch and that bar at the same time."

He swallowed some of the coffee. "I think I might have fixed that last night."

"Yeah?" She lifted an eyebrow. "Not with that piece of trash Artie you've had in there."

Quinn smiled, remembering Selene's attitude where Artie was concerned.

"No, Annette. Artie's history." Another gulp of coffee. "Got myself a new one who knows what she's doing."

"She?" Annette's jaw dropped. "I heard the boys saying something about it when they ate but I didn't pay it much attention. Where'd you get her? What makes you think a woman can handle those roughnecks, anyway?"

"She wandered in looking for a job. Can you believe it? By the end of the night she had everyone eating out of her hand."

Annette barked a short laugh. "This I gotta see."

"Maybe I can coax her out here for one of your meals sometime."

*When exactly would that be, you idiot?*

Last night he'd wanted very badly to spend the rest of it with her but she was adamant.

*"Vampires need to sleep. Alone."*

Vampires, for shit's sake.

Of course, between Sam's shaman stuff and his grandfather's tales, it didn't sound near as crazy as it should. He slugged down the rest of the coffee and picked up the two breakfast sandwiches. "I expect the boys are already out with the herd?"

"And probably cussing you for sleeping in."

Quinn looked at his watch. Six thirty. Yeah, she was right. But that damn dream—

"On my way."

He strode to the barn to retrieve his black gelding, Midnight, and saddle him. While he was doing that, Kevin Lang limped out of the barn. Unable to work the cattle after an accident, he now kept the tack in shape and made sure the stalls were mucked and the horses fed.

"They're all out in the west pasture, Quinn." The old man squinted up at him. "Heard you drive in real late last night. I'm surprised you can even sit a horse today."

"I'm fine, old man." *About to get better.* "See you later."

He wolfed down one of the breakfast sandwiches before swinging up into the saddle and urging Midnight forward. As he cantered past the barn, Annette's little place and the bunkhouse, he skirted around the big steel building that held his small private plane.

Along with having a ranch, flying his own plane had been another deep-seated goal. He'd taken some of his rodeo winnings and bought the little two-seater for a good price, had the steel building thrown up, tarmac poured for the runway and some landing lights installed. Though he used the plane sometimes to check fences and water holes, he hadn't had the opportunity to use it for pleasure, embrace the sense of freedom flying brought him. Maybe if Selene worked out at After Hours he'd be able to take off for some place now and then.

*With Selene.*

Yeah, he'd like that. Always supposing he could talk her into it.

Riding to the west pasture, he relished the feel of the big horse beneath him, muscles moving rhythmically between his thighs.

Unbidden, his mind called up the image of Selene straddling him last night, riding him as he rode this bronc, the silken fall of her hair like a curtain surrounding him. Did she get the same feeling when her thighs were pressed against his body? Did the same sense of dominance race through her, the edge of excitement at controlling such power with just a touch of the hand or a flex of thigh muscles?

There was that word again. Dominance. He hadn't been able to get it out of his head.

Quinn was far from a sexual novice and Lord knew he'd played his share of kinky games. But this thing with Selene was something way beyond that. When he drove his cock into her he'd felt like a bucking horse thrusting into a brood mare. Her being in complete control of the situation only ramped up the lust and desire boiling inside him.

He couldn't lie to himself. The sex had been amazing. No, beyond that. Mind-blowing. His mouth watered as he recalled the perfect deep rose of her nipples and the sweet pink flesh of her cunt.

*Business, Pedraza. Pay attention. You have a ranch to run.*

The men were already rounding up the cattle when he reached the west pasture. He kept a crew of four experienced and dependable hands who needed little supervision from him. They'd taught him everything he now knew about ranching, all the things he'd refused to learn as a boy. He shook his head over the memory of that sullen adolescent, the rebellious teenager who could have ended up doing nothing with his life, if other factors hadn't intervened. Well, one major factor. *Sam.*

He wondered what the old shaman would think of Selene. He'd probably get that sage look on his face but say something smartass, like a 1950s cheesy western flick. *"White man who thinks with his little head ends up losing his big one."*

"Hey, Quinn." Johnny Barragan urged his horse forward and trotted over to greet him. His foreman had worked for the old man who owned Last Chance before Quinn and knew more about ranching than even Quinn's dad had. "Planning to wait until we got all the cows moved before you got your ass out of bed?"

Moving part of the herd from one pasture to the other in preparation for planting new grain was something they could almost do in their sleep. Considering his schedule lately, today he was more than grateful for that. Even so, he had to give the guys a hard time. Part of the comfortable routine of the day.

"Yeah." Quinn grinned at Johnny. "Thought I'd let you guys do all the hard work before I showed up."

"Heard you got a fine new bartender."

Quinn frowned. "News sure travels fast. I just hired her last night."

Johnny nodded. "Word is Artie's been blabbing to everyone how he got thrown out on his ass for no good reason."

"Artie needs to shut his mouth before I punch his head down where the sun don't shine. But yeah, he's out. Thank God. Got someone in there who knows how to run a bar. Tamed the help and the customers without even raising her voice."

*And me.*

"We could sure use a fine-looking woman around here," the cowboy said.

Quinn's fists knotted on the reins. "Pass the word the rule is hands off, Johnny. No one touches her or they'll have to go through me."

The man's eyes rose almost to the Stetson that sat on his head. "That so? Any special reason?"

"Because I said so. Now let's get to work."

Johnny gave him a speculative look but trotted back off. As

they all fell into a working rhythm like a choreographed ballet, Quinn was nevertheless glad that they were only moving a small part of the herd today, because his mind kept wandering. He had the feeling he'd been bewitched.

*"I'm a vampire."*

Had she really said that? Did she even expect him to take her seriously?

In Texas, outrageous legends were as common as household pets. So many had been handed down by the Comanche who had settled this particular area of the state. His grandfather had told him plenty of those stories. The one uppermost in his mind was the chupacabra, the bloodsucking beast who wreaked havoc wherever it went.

*Legends are not necessarily fantasy, haitsi.*

Sam again. Given how tumultuous his thoughts were today, it was no wonder that the man who'd shown him how to find a quiet inside, who'd helped point him toward better goals than rebelling against his father's hardness, would be coming to mind again.

He wondered if Sam would believe Selene was a vampire. If he did, Quinn knew he might just do the same, without question. That was how much faith he had in Sam's judgment.

He still remembered the day Sam had first shown up in his life. One of the hands, out riding fence line, had radioed in to Quinn's dad that there was an intruder who'd set up camp on the edge of the north pasture by a tiny stream. Quinn's father had gone out there with couple of hands to send him on his way. Curiously, when he returned, he'd merely said the man meant no harm and suggested the owner allow him to camp there a couple weeks. He'd also told Quinn and his brothers not to bother him.

Which meant Quinn went out there to get a look. The man was anywhere from sixty to a hundred and sixty, white hair flowing past his shoulders, creased skin leathered by the sun. Piercing blue eyes looked Quinn up and down when he rode up as if *he* was the stranger.

Then the stranger rose gracefully and held out his hand.

"I'm Sam," he said in a voice that, hand to God, sounded as if it rolled out of the deep earth where centuries of his ancestors might be buried.

Quinn's grandfather had told him stories of men like Sam Red Elk. Not shamans, but Native American philosophers. His grandfather had died when Quinn was very young, no more than seven or eight, but he'd made an indelible impression on him, a stark contrast to his own father. Maybe for that reason and some inexplicable others, he'd sneaked out and camped overnight with Sam more than once. On that handful of nights, Sam had taught Quinn what peace and serenity was. He'd helped Quinn let go of his angers from his many clashes with his father and helped him find the quiet he'd needed to center himself, decide what he wanted to do with his life.

Ironically—given how much he'd always thought he hated this life—what he'd realized he'd wanted was to own his own ranch.

But it wasn't necessarily those memories of Sam that were dogging Quinn's mind today. It was the glimpse of a different world where outlandish things were possible, and the stories Sam had told him that supported that idea. Stories so unbelievable Quinn had to believe they were true. No one could make up such fanciful things.

A land so big and open as this, with so many empty spaces, made a man consider things other people scoffed at. But he'd had a real live piece of it up close and personal. After Quinn had bought the Last Chance Ranch, Sam had come back into his life, camped out on the edge of the property for nearly a year. He'd said he was monitoring some kind of magical fault line, one of the things that had made him recommend the place for Quinn. *It has good energy, haitsi. You'll be happy here.*

Quinn hadn't known how to process that, at least not until he'd seen firsthand what Sam had meant about "monitoring". He could say it was tricks played by the dusk hours, but he still vividly remembered the night he'd stayed with the shaman on the spring solstice. Sam had laid a hand on him while his eyes were closed and

Quinn had felt the energy of the earth beneath them. That fault line was a living, breathing snake the size of a river, coiling and moving, carrying them. It filled Quinn up, held him under, held him still in every part of him and told him the world was way damn more than he'd ever know, even if he lived a thousand years.

Sam had opened his eyes at one point, and Quinn had looked deep into the center of the earth. Maybe the man had spoken, maybe he hadn't, but he'd heard the words as if they were writing themselves across his soul.

*You will find your heart in the otherworld, Quinn. The world men deny because they fear its strength. They fear losing control of what they know. Be brave, Quinn, and find your heart.*

If Selene was a vampire, that would qualify as the otherworld, wouldn't it?

He wanted to scoff at himself, but he remembered those energies uncoiling beneath his feet, in Sam's eyes, inside of Quinn himself. Damn, he sure could use some advice from Sam. He lived in Nevada now. Quinn missed him, but he knew the man was as close as a phone call or a day trip in his plane. The line with Sam had always felt sure and strong.

Lifting a hand, Quinn touched the bite mark on his neck. He could easily dismiss it as a love bite. Other women had marked him that way before. But this one appeared more detailed and precise. That had been no nip, but a full, locking penetration that set a tingle to his balls just thinking about it. Had she actually drunk his blood? When her silky skin had pressed against his and her sensuous lips caressed his neck, he'd felt lightheaded. Last night he'd chalked it up to the incredible intensity of the orgasm, but was it more than that?

Maybe she was just one of those Goth freaks who liked to pretend she was a vampire. There were towns in Texas where whole groups of people dressed in black and red and made themselves up to look like denizens of another world. Even brewed bloodlike concoctions they drank, saying it empowered them. Quinn thought they were crazy, but to each his own. Selene seemed as far from those people as it was possible to be, but she'd given no clue as to where she came from.

Whatever she was, she'd mesmerized him last night, leading him in an exquisite erotic dance.

When had he ever seen himself as a submissive? Yeah, he knew what the word submissive meant. You didn't get to be his age with his experience and not know a whole lot about the different sides of sex. Or the fantasies that just being near her seemed to evoke. He could still feel the press of the leather belt confining his wrists.

Okay, the sex with Selene, both real and imagined, was beyond amazing, but regardless of last night's play and his early morning dream, he was still a guy. He needed to establish more balance between them if they were to continue on with this—whatever it was. There was no question that they'd be moving forward. The lust and hunger boiling between them wasn't going to disappear.

He should take the reins a whole lot more. Right? Last night he'd been willing to let her lead the dance because, truth be told, he wanted her with a hunger he wasn't sure would ever be appeased. But tonight would be different. The roles would be reversed. He would be in charge and the lovely Selene would do his bidding. Count on it.

A sharp whistle pierced the air, interrupting his conversational duel with himself. "Hey, Quinn."

As Dave Ojeda spurred his horse in Quinn's direction, Quinn pulled up on Midnight's reins and waited for the hand to join him. "What's up? Looks like we're in good shape here." The herd was moving slowly but compactly. They hadn't had to chase dogies or look for lost calves.

"We are, but Johnny and I wondered if you want us to head them a little farther north. The next pasture is still showing signs of a lot of new growth. We might want to give it a little more time to fully mature."

Quinn lifted his Stetson, wiped his forehead with his forearm and resettled his hat on his head. "I guess. If you guys don't mind the extra time. It means making sure we get them through two gates."

Dave chuckled. "They're just moseying along in this heat. I don't think they'll give us any trouble."

"Okay then. Thanks for noticing. I'll go on ahead and open the gate and ride sentry."

As Dave nodded, Quinn turned Midnight in that direction. Then Dave hollered after him again.

"While you're going that way, can you give that cow that's decided to wander a nudge back with her friends?"

"Sure. No problem."

Quinn urged Midnight forward with the pressure of his knees to where the stray cow was ambling from the herd. When it refused to respond to Midnight's insistent movements, Quinn uncoiled the single-tail whip hooked at the side of the saddle and cracked it in the air. The cow gave him a *what the hell* look but turned and moved back to the others. He flicked the whip once more for good measure.

Looping the whip onto his saddle again, he recalled Selene's words from the night before. *"Do you own a whip?"*

Exactly what the hell did she think she was going to do with it? He wasn't into pain. Was he?

This was ridiculous. He never let himself get distracted while he was working. The ranch was serious business to him. He'd known this woman less than twenty-four hours, spent only a brief time with her in bed, yet his body burned for her and his mind kept drifting back to her. On sex. With her. Hunger simmered constantly beneath the surface like liquid on a slow flame.

Enough. He needed to get his mind back on work. Right now.

Giving himself a mental shake, he coaxed Midnight into a canter, heading toward the other side of the meadow where the gate to the next pasture was located. It was turning out to be a good day weather-wise, the sun coming up, a touch of breeze, the kind of day he liked. In the distance he could see the rise of the low mountains that gave the Hill Country its name, dotted with thick stands of mountain cedar.

The temperature had climbed to the high seventies, about average for late spring in south-central Texas. Before too long though, they'd be crowding triple digits. Texas wasn't known for long spring seasons. Summer could be a bitch, like living in an oven, so he tried to schedule chores with the herd accordingly.

Then Midnight hit a pothole and stumbled.

His fault. It was a fucking greenhorn mistake. With ranch work, there was no such thing as not paying attention, even when things seemed to be going smooth. Men who didn't pay attention ended up going ass over teakettle over their horse's head or worse, permanently injuring a horse Quinn considered worth three of himself.

"Fuck, whoa, boy. Christ."

It all happened in a blink, worst-case scenarios flashing through his head, and then Midnight shied back, righting himself. Experienced as he was, Quinn was nearly unhorsed by the sudden jolt, but then they were right as rain, just like that. Midnight dropped to a trot but kept heading toward the gate, obviously more focused on the job than Quinn was. As he said, the horse was worth three of him.

Then he saw what had made Midnight shy back on course. A butterfly of all things. It fluttered up past the left side of Midnight's head, the horse giving it a snort and head shake.

Quinn was used to seeing the beautiful little creatures. Texas had more species of butterflies and a larger population of them than any other state. Every year millions of Monarch butterflies migrated through the Hill Country, heading south for the winter and back to their habitat for the spring and summer. Midnight saw them all the time too, but this one had apparently almost flown up his nose when he hit that pothole.

Quinn was familiar with the variety of designs on their wings, but this one had a different blend of colors than he'd ever seen before. The larger part of the wingspan was a smoky blue, almost the exact color of Selene's eyes. The border at the bottom was a shimmery pale gold, like her hair.

Okay, he was going loopy if he was comparing a woman's eyes and hair to a butterfly. Still, as he halted Midnight, giving them both a moment to recoup from the near miss, he kept an eye on the creature. The butterfly made a graceful turn, riding an air current to land on his hand, which rested on the pommel of the saddle, reins wrapped over his knuckles. The insect perched there, its delicate wings rippling. Then it took off, brushing his hat brim before heading off on its daily business.

Almost like it was sending him a message. *Okay, cowboy, get your mind back on your business. I can't hang around all day to save your ass.*

His lips twisted. He'd given the butterfly Selene's imperious, sultry voice, which proved he had his head caught up in his dick. Definitely not on the job at hand. Nudging Midnight into a canter back toward the gate, he told himself to get down to business. Running a ranch was hard work; immersing himself in that would get him back on track better than anything else.

He actually did pretty well in that regard until the day started winding down. At that point, every time he touched the whip coiled on his saddle or felt the belting of his chaps press across his pelvis, he thought of Selene, demanding he bring the chaps and whip with him. Usually he dreaded going to After Hours. Today, when the cattle were finally settled and he could ride back to the ranch with the hands, he was chafing at the bit to be at the saloon.

Quite frankly, that pissed him off. During the afternoon he had caught the men sending peculiar glances his way and he knew his distraction was obvious to them. He was too old to be led around by his dick, and he sure as hell couldn't afford for his men to see him that way. He needed to shower, change, get his shit together. The main reason he needed to go to After Hours tonight was not to get laid or let some pint-sized girl boss him around. He needed to make sure last night wasn't some kind of fluke, and that she really did know what she was doing with the bar. Everything else was secondary. Ridiculous as it might be, it felt like his goals for the ranch, the saloon, his whole life plan, were all teetering in the balance.

Maybe he shouldn't take the whip, make it clear he wasn't going to do everything she said. Or maybe he would take it, just to turn the tables. He imagined wrapping the fall around her luscious backside, holding it tight to keep her pressed against his cock. He wouldn't use it on her. God no. But he idly considered putting her over his knee, giving her a spanking, watching her thrash.

That was kind of fun to imagine. He'd gone that route before with women. But as he chose a clean shirt from his closet, his movements slowed, and he only got as far in his mind as closing his hand around her delicate wrist and pulling her forward between his knees. Then she took over the fantasy the same way she seemed to take over his reality. Sliding her hands free to frame his face, she'd bend down and brush his lips with hers, whispering the command to keep his hands on his knees, off her until she said okay, while things built inside him like a cyclone threatening to tear out his foundation.

Time to head to After Hours and Selene. And what was sure to be an erotic battle of wills. He couldn't wait.

The dashboard clock on Quinn's truck read eleven o'clock when he finally pulled into the parking area at the rear of After Hours and let himself in through the backdoor. Despite his full intent to be there earlier, Johnny had intercepted him to go over some things, which led to a couple phone calls in his office, where the stack of paperwork waiting for his attention couldn't be ignored.

So here he was, three hours later than he'd intended. He reasoned that was okay though. If this—hiring her as manager— was to work, he needed to give her room to establish herself. Let the patrons see her as the person in charge. He'd still come early enough to see how she was doing. All in all, this was probably the best time to do it. Any problems she'd had would be obvious.

He looked at the coiled whip he held in his hand and the leather chaps draped over one arm and shook his head, hardly able to believe he had actually brought them with him. A kaleidoscope of erotic images danced in his head as he opened the office door and placed them on his desk. He visualized her naked with the whip in her hand, flicking her wrist to make the thin strip of leather dance in the air as he did when herding cattle. In his mind he was also naked, except for the chaps, and facing away from her, hands pressed to the wall. He could almost hear the hiss of the single tail in the air and his buttocks clenched in anticipation.

*Jesus, Pedraza.* Despite all his self admonitions, the second he stepped into the building, those desires surged back to the forefront. *Don't be a pussy. Unless that's part of wanting to be a sissy-boy submissive too.*

His jaw hardened along with his resolve. *She's* only *in charge of the bar.*

The office had already been reorganized, a new system in place that made it easy to see which invoices were paid, which were pending, everything in a commonsense, neat filing system. She'd also laid out reports on the now clean desk that made it clear she'd expected him to come in and take a look. Reports evaluating inventory versus sales, legible notes in the margins of what product could be cut, which should be added. A cost estimate and sketch of interior design adjustments to spruce up the bar area and encourage more liquor purchases. A scaled-down but more appealing menu of bar food choices, integrating some local flavor with traditional comfort foods.

All in less than twenty-four hours. Was the woman even real?

He couldn't find anything that didn't seem like a good idea or not affordable on the current income level. Given that word of mouth had obviously turned out a big local crowd this week to check out the new help, it was a good bet they'd keep coming back.

As he left the office and headed to the main floor, the good impressions just multiplied. The air was filled with a mixture of voices and music, but tonight they seemed to be less raucous than usual. Not subdued, exactly, but...tempered. People having a good time, but not out of control like rowdy schoolchildren.

Standing at the hallway entrance, he assessed the situation. All the tables were taken, as were most of the bar stools. A few couples were on the dance floor moving to the music. He wasn't sure what they were doing could actually be called dancing, but they seemed to be enjoying themselves. Laughter was a punctuation mark in the blend of noises and shockingly no one was fighting or falling-down drunk.

Maria wove between the tables, serving tray balanced on one hand, smiling as she delivered the orders. A pink t-shirt with some kind of sparkle on it and boot-cut jeans covered her curves. Her thick hair was pulled back in a ponytail that bounced with each step. No one was grabbing for her body parts or making lewd remarks.

The tantalizing aroma of barbecue drifted from the kitchen and when he slid along the back wall to peek into the kitchen, he was stunned to see Manuel in not only a clean shirt but a new cook's apron, piling barbecue on heated buns and sliding the plates onto the pass-through for Selene or Maria to pull them through.

Another transformation.

But what drew his attention and mesmerized him was the manager herself. Selene wore the same jeans from the night before but tonight she'd paired them with a black t-shirt that made the gold of her hair even more pronounced.

Even though there was a sizeable crowd, her gaze pinned him the second he approached the bar. Her lips curved, the blue eyes reflecting...he wouldn't describe it as the easy warmth of a hearth fire. More like a she-wolf realizing dinner was within range of her jaws. Why that turned him on, he wasn't sure. For a brief moment he remembered the butterfly and a strange mixture of emotions surged through him like a waterfall tumbling along sparkling rock.

Selene never missed a beat, even though he was sure she was aware of his eyes on her every minute. She moved easily up and down behind the bar, working the beer taps, serving drinks, cleaning as she went and making sure she collected every dime due to the bar.

Quinn shook his head. Just like last night, it seemed to be her tone of voice, her smile, just the right touch of professional reserve and friendly barkeep, that kept people behaving and gravitating to her. While his customers wouldn't appreciate the comparison, it was a lot like the way cows responded to an experienced hand. If he showed weakness or fear, they picked up on it and took advantage or got out of control fast. Feeling uncertain and nervous, unguided or unprotected was the worst situation for a herd. If a hand knew what he was doing, the cows knew he was in charge and responded accordingly, staying pretty manageable even when things got riled up.

Her smile had a core of steel behind it, which she'd made evident to everyone. She'd cast a magic net over them, earning their respect and turning a mob into a friendly group of people. She was such a paradox. Look what she was doing to him.

*Fuck.*

He hadn't been this conflicted since he left rodeoing and took ownership of the ranch. At least in that area he had some working knowledge of what was required. With Selene he was drifting rudderless, trying to find his footing.

Moving into the barback area, he fetched an empty mug and poured a beer for himself. Selene turned in his direction and unleashed her bewitching smile. Heat surged through him and he took a healthy swallow of his beer. Trying to look casual and unaffected.

"You're early, boss," she said, with just a touch of sultry taunt on the title. "Come to check up on the help?"

"Thought I'd make sure the other night wasn't a one-hit-wonder performance. That you weren't just selling me a bill of goods."

Something dark flashed in her eyes, there then gone. "You've nothing to worry about. Why don't you take your beer and socialize with some of your patrons? They can tell you how much better things are running since that disgrace of a manager *you* hired is gone."

She headed back down along the bar, the muscles of her very fine ass flexing with each stride, her hair moving around her like a pale golden cloud.

Quinn grinned. Put him in his place, didn't she? When she turned back, he made sure she saw him still leaning against the wall, one boot hooked over the other as he lifted his beer to his lips and kept his eyes glued on her. He had no intention of hanging out with his customers. He planned to stand here and drive himself crazy with thoughts of what would happen upstairs after the bar closed.

Her brow arched, her eyes sliding over him as if sizing him up for what she had planned. He forced himself to give back some of the same, and felt his cock jump at the spark in her eyes. *Yeah, it's going to be a bit more of a tug of war tonight, honey.* If the balance shifted it would be at his design, not hers.

The next couple of hours dragged by such that Quinn thought time might have stood still. Yet it wasn't a chore. He moved to that back table she'd preferred the other night, one booted foot propped on a seat, and then he did chat up a few customers. But while he did that, he kept his eye on her, drinking in everything she was doing. There were still some hiccups, mostly having to do with Manuel and Maria's learning curves as they struggled to adapt to new skills. However, she was patient and encouraging with them, and he'd have to be blind not to see those types of hiccups were temporary drawbacks. Things were already three hundred percent improved.

A couple times some of the more troublesome regulars started to get out of hand, but before he could act, she was on top of that.

A firm hand placed on a shoulder, her steely look mixed with a warm but pointed direction to behave—or get the hell out of his bar. Barely five feet tall and he'd bet she'd make a hell of a cooler. He wouldn't be surprised if she'd been one.

So at least, job-wise, she seemed to be the real bill of goods. Still way too good to be true though. He reminded himself how deftly she'd avoided his questions. He knew the signs of someone running, no matter what she'd said. But from what? Or who? What was so terrible that she couldn't tell him? He would simply win her confidence, one step at a time, before he addressed the question again.

The only other problem with his quickly met satisfaction at the changes was it left his mind open to consider other things. He made a move once to help with clearing tables, just to distract himself, but Selene gave him a quick head shake. It was clear she was teaching Maria to manage her time covering the floor without help, and when she did truly need help, it was Selene's job to assist. Exactly what he'd hoped to see happen at the bar so he didn't have to be here every night. But he made a note it might be time to hire a busboy, especially if the income increased the way it looked like it would.

Because of how involved he'd had to be in the past, it felt odd sitting here with his feet up, slouched down comfortably to nurse his beer as she did it all. The way her gaze passed over him said she was cognizant of the message it sent to the patrons—he was the boss, and she was the employee. Given his earlier resolve, he should be pleased he was underscoring that message. He was the one in control. Instead he kept thinking about what would happen when—not if—those roles were reversed. How he'd serve her at the end of the night.

She was able to get the last one out the door by midnight. His other girl, Carol, would be coming in tomorrow, and Quinn was amazed to hear Maria offer to come in without pay to help train her so Selene wouldn't be overwhelmed. Selene agreed, but firmly indicated Maria would be compensated after a brief glance toward him to see that he concurred. She obviously deferred to the things that were his call as owner, showing him respect in front of his people. But was it an act? He remembered that little taunt when he got here, saying "boss".

Oh yeah, he'd show her who was boss tonight. As dumbass Neanderthal as that sounded, even in his own head, it helped steady him a bit.

"Good night, Selene."

Selene lifted a hand, acknowledging Maria's farewell as the girl and Manuel disappeared. She followed them to the foyer doors, flipped the locks, pulled down the security shades. Then she turned around and looked at him, the length of the mopped bar floor between them.

Honest to God, he was ready to toss her to the floor. Rip off her jeans and thrust himself into her as deeply as he could. He was so busy imagining her naked it startled him when she flicked off the lights and appeared right in front of him. Had he zoned out, or had it seemed she hadn't even moved, just materialized right there? His brain was fogged with lust. She pressed herself against him.

"Upstairs, cowboy. We have business to conduct." She tilted her head. "You brought the whip and chaps?"

"I did."

Her lips curved. "Excellent. Then let's get to it."

"Why wait?" He clamped both hands on her waist and set her on one of the stools, pushing his way between her knees that spread to accommodate him. In the next blink, his mouth was fused on hers.

Oh God yes. It was like he hadn't had her in months, let alone less than a day. Her lips parted beneath his, her breath sweet and whiskey tinged from where she'd sampled her drinks or let a customer pay for a shot just to see her tip it back in one smooth move like last night. She didn't chase it or spit it out, yet she was as clear and levelheaded now as a teetotaler. How did someone so petite tolerate alcohol like a linebacker?

He was good at taking over a woman, making her feel good.

His large hands slid from her waist to her hips, curved back over her ass, kneaded in that way that shot sensation up a woman's rim, right straight to her pussy, making her wiggle and squirm. She did writhe under his hands, her breasts pressing into his chest, and he groaned with the pleasure of it.

"Come on." He lifted her from the stool and clasped her hand, pulling her after him to the office. He grabbed the stuff from there, the whip and the chaps, and met her gaze, all smoky and mysterious.

"Looks like you planned a couple of your own surprises for me tonight," she said.

"You bet your gorgeous ass." He took her to the back stairs, pushed her gently ahead of him, even as he muttered, "And I want to see you work that all the way up to your room."

She glanced over her shoulder at him, and he didn't want the ponytail. He caught her around the waist, holding her there with the chaps and whip slung over his shoulder so he could pull the tie free, comb his fingers through her loose hair, see how it framed her profile. He buried his nose in the thick strands, pressed his cock up against the lower curve of her ass.

"I could fuck you right here, on all fours."

"Why don't you?" she whispered, and there was something in her blue gaze that challenged him.

His resolve faltered, something out of sync, but a surge of testosterone shoved it away.

"Walk," he ordered.

She smiled then and did just that, proceeding up the stairs and working that denim molded over her buttocks to the point his dick could have used a lot more breathing room. Or maybe not. He just wanted to sink it into her tight, wet pussy.

As the door to the apartment closed behind them, he dropped the whip and chaps on the floor, grabbed her waist and turned her so she faced him. Wrapping his fingers around her wrists, he pressed her against the wall. Her breath caressed his face as he lowered his head and captured her lips in a hot, hungry kiss. He invaded her mouth with a hard thrust, the delicious taste of her bursting on his tongue like heavenly elixir. He sucked, he glided, he drank, the heady flavor going straight to his head and his groin.

When he had fed to excess, when he was at the point of taking her up against the wall, he forced himself to step back. He lifted her in his arms, realizing how much he'd wanted to do that again, though just like last night he was surprised to find she was heavier than she looked. Nothing he couldn't handle, but what looked like maybe one hundred ten pounds had more density to it. Like the woman herself.

Placing her on the bed, he closed his hand around the fragile bones of her wrist, bemused. But he had more pressing things to do than contemplate that. Trailing his mouth along the line of her jaw and down her neck, he placed tiny nips on her skin here and there, soothing them with his tongue.

Yeah, she liked that. Particularly when he was nipping at her neck pulse, biting her. Those blue eyes honed in on him, and her lips parted. For the first time he saw the tips of her fangs, rather than just feeling them. Maybe they were filed teeth, whatever. He wasn't into any of that body modification stuff, but on her...hell, anything about her got him hot, apparently.

Her skin was like the petals of a flower, but sweet as vanilla to the tongue. He wanted to lick her all over, every inch of her. Plunge his tongue into her cunt and lap every bit of her incredible juice. Drive his cock into her, burying himself to the balls, feel the clasp of her pussy around him like a wet vise.

He yanked at her t-shirt, tugging it upward so he could find a breast and pinch the bud of her nipple between thumb and forefinger. He wanted—

*Jesus.* This was all wrong.

He wanted what they had the night before. As hot and aroused as he was now, it was nothing compared to the peak of excitement he'd reached then. It was like the first time he'd made love to a woman the way a man should, versus breaking his cherry in the hormone rush of being a teenager, quick and over in an instant.

Yeah, he'd gotten off in both cases, but there was no comparison to the quality, the lasting value of the one experience versus the other.

As the thought stabbed into his barely functioning brain, another followed. He was not in control here, not in the least. *Good Christ.* What made him think that was even a possibility? Selene was permitting him to exert his power. Allowing him to do as he wished. Proving it, he realized he was staring into her eyes, his chest rising and falling fast, but other than that, he'd gone still as a stone. Waiting.

Last night, doing her bidding, he hadn't felt trapped. When he gave her the reins, she had made him feel as if he was giving her a precious gift, as well as freeing himself. *That* was what had heated his blood and made his cock swell to painful proportions.

He pushed himself back and sat on his haunches, his legs still straddling hers as he studied her eyes. Watched her face. Waiting for instructions?

Selene made no attempt to rearrange her clothing. He might have thought none of this had affected her, except for the rapid beating of her pulse at the base of her throat and the flush that suffused her pale skin.

"Are you through with your little charade yet?" A laugh bubbled up from her throat, a sound that eased his sense of wrongness in an instant, the trapped feeling. "Had as much fun as you want?"

His mouth was so dry he had to swallow twice before finding enough moisture to speak. Male pride meant he wouldn't answer the first question, but he responded to the second one without hesitation.

"Not yet," he said.

"Get up," she ordered. "Strip off every bit of your clothing. Now," she added when he hesitated.

With his gaze still on her, he left the bed, toed off his boots and pulled off his clothing, tossing it to the floor.

"Put on the chaps." Her voice stayed low, but there was no mistaking the power in it.

Quinn eased the leather onto his body, making sure he didn't catch any of his pubic hair in the edges or trap his cock in an uncomfortable position. When he fastened the single button at the top he let his arms fall to his sides and waited for what came next.

Selene slipped from the bed and walked around him, her eyes darkening as they coursed over his almost naked body. She trailed her fingers against the taut muscles of his buttocks, letting the tips trace the crevice separating the cheeks. When he clenched his ass to hold her there, she pulled her hand away and gave him a light slap.

"Do you want my fingers in there, cowboy?" she teased. "Touching that tender skin? Probing the darkest opening of your body?"

"Yes." The word escaped from his mouth as if on its own.

"Perhaps if you are a very good boy I might give you a treat." She bent, holding her hair back with one hand to press her lips to first one cheek then the other. "But you must be very, very good."

When she was standing in front of him again he saw that she had the single-tail whip in one hand, caressing the leather of the handle with the other. The tip of her tongue touched her pink lower lip, moistening it in a way that made him think of her pussy. Her eyes took in every bit of his body as if she was devouring him, resting for long moments on his penis protruding thick and heavy from the chaps.

"The whip handled properly is a valuable instrument of pleasure." She made the statement as if she were telling him how fine a particular liquor would taste. "Turn around and place your hands on the wall."

His heart rate accelerated, and his feet seemed stuck to the floor. Selene's smile this time was hungry. "Do you trust me, Quinn?"

Did he? Fucking damn, he must to get himself in this position so willingly.

"I'll take your silence as a yes. So do as I say. Hands against the wall."

His palms were sweating as he pressed them against the wood. His pulse pounded so hard he could hear the roar of blood in his ears.

"No safeword discussion?" he ventured.

"There's nothing safe about playing with a vampire."

He heard the hiss and crack of the whip. His whole body tensed against the strike, jolting to register pain.

But nothing had touched him.

"The sound itself is quite arousing," Selene said. "When you hear it, the tail is only contacting air. When you use the whip on your cattle do you always hear that crisp noise?"

He shook his head. "No."

"Right. Because most often it's the whip splitting the air that catches their attention and urges them to do your bidding. So remember, the sharper the sound, the farther away from your body it lands."

Quinn drew in a deep breath and let it out. His testicles throbbed in cadence with his pulse and he knew pre-cum was dripping from his cock. Anticipation had never been so arousing, especially for something he had never experienced before.

Twice more she split the air with the whip, but then he felt a sting on one of his buttocks like a small pinch. His muscles tightened and heat roared through his body. Again he felt the kiss of the whip, applied with the same intensity. Any pain was immediately replaced by a rush of endorphins that fed his burgeoning lust.

He anticipated the next bite but when nothing came a groan rumbled up from his throat.

"There." He could hear her smile in her voice. "See that, cowboy? Just a tiny taste and already you want more." She ran her fingers over the spots where the whip had landed. "Small kisses bring small pain. We don't want to rush things, do we?"

*Yes. Yes, we do.*

He ground his teeth together, shocked at the explosion of desire both his situation and the whip itself provoked.

"I see you disagree. Let's move it along a little, shall we?"

Before he could prepare himself, the lash bit into him again, harder this time, the sting greater, the burn hotter. Selene was silent as she gave him a series of four strikes. Adrenaline surged through him, mingling with the rush of endorphins. The surroundings faded away until all he was aware of was the needle bite of the whip and the insane pleasure it brought. When she stopped, the pain was so stimulating he wanted to beg her to keep going, unbelievable need consuming him.

"The pain gets overridden by intense pleasure, doesn't it? My cruelty unlocks things inside you. Things you need, Quinn. I love watching it happen. Turn around, cowboy. See what I'm talking about."

*No more whip?*

Flummoxed by the truth of her words, he wanted to protest them, but his mouth couldn't seem to form the words. Facing her, the combination of hunger and pleasure in her eyes nearly did him in. Without touching her, he had aroused her to a need almost as great as his own.

She had removed her own clothing and stood naked before him, her nipples darkened to the color of an heirloom rose. She held the whip curled loosely in one hand and with the other she ran her fingers between the lips of her cunt. When she lifted them they were glistening with her juices. She moved forward and painted his lips with the liquid.

"See how you affect me when you do my bidding?"

His nostrils flared as the scent drifted up to him.

"Lick your lips, bronc. Taste me. If you are very, very good I will let you fuck me with your tongue." She took a step closer, her next words whispered. "And your cock. But only after I show you how intense the pleasure of the whip can be. I want to drive you to the point where you're entirely under my control." Pressing a hand against his chest, she held him place as she dipped her head, licked one of his nipples, causing him to shudder. Her hand slipped up, collared his throat, squeezed. "Let's see how high a level we can take you." She licked the other nipple. "Trust me to know just how far to go this first time. Tell me you understand."

"Yeah. Yes. God, yes."

She lifted her head, her hair brushing his flesh. "Did you make yourself come since you saw me last?"

"Couldn't help it. Woke up with a hard-on so bad I couldn't have ridden my horse without scaring him."

Her lips curved. "Far be it from me to traumatize your horse. But we're going to set a few rules going forward. You want to masturbate when you're not with me, you have to call me. I want to listen to you do it. If I don't answer, you do it for my voicemail. I want to hear every dirty thought going through your head as you're doing it." Her voice dropped to a whisper as she rose on her toes, nuzzled his throat, pricked him with one of those filed teeth of hers. Funny, though, they hadn't seemed so prominent when she was working the bar, flashing that mesmerizing smile of hers. "So I can listen to your voice later when *I'm* masturbating," she said.

"What if I want you to call me when you do that?"

"Tough. You can just imagine it, until we're together. When you're good, I might occasionally let you watch. You understand me, Quinn? If you need to jerk off ten times a day, you'll call me ten times a day. But if you call and I say no, you'll just have to figure out how to help your horse cope. Your climax belongs to me, every drop."

He swallowed as those fangs pricked him again. "You're hungry," he muttered, cupping the back of her head. "Do what you gotta do."

He couldn't explain what the hell he was doing, playing into whatever delusion she had about that, but he had a burning need for her to nourish herself from him. She stilled at his comment, her fingers spreading across his chest, lingering there before she pushed away.

"Maybe later. You're not a marked servant, and I want you to conserve your energy. For now, I have other hungers to satisfy."

He blinked, not sure what to say to that, but she wasn't in the mood to explain herself.

"Stay just like that." She paced back again, slid the whip through her fingers. "Another night, I'll tie you up tight, and make you watch the lash come at your front. Let it kiss your thighs, your ball sac, your nipples. You'll come from the pain and my command alone. Would you like that?"

"Yes."

She cupped her breast, ran the whip handle down her body and then, mother of God, it disappeared inside her. She hummed, dropped her head back on her shoulders, rotated her hips with the movement, her thumb sliding over her swollen clit.

"I can do that for you," he said hoarsely.

She cracked open an eye, a lock of blonde hair falling over her blue eye. "Better than the handle?"

"Hell yes."

"Hell yes, what?"

"Yes...ma'am."

"Nice. I don't always need that, but I do love the way you say it, cowboy." She drew the handle out, touched her lips to it. "I expect you'll have to oil and clean that now, but you'll remember where it's been." She set it aside and sauntered toward him. He fisted his hands at his sides.

"On your knees, wonderful man."

He sank there, his head tilted up to watch her approach. As she stepped in front of him, she reached out, stroked his hair back. He closed his eyes and didn't think he'd ever felt so aroused...or at peace, under that oddly soothing touch.

"You've worked so hard for what you want, Quinn. I listen to people, and I know they respect you, look to you as a leader in this community. Your opinion counts, because you've earned it. But you have no woman, no family close by. Don't even seem to really have many close friends. Why is that, Quinn? Why do you prefer your silent pastures to being around your own kind? Keep your eyes closed. Tell me in the darkness. It's easier that way."

He wasn't sure anything would make it easier, but he kept his eyes closed. "Why do you need to know?" he asked, fighting the tense weight in his chest trying to disrupt the moment.

Fortunately, she continued to stroke him. By keeping his eyes closed he felt he was back in that erotic dream state from this morning, her voice like a ribbon of silk weaving around him.

"You're not a man who talks about his emotions. I like those traditional qualities to you. You're a man's man, Quinn. But to do this right, I need to know the emotional makeup below the surface. Why you do certain things and how it will affect what goes on between us. So I'll push to get to the root of who you are." Her voice took on an edgy purr. "I can be gentle about that, or not-so-gentle. Because it's to give us both pleasure. But I want truth from you, always. Tell me."

God help him, his mouth was already opening to let the words spill out, as if the stroke of her hand was a sorceress's compulsion.

"I'm not sure I can make you understand," he began. "When I was growing up we lived in the foreman's house on the ranch where my dad worked. Our home was the noisiest place in the world. At least it felt that way to me. There were four of us, all boys, and I was the youngest. I was kind of an accident, so my next oldest brother was about eight years older than me. We never really connected as siblings. We barely even keep in touch with each other."

"I'm sorry. That must make you sad sometimes." Her voice was a calming caress.

"I got used to it. If someone wanted to be heard, shouting was the only answer. Then there were the hands, just as wild and noisy as we were. There was no place to get away from it. I think I was the only one in the family who ever found it...jarring. Distressing. Privacy was nonexistent. Everyone was in your business all the time."

"I can understand that." Her voice was edged with hidden meaning.

"My dad was a hard man. He raised us the way he'd been brought up, with a lot of shouting and a good strapping with a belt when we misbehaved. It seemed a day hardly passed without one of us feeling the leather on our backsides." He shook his head as if to clear it. The ranch had always been a maelstrom of sound, exploding around him with the force of a tornado. "I felt, I don't know, I guess you'd say I got lost in it all. And Dad and I just never saw eye to eye on anything. We were always at each other's throats when I was a teen. It came to blows a couple times, made my mother cry over both of us, because we couldn't get along."

"Oh Quinn." But her tone stayed low, as if raising it beyond a certain level would fracture his thoughts.

"I'm not sure how my mom ever stood it. She was an amazing woman, and the only one who could keep order. Who could make my dad shake in his boots."

Selene's lips curved in a knowing smile. "I think I would have liked her."

"Yes. You probably would."

"But then you left home," she prompted.

"Yeah, to try to be something more than part of a crowd. Only being on the rodeo circuit wasn't any different. The only thing that changed was the geography. All that shouting and screaming. The noise of the animals and the competitors just invaded your head and swelled in your brain. The ever-present crowds. For a long time I never had the money to stay in a motel so I slept in my truck. Let me tell you, that's no place to get away from the constant sounds of the rodeo."

He paused and let out a slow breath. A muscle ticked just beneath his left eye. "You say my kind. I don't even know what my kind is. I just know the silence of the land, even with the cattle, is the first peace I've known in my life. It's like being in a healing place."

She stroked her slim fingers over his forehead. "Peace can be found in many ways. Perhaps giving control to me, allowing me to lead this dance, will be a kind of peace for you. A place where you don't always have to call the shots. Where you can just be. Will that work for you, Quinn?"

He shrugged, as if giving voice to the answer was a step he couldn't yet take, despite the admissions he'd already given to her.

"You seem a little isolated yourself," he said instead, opening his eyes and looking up at her. "You work a crowded room like the friendliest person alive, but the reserve is there, keeping them all at arms' length."

"Vampires aren't social," she said. "Not even with each other, at least not that way. When we get together it's more politics than potluck. Usually someone ends up dead or wishing they were."

He held her gaze. "I don't know what to believe when you talk like that."

"It doesn't seem to bother you all that much. Which means you have an exceptional tolerance for someone crazy running your bar or," she slid her finger down the side of his throat, tracing his pounding pulse there, "something in you already knows the truth and is okay with it. Which both intrigues me and tells me I should leave before bad things happen to you."

He closed his hand over her wrist, a gentle hold. "No. That's not what I want."

"Since when is anything about what you want?" But her brittle smile wasn't unkind, and he saw a trace of sadness in her eyes. That flash impression of the many things moving at too deep a level inside her for him to get a handle on it had his fingers tightening on her.

"Let me give you pleasure."

She cocked her head, considered. "I notice your staff here calls you 'boss'. Is that what everyone who works for you calls you?"

"Yeah. Pretty much."

She nodded. "Will you call me Mistress, Quinn?" Withdrawing her hand from his touch she stepped back, gloriously naked, her gaze sweeping him. She answered before he could.

"Whether you will or not, that big cock of yours jumped at the idea of it. You can't imagine how amazing you look in only those chaps. I want to eat you alive. Stretch out on the bed. I'm ready for a hard ride."

# CHAPTER FIVE

$\mathcal{S}$elene watched him comply, moving onto his heels and then standing. In that position he towered over her, but she didn't retreat. He paused, his expression gripped by an amazement that caused her to lift a quizzical brow. Setting his jaw, he put his hands to her waist, slowly lifted her off her feet, biceps flexing in a very attractive manner as he raised her over his head.

She was reminded of the *Dirty Dancing* scene when Patrick Swayze lifted "Baby" over his head. Quinn's expression was almost as absorbed as "Johnny's" and made butterflies jump in her stomach. She tried to stay away from movies and TV, because Laurent had frowned on it, saying it was never a good idea for vampires to get too involved in human culture, but she'd watched that one in defiance, curled up in her crappy hotel room, in need of some sense of controlling her own destiny...even if it was simply watching a goddamn movie.

Quinn held her there. "There's nothing to you," he said in a wondering voice. "You're just this little girl, but you have the eyes of a chupacabra."

"What or who is that?"

"A creature of supernatural legend that kills its victims by piercing their throats and draining their blood."

She stared at him. "That's what I remind you of?"

"Only the eyes," he told her. "You have the same hungry look in your eyes."

"Maybe it's you I'm hungry for," she murmured.

Still holding her gaze, he lowered her back to the floor, their bare bodies so close. "The bed, cowboy," she said.

He released her waist but held onto her hand, so that when he moved to comply, he drew her along with him. She stood at the side of the bed as he stretched out, and when his fingers slipped from hers, she felt their loss. "Arms over your head. Grip the rails, just like before. I don't want anything in the way of taking my pleasure."

As he obeyed, she had to draw in a breath at the beauty of his rugged male form. The mileage and scars just made him all the more appealing to her. She traced every muscle of the six-pack abs, the crescents of his pectorals, the bump of his nipples and the light layering of gleaming hair across that terrain. She teased his navel with a fingernail and earned a squirm, a half-snort, half-chuckle that made her smile. Then she curled her fingers around the thick root of his penis, and his face got intent again. He breathed her name as she tugged on him, dug her nails into his balls, made him arch up with a hiss.

"Spread your legs out wider."

The pleasure of his obedience speared her. He understood it, deep down, and seeing it come to the surface of his consciousness was as great a pleasure as the response of his cock. More. When he'd made that shift earlier, from what he thought was expected of him to what he truly wanted, she'd wanted to fuck him to oblivion right then and there. The willingness to set aside his perceived greater strength and size, the capitulation of his mind, handed to her with trust in where she would take him...it was all the best parts of power and pleasure.

When she'd been turned into a vampire, she'd learned the meaning of the word helplessness. It was only when she discovered that vampires had a genetic disposition toward sexual Dominance, and even the weakest vampire had the right to exercise that over humans of her or his choosing, that she found an escape from how nightmarish her life became at times.

It also put her in touch with something about herself that made her not regret so much the circumstances that had brought her to that state. She just resented the assholes who had seemed to inundate her life since then. She wasn't running from what a vampire truly was—only what the vampire world demanded she be. It was a shame Laurent and his ilk didn't comprehend the difference, and she was nowhere near high enough on the food chain to teach it to them.

So it was time to focus on the here and now. "What do you want, Quinn?" she asked, putting her hands on the bed and sliding onto it on all fours over him like the dominant predator she was. She bent her elbows, blew lightly on his testicles and all up along his shaft.

"To fuck you."

"Hmm. The right intent, but not quite the right answer. Try again. Here's a hint. Who am I?"

Those dark eyes fastened on her face. She saw him struggle with it. Was it too soon? Or had it been locked away in him for so long, in this moment clogged by lust and intensity, it would shove past his reservations and logic, all vestiges of caution?

He swallowed, and she realized she'd gone preternaturally still, something she tried to stay aware of and avoid, but in a highly charged physical or emotional state, her youth as a vampire showed. She was holding breath she didn't have to take.

"My Mistress."

Fire swept her, and she knew he saw it in her eyes, because his cock did that eager jerk again, his balls drawing up as she scraped her fangs along them. In their normal state, her fangs looked like sharpened canines, but for feeding they gained a quarter inch, giving her a deeper penetration. His eyes widened as she lifted her head and he saw them.

"Again." She realized her voice sounded like a growl, and his breath rasped in his throat.

"My Mistress. Mine. Please...fuck me. Let me give you the ride of your fucking life."

Her cowboy, being possessive. It twisted him even deeper into her heart. She slid up his body, dragging her breasts over his cock, cupping them around his shaft, using his pre-cum to lubricate the movement. He thrust in instinctive reaction and she chuckled.

"No movement unless I say," she chided. She made him keep his ass glued to the bed as she worked his cock between her breasts, fingering her nipples as he watched with glazed fascination. His whole body was one quivering cord of male power, waiting to be unleashed.

Rising onto her knees, she took hold of his cock. He was right about the differences in their sizes. Her fingers barely wrapped around his base, and when she straddled him, she felt the pleasurable strain as she spread her thighs over him. He was a big man and she loved that about him. A big, rough man who worked with his hands, whose ambition was a successful ranch and the ability to enjoy quiet, open spaces. His idea of a romantic night would be lying in his truck bed, staring up at a star-filled sky, sharing a six-pack and talking until dawn came. She couldn't imagine anything more simply perfect than that. Even if she couldn't stay until the rising of the sun. Even if she could never be the woman in that truck with him, planning a life of babies and what to make for dinner.

*Selene, shut up and fuck him.*

She lowered herself onto him, letting pure lust-filled bliss take over as that meaty cock stretched and filled her.

"I want to touch you." He sounded as fierce as she had a moment before, that same growl in his voice.

"No," she said, soft as a whispered breeze, her eyes locking with his. It was part of the pleasure, seeing a man obey, not from barked orders or because his hands were tied, but because he hungered for the restraint of his Mistress' will. "Stay still."

She rose and fell while he shuddered beneath her, grunts escaping his lips at the effort it took. For her part, she thoroughly enjoyed every solid inch of him, every reaction on his face. He was clenching the headboard rails so hard, they would bite into his hands, leave lasting imprints.

"This is how you're going to come," she said. "You'll wait until I come, and then I'll keep moving on you until you climax. But you don't get to thrust until you start to come. Tell me you understand. Tell me in the way you know I want to hear."

"Yes, Mistress. Fuck..."

"Don't close your eyes," she said, pinching his nipple sharp enough that his gaze sprang open as he flinched. "You watch me."

Rise and fall. Up and down. The friction of his corona on her opening, the hard stroke of impact against her clit as her movements became fiercer, built the climax in her like a storm. Seeing a reflection of it gather in his eyes, in his body, just egged it on. When she went over, she cried out her pleasure, but she still heard his raw voice.

"Yeah...that's it, baby. Come for me. Come...you're fucking... beautiful...Mistress. My Mistress."

He kept saying that. As she savored her aftershocks, she sensed his climax, his face getting that tight look, the eyes starting to glaze over.

"Now, Quinn. Go over for me. You can thrust."

His hips bucked up, thrusting his cock so deep into her it hit her cervix, not necessarily a pleasurable thing for most women, but for vampires there was a translation point from pain to pleasure that made them understand sadism in a way most humans never could. Except for a vampire's full human servant. Servants learned the way of it...if they were meant for that life.

That thought, which she should banish far, far away, was obliterated by her cowboy, whose animal nature had taken over. He interpreted "Go over" in his own way, releasing the headboard and seizing her hips to flip them, so he was between her legs and plowing her like a field of moist earth. He came, his breath hot against her ear, his ass flexing under the lock of her legs. As she raked his back with her nails, she relished his guttural noises. She flipped them again, seeing the surprise in his gaze when she did it so easily, shoving him back down with a hand locked around his throat. She worked herself on him, squeezing and circling her hips, grinding down on him, milking the last bit of climax out of him as he held on to her hips with bruising fingers.

When she at last slowed down, she knew she'd acquired the last drop. That surfeit slid down her vaginal walls, where it would make a lovely, heated, sticky pool between cock and cunt. Even as she loosened her grip, she knew she wanted to feed on him again, which concerned her, because she *wanted* to feed on him. Didn't need to do so. She shouldn't need to feed again for another day or so and when she did, she needed to take it from elsewhere. Food was always easy for a vampire bartender. One of those last call customers could be asked to stay a little longer to help the cute little barkeep move a couple heavy boxes. The next day, he'd have a pleasantly hazy hangover, where details were missing, such as the quick pint she'd taken from his throat.

The idea had no appeal to her at all, not with Quinn right here. So available, and learning to respond to her in so many irresistible ways.

Which was exactly why she needed to resist.

She slid off him, picked up her clothes. Coiling up the whip, she tossed it on the bed next to him. "You're right. You give a mighty nice ride, cowboy. Now it's time for this girl to get some sleep."

She saw the *what the fuck* look at her transition, knew she'd been too abrupt. But he wanted to stay with her, she could see it. That was the danger of Quinn Pedraza. A whole bar full of men wanting one-night stands, and the one who'd caught her eye was the forty-two-year-old with deep brown eyes, a heart of gold and a need for love and family. She was self-aware enough to know that was part of what appealed to her. Maybe she had become far more of a vampire than she realized, that she couldn't bring herself to care enough to stop this. But at least she could avoid the things that encouraged the wrong kind of intimacy. Like sleepovers.

"Did you see the reports I left you?" she said casually. "Everything look good on those?"

He blinked, sitting up, putting his feet on the floor. "Yeah," he said at last. "Yeah, looked good."

"Good." She was dressed now. "That's separate from this. All professional. This is your place, so if you have any concerns, you talk to me about them. Don't hold back."

He stood, stripped the chaps as if wearing them now and nothing else made him uncomfortable. His gaze was studying her, measuring. Caught between confusion and calculation of her intent. He was a smart man. He'd understand the boundaries she was setting. She just didn't know if he'd pay attention to them. Because he had that side to him as well, the alpha male she found far too irresistible.

She moved to the doorway, looking back over her shoulder as he pulled on the jeans, threaded his arms into his shirt, shrugged it on, leaving it unbuttoned. He hadn't yet buttoned the jeans, and all of it made her ache. *No. No more candy tonight. It will spoil your dinner.*

"Remember what I said, Quinn. You want to come before you see me again, you call me. That's an order. I can make that single tail hurt a lot worse." She gave him a deliberate look, lingering on his cock. "As much as that thought might turn you on, I can promise you there's a difference between punishment for disobeying your Mistress and punishment for pleasure."

The look in his eyes, an echo of the way he'd reacted to the lash, begging her for more with every twitch of body language, told her she was in trouble. Because he'd crave it either way, for pleasure or punishment. As a result, she had no idea if he would obey her...or not.

She turned and left him.

❧

She hadn't said anything about when they'd get together again. Tomorrow night, every night, only when he was available...

It had been a couple days since he'd seen her, because he had some major issues at the ranch that kept him working well past dark. Much as his cock railed against him, he was just too worn out to go to After Hours when the day was done. Maybe that was good. The way she'd drawn back from him had left him a little ticked. Well, fine. He could prove he could control his urges just as much. He'd seen enough to know the bar was in good hands, and if she did a one-eighty on him, it'd get back to him, because at least one or more of his hands went there every day or two.

By asking them the right questions and during his trips to town, he'd learned a couple more interesting facts about her. None of the merchants who had only daylight hours had met her. Selene had sent Maria to the hardware store for a bucket of paint and brushes. She'd also sent the girl to the handicrafts store to get hand-woven rugs and the little accessories boutique to find hand towels and some other things. All of it no doubt to spruce up the apartment.

So far, she was sticking to the whole vampire lore pretty good. She might be nuts, but if she was, he was apparently a rabid squirrel. He hadn't thrown her out, even knowing such blatant signs of a mental disorder couldn't bode well for the long-term future of his bar. No matter how much of an improvement she was over Artie. But what had she said? *Something in you already knows the truth and is okay with it.*

Yeah, he was tired as hell from the ranch work and determined to show her he had a life beyond sniffing after her, but he wasn't too chickenshit to accept it was more than that keeping him away. He'd gone back to After Dark that very second day to put things under his control again and essentially got his ass handed to him. Marked with some stripes and dings that he twisted around like a snake to stare at in the mirror the next day. He needed a few days for a reality check.

Unfortunately, his dick decided two was the max he was going to get, no matter how exhausted he was.

He woke up that morning, caught up in another of those near wet dreams about her, his cock throbbing and his hand already on it, muscle memory kicking in because his brain assumed Quinn was on board with keeping his dick calmed down in the usual way. Then he remembered what she'd said. Hell no, he wasn't calling her to ask her to jerk off. What kind of man did that?

But God, when he'd turned around after he submitted to that single tail, the way she'd looked...it was as if he'd given her the best gift any woman could ever get, way beyond diamonds, chocolates... anything. Would it be like that to her, him asking if he could come for her?

He wasn't sure if that was why he reached for his phone. He wanted to be fucked, yes, but he'd had plenty of that in his life. Copious amounts of fucking, more than most men ever did. He wanted to hear her voice, see how she was doing. She stimulated him in a lot of ways, fascinated him. He missed her.

The phone rang. It was about four a.m., still dark, and he was giving up a precious extra hour of sleep he needed, but he needed her more.

"Quinn." Her voice was a bit slurred. He was a bastard. She'd put in a full day, had probably only gotten to bed several hours ago, whereas he'd had the benefit of hitting the hay about ten.

"Hey. I didn't mean to wake you. Or catch you before you go to bed."

"Are you hard, Quinn?"

Wow. She didn't believe in preliminaries, and there was no derision to her tone, as if irritated that he'd called just for that purpose. But he didn't want her thinking that, regardless. "Yeah. But that's not why—"

"I don't care why else you called. I want to hear you come for me. Wrap your hand around your cock and turn on your side."

His brow furrowed. He was tempted to resist. Then he bit back the other words and complied.

"Are you wearing anything?"

"No."

"Is that how you usually sleep?"

"Sometimes boxers, but it's easier to jump right in the shower first thing in the morning if you're already bare-assed."

"Such a practical man. Do you keep any lube near your bed? Anything you can use as lube?"

He blinked. "Uh, there's this balm I put on my hands or lips sometime when they get real chapped and cracked. It's in the nightstand drawer."

"Perfect. Spread a good amount on your hands, and then grip your cock with one of them, and put two fingers of the other hand up your ass. All the way to the bottom knuckle."

"What?"

"You've had a woman lick your rim. Penetrate you with her fingers?"

Some of his more experienced bed partners had introduced him to it. But he'd actually never put his own fingers up his ass.

"Yeah. A couple times. Just haven't done it with my own."

"No time like the present. I want you to start getting your ass ready for when I'll put on a nice thick strap-on and fuck your brains out, the way you've fucked your cute little buckle bunnies. Your fingers are nice and thick, much better than mine for that purpose. So do it."

Again he hesitated, but the erotic lure of it was too much for him to resist. The internal muscles of his ass already clenched with anticipation. "Okay."

"Hmm. I'm thinking I'd like to hear something a little more along the lines of 'Yes ma'am'. Think you can manage that?"

He paused, thought it over, and then it came to his lips as if it had just been waiting there to be said. "Yes ma'am." He'd called her Mistress the other night in the heat of the moment. Some part of him wanted to say that now too. But he restrained himself with "ma'am".

She purred. "God, hearing a cowboy say 'Yes, ma'am' in that

drawl. It makes me want to have you stand in a corner and just say it all day long while I play with myself."

"I'd be happy to do the playing. Ma'am."

She laughed then, a throaty sound. "You like to flirt, Quinn. I like that."

Actually, he'd never been much in that department, but the edgy way she played at it herself inspired him. Then her voice sharpened to that sultry demand again. "Have you done what I told you to do?"

He slathered the udder balm on his fingers and gripped his cock, which was already nice and aching, like the skin was going to split right off it. Then he reached back, eased his other greased-up fingers into himself. His cock convulsed, cream blooming on the top, and a rasping breath escaped his lips.

"Nice." Her voice had that hum to it that he could feel vibrating all the way to his testicles. "The first time I fuck you, Quinn, I'm going to have you lying face down on your bed. I'm going to tie your wrists and ankles, spread you out wide. Then I'm going to put myself against your back, drag my nice big rubber cock down your spine, put it between your cheeks and push in so, so slow, until you're stretched and burning. Until your mind is completely breaking apart from the way it feels to have me fucking you like a man while my breasts press against your back and my hair brushes your shoulder, and you smell my cunt getting so wet..."

"God...Mistress."

"You can come for me now, Quinn. But you have to do it within five minutes or you don't get to do it at all. Remember what I said. I want to hear every filthy, uncensored thing going through your mind."

So he did just that. He described exactly what he was doing, the grip he had on his dick, how he was pushing the taut skin up to the head, stroking just the right spot firm and intent, and he said all sorts of delightful filthy things. How he wanted to fuck her cunt, her ass, shove himself into her mouth, come all over her tits...how he wanted her to fuck him...down on his knees, her behind him, fingers shoving into his ass, tongue there, then using the handle of his whip, making him shudder and bite back pleas for mercy as she worked him, his balls drew up and...

He spewed all over himself as she whispered the words to him. "Now, Quinn. Now."

The hot syrup clung to his fingers and dripped onto his balls. His skin was on fire wherever it touched. He felt as if every bit of energy had drained from his body through his cock and spilled around him. He'd had all kinds of sex—down and dirty, hot and sexy, even passable phone sex. But this? She had gotten into his mind, into his body, and taken over his senses. He had been power-less to do anything but what she commanded.

He was barely catching his breath when she spoke. "Remember, you call me whenever you need to do that."

She hung up. Just like that, leaving him hanging on to the throaty sound of her voice, which told him she was just as aroused. It tormented him as visions of her naked body shimmered in the air, her slender hips, her smooth pussy, her breasts swollen, her nipples hard and begging for his mouth. He imagined her pinching each of those nipples until they were engorged and stiff, then letting those fingers drift down the silken flesh of her stomach to her pussy. Separating the plump lips with the fingers of one hand while with the other she caressed her glistening slit in a long glide.

Christ! Heat jolted right into his balls and the vein feeding his shaft pulsed as his blood surged through it.

He closed his eyes and in his mind saw her bend her legs to give herself better access. Slip two then three fingers into her waiting cunt. His heart thudded as she fucked herself, now pinching her clit with her other hand and tugging and rolling it, bringing herself to climax with her slim fingers.

When she convulsed, spasms rippling over her body, his cock hardened to the point he was afraid to touch it for fear of damaging himself. At this rate, he'd have her on the phone all the damn time. He forced his eyes open, wiping away the image.

He needed more. Much more. Even if it meant letting her call the shots.

He couldn't leave it there so he dialed her again. She picked up on the first ring.

"Even your recovery time couldn't be that good."

"It just might be, baby." He grinned at the sound of her chuckle. "How are you?"

She paused. "What?"

"I asked how you're doing. Are you okay? Did your day go okay? I've been pretty busy with the ranch, and I haven't had a chance to check in."

He sensed the change in subject matter surprised her but she answered him. "You've checked in with Maria and your ranch hands to see how I'm doing, what I've been buying."

"Yeah."

"Then you know how I'm doing." She hung up again.

He stared at the phone. Was she pissed at him? She hadn't sounded that way. It sounded like she'd chuckled at him again before she ended the call. She was hard to figure. It took an act of will not to call back again, for more than one reason.

Sleep eluded him. Every scene with her played over and over in his mind. He felt the bite of the lash on his back, her touch on his bare ass, the sensation of her mouth. The unbelievable ability she had to bend him to her will. At last, he gave up and left the bed, getting an early jump on the day.

As he went about his work throughout the morning and afternoon, knowing he had to call her to get off kept him in a constant semi-aroused state. Perversely, it also helped him suppress the urge to call so he wouldn't seem like some sex-crazed lunatic. At least until evening.

Once he was in the shower that night, the water running down his bare body, the meanderings of his tired mind went right to his cock, and before he knew it, he was throbbing again. Her words in the darkness of early morning played out in his mind.

*"I'll put on a nice thick strap-on and fuck your brains out."*

Again his inner muscles tightened and a bolt of lust speared him. Fucking a woman's ass always turned him on, but what would it be like to experience it from the other side? Allowing that had never even been on his sexual horizon but now that Selene had planted the image in his mind...

*No, you can't call. You don't want to come off as some kind of dog begging for scraps.*

He held out until he'd gotten out, mostly dried off, and saw his phone sitting on the counter. His hand reached for it as if it had a mind of its own.

She picked up on the second ring, but she was already talking. "Yeah, put that back there. Thanks, Robert. I'd like to change the shipment rate...hold on. Mr. Pedraza?"

She was dealing with the beer delivery guy. Just like the previous night in front of the customers, she was calling him boss or Mr. Pedraza. It fucking turned him on, knowing behind closed doors, it was something entirely different. He decided to give back tit for tat. "Yes ma'am?" he drawled.

There was laughter in her voice at that, but she kept on track. "So do you need the same order you requested this morning?"

Okay, she was better at this than him. Was she really going to have him do this while she was doing business? "I'll call you back."

"No. I'm accepting that delivery only at the proscribed time, boss. Just as we discussed. I can do this at the same time. Go ahead and give me what you need. Now."

Her voice was conversational, yet he heard the trace of steel, that hint of command that probably passed unnoticed to the beer guy. In contrast, Quinn heard it as clear as a drill sergeant's bark.

"Fuck, I can't do this."

"Yes, Mr. Pedraza. I'm very confident that can happen. Robert, here's the order change. Can you put that in the back?"

Robert must have walked away, because her voice changed immediately. "I want to hear you, Quinn. Want to hear every groan, every curse, the way you say 'I want to fuck your cunt' like a sacred promise. Obey me, cowboy."

"Are you wet?" he demanded. "Christ, give me something. I feel like a fucking dumbass teenager here, chasing a cheerleader's skirts." He should hang up. He was just too damn horny to do so. But he wasn't going to beg. He'd never been that kind of guy with a woman, and he wasn't starting now.

"I'm so wet that if I buried your face in my pussy right now, you'd drown," she said. "Give me a gift, Quinn. Give me everything you are in this moment. You're not a teenager. You're a powerful, tough-as-nails man who makes me hot just to hear your voice on the phone, begging me in that rough way of yours to let you come."

Just like that, hearing the urgency in her tone made all his uneasiness disappear. Was it his imagination, or did showing her desires so blatantly freak her out a little bit too? All he knew was hearing that note in her voice made things feel more balanced, though he was sure she wouldn't appreciate hearing that at all.

Over the next five minutes, he worked his cock in his hand, the shower steam still misting his flesh. During that time, Robert returned, she worked out a freaking new order schedule with him and told him to check the cooling lines on their tap system. When Quinn came at her veiled order, "Yes, boss. Now's the perfect time," he barely had time to cover himself with a towel to save a night of mopping up the floor.

While he was still catching his breath, she put Robert on the line so he could verify she was the new barkeep and not some wet-dream fantasy who'd wandered in straight from the pages of every guy's fave skin mag. Robert didn't put it that way, but Quinn was sure that was what he was thinking. It sure as hell was what he was thinking. He managed the, "Hey, Bob, yeah she's my new help, and unless she asks for the freaking moon, we're all good." Though he might just give her the entire universe, not just the moon. Selene took the phone back from Robert.

"All right, sounds like we're all done, Mr. Pedraza. Call me back if you need me again." The connection was cut.

It wasn't until about an hour later he started having weird feelings about it. Yeah, typical guy, getting off, then having regrets. But Jesus, while she was dealing with a vendor? He wished he could go see her tonight, but it just wasn't in the cards. He still had a few hours to go on paperwork for the ranch and a full day tomorrow. He sighed, put his head in his hands. In a matter of a few days, he'd gotten himself hung up in a pretty complicated set of feelings. Having those feelings for someone who worked for him was never a good idea.

Once again he was back to the idea it was probably good to put some physical distance between them. So he promised himself no more phone calls. At least until he actually had time to go see her again.

# CHAPTER SIX

*T*he next morning, the men rode out early to get the herd moving. One of the hands called and told him they had finished mending a broken spot in the fence on the north pasture and were getting ready to drive the cattle there. While Quinn knew they would have done their usual efficient job and didn't need his stamp of approval, he was tired of wrestling with paperwork and forcing himself to leave the telephone alone. Checking out the repairs provided the perfect excuse to take in some steadying solitude.

The sun was bathing everything in its warm golden glow when he saddled Midnight and headed out of the barn. He didn't take his phone with him, on purpose. As he rode out through the meadows waiting to be filled by part of the herd, he drew the air deep in his lungs, let the underlying quiet beneath the sounds of nature ease his mind, his gut.

He walked Midnight along the fence, checking for other weak spots, but at a certain point, he closed his eyes, let Midnight walk about a quarter mile, his mind lulled by the horse's movement. When Quinn finally opened his eyes, he found one small detail in the landscape had changed. One that made him smile.

"Well, looks like there's more than one of you after all. Must be a new strain."

It was the same type of butterfly he'd seen a few days before. Midnight's ears flickered as the delicate winged insect beat a determined track right for the two of them, almost emanating the attitude, *"Why on earth did I have to bring my ass all the way out here to find you?"*

Bemused, Quinn watched the creature perch right on his rein-wrapped hand on the pommel, just as before. It fluttered its wings, settling down. It was rare a man got to look at a butterfly this up close and personal, so still, and in his current contemplative state, he was impressed, almost hypnotized by its beauty, by the subtle blending of the colors. The usual tracery of black was missing. Every butterfly he'd ever seen had at least a touch of it in its palette, but not this one.

Keeping still, he cast his gaze around, seeking others, but didn't find any. Weird. They always traveled in flights, never alone. Not that he remembered.

He lifted his hand, expecting the delicate creature to skedaddle, and was surprised it stayed in place. When he flexed his fingers, moving the knuckle the butterfly rested on, instead of skittering off, it fluttered its wings. Hovered in front of him before coming to rest on his shoulder.

He freed his hands from the reins, knowing Midnight would stay still until bid otherwise, though the horse's ears were swept back, as if listening with animal radar to the silent byplay between his master and the intriguing insect. Quinn turned his hand palm up, realizing he was holding his breath. The butterfly lifted off, floated down and landed right in the cup of his hand.

He stared at it. Slowly, he closed his fingers into a curved basket around it. It didn't move. At the faint brush of the wings, he opened his grasp, remembering something about a human touching a butterfly's wings could take away its ability to fly. The thought gave him a moment of consternation, then the butterfly lifted off, relieving him.

A piercing whistle caught his attention and he looked up to see the mass of cattle coming up over the crest of the hill, the hands in loose formation around them.

"Well look at that. I timed that just right, little lady. I assume you're a little lady. You just don't strike me as a guy."

When he moved to unlatch the gate so the herd could move through, he expected the butterfly to whisk away, but it sat on his shoulder, now on his hat, now performing a delicate dance around his head. When it landed once on Midnight's forelock, he tightened his grip on the reins, expecting the big black gelding to protest. But the magnificent animal just twitched his ears and bobbed his head once, as if having a private conversation with the little creature.

*Okay, now I am really losing my mind.*

It remained in its place even as he backed Midnight away out of the swarm of cattle. Then, once he was clear, it went back to resting on his hand. He kept it as still as possible, giving it that resting spot as he called out direction to the men. Fortunately, none were close enough to notice, so he didn't have to explain what the hell he was doing playing with butterflies.

When Kevin brought lunch out to them in the four-wheel pickup, Quinn dismounted and waited for the butterfly to move off. Instead it simply changed its position, settling on the brim of his Stetson. A strange feeling whispered through his system. The men made a joke about it, and Kevin lifted a hand to swat at it. "Let me take care of that, boss."

Quinn caught his arm, quick as he'd rope a calf out of the shoot. A startled look crossed Kevin's face, and Quinn swallowed, hoping the dull flush he thought was on his face wasn't. "Don't. It's bringing me luck. Haven't had a damn thing go wrong since it showed up a few days ago." Because he was somehow sure it was the same one.

Well, at least that was something cowhands understood. They all had their superstitions, and though they ribbed him about it, not a one of them did anything like Kevin had again. They started looking a little amazed themselves at the way the butterfly stayed with him, just doing that gentle wing pump, sometimes barely moving at all.

"I think it's tired, boss," Dave said, pointing with his fork. "I saw one once get all buffeted about by a windy day, and when it lighted on a protected branch, it did just like that. The wing movement's like them catching their breath."

"Well, last time I saw it, it was clear on the other side of the property, so maybe it had a big trip today." Taking of his hat, Quinn set it on the rock next to him so he could study the creature. Per his request, Kevin had brought him his phone, so Quinn took a picture of the insect, examined it. He made it into his screen background, because he liked looking at it. He'd show it to Selene, tell her it had her eye color.

Damn, he missed that woman. Today was the last day they had to work such long hours. He was going to go see her at After Hours. No, forget that. He was going to call her, offer to take her out to dinner Sunday night. She was new in town and he'd been a selfish bastard, making it all about the sex and not being a proper gentleman. Never mind she hadn't seemed to mind making some pretty hefty sexual demands herself, a man knew the right thing to do by a woman. He wasn't going to call her in front of all his men, and by the time he got back, she'd be hip deep in the bar's operating hours. He'd send her a text, even though that wasn't as proper as asking her voice to voice. Truth, he wanted to call her for a reason other than whacking off.

He typed out a quick text. *Like to take you to dinner Sunday night. Place that has good music.*

He closed the phone, put it aside. She was probably sleeping, wouldn't answer until later tonight. When she did, she'd probably tell him she'd already arranged to have musical entertainment at the bar, because he knew she was working on that. He wouldn't be surprised if she'd gotten Alan Jackson himself. The woman seemed capable of anything.

"Boss is grinning like he's thinking about a woman," Johnny said. "We know which one."

"Which is why we can't blame him for grinning like a fool." Kevin elbowed him. "She's only been here a few days and every man in the county has an eye for her."

Quinn scowled at that, and they all chuckled at his obvious displeasure.

"Looks like boss has already put his brand on her," Dave said.

If they only knew. Quinn thought it far more likely that Selene was thinking of putting a brand on his flanks. He better not plant that idea in her head, though his buttock gave an alarming little tingle at the idea, echoed by a turgid response from his cock. Yep, he'd definitely lost his mind.

"She seems to like him okay. Though she had Turley stay after hours last night and help her move some boxes around, and all he remembers about it is waking up with a smile on his face."

Quinn pinned him with a dark look. "What the fuck's that supposed to mean?"

"Nothing, boss." Kevin's face shifted to uncertainty. "We're just messing with you. I'm sure he was just helping her move boxes."

"Time to get back to work," Quinn said shortly, rising and picking up his hat. The butterfly had apparently had her rest. She lifted off, all the men likewise stirring themselves for the grueling afternoon ahead. Quinn watched the delicate creature float away, then returned to Midnight.

He couldn't explain his possessive feelings toward a woman he'd barely just met, but in truth, when he spent time with a woman, even if he wasn't planning to set up house together, he expected it to be just the two of them until one or the other called it quits. He put the image out of his mind of the husky Turley coming anywhere near that lush body, feeling the tips of her fangs at his throat...

Midnight snorted as he mounted and sat his ass in the saddle a little harder than he'd intended. "Sorry, boy."

He had a busy day ahead. His best strategy was to work himself into full exhaustion by the end of it so he wouldn't have enough energy to wind himself up over stupid shit like this.

~

Mission accomplished.

He barely got enough of a shower to wash off the muck before falling face forward into the bed. He'd contemplated just sleeping in the barn and saving the cleanup, but the bed was too inviting to pass up. Christ, his past life as a rodeo cowboy had a way of hitting him hard on the more strenuous ranch days. He wasn't twenty anymore, yet now he felt every stupid thing he'd done to himself between twenty and thirty.

He was an easy sleeper, his internal timer rigged to wake him up when it was time to get up. He didn't do a lot of waking up in the middle of the night. Unless something was amiss. His eyes opened in darkness, the clock reading two a.m. in his peripheral vision. And he knew he wasn't alone.

The funny thing was the lack of alarm he felt. He'd known it was her even before he'd opened his eyes, which suggested he was still sleeping, dreaming.

"Aren't vampires supposed to be invited before they come into someone's house?" he said groggily.

"That's a myth to make people feel safer." Selene gazed at him from the foot of his bed. "You wouldn't invite me into your home?"

"My house, my bed. Anywhere you want to be. How'd you get in?"

"Came down the chimney."

"Like Santa Claus. A sexy, blonde Santa."

As she moved around to the side of the bed, he saw her suppress a smile. He was so out of it, he was like a drunk, saying whatever came to mind. He turned toward her, biting back a groan at his stiff muscles, but he wanted to see her. She stopped just out of reach, still studying him. "You haven't come to me in three days. I got impatient."

"I wouldn't have been worth much to you. Been working my ass off. Probably not much good to you tonight."

"Turn over onto your stomach," she said.

He flashed on what she'd said on the phone, about fucking him that way. The surge of worry and anticipation woke him up a little more. But she didn't appear to be carrying any strap-ons with her. All she wore was a thin, short dress, and she was barefoot.

He complied and the mattress shifted as she slid onto it. She tugged his sheet all the way down. "You do sleep bare-assed naked," she said, amusement in her voice. "I like that."

Then she straddled his thighs and began to give him a massage, starting at his neck and shoulders and working her way down. It was fucking bliss. He practically whimpered but managed to choke back the unmanly sound. He realized when she sat down on his legs that he wasn't the only one bare-assed. She was naked under the dress. It made him realize, though she was any man's dream, she was not a dream. She was really here, in his room.

He turned, and she adjusted so he could be on his back, looking up at her. She stayed on his thighs, but he stretched out his longer arms, slid her up so he could take a better hold of her. It put her right on the length of his stiff cock, but that wasn't his intent. He just wanted her closer.

"Christ, I missed you," he murmured. "I wish I wasn't so tired."

She pressed her mouth against the palm he had cupping the side of her face, and then rotated her hips. His dick, brainless as it was, just got harder.

"Honey, I—" He couldn't do right by her tonight. But she'd come all the way out here. He needed to try.

"Ssh." She shook her head at him. "It's not a matter of you being able to give, Quinn. I'm your Mistress, and I take when and what I desire. It's that simple. You're going to learn I'm not going to be denied. Your only job is to follow the flow of the current."

She lowered herself onto his body, breasts against his chest, and rotated her hips again. She was able to fit the head of his cock into the mouth of her pussy, and then she was sliding down on him, inch by inch, her face so close to his. He stared up into her eyes, gripped her hips, and then he was hilt deep in her, her so still, their bodies fused together. The quiet darkness of the room closed around them. Powerful as his growing arousal was, the energy between their locked gazes was ten times that.

"I almost called you a hundred times."

"You should have."

"You have a bar to run. And I happen to know your boss is a real bastard."

She smiled at that, put her mouth on his. It was a slow, deep kiss, and he wondered if she lost herself in it as much as he did, because it seemed to go on for quite a while. They made incremental movements on one another, stoking that joining point down below, but their mouths nipped, played, flirted then dove deep, that all-absorbing rhythm of motion and timing to a really good kiss. By the time it was over, her hands were fisted in his hair and he had his arms banded across her back, one hand sliding down to cup her buttock, stroke the silk of it as she moved on him.

"You're heaven," he told her, too lost in a haze of exhaustion, arousal and half-sleep to worry about sounding stupid.

Her gaze softened. When she started to rise, he noticed she seemed a little unsteady. Tightening his hold to give her time to regain strength also kept her close. "What did you mean?" he asked, his voice a low rumble. "That night you said you couldn't feed from me because I wasn't a marked servant."

"I could have fed from you, but it was a little soon after the last time." She paused as if she was considering whether she wanted to explain. Or maybe if he was asking seriously or just yanking her chain. While he wasn't sure if he did believe any of it, he wasn't yanking her chain. The thought had drifted into his mind like everything else tonight. Random, unfiltered and yet somehow significant.

"At a certain age, most vampires consider taking a fully marked human servant. It lets them have a regular blood source, among other things." Her fingers whispered along his throat. "A vampire has to mark a human three times for him to be her full servant."

"You mean...drink from him three times?"

She shook her head. "A serum is released in the blood. It's best to do it three different times, because all together, they can be painful. In a not-so-good way." Her faint smile reminded him how he'd embraced the pain of the lash. "I've thought about that a lot," she murmured, following his thoughts there. "I want to do that to you again. I want to give you more pain, watch how hard it makes you."

She pulled the dress over her head, her hair funneling along her pale left shoulder as she finished the motion, let the garment flutter to the bedding beside them. He reached up, dove his fingers into the thick silk of her hair. Her vibrant blue eyes rested on his face, watching everything he was doing. His body was beat all to hell from the day, but he found he wanted to do everything to her, for her. Suddenly her words made more sense to him. *"It's not a matter of you being able to give."*

"I felt you here, even before I saw you in my room."

"That's the first mark." She paused, as if she'd thought better of having said that, but then lifted her shoulder, which caused an interesting movement with her breasts. He cupped the weight of one, enjoying the simple pleasure of stroking the curve. It really was like they were floating tonight. That edgy urgency that had brought them together before wasn't here, but that didn't make this less intense. Just intense in a different way that kept his throat thick, his movements dreamlike.

"I gave you the first mark, the other night. It's only a geographical locater. It tells me where you are, within a thousand miles or so."

"Is that all? The government's secret microchips do a better job than that."

When she made a face at him, he twined a lock of hair around his forefinger, splaying the others over her left breast. He did a slow, teasing pass over her nipple, watched it harden and her catch her lip in her teeth, felt her pussy contract on him. He wanted to do this all night, swim in languid arousal. "What do the other two marks do?"

"After a vampire gives the second mark, she can speak in her servant's head and allow him to hear her thoughts, when she wants him to do that."

"Hearing your voice in my head. That would be nice." He smiled absently and she caressed his jaw.

"You're half asleep, cowboy. No man wants a woman's voice in his head all the time. She'd devil him to death."

"True. But I think...when she's the right one, her voice is there all the time anyway. Right?"

She studied him. It was a surreal conversation, vampires and marks, but all of it fit together, in a way that fit her. He tried to grasp that, and was too sleepy. She stroked his face.

"You're a romantic, Quinn. I want to say it's unexpected, but it was obvious the first time I walked into your bar. You believe in things being how they should be, even if it's hard to find them set up that way."

Catching both his hands, she molded them around her breasts, a direction he was more than pleased to follow, kneading her curves, thumbing the nipples, lifting and bringing together the two curves as she made a sweet moan. He lifted his hips, embedded himself a little more deeply in her.

"When the third mark is given," she continued breathlessly, "a human becomes fully submissive to the vampire. Her property. She can hold his soul in her hand, crush it, possess it. His life force is linked to hers." Her gaze came back to his. "If she dies, he dies."

"I know a lot of old couples who would like that, so one of them isn't left behind." He sighed. "I think my folks worry about that now and then."

She tilted her head, the silken fall of her hair sweeping over one shoulder. "Where are they, your parents?"

"Happily living out their lives in a senior community in Arizona. When he was still working, they used to catch me on the rodeo circuit as often as they could." He'd seen a different side of his father then. The old man would never be a friend to his sons or offer praise easily, but showing up for those events and treating Quinn with rough approval had changed things. Though they couldn't find common ground as man and child, they'd made their peace with one another as men.

"They don't miss the ranch?"

"No. Surprised the hell out of me. But when Dad hit sixty-five he said he'd seen enough of horseshit and roughnecks and they headed for the place a lot of their friends had found."

"Your parents are close," she guessed. "They have that connection."

"Yes. I didn't get it for a long time, because he seemed so hard, but I guess the key was in how he listened to her even when he didn't seem to listen to anyone else. Love can be a powerful thing." He fixed his gaze on her.

Now her hands closed over his, stilling them. "It can't be like that for us," she said. "Vampires don't fall in love with humans. Humans are their servants."

"What if the human servant falls in love with the vampire?"

"That's acceptable, as long as the vampire isn't swayed by it, as long as she never forgets that the human is not her equal, that he belongs to her."

He studied her. "You believe that bullshit, that people— vampires, humans—can shut it down like that?"

"If they know that the alternative is far worse." The shadows that crossed her face had him sliding his hands to her shoulders.

"Come down here."

She gave him a look at that, as if she was going to put him in his place, tell him she was the one who gave the orders around here, but in the end she surprised him, letting him draw her down so her face was nestled against his throat. When both his arms banded around her, she slid hers under his shoulders, held on, their bodies now linked as intimately above as below. Maybe she was right about him being a romantic, because it felt more important, a stronger desire right now, just to hold her as close as he could, than to thrust to completion where he was buried to the hilt inside her.

"Have you...fed lately?" he asked.

Her fingers curled against his skin and he ran his hand down her bare back. When she didn't respond, he added, "It might just be the moonlight, but you look a little paler than usual."

Lifting his chin, he made it clear he was giving her better access. He stroked her cheek, applied pressure to guide her. Offering.

Selene could close her eyes and hear the thud of his heart, the coursing of blood through his veins. During broad daylight, she was sure he was still questioning her sanity, or determining how much of her vampire delusion he could handle. However here, in the shadows, with that touch and look, it was clear he'd already accepted what she was...what he was becoming to her.

She'd been told by other vampires it could happen this fast. Most of them had acquired their human servant within only a handful of days of meeting them, an unbreakable bond that could span over three hundred years. Vampires didn't indulge in romanticism, not when it came to humans, but Laurent had used those terms so she could understand.

"*You were a human,*" his lip curled as if reacting to something distasteful, "*so love at first sight is the closest approximate, though it has nothing else in common with that other than the quick ignition of the attraction. Lord Brian, who conducts scientific studies on vampires, says there may be some chemical inside certain humans that makes them more amenable to the idea of becoming a vampire's servant, and that chemical may attract vampires to them. In fact, in some of these chemically compatible humans, he's noted their libido increases considerably after only the first mark from the vampire who will become their Master.*" Laurent's gaze had gleamed with indifferent amusement. "*It's as if they're preparing themselves for the demands we will put upon them, despite their bodies still lacking the second and third marks needed to handle that demand physically. You could fuck a first mark to death in no time.*

*"In short, the powers-that-be have ensured we have a pool of human servants willing to serve our needs, even if they don't realize it as quickly as we do."*

She wanted to give Quinn the second mark, badly. It was the only thing that could explain it, some kind of chemical receptor. She wanted to talk in his head, hear him speak inside hers.

But a decision like that would impact Quinn's life dramatically. Quinn, who'd worked so hard for his ranch, whose body bore the dangerous roadmap of his rodeo life to meet that goal. She wasn't an impulsive teenager, no matter that sixty was considered little better than a college student in the vampire world. She was his bar manager, his sex partner. His Mistress for playtime, not for real life. No matter how it felt otherwise.

Instead of taking the vein offered, she pushed up, sitting astride him, and leveled a gaze on him. Saying nothing, she began to pleasure herself, gripping him with her internal muscles, sliding up his shaft, commanding him to service her as she desired. His brown eyes got that intent look that sent a thrill of pleasure through her, and he put his hands to her hips, adding strength to the rhythm she was setting.

She'd told him she'd take, no matter what, that she'd never be denied. But with every movement in sync with her, the way his body arched to drive up into her, how his eyes stayed on hers, making sure he was satisfying her, he told her he'd give even beyond the point when the well was dry. That was the type of man he was, not just when he wanted or desired, but when he loved. It wasn't until now she'd realized what a dangerous drug that was, offered so freely to a vampire. Nigh irresistible.

She dug her nails into his chest, hard enough to draw blood, and his pulse leaped, his cock thickening inside her. She wanted to do everything to him, use the whip on him again, tie him down and fuck him, just like she'd described. She could see staying in this little corner of Texas her entire life, running his bar...

Her entire life? Centuries of it, long after his bones were dust?

She was no longer human. She couldn't afford to think this way. She translated emotional needs into physical ones, redoubling her efforts, driving them ruthlessly, pulling the climax out of him that his exhausted body was going to give her, come hell or high water.

He kept up with her, eyes still on her face. How much did he see or understand? "Take your hands off me," she ordered. "I want them over your head."

"No." He gripped her harder, brought her down on him, so the resulting impact between her clit and his pelvis sent a searing jolt of pleasure through her.

She was going to get meaner about it, but then that softening happened in his eyes. "I want to touch you," he said. "Let me touch you."

He was, in far too many ways. But she let it go. She let herself go instead, going up to that edge, ready to soar. She tightened on him like a vise, felt every delicious inch of him.

"You come for me, Quinn. Right now. Your Mistress commands it."

It took a few seconds, because the man had truly worn himself out these past several days, but there it came, at last, his hips bucking up, a groan tearing from his throat as she matched it with her own cries. The moonlight played over his face, his tanned skin and rippling muscles, and she felt the imprint of his fingers, holding her sure and strong, taking them both all the way past the finish line.

When she at last slowed, she felt a little lightheaded. Yeah, she did need to feed. She'd had Turley right there in the bar cellar, had even started the process of messing up his faculties enough he wouldn't remember what would happen, had put her lips up to his throat, and the second she inhaled and didn't smell Quinn...she couldn't.

She was going to have to get past that quick, because obviously

Quinn was in no condition to give her blood...unless she gave him the second mark. That mark would not only augment his strength so she could feed from him more frequently without adverse effect, it would supplement his strength on the ranch, which he obviously needed.

*Rationalize much, Selene?* There was no going back from the second mark. Even though the Vampire Council frowned on giving the first mark without the intent of bringing a human into a vampire's service, there were plenty of humans running around with that geographical marker who remained oblivious to the vampire world. As a result, they were left alone. A second marked human might ascribe hearing a vampire's voice in his head to special telepathy, but since a second marking usually also accompanied the blood drinking and other inroads into the life of a vampire, only a human in an advanced state of denial, or an idiot, wouldn't realize they'd been marked by a vampire. Quinn was no idiot.

If she second marked him, then eventually left him, and another vampire stumbled on him, scented the marks...it was a death sentence, unless the vampire chose to make him a full servant and complete the process.

Her fingers tightened on him, cutting into those crescent marks she'd already left. It was in these moments she knew she'd become more vampire than human, because her fangs lengthened with savage intent at the idea of him belonging to another. *If* she marked him, which she wasn't going to do.

"So...no blood drinking tonight? Not hungry for that kind of food?" He was teasing her. Tired as he was, he'd obviously realized something had shifted in her mood and was trying to get her in a better place. She gave him a hooded look.

"I only have to drink every several days, unless something stresses me out or causes me additional exertion."

His thumb passed over her lips, her pale cheek. "I'm guessing you had an exerting day."

"It's not your concern. You won't be my only blood source."

"What does that mean?"

In an instant her cowboy's exhaustion vanished. She wondered if he realized he'd wrapped his fist in her hair. He pushed up to a sitting position, curling the other arm around her hips.

She knew he worried that he was somehow less a man because he was discovering he liked submitting sexually to a woman. She wished he could see his expression and body language now, because the thought of another man touching her had him reacting like a rutting bull, telling every male around *hands off*.

She found it far too stimulating.

She laid her hand on his chest, her eyes heating, mouth firming. "I can't drain you like that on a regular basis unless you're marked in a way to compensate for it. Don't worry, cowboy. You're the only one I want in my bed. If I have to take blood from a customer, they won't remember much except a pleasant, hazy dream."

"Was that what you were doing with Turley in the back room?"

Her fingers curved inward again, a reminder of claws. "Your spies are a little too aggressive."

"You could have done that to me? Made me forget it happened, that first night?"

"Probably. It would have been harder since we're more than a passing relationship, now that I'm working for you. It means I make a bigger imprint on you." She shifted. It was getting too real. They were having a serious discussion about the specifics of the vampire world, and she didn't see that faint flicker of skepticism necessary to restore him to a state of disbelief after she left. She couldn't let him go too far down that road. By letting herself get caught up in a fantasy, she was drawing him too deeply into her reality.

"It's time to change the subject, cowboy. I'll be tempted to show you my shrine to Satan and my Dracula movie collection." She gave him a half-smile.

Quinn kept his grip on her hair, though it eased into a more caressing hold. Still, there was enough pressure she remained tight up against him.

"You're so strong. Yet, right now, like other times, I get this glimpse of something...vulnerable." Before she could stiffen up over that, he added, "How is it you make me want to be on my knees, and yet I can't think of anything but wanting to protect you?"

His bluntness surprised her. "They're not mutually exclusive, cowboy." She touched his mouth, fingertips lingering there. "You think a man who submits is weak, less of a man? Someone who needs a woman's skirts to hide behind? There are monks throughout history who will tell you there's no greater courage in the world than that found in full, willing submission."

His hand tightened again, his other one curling around her back, bringing her to his mouth. She allowed it, making a sound in the back of her throat when he closed his eyes, gave himself to the kiss. And to her, even as he held her secure in the circle of his arms. She welcomed his strength, her body melting against his. He spoke against her lips.

"Whatever you are, whatever you need, Selene...you take it from me. I don't care what you have to do to make it work."

She drew back, gave him a serious look. "I can't mark you again, Quinn."

"Yeah, you can."

"You only say that because you don't believe any of this." She hoped so, desperately, even as she worried just the opposite was true. And worse, that she wanted him to believe her. Wanted to share all of who she was with him.

"I say it because the idea of any other guy with his hands on you, with your lips on his throat, makes me want to tear him apart. It tears me apart. That's all I know."

"Just...shut up. Go to sleep." She coiled her arms around his shoulders, pressed his head into her throat, against her chest. He kissed her sternum, squeezed her, but took them both down, sinking back into the covers, holding her close. They were still joined, his cock still hard enough to stay inside her. She stroked his hair, maintaining the embrace. He didn't say anything further, but as his hands moved on her, his rhythm eventually slowed, became more erratic. When his breath evened out, a painful smile curved her lips. Exhaustion had reclaimed him.

She'd had temporary relationships where she served as a man's Mistress without him knowing she was a vampire. It had assuaged the sexual need while she sought the blood need elsewhere. It was tough to keep the two separate, but she'd learned it was smarter to do it like that. She could say her options were too limited in this more rural area, but she wasn't in the habit of bullshitting herself.

Sliding off him, she curled up next to his body and continued to stroke his hair. She wanted the soothing motion to add to his rest. She *was* young for a vampire, young enough to learn new things about herself. Taking care of him—giving him the massage, tending his sore muscles, watching over him while he slept—that was part of having a servant too. She realized it made her no less dominant or in control to want to care for him.

What's more, if he gave her the gift of his submission, it was her responsibility to care for him. For the most part, she'd always just taken care of herself. Caring for a man during sex the way a Mistress should was the beginning and end of it. Now she was on the run from Laurent, a vital time for her to keep her human interactions limited to just that. Yet here she was, wanting to tie Quinn to her in a way that might endanger him. She stared at that vein in his throat, forced her fangs to sheathe. Yes, she was hungry, but she didn't trust herself not to give him the second mark if she did feed.

Instead, she forced herself to get out of bed, locate the pocket knife she knew he'd have on his dresser. It lay there among the other items he'd tossed down when he stripped. A used bit he'd changed out and forgotten to leave in the tack room. The sweaty bandanna he wiped his face and neck with. The thick leather gloves that protected his hands when he fixed pieces of fencing. She touched those things, enjoying that simple intimacy, then she recalled herself, picking up the knife. He kept it razor sharp, which pleased her.

Coming back to the bed, she sat on the edge next to him and curled her fingers around his forearm. She cut the wrist vein she wanted so smooth and quick he only murmured in his sleep. Bringing it to her lips, she inhaled the rich aroma of his blood, but then she closed her eyes, forced all the churning emotions to shut down and took a quick draught. At least that was her intent. But once she had the taste of his blood in her mouth, she wanted more. She wanted all of him.

She broke the contact with an oath, realizing she'd taken too much. He wouldn't be worth much energy-wise in the coming day, especially as tired as he already was. *Nice going, Selene.* Cursing her lack of control, she clotted the wound, fighting the urge to sink her teeth right back into him. He was like an elixir she couldn't get enough of. Forcing herself to stand, she tucked his arm under the covers, slid them more securely up over him, then left him sleeping.

It was time to return to her cellar, a reminder of all the things she couldn't be to him. She should just take her leave tonight, keep running. Yet she couldn't leave him, not yet. She was too selfish to give him or After Hours up. It was so good to be running a bar again. Almost as good as having her own place.

Wandering through his house, she absorbed every detail, seeing the stamp of the man who lived here. The house was a mixture of old and new, like Quinn himself. He had told her the house had been in the previous owner's family for generations. The wood floor was scarred by years of boots marking it, but it shone with a polished gleam.

Two other bedrooms were furnished simply with a large bed, a dresser, nightstand and chair. They had the look of guestrooms that seldom saw guests. Quinn didn't impress her as a man who entertained much. Comfortable furniture filled the living room, leather and wood and heavy woven fabric in all the colors of sunset. It looked new enough that she was sure he'd bought it himself. He'd done a good job.

She could imagine him in the big armchair wrapped in a burnt orange color, his feet resting on the matching ottoman. On the lamp table next to it she spotted a stack of ranch and cattle magazines. The couch was extra long to accommodate his height when he chose to stretch out on it. A big-screen television hung on the lime rock over the fireplace.

*Men and their toys.*

A partially open door off the living room tempted her and she poked her head inside. At once she realized that here was the heart of the man. The massive desk covered with stacks of folders and papers and the computer to one side let her know this was his office, where he managed the business of the ranch. It also held his memorabilia. Two gold buckles proclaiming him rodeo champion hung side by side in shadow box frames. Next to them were framed articles about his rodeo exploits. The paper was worn and creased, an indication he'd carried them around for quite a while before taking steps to preserve them. A bookcase against one wall held a combination of books on ranching and cattle mixed with classics by Zane Grey and Bret Harte. On the top were other rodeo awards he'd won, most of them statues of a rider on a bucking bronc with an inscribed plate on the base.

Finally there were the pictures, Quinn as a young greenhorn competitor, all the way to the mature man she knew now. She saw him on a bucking horse, his one hand in the air, the horse's head dipped low. She suspected that one-handed grip was part of the rules, because she couldn't imagine doing something as crazy as holding on to a gyrating horse one-handed. Reaching out, she touched the image of her cowboy, sure she could smell the sweat on his body, the aroma of horseflesh, feel the grit of the dust on the ground. Other photos showed him accepting various awards and trophies.

Most of those pictures had a note in feminine script in the matting. "So proud of you"... "All our love". Her lips curved. Of course. He wasn't the type of man to put pictures of himself on the wall, but if his mother had given them to him, she'd expect to have them displayed. It reminded him who he was, how far he'd come... the things that mattered.

Proving it, on a low table she spotted the framed photo of an older couple she assumed to be Quinn's parents. She studied the stern mouth and lines of hard work around his father's eyes. Not a giving man, but his arm was around his wife, and her serene face, as well as the lines on it, told of a continuing battle between sorrows and joys. It suggested what Quinn had already implied, that his mother's strength and enduring love had kept their dysfunctional family together.

Sitting in the big chair at his desk, Selene smoothed her hands over the butter-soft leather and inhaled Quinn's scent. She closed her eyes, trying to imagine him at every stage of his life. Learn all the things that had gone into making him the complex man he was now.

When she was satisfied she'd absorbed enough of him—or all that she could take the time to do tonight—she pushed out of the chair and passed through the rest of the house. The dining room was furnished in the same oak as the living room. As Selene ran her hand over the surface of the table that carried the trace aroma of lemon oil, she could easily see Quinn sitting at its head, coffee mug in his hand as he chewed over the day with his ranch hands. She could practically smell delicious aromas wafting from the kitchen. Chili and hearty stew and soup and other stick-to-your-ribs food that would fill up his men, things Manuel had discussed with her when she asked about favorite local fare.

Since she scented a woman, and Quinn, while not a slob, wasn't likely to keep a house this clean, Selene guessed he had a female cook and housekeeper. Fortunately for Quinn's survival, the scent was that of a much older woman.

The possessive thought gave Selene a tight smile. Ambling onward, she found the large window in the kitchen gave a view of the yard and the barn and the corral beyond, where during the day horses probably gamboled and played. The peace of it, the serenity, made her wish for things she was sure she could never have. Laurent would find her and see to that.

But meanwhile...

She'd circled back to the living area, to the chimney. Dipping her knees, she measured the small crack in the flue. Considering her exit strategy turned her mind from her unwise thoughts about Quinn back to the reasons she really should give him up. This was one of the major ones. With all the complications being a vampire brought to their relationship, she had even more dangers associated with her than most of her kind.

She was a turned vampire, which already carried its share of prejudices in her world, but the real taboo in the vampire world, the most closely guarded secret she carried, was that she hadn't been wholly human.

Her form shimmered, and the woman disappeared, replaced by the butterfly. It paused, hovering, the wings fluttering, then it slipped through the crack of the flue and headed out the way it had come.

# CHAPTER SEVEN

*he wet, tight skin of Selene's pussy clamped around his cock, squeezing it, milking it, making his balls draw up as his body prepared to explode. Her hot liquid bathed him and just like that he erupted like a geyser. God, she was tighter than a fist, gripping him so hard—*

Quinn's eyes flew open, sunshine slanting in from the window and temporarily blinding him.

Shit. Another dream.

His hand was wrapped tightly around his penis and his fingers were covered with thick drops of cum. While it had been worth it, even in a dream, to bury himself in Selene's cunt, he was exhausted, as if he hadn't had a minute of sleep. He was stunned he'd had the energy for such an intense wet dream. Even more so that he still wanted Selene with a fierceness that threatened to consume him. His hunger for her went beyond any sexual need in his memory. Was that a vampire thing?

Squinting against the bright sunlight, he looked around the bedroom. She was gone, no sign of her anywhere, just the faint lingering trace of her scent on the sheets. He had an insane desire to wrap himself in the bedclothes as if he could rub her essence all over his body.

He glanced at the dresser, hoping she'd left a note for him, but there was nothing on the surface except the lamp and his usual junk. Though his pocket knife had been moved to the nightstand. Frowning, he picked it up.

Her words from the previous night sat in his brain with the weight of a boulder. All that talk about marking, about possessing. About eternal connections. He recalled his unexpected roar of jealousy that she'd consider engaging in such an intimate act with someone other than himself. He didn't want another man's hands on her. Or her mouth on anyone else. She was his, and he had to make damn sure she knew that. But even more than that he was hers, in a way he'd never belonged to anyone else in his life. Rationally he wanted to discard all that shit about vampires, but emotionally? He wanted to be her servant. Real or conjured up, he wanted her to do whatever was necessary to make him a permanent part of her.

The last thing he remembered was placing a kiss on her delicate breastbone as he wrapped his arms around her and lay back with her warm against his body. His cock, semi-hard by then, had still been nestled in the wet heat of her pussy. He could still feel her hands on his cheeks and forehead, the whisper of her voice urging him to sleep.

He wondered if she was angry that he'd fallen asleep during sex.

*Of course she is, asshole.*

Well, he'd done that all right. No wonder she'd left him without a word. In his entire life he'd never fallen asleep during sex, but he'd felt as if she drained every bit of energy from him. He'd have to find a way to apologize to her. Hell, he'd strip down and let her tie him up like a calf during team roping if that would make her happy. Anything she wanted.

With great reluctance, he heaved himself out of bed and headed for the shower. By the time he had the water turned on full force he was hard as a steel rod again. It seemed all he had to do was think of the ethereal Selene, and his cock stood up and saluted. Leaning against the tile wall, the spray beating down on his body, he cupped his balls with one hand while he rubbed his cock with the other.

Yeah, he knew he was supposed to call her to do this, but if she was mad at him, that was probably just yesterday's game, everything re-set now. If he didn't release some of this pressure, he wasn't going to be able to focus.

As her image danced in his brain he stroked himself, another orgasm gathering deep inside his body like a coil of steel set to spring. He saw her fingers wrapped around him, her lips surrounding the head of his shaft, her tongue lapping the flesh sheathing the hard rod of his penis. The muscles at the base of his spine stiffened, his balls tightened and he erupted like a geyser, spewing the thick liquid over his hand.

He struggled to even out his breathing as the water washed away the semen, evidence of his body's addiction to this woman. It took awhile before he could draw a full breath, his heartbeat steadying down to something close to normal. But it took him longer to dry himself off, his limbs heavy, his body protesting his demands on it.

Wiping the steam from the mirror over the sink, he stared at himself. Then his gaze landed on the mark on his wrist, no bigger than the sting of an insect. It jumped out at him as if bathed in a spotlight. Vaguely, he remembered her nicking him with his pocket knife, then her mouth sealing over the spot, but he'd thought it was part of his dreams. Well, that explained the relocation of his pocket knife. Was that why he was so weak? Was he crazy to let someone drink his blood, play into her fantasy about being a vampire? He had a ranch to run.

*After a vampire gives the second mark, she can speak in her servant's head and allow him to hear her thoughts, when she wants him to do that.* Her words from the night before were as distinct as if she had just uttered them. But last night she had refused to give him that second mark. She had laid out all the reasons why it wouldn't be a good idea. Accused him of being a romantic when he embraced the idea of hearing her voice in his head. But he wouldn't mind carrying her voice around with him all the time. It soothed him, calmed him, even as her touch drove him to extreme peaks of sexual arousal.

If serving her was the key to their intense physical pleasure, he was definitely all for it. Even if it meant serving her on his knees. Who the hell would have ever thought that would be such a turn-on for him?

His buttocks clenched again as he remembered her promise to fuck his ass with a strap-on, wrists bound to restrain him. His poor exhausted dick tried its best to harden again. The feel of his fingers in that hot dark tunnel had been so arousing he'd had to grit his teeth to maintain some semblance of control. And they were his own damn fingers. His breathing accelerated and he gripped the edge of the sink. It seemed Selene might be other-worldly after all, since she apparently had cast some kind of spell on him.

He touched the mark on his wrist, enraged again at the thought of her marking Turley so she could feed. Feed, for shit's sake. Whether he truly believed everything she told him, he planned to do whatever it took so her mouth never touched anyone again except him. He would tell her so, tonight. Make damn sure she understood.

Annette was cleaning up the counters when he finally made it into the kitchen. She gave him a hard look but said only, "I kept your breakfast warm in the oven. You look like you need it. The coffee's fresh."

"Thanks."

There was no way he could put his body through the rigors of ranch work today. Anyway, he still had records to update—weight gain, feed mixture and myriad minutiae that went into breeding saleable stock. He called Dave Ojeda on the two-way and told him to take care of whatever needed doing out there. He, Quinn, would be in his office if they needed him.

But even the paperwork seemed to tax him. His mind kept wandering, remembering Selene's body, her satiny skin, the brush of her glossy hair against his body. The incredibly gentle touch of her fingers even as she drew yet another exhausting climax from him.

In her joke about her shrine to Satan he'd detected an odd anxiety, as if she *wanted* to discourage him from fully believing in the vampire thing. He was a practical man all in all, not one to be drawn in by hustlers, promises of easy money or miracles too good to be true, but he also knew how to draw conclusions from the available evidence, and there was a lot of evidence gathering when it came to Selene. Her obvious worry last night that he was actually starting to believe her might just be one of the biggest indications it *could* be true. If he were a vampire trying to blend, wouldn't he depend on people's skepticism, their easy dismissal that someone who thought they were a vampire actually wasn't, to protect the truth?

But his open-mindedness to the otherworldly was only part of why he was going along with this. The real reason, he was sure, was the unexpected bond he felt with Selene. The idea of being her servant wasn't at all unappealing. And the craziest thing? He was beginning to feel comfortable with the concept. The big alpha cowboy was actually settling in to the idea of giving control to a woman who was as insubstantial as a faery and barely came up to his chest.

*You're addicted to the sex.*

Well, yeah. Maybe. It was certainly better than any he'd ever had in his life. But it was more than that. She had a power over him that bound him more tightly than any lariat or whip yet he welcomed the restraint.

*I am so fucked.*

He finally lay down on the couch across from his desk, where he fell into a half-doze. But he was restless, taunted by thoughts of a naked Selene straddling him. Giving up, he went to sit on the back porch, hoping fresh air would cleanse his addled brain. It might have, if the butterfly hadn't appeared, riding a current of air to land on his knee.

Quinn stared at the gossamer wings, that same smoky blue of Selene's tempting eyes and the liquid gold of her hair. Damn. He could almost hear her regal voice, commanding him.

*Would you take off your clothes out here if I told you to, cowboy?*

Quinn shook his head. He was losing his fucking mind.

Annette gave him an odd look when he gave dinner a quick pass, excusing himself and muttering something about lack of appetite.

"You feeling okay, Quinn?" she asked.

"Yes. Fine. Good." Horny. "I just need to get down to the bar."

"I thought that new manager you hired had everything under control. Rumor is she's some hot piece."

Rage boiled up inside him. "You tell anyone who runs their mouth that Selene is a lady, a sharp one, too smart to fiddle with the likes of anyone around here. If I hear any talk or see anyone taking liberties they'll be looking up at the sky from a dumpster."

"Okay, okay!" She held up her hands. "Pardon me all to hell."

"She's doing a damn fine job, in case you wanted to know. I just thought I'd see if she needed a hand."

He could feel Annette's eyes boring holes in him as he headed out of the kitchen. The woman was too smart for her own good.

He showered once more, even though he hadn't done any hard work during the day, and shaved carefully. Again he touched the mark on his wrist. According to Selene the third mark was the one that made him fully her servant. So if the second mark was an interim step that would give them both more energy but not completely bind him, why wouldn't she do it?

Whether he believed everything she said or not, it stunned him to realize how intensely he craved that second mark. Maybe even the third one. As he brushed his teeth, splashed on aftershave and dressed in clean clothes, he was besieged with an urgency to see her, so much so that he had to stop himself from speeding as he headed down the highway into town.

Despite it being a weeknight, After Hours was busy. Carol was on shift tonight and moving easily from table to table, serving drinks and bussing the empties efficiently. Apparently she'd had the Selene speed-training program. Selene was behind the bar, mixing drinks, working the cash register and bestowing her public smile on each customer who ordered.

He moved into the barback with her, filled two beers for customers and tapped her on the shoulder. When she gave him a cool stare, it was clear she'd been fully aware of his arrival. As usual.

"You're in my way, cowboy."

Whoa. What the hell? "Just wanted to make sure you had everything you needed."

"Of course I do. I don't need you hovering." She frowned. "Or are you doubting my abilities?"

Okay, this was not about getting in her space. It had to be about him falling asleep. Damn it, this was what he'd been afraid of. But she had to know she'd worn him out. Hadn't it been her telling him to close his eyes?

"Listen." He drew a breath. "I want to apologize—"

She bumped into him as she took a bottle down from a back shelf. "Not now. I have customers to serve."

Though he bristled at her tone, a glance around showed way too many interested ears perked. This was getting him nowhere fast. He'd best wait until the crowd died down and he could get her alone.

"Fine. I'll be in the office," he told her shortly and headed down the hallway.

If he lived to be a hundred he didn't think he'd ever understand women. He'd roped steers that weren't as cantankerous. Last night when she showed up at the ranch with no warning, he'd thought he was dreaming. He'd been lying in bed half asleep and suddenly there she was, in his room, as if he'd just conjured her up.

His cock swelled and pressed against his fly at the memory of her hands on his body, massaging and rubbing. He hadn't thought he'd be able to participate, as worn out as he was, but Selene managed to coax his body to mate with her in a hot, lazy coupling. Her voice had enveloped him like molasses as she took him into the wetness of her cunt and drew his response out of him.

Like a Mistress. Like the Mistress she told him she was.

It had all been so good, and then he'd gone and fallen asleep, asshole that he was. He'd make it up to her, if he could just get her to talk to him.

The hours dragged by as he did his best to pass the time in the office. A few times he lounged in the entrance to the main room, checking out the crowd. Checking out Selene. But she either scowled at him or ignored him completely.

He crafted a few apologies in his head, but as time passed, he couldn't help feeling the punishment wasn't exactly matching the crime. He'd been worn out, and at least he'd made sure she'd had pleasure before he dropped off. She was the one who'd shown up unexpected. Damn it, he wasn't a cringing doormat, and if she thought she could talk to him like dirt just because he let her tie him up, they needed to talk that shit out.

He'd reached the end of his patience by the time he heard the sound of people leaving, Carol and Manuel calling good night. Finally—*finally!*—he heard the tap of Selene's heels on the concrete floor as she headed for the office. He forced himself to wait, sitting at his desk, as she opened the door and stepped in, carrying the drawer from the cash register.

"I see you're still here."

How could someone who looked so fragile exude such strength and control? *But isn't that part of what draws me to her?*

"In case you forgot," he drawled, "I own the place."

"In that case," she retorted, "you'll want this tallied and locked up for the bank. That means moving out of that chair."

He dropped his booted feet from the desk where they'd been resting and leaned forward. Taking the cash drawer from her, he set it on the desk and rose to come around it. Before she could move away, he'd curled his fingers around her wrists. When she tried to tug free, he tightened his hold.

"Enough," he said. "I know why you're pissed off at me and I should at least get a chance to apologize."

Her eyes widened. "Excuse me?"

"I'm sorry I fell asleep, okay? It was more than rude of me." Sitting his ass on the edge of the desk, he reeled her in closer until she was standing between his thighs. "My only explanation is I was worn out from a hard day of work and you took what little energy I had left. It won't happen again. You have my word."

"What are you talking about?"

"Last night. I owe you an apology." He frowned. "Isn't that why you're so pissed off at me?"

She took so long to answer him, the regret he'd battled all day surged over the irritation. Had he lost her already? He was seized with an uncommon need to pull her tightly to his body and demand she forgive him. To tell her she belonged to him. That she was his and no one else's. But for once in his life, common sense took over. He had an innate sense that was exactly the wrong tack to take. As hard as it was, he had to force himself to wait for her to say something. Anything.

Her mouth had tightened, and she suddenly looked drawn, tired. "This isn't your fault. I told you to go to sleep and you did."

He stared at her, puzzled. "Then what's this all about? I ask you out on a date, you show up in my bedroom and fuck my brains out. Now you won't talk to me."

She shifted her attention to where his fingers gripped her wrists. At once he released her, although he was afraid she'd turn and run out the door.

Selene backed away from him, that inner battle reflected in the turmoil in her eyes. She inhaled and let her breath out, the movement tightening the fabric of her dress across her breasts. Normally it would have been distracting, but there was something far bigger in the room, making it hard to breathe for the wrong reasons.

"I can't do this, Quinn. I know this is hard to understand, and I shouldn't be taking it out on you. In my world..." She gave a half laugh, tinged with bitterness. "In your world, I'd be eligible for retirement. Yet in my world...I always thought it was bullshit, what they said about age, made vampires, all that."

His brow creased, but he held his tongue. If he started asking stupid questions, she might stop talking, and fortunately, whatever she'd been holding inside looked like it was ready to boil forth.

She paced to the back of the office, turned and leaned against the wall. She settled her hands in a fold behind her, which raised her breasts, accentuated every lovely line of her body. What made it even more provocative was how unconscious it was.

"I'm sixty-two years old, Quinn. Given the average lifespan for a made vampire is four hundred to six hundred years old, I'm barely out of my teens. When I was made, it was explained to me that made vampires have impulse problems, especially in the first hundred years. It's why we're kept so close to our sire or mentor during the first fifty or sixty years, and then it's up to that sire to decide when to loosen the reins, give a young vampire more independence, the ability to move more freely around your assigned territory. Have your own career, job, relationships, what have you. If you don't have a sire, you're assigned a mentor who takes on that role. A mentor isn't held as strictly responsible if you screw up as your sire would be, but it's still a heavy responsibility."

"You had a mentor instead of a sire?" he ventured. She nodded.

"There's a prejudice toward made vampires in our world. The born vampires are our aristocracy. If you're merely *born* a vampire, you're given the title 'lord' or 'lady' at birth." Her lip curled derisively. "You have to become an overlord to earn that as a made vampire, and very few of us do that. So I didn't give the issue of 'impulse control' much credit. Just figured it was more of the snooty born vampire bullshit, trying to make us feel inferior. I should have listened better."

Her gaze locked with his. "Last night I almost second marked you when you were awake, and then, when you went to sleep, I came so damn close. Too close. It would have been inappropriate of me to mark you without giving you a choice. A fully informed choice."

Quinn didn't know whether to rejoice that the problem here was not with him or to turn her over his knee and paddle her ass for putting him through this. He straightened.

"Selene, I told you last night, I want whatever it takes to bind us together. Anything. I've *made* my choice."

She shook her head, flattened herself against the wall as if she'd step back farther if she could. "Stop it. You don't understand."

"Then explain it to me, because whatever it is, it's eating away at you."

Again a silence stretched between them. This time when she raised her lashes he saw her eyes had gone cold, empty. Eerie and still.

"In my world, your consent is the *only* thing required," she said, low. "After that, *every* choice belongs to me. Do you understand that, Quinn? There's no law against me killing you if you displease me, whether it's quick, or I torture you for days. It's ironic that they give you the choice to become a slave, but that's the only choice you have. Then there's my own status. I am nothing in my world, the lowest on the feeding chain. If another vampire wants to use my servant for himself or herself, I have no choice but to allow it, a twisted form of hospitality rule."

She gave a short, bitter laugh. "Every vampire is required to attend his or her overlord's gathering once yearly, where that can and will happen, with a multitude of other servants."

He digested that. Did he believe all this? It was getting hard to discount it, especially with the complexity of it, the depth of her obvious belief. He supposed that was her point, to shove him toward the "bitch is crazy and back away" side of things. He cleared his throat. "I'm guessing made vampires think about this stuff more than born vampires. You're still human enough to have a conscience about it. Obviously."

Pain crossed her gaze. "Yes. Though that feeling goes away with the years. I was told that as well, didn't believe it either, and now I've already done more than I should with you, than conscience should allow."

"But other than that, what's the problem?"

She stared at him. "I get that you don't believe any of this, Quinn. But don't make light of this or mock me."

"I'm not." He injected enough steel into his tone to win an answering spark in her eyes. "I honestly don't know what to believe, Selene. Yeah, a part of me keeps wanting to say you're just some insane, hot woman with the delusion she's a vampire. But maybe I'm just as crazy, because there are things about you that tell me that might not be the case. I might not be to the point I can say out loud I believe it, but I'm not entirely on the not-believing side of the fence. But that's not the point. You are. There's more to this for you. I feel it. What is it?"

She sighed. For the first time since he'd met her, she assumed a defensive posture, crossing her arms over her chest and taking a step closer to the door. It was the pose of a woman who felt entirely too vulnerable, and his gaze narrowed. Any man with radar for it knew the signs of a woman who'd learned what being helpless truly meant. It was such an unexpected look on his Mistress, he took a step toward her before he could stop himself. Goddamn it, who the hell...

She held up a hand, drew a breath and spoke, her voice monotone. "I was turned into a vampire against my will. I worked in a bar up in New Jersey, and he was the cooler. I didn't know what he was, never did until that night. He was mesmerizing, amazing and yet...almost unreal. I thought...we didn't have a deep relationship, just a few steps above friends with benefits, but I thought at least he was my friend. Another thing a human learns quickly about a vampire." Her gaze met his, brushed and became distant again. "Vampires are never friends to humans. Not even to each other, not really.

"Yet there is a code. It's against Council law to turn a human into a vampire without their approval or the human's consent. He sought neither and was executed by the Council as a result. In our bedroom. It was in my first days, where I was nearly mad with bloodlust. He too was young by vampire standards, and he had no idea what he was doing. He just wanted another vampire to be his constant companion, his friend in a cold world. He had a female friend who worked in the bar with him, who tried to dissuade him. I thought she was a jealous former lover. After, I realized she was his human servant and was trying to save him."

He saw the shadows in her eyes, the memories of a night that haunted her. "The first days...the bloodlust is indescribable, but it's manageable. That's what I was told later, because it's only manageable if your sire knows what he's doing. He didn't."

Her voice went back to that dead tone as she obviously sought to just get it out, make him understand. "A week into it, someone was sent to deal with it. If the executioner hadn't gotten there in time, I likely would have killed humans indiscriminately, revealed vampire kind, done unimaginable harm. It's hard for me to accept how he was killed, so decisively, without remorse. However, when I was restored to some level of sanity and self-control, I understood why they punish the act so severely. The assassin..."

She shook her head. "He makes the determination whether the made vampire is a stable turning, stable enough to live. He was the first vampire who showed me true kindness and compassion, and I don't even know his name. Ironic, given that if I was one of those made vampires that turn badly—another reason the act requires approval—he would have ended me as quickly. Yet John didn't suffer. It was punishment, but not done without mercy."

When she remained silent for a prolonged period, Quinn spoke, a quiet prod. "But they didn't punish you?"

"No. Not essentially. A forced vampire is considered the victim." The word came out like a curse. "A stigma that takes a long time to overcome. When you're a forced vampire, you're like a poor relation. No one really wants you in their territory, and those who do want you, you don't want to attract their attention."

He'd thought her in control of everything, and apparently she'd been powerless for a long time. Yet she'd overcome it.

"The approved made vampires look down upon you," she continued. "You're the bottom of the feeding chain, but I had a talent for making money at running a bar, and that appealed to the territory overlord who agreed to be my mentor. Laurent."

The way she said his name, part curse, part dread, had his attention sharpening on her again, his protective instincts bristling. "He's more than four hundred years old. Very powerful. With vampires, strength comes with age. The relationship didn't start out so badly," she added, with forced casualness, "but over time I tired of him reaping the benefits of my talents and still being treated as less than nothing. So I left."

She closed her eyes, shook her head, as if in self-admonishment. Opened them again, looked him straight on. "I ran away. Left his territory without permission, and got as far outside the range of his marking as I could, because overlords impose a blood-link on all in their territory. But if he moves in the right direction, gets close enough, he can find me. I have staked my life, no pun intended, on him continuing to consider me nothing, not worth the effort. As well as on his notable distaste for any state below the Mason-Dixon Line. In his mind, New York City is the center of the world."

"Nice to know vampire New Yorkers are no different from human ones," Quinn said dryly. "They don't realize Texas is the center of the universe."

She gave him a look tinged with despair, as if he was too dense to comprehend what she was saying. He dared to reach out, clasp her hand. She was rigid, her fingers cold, but he gave the grip a little shake to loosen her up. "Hey. Look at me."

Her lashes lifted, and he saw it then. Hunger, at the mere contact between them. Not just for blood or sex, but deeper things, things he understood from wanting his place in the world for so long and having to fight to get it. Her hand quivered in his and with an oath she pulled away. Before he could blink, she was in the corner as far away from him as she could get in the small office space. As if realizing that wasn't enough, suddenly she just wasn't there.

He would have thought she'd just dematerialized like someone in a Harry Potter film, but he felt the light breeze, the scent of her against his body and realized she'd actually moved that damn fast.

"Selene." He strode up the hall, alarmed, wondering if she'd left the building entirely, then came up short.

She was behind the bar, armed with a rag and cleaning solution, and was rubbing vigorously.

Cleaning. She was cleaning.

When he was young, if Mom was pissed at Dad, or worried about something, she went after dust bunnies in the deepest crevices of the house, the ones that had been there long enough to set up house unnoticed and have dust bunny babies. Well, they did say a man was often instinctively attracted to someone like his mother. The thought caused a rueful twist to his lips, though a far less humorous feeling moved inside him. He approached the bar cautiously, gauging her mood, what was happening inside her head. Her vigorous scrubbing was giving him a nice show, her generous breasts working with the motion. The rhythmic way her whole body was moving with her efforts was how she'd be moving if he was fucking her from behind, that white-knuckled grip something entirely different.

Probably not something she'd appreciate him bringing up right now, but in a way, she'd started it. While that hunger in her eyes hadn't been only about blood and sex, those components had definitely been there. Her heated look had been sexual, possessive, needy...just the way he'd felt for her when he woke up this morning. As big a feeling as that had been, he had an inkling of what she meant about impulse control, because seeing all that sheer want in her eyes was overwhelming to him.

"Okay," he said quietly. "I get that being your servant might sometimes suck, if we had to do that overlord thing, or a bigger, badder vampire sauntered this way. But using your own logic on that, we're here in the middle of nowhere. What's the chance of another vampire ever deciding to go to fry-an-egg-on-your-ass middle Texas to find a low-totem-pole vampire and her servant, and asking to be put up in the guestroom? Or up my ass?"

She came to a full stop and stared at the bar, shining like a new penny. "Quinn, I warned you about making light of this."

"I told you I'm not goddamn doing that." He slammed his hand down on the bar between her braced palms. She flinched, and it made him madder. "You've been on top of me, literally and figuratively, since you arrived, Selene. Now you're not meeting my gaze like you're some kind of fucking timid virgin. *Look at me.*"

How many times had he argued with himself about whether his acceptance of her vampire craziness was just his dick getting in the way of his head? Then he'd gone past his dick deep into emotional territory, far faster and deeper than he'd ever gone with a woman, and he'd been concerned that was interfering with his judgment.

The next second ended the argument once and for all.

As if her disappearance from the office hadn't cinched it, this time he didn't have any warning at all. One second she was behind the bar cleaning, the next he found himself slammed against the wall thirty feet behind him, her right up against him, her hand on his throat, and his toes barely brushing the floor. The constriction on his windpipe was immediate and life-threatening. He grabbed at her wrist, stared down into eyes that were flickering with honest-to-God crimson flame. She had her fangs bared. What he'd only felt when they penetrated his throat he now saw fully unsheathed.

Yeah, they could be fakes. But he knew they weren't. No more than her moving that fast or holding someone twice her weight up against the wall like paper could be a trick. Holy God.

Spots had appeared in his vision and he was getting light-headed. "Selene," he choked. Survival instinct trumped acting like a gentleman. He twisted, striking out at her, and his fist met empty air as his feet hit the ground and he fell to one knee, struggling to breathe.

When he managed to lift his head, she was standing a few feet away, that still, expressionless look sliding chills up his spine, raising the hair on his neck.

"This is what I am, Quinn. Take a look. You're standing on the tip of the iceberg for a world that can get far darker and bloodier than you can imagine. You can't be part of that world. I don't want you to be part of it. You've done nothing to deserve that."

He pushed up to his feet, squared off with her. She still didn't move, as if she were a statue that had sprung up in the middle of his bar. Yet as he stared at the frightening image she was projecting, he was thinking of other ones. Her in his bed in the middle of the night. The brief glimpses of vulnerability, the touch of humor and kindness in her makeup, her pride in the way she ran the bar, such that he could pick on her some about it. Her kind and firm behavior toward Maria, Carol and Manuel.

She might be twenty years older than him, but he'd been around long enough to know people weren't just monsters or saints, but a whole compilation of things in between. If they projected themselves as a monster, there was a reason for it.

She said she didn't want him to be a part of her world, but she hadn't packed her bags either. She wanted this bar. She wanted him.

"You know, I don't get the whole 'o woe is me, I'm a vampire' vibe off you," he said. "So there's a big part of you that's embraced that world, tangled it up with the type of woman you are. The type of Mistress you are."

Her gaze flickered, but he continued. "I think what's got you so pissed is you want something bad and you don't like not being in control of your impulses. Humans are all about figuring out which impulses to follow and which to contain."

As he spoke, he was closing the distance between the two of them. He might be crazy, because she wasn't moving, retracting the fangs or looking one whit less scary. But with every step he made toward her, he saw that hunger rising in her eyes. He even noted a slight tremor sweeping through her body, like the quiver before a predator sprang. God help him, it drew him like a magnet. He stopped in front of her, toe to toe.

Her lashes rose, those fiery eyes resting on his face. No, not his face. She was staring at his throat. He swallowed.

"I'm not doing it," she said, sharp as a razor blade. "I won't make you my full servant, Quinn."

"I'm saying yes, Selene. Maybe I haven't thought it through. Maybe I'm not supposed to. It's like the decision to have kids, get married, name-your-life-fork moment. Some level of thinking is smart, but at a certain point, when the desire is strong enough, you just push past it all and say fuck it, make the leap. You're not turning me to a vampire against my will, like your sire. I'm so goddamn sorry that happened to you. But we're talking about you turning me into your servant, and I'm saying yes."

"You need to leave." She looked as if she were made of glass, and if he so much as touched her, she'd shatter like an explosion, cutting them both to pieces.

"How about this?" Despite the volatility of their emotions, he went with a conversational tone. "Concede I have enough of a point about us being in the middle of nowhere to give me the second mark. Let me at least lend you energy and connect to you that way."

"When I leave, if you encounter another vampire and they detect that second mark, they would kill you. Or make you their servant."

He digested that, took a breath. "Again, what are the chances, if you move on," not happening without him, but that was another argument for another day, "that some vampire will be in this part of the world someday and get close enough to me to find that out? The risk has got to be pretty low, right? Let me make that choice, accept that risk. Let me help you, be close to you. This is where I live, where I'm going to be, Selene."

His yearning to connect so intimately to her was rising hard and strong, impossible to resist. He willed her not to resist it as well. He wasn't the type of man who petitioned or pleaded, begged for anything. But as he exhorted her to give him that second mark, he knew he was striking a match against the Mistress side of her, the one that would have a hard time resisting a plea from the man she knew belonged to her.

Because he knew it now too and that made it even more potent.

At long last, she lifted her gaze. "Quinn."

"Do it. Please." He whispered it, sliding his arm around her waist, drawing her closer. Cupping her face, he caressed her cheek with his thumb, found the tip of her fang. It was sharp enough to prick, and thinking on that, he pressed harder. The drop of blood welled up, and he traced her lips with it, watched them part and her delicate tongue take the drop away, making his cock get even harder, though it was pretty much at full tilt now. She'd gone even more still, yet he sensed a soul-deep tremor from her, the energy building, close to conflagration point. He pushed his thumb into her mouth, drew in a breath as her lips closed over it, sucked, making him bite back a groan.

He wanted whatever would bind her to him. The intense feeling of possession he felt for her was so unusual it rocked him.

"Selene. Please. Mistress." If she didn't stop running her sweet tongue over his thumb he was going to strip off her clothes and bury his face in her cunt.

With a cry, she wrested away from him, but this time an answering fire surged up in him. Before she could do that vampire sprint, he'd seized her wrist, turned her and slammed her against the same wall she'd held him against. He saw her eyes fire at the challenge, but he was the one on the bull now, not her.

"Goddamn it, Selene." He gripped her slender shoulders, holding her. "This is what I want. Whatever you have to do, do it, so I'll know every minute of every day and night you are mine, and only mine."

He took her mouth with a voracious hunger so intense it shook him. Lifting her off her feet, he shoved himself against her core, ground there with crude, undeniable intent. As he did, he stroked his tongue in her mouth. He was doing his own feeding now, drawing her into himself. His fingers dug into her shoulders as he pressed his body hard against hers.

"Feel that?" he gasped when he lifted his mouth. "Feel my cock? I'm so damn hard for you one touch and I could explode." He nipped the tender line of her jaw. "And that? I'm doing my own marking. Here." He trailed his mouth down her neck and tasted a delicious morsel of skin. "And here?" He licked the spot then scored her with his teeth. "And here?" He nipped at the hollow of her throat, the beat of her pulse thrumming against his tongue.

"Quinn." She shook her head, a wild thrashing. "It's not—"

"The same thing?" He stared into her eyes, knowing he was as close to being out of control as she was. "I don't care. I'm giving you my mark. I want yours, damn it."

Frantically, as if she'd disappear unless he branded her in some way, he reached down and yanked up the hem of her dress. Though she could work a pair of jeans well enough to make a man drool, he was glad she was wearing one of her short dresses tonight. He thrust his hand between her slender thighs, searching for the wet heat of her pussy. Yanked so hard on the insubstantial silk of her panties that the fabric tore and he tossed it aside. When he thrust his fingers into her and her muscles clamped down on him it took every shred of his control not to come in his jeans.

This woman was not only addictive. She brought out an over-the-top sense of possessiveness he'd never felt with any other woman.

But then she gave him what he wanted. She turned the tables to possess him.

He hit the table behind him as she shoved him back, but she was following right behind, and put him through the damn thing, turning it into kindling as she brought him down on the debris and straddled him. He felt rough wood dig into his back and didn't care.

She held him down, stared at him. "Second mark," she said. "That's it."

*Whatever helps you sleep at night, honey*, he thought. Then he realized if she was going to be in his mind soon, he'd probably have to
learn how to curtail such thoughts. Unless he wanted one of those
broken table legs shoved up his ass.

He slid one hand up her thigh, back under the edge of her
skirt. He slowly, slowly, pushed his fingers into her wet core. She
bit her lip, eyes fastened on his. As he stroked her, she made a
little humming noise. Her heavy-lidded eyes heated, her kiss-
swollen lips curving in a tiny smile. It told him her decision had
been made. His gut loosened as he saw she was back in control.

"My cowboy takes what he wants," she told him, "but only
because I allow it. Remember that."

Sliding his fingers free, he tightened his stomach muscles and
used them to lever himself up to a sitting position. Once there, he
twisted a hand in her hair, used that hold to tilt her head back as
his other arm banded hard around her waist. His heart was
pounding so hard he could barely get the words out.

"Is that right?" he growled.

"Yes. It is. And if you want to fuck me, you'll wait for my
permission."

She was going to do it. She knew she was. Praying she was not
making a mistake that would betray them both, reassuring herself
this was just the second mark, not one that irreparably bound his
life to hers, she bent forward, brought her lips to his cheek. A bolt
of sweet inevitability hit her as he raised his jaw, his hands gripping
her hips. Now that she was certain of her course, the clawing urge
morphed to anticipation. She straightened with just a tiny scrape
of his skin and eyed him. Her restless male animal, trapped
between her thighs.

"Take off your shirt, Quinn."

As he managed it, she rode the sinuous rolls of his muscular
body, feeling the shift of his hard cock beneath denim. "Now put

me up against the wall. I want to see all those fine muscles working for me. A bit more gently this time. You were rough with your Mistress."

He gave her a tight half chuckle at that. "I think she likes that."

"Hmm." She twined her arms around his neck as he got them both up, all those muscles tightening beneath the grip of her arms and legs. She pressed her face against his hair, suddenly holding him so close that she could feel his heartbeat.

*Stop, Selene. Don't do this. Don't do it.*

But he'd said yes, and the urgent beat inside herself would no longer be denied. *It's only the second mark. Only the second mark... We're in the middle of nowhere. I've never wanted anything for myself like I want him. Can't I have this one thing? For just a little while?*

*Oh God. Can you hear yourself, Selene?*

*Shut up. Just shut up.*

The wall pressed into her back, him into her front. She arched a brow at him. "I want you inside me when I do this. All the way to your balls. Then you stay utterly, completely still."

He let go of her to open his jeans, take hold of his cock and find her bare pussy. When his broad head pushed into her, she swallowed a hum of pure satisfaction. He was hard and thick, every part of him sending the irresistible message *he's yours he's yours...*

She slid her cheek forward, against his. She felt the anticipation of his taut body, his struggle against the desire to thrust. "It will hurt the first second, but then...it will be different."

She teased his throat with her lips. The beat of that artery was so urgent, intense like the man himself, as if calling to her. *Oh Quinn...*

As if her savage subconscious anticipated the interference of her residual human notions of right and wrong, her fangs elongated once again, her pulse accelerated and hunger drove away everything but the need to take. She bit down, harder than she'd intended, and he stiffened, but only in a way that made her want to tear into him even more. She felt his cock get harder, thicker, his fingers digging into her buttocks, his body pressing more insistently against her. A lovely ripple of sensation gripped her like a fever ache. She pressed her tongue against the glands in the back of her mouth, something she'd never done but the once, with the geographic marker, and yet it was as if animal instinct told her exactly what to do. Right on the heels of that, she also released a hard, heavy surge of pheromones, because she wanted to see the results. She'd told him not to move. She'd not told him she intended to make him climax.

As the second mark serum surged into his blood stream, the pheromones rushed right over it. He jerked, groaned. "Fuck, Selene...I can't..."

She swallowed the precious mouthful of blood and, as his desires overcame his will and his cock started spurting inside her, his mind opened to her in a flash of images. Primitive needs and desires, his vision of what they were doing, what he wanted to do to her, endless explorations of both their carnal appetites. Then there was more feeling than images, hard, driving need... God, he wanted to move. She wanted him to move. But she held him locked in her arms, her thighs a tight vise over his hips, fingers dropping there to dig into his ass, reminding him.

*Feel it all, cowboy. Try not to move... Let me see it all in your mind... how you're feeling it...*

His mind twined with hers. What she'd derived from his words and body language, she now felt as full truth, his deep craving to submit to a strong Mistress, one with enough cruelty to her to let him be rough when he wanted to be—and take it— rough. Yet he was strong, in charge, not a man to ever stand behind a woman in a fight. Maybe now that she was in his mind she could show him those two things weren't mutually exclusive at all.

Her pussy clamped down on him, wanting to follow him over that cliff, but now she had something else she wanted, and she didn't mind denying herself for the pleasure of it.

She gripped the side of his head, pressed a slight blood imprint on the line of his jaw, licked it away, not willing to waste even a taste. *Whatever happens from here forward...you're mine, Quinn. You understand?*

*I have been since you walked in the place.*

Did he realize he'd just spoken directly in her mind? She'd heard secondhand what servants felt at receiving the second mark, but she hadn't thought much about what the vampire would feel. She could hear the call of that third mark like a siren's call in a treasure cavern full of delicious possibilities. It made her want to finish it, because as the second mark unfurled in his blood and his mind opened to hers...it was indescribable. She could come to rest at the lower levels of his consciousness, was aware of the floor beneath that point, knew the third mark would take away all ceilings and floors in his soul, that there would be no corner of him that could retreat from her, that would not utterly belong to her. He didn't understand that or maybe...maybe he did. As much as either of them could understand it, with him having a hunger for submission to the right Mistress, yet never having been a vampire's servant, and her, a young vampire who'd never yet taken one.

He shifted his head, pressing his forehead to hers as he drew in a ragged breath. His voice came out a whisper. "Mistress."

# CHAPTER EIGHT

*a* capitulation, or maybe an acknowledgement. Certainly, at last, an acceptance that without her his life would be colorless. If his submission was the price to pay, he paid it willingly. With unexpected, startling pleasure.

*What do you have to say to your Mistress, Quinn?*

Her voice was in his head. Quinn was realizing that the last few things she'd said, that he'd assumed were simply his own thoughts anticipating her own mind, hadn't been those at all. She'd been right. Her bite had been more painful than the previous ones, driven by her hunger, but it hadn't been anything next to that brief second afterward, when fire had been injected into his veins. It had only been a blink, though, then a wave of arousal had crashed down, wrapped itself up with it, a continuation of the lesson she'd been teaching him, that pain and pleasure would go hand in hand with her. And she'd teach him to love both in equal measures, no matter how high either went.

Yet it wasn't a one-way street. Her earlier distress, the conflict, was over for now, and he'd given her something she needed. He was sure of it.

*I need something now. Are you willing to give me whatever I want, Quinn?*

She had a gleam in her eye, and he could feel her body revved and waiting. She wanted to use him, use him hard. He was more than ready for it.

He still had her pushed against the wall, one hand twisting in her hair, his cock buried in her wet heat. "Whatever you want."

"Put me down and take off your clothes," she ordered in that imperial voice. "All of them. You'll leave them here. Inside my room, I want my servant accessible to me in all ways."

Reluctantly he withdrew from her, sliding her back to the floor. She'd kicked off her sandals and stood in her bare feet. Despite that, and the scraps of her panties lying on the floor, her hair and clothes in disarray, she looked every inch the queen. With hands that shook, Quinn toed off his boots and stripped away his jeans.

Selene licked her lips. "Commando. Thought I didn't feel anything between you and those jeans. Shameless."

"Less to take off."

She curled her fingers around his wrist, drew his hand to her even as she laid her other hand on his chest, holding him in place. Making him watch, she guided his hand between her legs, controlled the movement of his fingers as she dipped them inside herself, turned them in that heated slickness. She dropped her head back on her shoulders, humming a little before she withdrew his touch, gave him back his hand.

"Now lick your fingers and tell me how I taste."

He was ready to explode but deliberately swiped his tongue over each finger, lapping her syrup that coated them. Her scent drifted up to his nostrils, sending urgent messages to his balls.

"Carry me upstairs," she said.

He didn't have to be told twice. Lifting her in his arms, he headed for the stairway. If any other woman took that commanding tone with him, his penis would have deflated like a punctured balloon, but with Selene it only made him harder. More aroused and starving for her, if that was even possible. The same emotions he'd felt when she used the whip on him, when she taunted him with images of the strap-on, when he lay in bed totally at her mercy, those emotions swirled through him like a sensual tornado and he had to stop himself from dropping to his knees.

In the small flat he didn't stop himself. When he stood her beside the bed, without even thinking, he dropped to his knees before her. Her gaze kindled like hearth light.

"Do you want to fuck me, Quinn?"

"Yes." More than he wanted his next breath.

"Yes, who?" she prompted.

"Yes, Mistress. Just tell me what you want."

"I want you to get up on the bed on your hands and knees. No questions or speaking until I say, or I will send you home just like this." A hint of amusement touched her lips as her gaze swept his naked body. "Perhaps exactly like this."

Was she going to have him finger his ass again? The memory of those sensations made his balls ache. As he complied, she opened the drawer on the small bedside table and took out a tube of what he recognized as anal lube. It made him clench inside.

Uncapping the tube, she climbed onto the bed behind him, still wearing the short dress. He braced himself for intrusion but instead felt her lips on his buttocks, first one cheek then the other. Her lips were cool but each place they touched his skin felt as if a hot brand had been applied. His cock, which should have needed a far longer recuperation, started to stiffen again.

"You shouldn't feel as lethargic after I feed from you now. You'll find your libido can mostly keep up with mine."

"I wasn't doing too shabby on that without the mark."

"No, you weren't." She sent him a sultry look beneath her lashes. "But I wasn't being half as demanding as I can be."

"But I can handle all those demands now." Male pride said he could have handled it even before, and he could tell she heard that thought, because her lips gave that twitch again.

"We'll see."

He didn't know what the hell that meant, but it better not mean she was going to share those favors. He saw a shadow cross her eyes, reminding him of the conflict she'd explained to him. *That's your only choice, to become my servant. After that all other choices are mine.* Though not all, because a bigger, badder vampire could take those choices from her as well. From Quinn as well.

He didn't want either of them to go back to that moment, but she leaned over the bed, touched his face. He saw a slight softening of her eyes and mouth, the human side of Selene surfacing enough to give him a qualified gift. "As long as I claim your obedience as my second mark, Quinn, you are the only male from whom I will make demands. I can't give you many promises, but I can give you that one."

The words suggested again she might not be here forever, that one day Quinn would find her gone. But her eyes warned him of confronting that now and, truth, in this position, he wasn't in the mood for a full out argument.

"Good choice," she murmured, drawing back and giving his buttock a smart slap. The impact sang through his haunch like a bruise and he bit back an oath. She might have a slender, female hand, but there was a vampire's strength in it.

"We have a problem to discuss." She straightened, eying him. "While in your mind, I caught a couple things that didn't please me."

"Hey, no man can help noticing Carol's boobs. She wears those tight, low-cut shirts—"

She chuckled, her blue eyes narrowing. "No argument. I've enjoyed looking at them myself. No, cowboy. I'm talking about how you woke up this morning and what you did in your shower. What was the rule?"

*Oh shit.* "I thought you were mad at me, and I didn't want to come here all revved up—"

"That's where you made your mistake. *You* didn't want. What did your Mistress want? Think about that for one little second."

Maybe one little blink. She was there, then she wasn't. She was back, two blinks later, the fabric of her dress ruffling over her thighs. There were no panties under that dress and, as his gaze coursed up her thighs, he saw the tracks where his release and her arousal had marked the flesh. It made his cock get stiffer. Then his gaze rose to see where she'd gone.

She had his belt in her hand, doubled over. *Fuck.* "I asked you a question, Quinn. What did your Mistress want? What did she demand of you?"

"That I call her whenever I wanted to come."

"Exactly." She slid the belt through her fingertips, let the tongue fall to the floor, then slid it up through her fingertips again, doubling it over once more as she shifted closer. She trailed it along the valley of his spine, down the crack of his ass. "Spread out your knees. I want to see that fine, tight ass of yours lifted. Show me what all's mine to play with. Torment if I want."

Okay, she was taking this up a notch. Maybe trying to see just how serious he was about this second mark stuff. But it wasn't a matter of that for him. His body was responding to everything she was demanding, even as his mind was scrambling, giving him the *WTF, have you lost your fucking mind* screech.

"Say it, Quinn. Who does your climax belong to?"

"My Mistress."

"What else belongs to me? Be detailed." The belt slid down his thigh, back up again.

"Everything. My cock."

Crack!

The belt hit his buttocks square across, and hell, his dad had apparently been an amateur compared to Selene. Which was saying something, since he and his brothers lived in healthy fear of that leather strap. He bit back the oath. "What else?" she said, her voice that silky demand.

"My ass." Which was hurting like a son of a bitch and about to hurt more.

Crack!

"More. Lay it out for me, Quinn. Every body part you can name."

Jesus Christ. He got through arms, legs, feet, hands, mouth, lips... Between hands and mouth, she stepped close enough she put her hand on the back of his neck, exerting gentle pressure to take him down to his elbows. She tapped his carotid. "Throat," he managed thickly.

He tensed for the next blow, but she bent forward, put her lips on the valley of his spine, holding her hand on his nape as she teased that channel, down to his abused ass, at which point her hand slid to his hip.

"You remember I told you I'd eventually fuck you with a strap-on."

"Yes ma'am." The words came naturally, and she let out a purr of satisfaction that spread warmth through his chest. He really had lost his mind.

"No strap-on tonight, cowboy, but I want you to live with the anticipation."

Oh, no problem there. Since Selene had blown into his life, anticipation had been his middle name.

She'd put the belt aside. Her hands were gentle, massaging the cheeks of his ass, much as she'd kneaded his muscles the night before.

"I trust I won't have to repeat that lesson again. You know who to call if you want to come."

"Yes ma'am."

"I'm cruel, Quinn, but not about that. However, I expect you'll get to the point you won't want to come except in my presence, because you'll understand what a gift your self-control is to me."

Slim fingers traced a light line from the base of his spine down through the crevice, pausing at the tight opening, circling before reaching down to cup his balls. His shaft bobbed and a tiny bead of pre-cum dropped to the sheet.

Over and over she followed the cleft, stopping each time for a millisecond at that sensitive spot. Quinn clenched his fists in frustration, hanging onto his control by a thread. But he felt this was some kind of test, and failure would be disastrous.

When she removed her finger he wanted to cry out in protest, but he felt the cool touch of the tube at his rectum and the cream. Then the pressure of her slender finger as she eased it into his tight passage, spreading the balm into his tissues. She added a second finger, scissoring them to stretch him. He gritted his teeth, imagining how it would feel when she used the actual toy on him.

As she continued to stroke her fingers in and out, she slipped a hand between his thighs to cup and squeeze his balls again. "When I fuck you here," she told him, "I want you to be good and ready for me. Before every shower, I want you to take that balm you used the other night and stretch yourself just as you did then. Just as I'm doing now." She pinched his sac. "Because when that dildo slides into your rectum you'll come until you scream for relief."

"Jesus, Selene."

Her hand tightened painfully on his balls. "Proper form of address, cowboy."

"Jesus, *Mistress.*" He'd call her Queen of the May if it brought him some relief. Those magic fingers in his ass were driving him nuts. If anyone had told him even a month ago that he'd be here, like this, reveling in his submission to a woman—any woman—he'd have beaten the shit out of them. Yet here he was, craving her touch, her commands.

He swallowed his protest when she withdrew her fingers, giving his balls one last squeeze.

"Don't move." Slipping off the bed, she took care of the tube, went and washed her hands in the bathroom, leaving him in that position. Then she slid onto the bed to a position beneath him, her legs spread wide on either side of his knees. She did it with a mouthwatering, flexible grace.

"I want you to fuck me now." Her eyes had darkened almost to navy. "But slow. If you try to move too fast, we'll stop and that will be it for the night."

*Holy shit!* If he didn't come pretty soon his body might self-destruct. He had enough problems dealing with the touch of her fingers as she caressed him.

Quinn took a moment to center himself, lifting her legs so the head of his cock was positioned directly at her opening. Then, eyes locked with hers, he slid very slowly into her hot, waiting cunt.

Heaven. That's all he could think when the wet tissues gripped down on him and his penis bumped the mouth of her womb. Selene raised her legs so her ankles locked behind his neck, the position allowing him to drive deep into her body.

Slow, he reminded himself. Take it slow.

But it was torture, that deliberate thrust and retreat, in and out, her inner tissues hugging him like a wet fist. He never took his eyes from hers, the contact the only thing that centered him. She held the power over him, and the more time he spent with her the more he realized he wanted it that way.

"Selene." He let out a ragged breath. "I can't—"

"Not yet," she warned. "Not until I give permission. Touch my clit. Pinch it. Hard."

Quinn adjusted his position to slide one hand to her pink slit, finding that hot button of nerves and rubbing and squeezing it. Stroke, stroke, stroke. He saw the impending climax in her eyes, in the flare of heat in her irises. Her gasp of breath. He was ready to beg when she finally said, "Now. Hard and fast."

He drove into her like a stallion mounting a mare, his thrusts so strong the headboard of the bed slammed into the wall. Over and over he plunged into her wet heat. With her ankles as leverage she lifted her hips until he was sure he could drive straight through her body. The second he felt her orgasm grip her and her breathless "Now, Quinn", he let go, every muscle spasming as his cock flexed and spurts of semen filled her.

He collapsed forward, grateful that Selene eased her legs down, permitting him to do so. A sheen of perspiration coated his skin, his heart trip-hammering so fast he thought it might pound its way out of his body.

With sex this intense, he'd expect to feel like he'd never be able to move a muscle again. In that first second, he barely had strength to ease himself from her body, but as he lay there he realized he wasn't as tired as he normally would be. He felt more like he had ten years ago, when he'd already be thinking about the next way he'd take the buckle bunny lying next to him.

"I think it's best you censor some of those thoughts," she warned, her lips curving with that sensual set that suggested she was thinking of ways to teach him just how to do that. His ass was still throbbing.

She pushed him onto his back. Drawing a line of kisses from his groin to the hollow of his throat and then along the line of his jaw made him go still, touched and aroused at once.

"Mistress," he murmured.

She straddled him, leaning down to lick the underside of his jaw. "Sleep now," she told him. "I think you'll find if you close your eyes, you're more tired than you expect. The second marking needs time to get fully through your system."

His eyes closed, and he found she was right. With that signal that he was preparing to sleep, his body seemed to sink an extra inch into the mattress. But just as he was about to tumble into the black void, the whisper of her voice drew him back.

*You make me feel safe, cowboy.*

Did she actually say that? He wished he could get his fucking brain to work, because he had a feeling he was missing something important. Safe from what?

He must have mumbled something because she brushed her mouth over his. "Not my body. My heart. I never thought to have that, yet here you are."

"Heart," he said sleepily. "Safe with me."

Her fingers curled into his chest. *I know. It's yours that isn't safe with me. I'm sorry. But I promise I'll do everything in my power to keep and protect you.*

*That's all any of us can do.* His mind drifted around hers, a floating, dreamlike dance. *Human or vampire. Right?*

Before he could hear her answer, he fell into a dreamless sleep.

Selene stroked his chest. In the random swirl of his thoughts as he drifted to sleep, she saw that he still wanted to take her to dinner Sunday night. Then he wanted her to come spend the night at the ranch with him. He wanted her to meet Annette, the housekeeper and cook, obviously an important person in his life. She supposed it could be worse. He could be trying to introduce her to his parents. What the hell was she doing?

She was trying to pretend she was still a human, where she could conduct this relationship like that. She could block Quinn from the thoughts in her head, all while fully monitoring his every thought without him having any ability to stop her. Yet she'd kept her mind open when she'd second marked him, and said the words that had just come into her mind, so sweet, simple and true. So terribly dangerous. Even as she whispered them again aloud now.

"You make me feel safe."

She'd told him the truth, that she meant her heart. She'd learned the heart's safety was more important than physical well-being, because physical power was an illusion. There was always someone more powerful who could threaten the body or mind. But with the right person, the heart could feel safe, inviolate. A rare, precious gift, one that made her afraid, but not at all for herself. All for him.

Just before dawn, she retrieved his clothes from the bar to put them neatly folded just inside the bedroom door. When she left him to retreat to her cellar room, out of habit, she locked it. Though Quinn had keys at his ranch, she didn't expect he'd brought them with him and so she'd be left undisturbed. She needed to keep sending him the message that everything was on her terms.

While it was a rational decision, she knew more than logic was driving the decision. She liked the idea that he was hers to command. Not only like a Mistress, but like a vampire. She just couldn't decide if holding on to her humanity or relinquishing it all to her vampire side was the best path for Quinn. Or if she'd damned him regardless.

*God help us both.*

~

Mid-morning, Quinn sat at his home office desk, booted foot propped on an open drawer, staring at a stack of paperwork, unseeing. He was thinking about the way they'd joked about the difference between Texans and New Yorkers. Yeah, people up North talked and acted fast, and they could be as sharp as they appeared. But his people weren't any less sharp. They thought things through, long and hard, from all different directions. Sometimes that could take a piece of time. Sometimes it only took a blink, especially if a man had had a lot of practice at having to make important decisions that might or might not land him under a bull's feet.

He was running through everything he'd heard in Selene's voice, seen in her body language when she talked about her life before. She was tough, his Mistress, but he could tell until she resolved this thing with Laurent and her past life, she was going to have to keep running and living scared. Yeah, there wasn't a timid bone in her body, but he could feel the fear, way down deep, when she held him, and whispered those potent words, *You make me feel safe.* There was too much sadness in it, as if she understood the feeling was deceptive. Even worse, he could tell she thought she'd somehow failed by marking him twice, looping him into her world.

Everybody needed somebody, and he was damn proud she'd chosen him. No matter how fool crazy it seemed, he wanted that third mark too. But first things first. He had an idea, and it seemed best to exercise it during daylight when she should be fast asleep and couldn't come traipsing into his head ordering a cease-and-desist.

*Yeah. Like to see you enforce that in the bright sunlight, honey.*

Picking up his phone from next to the steaming mug of coffee Annette had left him, he dialed. Time zone was off by a couple hours, but Sam got up with the dawn every damn day.

"I can almost smell Annette's coffee from here." The old man picked up with that greeting. With Sam it could be caller ID or damn telepathy. Quinn didn't question it.

"She probably waves it in your direction out the kitchen window. You know she was pretty taken with you. You probably could have tapped that."

Sam scoffed, affecting an old cowboy-western movie Indian monotone. "You hold out forbidden fruit, white man. That squaw is heap big trouble."

Quinn grinned. "No argument there. She fussed nonstop about you being here, but I could tell she missed you after you left. Think she liked your throw-downs."

"They were debates."

"Sounded like chickens chasing each other around the yard to me and the boys. So how's it going up there in the middle of Nowhere, Nevada?"

"It's been an interesting couple of years. Maggie and Matt moved back east and the new neighbors are...stimulating."

"No shit? I know they said they'd eventually head back that way since Matt was from North Carolina, but they seemed real dug in. They were a big help to you."

"The new ones are as well. A goddess-in-training and her angel mate."

"Of course," Quinn said dryly. "Couldn't be your standard couple, him a tax attorney and her a real estate agent. You have to train to be a god or goddess? Who'd have thought?"

"Everything new requires a period of growth and learning. As well as a lot of meditation on the right path to take." Sam's voice sharpened. "Which brings us to why you're calling."

Yeah, that was Sam. He didn't do a lot of chitchat, but when Quinn had spent time at his campfire, he'd found he really liked those long silences, filled with nothing but the crackle of the flames and the energy that filled the world around them.

"So should I even ask my question, or have you already heard it on the wind?"

Sam snorted. "You answered the most important question before it left the lips of the universe, so your way is set there, for better or worse. You might as well ask the other ones you have, since those answers might help you survive your foolish impulses."

"Are all shamans cryptic and patronizing?"

"We take a special course. It adds to our mystery."

Quinn shook his head. He loved the old guy and missed him. He didn't know if Sam would give him a straight answer or tell him he was off the rails. Which he very much might be. But if he could ask anyone, it would be this man.

"Do you know anything about vampires?" A cowboy asking about a vampire. What the hell must Sam think of that?

The old man chuckled. "Would you like to narrow it down? That's like asking whether I know about cars."

"Still driving that '68 Chevelle?"

"I will do so until the close of time."

"Yeah, not sure the warranty stretches that far."

"Quinn, I like talking to you, or not talking, when it is time for us to enjoy company. You have a purpose in calling, and it's important. Let's get to it."

Quinn cleared his throat. "I'm seeing one. Dating one. Sort of. A vampire, I mean. She's in some trouble." Briefly, he gave Sam the details. "Goes without saying this is just between you and me. I'm just wondering...how does she get out of this? I get the feeling she's no more than a kid in that world, so for all that she stays about three steps ahead of me on everything, I'm thinking you might have some insight...or know someone who can give us some."

"So you don't doubt what she is."

"She didn't leave me much choice." He thought of that speed trick, the slamming against the wall. But deep down, she'd been right. He'd already known.

"Has she marked you, Quinn?" Hearing Sam know exactly what the problem was kind of confirmed all of it, gave Quinn a lightheaded sense of passing into a different dimension. He settled himself down with a firm admonishment to focus.

"Twice. She won't give me the third, so she says."

"But you're thinking you want that. You understand what that means?"

"Can we talk about me after we deal with the important stuff?"

A significant pause, then Sam spoke again. "That was a potent answer to the question, Quinn. A vampire's servant always thinks of the vampire first, their own well-being secondary. You have always been a hard worker, a man who cares deeply for those who matter to him, and will do whatever is needed. I can give you some advice, but do not proceed on it without that third mark. She'll know you need that as well, or she'll go alone."

"She's not going alone."

"You also have much to learn about a vampire, even a young one." Sam's voice held grim amusement. "Are you aware that the vampires have divided our world into territories, and each territory has a vampire overlord? Groups of territories are under Region Masters, and the whole structure is directed by a Vampire Council. There are not many vampires, but because of their power and nature, they operate in a feudal way. Each territory overlord demands tithes from vampires in his or her territory and in turn the overlord ensures they are all complying with the rules of the Council to ensure the safety of vampire kind, for everyone's mutual benefit."

"How do you know all this? Never mind. You're going to say something like 'how do I know the sun shines or the rain falls'. You have a goddess and an angel next door, after all."

"If you are going to answer your own questions, you could do so silently, so you're not interrupting," Sam retorted. "What I was going to say is, if she is in trouble and fleeing one overlord, your only solution, albeit an uncertain and dangerous one, is to seek asylum in another territory, petitioning *that* overlord for protection and advocacy. Does she have any skills that could benefit the Texas overlord in any way?"

"We have an overlord?"

"Have you been paying attention? Yes we do. Or rather, the vampires in this territory do. Answer the question."

"She's a hell of a bar manager. She was making the other guy big bucks running several of his places up in the New York and New Jersey area. She's already turning my place around and she's been here less than two weeks. Do they have some kind of compulsion thing?"

He knew he'd just taken a ninety-degree detour, but Sam had a way of bringing out those subconscious concerns, pushing them right to the top of the list. "I mean, I've never fallen so hard and fast...but I want it to be real, Sam. I want it to be real like I've never wanted anything in my life."

Another silence before Sam spoke. "When I first met you, Quinn, I felt strongly that the energies surrounding you were taking you toward an otherworld path, but the path was not clear for a long time. Your subconscious knew it too, for I sensed you were preparing the ranch not just for yourself, but for someone else as well, even when you did not see it. You're a man who enjoys his solitude and quiet spaces, but the right person is a complement to that space and solitude."

What should have sounded remarkable sounded like something Quinn had always known, hearing the words said aloud. But he wasn't going to jump completely on the Kool-Aid train yet. He waited for the answer to the question. Sam sighed.

"Yes, vampires have some compulsion ability, to help them feed, to help their food forget, but to make a man decide to give up his life to one of them, no. That requires human consent. There is a lot of evidence to suggest vampire servants are a specific subgroup of humans, a switch inside them somehow triggered by the presence of a vampire. Perhaps the right vampire, much the same way certain people are attracted to other people."

So whatever he was feeling for Selene...it was real. That loosened things in his gut, made him feel much more sure of all of it.

As long as she felt the same way, no matter what she said about vampires and humans.

"So we need to go visit this Texas overlord. You don't have a name, do you?"

"Caleb Buford Dorn."

"Butch Dorn? You're shitting me."

Quinn had met Butch Dorn years ago at a cattlemen's convention in Dallas. It had been a brief meet, the two of them hitting the bar at the same time and shooting the shit for a couple minutes. Quinn was as straight as they came, but he remembered the guy was a handsome bastard, with piercing gray-blue eyes, dark, short-cropped hair and a magnetic personality that seemed to go along with the large and successful spread in southwest Texas he owned, Blood Rock Ranch. Quinn also remembered that every time he'd seen Butch had been at night. During daytime he had a guy who represented him at the meetings, his right-hand man. What was his name...Dixon. Dixon Conner.

He leaned forward, flipped through the giant rolodex of business cards he insisted on keeping. He knew he should put them in his phone or on the computer, but he liked looking at the designs on the cards, and he'd remembered Dixon's. There it was. Christ. Talk about hiding in the open.

Dixon Conner, Ranch Manager, Blood Rock Ranch. The two Rs for "Rock" and "Ranch" had a stretched, sharp point. Almost like a pair of fangs, if you held it back a bit and knew what you were looking for. The card was red, the lettering black. He remembered arguing a couple points of order with Dixon over beer afterward, and he'd also asked about his boss, because it had been hard to get those piercing eyes out of his head. Now he thought about what Sam had said, about certain people gravitating toward vampires, and shifted uncomfortably. He remembered Dixon shooting him an odd, long look before they parted, and giving Quinn his card with a friendly, "Call if you're ever in the area."

World was full of crazy intersects, wasn't it? Almost made him believe what Sam had told him, countless times. *If you step back and could gaze at the universe like a god, you'd see all the threads cross other threads. They all circle, weave and spiral in ways that make the universe like a rippling flag.*

"Son of a bitch," he murmured. He realized Sam had been silent throughout his whole revelation. "Sam?"

"Have you found what you needed?"

"Yeah. Think so. You said this would be a dangerous way to go. Why?"

"Humans often craft societies that give the illusion of civility, rules, structures. Vampires have strict rules and structure, but violence and death are as much a part of their world as breathing."

Quinn thought of what Selene had said. *Vampires are more about power and politics, where people end up dead or wish they were.*

"Do not be misled by whatever you know of Butch Dorn. What you know of him is what he has presented to the human world. A vampire overlord is dictator to the vampires within his world. They live or die on his word. He also might decide to torture them for several years in his basement just to reinforce a point of order."

"Selene seemed pretty worried about what would happen if this Laurent character finds her."

"She should be. I wish you had not been drawn into this, Quinn. Though where you are meant to be is not always in line with the wishes of those who care for you."

"Hey, don't worry about me, pal. I've weathered my share of knocks."

"Yes you have. I can't assist you in this because I have no influence in that world. If I was simply a mortal with no connections to the magical realms, what I know of vampires would win me a death sentence, for they are very particular about who knows about them."

"Should we be worried about this phone conversation?"

"No. Anything that comes through the fault line is always disrupted from outside eavesdroppers. That's why you hear the static on the line."

"I just figured you have a crappy provider."

"I have one of the best providers there is." Sam's tone held reproof and his trademark dry humor. "You should come visit sometime, Quinn. What you felt that night...it's far stronger here. It might bring your soul strength and ease. I think you'll need both for the path you are taking. Remember," he added, voice sharpening, "if you go to see Butch Dorn, make sure you're third marked. Or let her go alone."

"Why?" *What the hell?*

"You won't survive the trip otherwise. She will need you afterward, no matter what happens. That is what I feel, though I don't see the path you'll follow." Sam paused. "But keep in mind, Quinn, if you let her make you her full servant, there is a dark, brutal side to that you don't fully grasp, that has nothing to do with love and romance. You have always been a self-determined man, and one to whom being a man has a particular meaning. When you are a vampire's servant, however you define yourself is secondary. You are hers, in every single way. To use, to loan, to determine your path for you for the rest of your life. Are you really prepared for that, Quinn?"

# CHAPTER NINE

*as anyone?* Well, shit. Yeah, Sam had hit the nail on the head. Some parts of this he didn't even have to think about. He wanted Selene, wanted to be with her, care for her, protect her. But then there were the parts he didn't *want* to think about. He was still coming to grips with the cravings that made him get off on being topped by her, strapped by her with a belt, for fuck's sake. Threatened to be fucked by her like a man. Jesus. It made him question his manhood, even as other things overrode it. He figured Sam's unspoken message had less to do with the mark and more with his state of mind. In other words, Quinn needed to figure that shit out before he went forward.

But first, he took her out to dinner Sunday night, just as he'd said. A cool little place with live music, dancing. He hadn't been on a real date in fuckall, such that when he picked her up he felt like a giddy schoolboy. Selene took his breath away. She wore a tiny little dress that made him want to drool on her, right before he tore it off her, but he managed to keep it in check and get her to the restaurant. After a steamy kiss.

Over dinner in a corner of the restaurant, in between band sets so she could hear his low tones, he casually mentioned that he'd talked to his friend Sam, and what they talked about. Then braced himself for the explosion of shrapnel.

Her eyes had narrowed, her jaw getting that tight look. He wanted to reach out, cover her hand, but her body language said that was about as good an idea as hugging a rattlesnake. Instead, he kept going, giving her all of it, as well as Sam's background. Fortunately, she showed she could listen as well as be pissed, because her expression grew thoughtful, and she started tapping her fingers meditatively on the wood surface of the table.

"I guess I should have realized your easy acceptance of things beyond your world had a concrete source. I just figured you were a dumbass cowboy with so much of a hard-on you'd overlook crazy."

She was teasing him, though there was an edge to it that said she hadn't made her mind up about any of it.

"Well, there was plenty of that too." He cocked his head. "You going to punch me now?"

"Still considering."

"Want to dance with me while you think about it?"

She followed his nod to the dance floor. "You dance?"

"I can Texas two-step with the best of them, honey. But forget about that fancy New York hip-hop, Zumba, ass-shaking crap."

She allowed a small smile at that, and he dared to close his hand over hers. "Come dance with me, Mistress. Please."

At her bare nod, he rose, taking her hand and leading her to the floor. They were doing one of Toby Keith's more upbeat tunes, so he swung her into that. She didn't know the steps, but she was fleet of foot and picked up on things fast, two things he already knew, though fleet of foot was probably an understatement.

He tightened his arm, enjoying the feel of her. She was still thinking about the things he'd told her, deciding how pissed she needed to be, but he saw her start to loosen up as they made the turns, give him a smile as he did an exaggerated misstep that threatened to step on her toes.

"You shouldn't have done that," she told him, and he knew she wasn't talking about clumsy dancing.

"I thought a servant is supposed to do things to watch out for his vampire."

"You're not my servant. I've marked you twice, once too many."

Maybe once too few. He met her gaze as he thought it. She bit back a response, her cheeks flushing, and he saw the frustration in her gaze, felt it in the tension of her body. She was about to pull back from him, probably tell him to pull his head out of his ass.

"You know," he said abruptly, "you may be about twenty years older, but it doesn't mean I don't know anything about life. I know how hard it is to find someone who makes you feel like they're the one you're meant to be with, a down to the balls-and-guts feeling."

*I'm a lot more than a dumb fucking cowboy. I also know how we all have to wear different faces to get along in the world, but if you have one person who knows your real face, no matter how many masks you wear, everything else is worth it.*

He'd added that in his mind, because it made it easier to say something like that. Her gaze lifted to his, held. Frustration turned to understanding, to sorrow and yearning, to the whole map of places she'd been and endured without having that person at her side.

The band finished and the female vocalist stepped up to the mike. "This is for those lovers out there. The ones who've been together so long they creak out of bed in the morning and still hold hands over breakfast, and the ones staring into each other's eyes right now, hoping they've found that person."

Quinn's jaw tightened as he recognized the intro to the Anne Murray song *Could I Have This Dance*. He switched to a Texas waltz, sliding one hand up to the side of Selene's neck as he closed his other hand over hers, molding it over his waist before he slid his arm around her, taking her into the flow of the dance and the song.

She kept staring at him. Her mind had remained still, still as her body seemed, even though they were moving together. "Quinn," she whispered.

"It's okay. All of it is okay."

She closed her eyes, shook her head, but put it on his shoulder, let her body meld into his. It made his chest tight, closed his throat up. He wasn't sure the exact message she was sending. It wasn't a capitulation, but for sure it was a message of wishing the world was way different.

*When the assassin killed my sire, his human servant died with him. Dropped like a stone in the same room. The third mark links you to my life force, Quinn.*

"If I die, you die."

She murmured it into his chest. With the music going, he shouldn't have been able to hear it. However, thanks to that second mark, he could, because he saw the words form in her mind even before they came to her lips. Christ. That was the biggest part of it, wasn't it? She'd seen the servant die, caught in the same assassination.

He tightened his arm around her. "I get it. But you don't stop riding because a horse throws you. The worse the throw, the more important it is to get back up there."

He nudged her temple so she shifted her gaze up to him. "So if you die, I die? And you only live to be about six hundred years? Man, that's a raw deal. No wonder you're trying to protect me from that."

She thumped him with her fist. It might look like she had a petite little hand, but she put enough behind it he was pretty sure he'd have a bruise. "Ow."

She sighed against him, but he was gratified she'd seemed to become more fluid again, her curves fitting into his angles. Brushing the crown of her head with his lips, he realized he felt very tender toward her right now, protective. The vibe that was making him react that way was coming from her, underscored by her next thought.

*Quinn, when Laurent finds me—and he eventually will, no matter what—there's probably a fifty-fifty chance he'll kill me as punishment for leaving his territory.* "It's something I accepted when I bolted."

When she lifted her head again, the vulnerability had vanished. Now her eyes were steel. "I won't take you down with me."

Stepping back and away from him, she turned and left the floor. When she picked up her wine and took it out onto the outdoor patio, he followed her, despite her stiff shoulders suggesting she might not want the company. She wound through the tables, occupied by a scattering of people, and found one in a back corner. Once there, she sat down, brought the wine to her lips for a healthy swallow. Then she turned her gaze to studying the sky. Making it clear she wanted her own space.

Too bad. He dragged a chair close enough his knee slid in front of hers, and tugged her chair around so she had to see his face, the cold resolution he knew was there.

"That's not going to happen. We'll go see Butch. You're amazing and strong, he'll help you. Hell, you show him how you run a bar, he'll want you in his territory. He might be no better than Laurent, but I'm banking he will be. I only had a moment's impression of him, but Dix seemed a decent sort, and if he's associated with him..."

"If he was acting on his behalf during daylight, Dixon is likely his servant."

Right. He didn't know why he hadn't put together the obvious. Butch would tell Dix what to say on his behalf during those meetings.

"So we're going to figure this out. You're going to live. I want to do everything to help make it happen, so I need to be with you. Sam was adamant that you need to third mark me for me to go."

"I am not going to let you twist the words of a shaman to get your way."

"There was no twisting to it, honey. He said it straight out. At least think about it."

"You're willing to become my slave, my property, possibly used by others in the vampire world. Yet you're still not sure you're comfortable with me dominating you, Quinn." She met his gaze, and he had to will himself not to flinch, though with that second mark she saw his desire to do just that, damn it. "In the heat of the moment you accept it, but until you're comfortable with it during daylight hours, it's not even a remote possibility."

"I'll figure it out as I go. I'm not an impulsive twenty-year-old, Selene. Everything in my life, I've made out the shape of it before I leap, so even if I don't know the full picture, I have enough of it. The most important thing to me is you." He cupped her chin. "With you I've found the first real emotional satisfaction I've ever known. Don't take that away from me."

"I'm not." She pulled away. "But telling you about being a servant and you experiencing it are two different things. There's no trial period for this. Once it's done, it's done. You don't even know me."

"Maybe I know the things I need to know. You've told me the worst of it, right?" He twisted the spaghetti strap of the thin dress around his fingertips. "You prefer the right side of the bed. You like to be on top. You like to wear yellows and blues."

At that, her mouth twitched, heartening him, but her eyes remained serious. "The hues I'm wearing bind to my wing color when I transform into a butterfly. I've tried to be consistent around you. Have I managed it?"

He blinked. Blinked again. Set down his beer. He thought of that butterfly, the way it had stayed, hanging out with him, almost seeming to watch out for him as well. The way he'd automatically imposed Selene's attitudes and voice onto the delicate creature's actions.

At his expression, she nodded. *Strange as it may seem to you, Quinn, I've just told you the worst thing about me. No one except you knows I have Fae blood. Not much, just a little on my grandmother's side, enough to give me the power to shift and travel in that form during daylight. But even that small amount of Fae blood is intolerable to vampires.*

Quinn stared at her, then his gaze clocked down to his hand, drawn there by a memory. Turning his hand palm up on his knee, he opened his fingers wide, then curled them up, remembering how the butterfly had stayed so still in his hand, trusting. She trusted him, she felt safe with him. She'd said so, hadn't she? It amazed and humbled him, even as he realized she was obviously conflicted about feeling that way, probably thinking a big, bad vampire like her was supposed to be beyond things like needing to feel safe. Loved. But maybe bigger, badder vampires had similar feelings. He didn't know a single being on the planet who didn't need to feel like they belonged, who didn't sometimes seek the company of others, need to feel loved. Except maybe badgers and Annette, but everyone knew they were ornery cusses.

"Why is that the worst thing about you?" He heard himself ask the question, even as his mind was still spinning over it.

"Because vampires despise the Fae. There was a rumor last year that Lady Lyssa, the highest-ranked among us and now head of the Vampire Council, is half-Fae, and the Council tried to execute her when they found out. She disappeared for a time, but when she returned and took over the Council, the rumor vanished. Those of us who have heard it secondhand assumed that was all it was. Even if it isn't, what will be tolerated in the most powerful of us is not likely to gain the same amount of acceptance in the lowest."

She'd been so fragile in his hand; he could have crushed her. Yet from the way she'd acted in that form, the way she gazed at him now, he knew she didn't feel it diminished her power.

Why did he feel he was any different? Deciding to submit to her, to trust her with every deep, dark longing he had, didn't make him weak. She brought out the need to be himself with her, and she'd already showed how much she liked who he was, every bit of it. Being submissive to her aroused him to the point he wanted to fuck her for days, protect and keep her forever, and nothing about that felt unmanly. Far from it.

She was obviously tracking his thoughts, because when he made that connection, when it all clicked together, that stillness was back, but there was a different quality to it now. When he saw a glint in her gaze, he caught her chin again, gently guided her face back to him. Leaning forward put them almost eye to eye, and when the tear slid free, he caught it on his thumb.

"Selene. Mistress." He placed his mouth on that tear track, moved to her lips, and they parted beneath his, her breath caressing him as they shared a kiss that awoke heart and loins together. Hell with it. Sliding his arm around her, he brought her onto his lap, the armless metal chair making it possible for her to straddle him there in the shadows as he cupped the back of her head, made the kiss deeper, savored the feel of her arms winding around him. Those arms could crush him like a boa constrictor, but she held on to him now like a vulnerable woman who needed to hold on.

*Give me that mark, Mistress. Doesn't matter, all the logic and arguments, my worries, your worries. You know it's meant to be. Knew it from the first.*

She lifted her head, her lips glistening from the demands of his. "I like everything about you except your stubbornness," she managed.

"Bullshit," he murmured. "If I wasn't so bullheaded, you wouldn't find me half as much fun. What excuse could you use to pull out that whip otherwise?"

"I'd think of something. I'm not above making things up."

"Actually, I think you're one of the most honest people I've ever met. You told me you were a vampire on your job interview." He lifted a brow. "Kind of a weird way to hide being a vampire, if it's such a big secret."

"Actually I've found it's the best way. People assume you're a bit crazy, ignore that part of you, your little 'quirks'. It's what you thought at first, wasn't it? Most people never go beyond that. Much easier than trying to hide the need to stay inside during daylight, the paleness. Thanks to reality TV and the Internet, it's easier to hide what you really are in plain sight than ever before. Everyone has seen everything and believes nothing. Since I was human, I can play human far better than a born vampire."

He couldn't argue with her logic. Cognizant of looking like

they were considering a quickie in the corner, he eased her back to her chair, grinning when she briefly tightened her thighs and arms, not letting him do it until she was good and ready. Which gave her time to do a sexy little rotation of her hips over his lap, confirming he was hard enough to make it embarrassing if he had to get up and go get her another drink from the bar.

*What an excellent suggestion, cowboy. I wouldn't mind letting these other ladies see what's mine and mine alone. As well as our waiter, who obviously prefers men, from how he kept batting his lashes at you.*

He winced. "You'd do it too. Sadistic wench."

When he focused on her expression, he found her gazing at him quizzically. "A mojito, please," she said.

"Christ."

Yet as he left her to get her drink, he knew she was doing more than teasing him. He was pretty sure he had her thinking about that third mark thing. Which meant until she gave him that third mark, he was being tested for the job.

When he went back inside, headed toward the bar, he saw what she'd seen, the waiter eyeing him like he was fried ice cream with a cherry on top. His gaze zeroed right in low, telling Quinn there was definitely not enough dim light in this restaurant. The guy's lips curved faintly. He obviously knew that hard-on wasn't for him, but that didn't keep him from appreciating the hell out of it.

Quinn knew his cheeks had to be red as a baboon's ass as he hit the bar and ordered the mojito and another beer. She could have waited for the waitstaff to make another round of the outside tables, but Selene wanted to see him wait upon her like this.

She'd said it was possible a vampire more powerful than her might "borrow" him. Female or male. He swallowed, thinking that through. *Could* he handle that? She'd said telling him something wasn't experiencing it, and if she could track his thoughts, then he needed to give thinking this stuff through a go. As she said, he couldn't manipulate her, and he wouldn't even try. He wanted it to be all honest and aboveboard between them. So he would handle this test. And the next, and every one she threw at him.

*Not everything is a test, cowboy. Some things are just your Mistress' desire to see you obey. It arouses me, knowing you're embarrassed but still willing to show off what's mine. Watching your ass flex in those jeans makes me want to take a nice healthy bite. I may have you lie face down on the bed tonight and draw blood right from that delectable butt cheek. Then I'll put my fingers up your ass, make you come as I feed off you.*

*Fuck.* He leaned against the bar because he figured his profile, even with the denim, was pretty obvious.

*Straighten up, cowboy.* Her voice was sharp. *Be proud of what pleasures your Mistress.*

Damn if he didn't do it, because as the command resounded through his head, he felt that response leap to life inside him. His response aroused her, and hers, his, a powerful, never-ending spiral.

That was the key to it, wasn't it? When he pictured himself bending over, letting some guy take him up the ass, he knew no way in hell could he do that. But when he put her in the picture...

That purring voice, those eyes so close as she drew him down upon her on the bed, telling him to fuck her as some guy approached behind, ran a hand down his back, parted his cheeks and... Quinn would plunge into her pussy, and it would be all about her. He'd come because she was using him for *her* pleasure.

If it was for her, he could do it.

Admittedly, only if it was once in a while, like for birthdays, Christmas and the annual head-vampire muckety-muck get-together. He much preferred it being just the two of them. He really didn't want to share or be shared. But he really didn't want to muck out stalls or prepare for taxes. He didn't like going to the dentist and having him stick his hands in his mouth. But he did those things because they went along with the things he really did want. A successful ranch, a job well done, a life worth living, the good and bad all part of it.

Knowing in his gut that Selene wanted it to be just the two of them, living their quiet life out here, would help make the distasteful stuff even more feasible to him.

His dad had given him the sex talk, but his mom had followed it up with the love and marriage talk.

*One day you'll want to be with a girl always, like your father and I have done. I see your heart. Out of all your brothers, you're the one with the deepest wish for a forever kind of thing, even though right now it's boiling among all those hormones.* She'd given him an affectionate swat as he flushed, ducked his head.

*That's normal, boy. But when you do find her, there's this odd thing about loving someone. Sometimes it's more bad than good. You have hard times together. It isn't easy, fitting your life together with another and making it work year after year. But I can promise you, if you're meant to be, you'll figure out one good moment is stronger than ten bad ones. Love is worth it, and if you have love, you figure out how to make things work. Then even the bad stuff becomes part of loving someone, as much as the good.*

"Here you go, boss." The bartender broke into his thoughts, pushing the two drinks across the bar to him.

Quinn nodded, handed over the money, then made his way back through the crowd. The dinner crowd had died off and was being replaced by the drinking and dancing crowd, making the noise level rowdier, the crowd bigger. He was startled but not entirely surprised when he passed a group of girls and one of them took the opportunity to grab his ass. Hell, big as his dick was, he was lucky she hadn't tried for that. He maneuvered out of her grasp, gave her a genial look and a faint grin, the courteous body language of "Appreciate it, honey, but not available" and took another couple steps. Then Selene was there.

Because of the crush of people, no one would have noted she'd gotten there so quick, but he saw the occupants of a couple tables behind her grabbing hold of their napkins as they seemed to flutter from a passing wind for no reason. But what had him putting the drinks down on a side table just as fast was her expression.

Those blue eyes were charged with those unnatural crimson flickers, and God above, he could see the tips of her fangs coming out as she got right up in the hapless half-drunk girl's face. The vibe she was putting off was scary enough to sober the kid right up.

"Not. Yours." Selene hissed, her hand curling around the edge of the table as if she might be a breath away from hurling it.

The girl's brown eyes were wide as saucers. On a usual day, facing something normal, she looked like the feisty sort who might have made a smart-ass remark, started a catfight, but every animal in the world, even human, knew when they were facing something far more dangerous than themselves.

She lifted both hands, palms up, and shrank back in the chair. "I-I'm sorry," she stammered. "We were just playing."

"Play with something else."

Not sure if it was the best decision, Quinn slid an arm around his Mistress' waist, gave it a faint squeeze, a pressure to move them toward the door. *She was just admiring your taste, Mistress. She's young and drunk. It's okay. She's just a kid.*

Something shuddered through Selene. She'd mentioned something about a marked servant being able to lend energy, and apparently a second mark could do some of that, because he actually felt her reach into him, dip into his calm like a well to quench thirst.

She might be his Mistress, but he also had power. To influence, encourage, persuade her where no one else might be able to do the same. He could use it right now, to help her in this situation. Tightening his grip, he brushed his lips against her temple as if it was just the two of them, no one else.

*Let's go somewhere else. My Mistress wants to fuck me, prove I'm hers. I'm all for that.*

Stiffly, Selene straightened. Taking the cue, Quinn gripped her hand, left the drinks behind and headed for the door. He'd have told the girls they could have the beer and mojito if they wanted them, but he thought it best if he just focused on Selene.

Once outside, he took them toward his truck. Selene was wooden and silent, perhaps fighting her emotions. Then she decided to turn the aggression outward.

She didn't push him back against the truck. She shoved him,

such that he almost had to dig his boot heels into the asphalt to keep from going through it. As it was, he was pretty sure his ass print was going to be permanently embedded in the door panel. But he had other things to occupy his mind other than body work. Well, body work on the truck.

She had herself against him, leaving her high heels behind to step on his feet, raise up and claim his mouth. He was more than willing to match her passion, bending to make it easier on her, his arms closing over her, both hands taking a nice handful of her ass and hiking her up his body. Her fingers dug into his shoulders, his back, his nape, tugging on his hair as she scored his lips with her fangs, delved deep with her tongue, stroking his. Her need washed over him, took everything else away.

He realized he was making a noise like a soothing growl, conveying his eager lust and confirming he was all hers.

*Right here. Now.* Keeping one arm looped over his neck, she reached down between them, tugged at his belt and slipped the top button of his jeans, pushing the zipper down so she could reach right in beneath his shorts, close her hot hand around his throbbing cock. She stroked it with clever, knowledgeable fingers, had his arms tightening around her, his hips bucking into it.

"Christ, Selene. Wait..."

"No waiting. You'll come for your Mistress like this, any way she wants it."

"Let me be inside you." He grabbed a fistful of her hair, yanked her head back to look at him. She made that dangerous hiss at him, showing her fangs, and he closed his mouth back over hers, growling more aggressively this time as she bit him, tasted his blood. *I want to fuck you. Make you scream, Mistress.*

*In the truck. That's as long as I'll wait.*

He didn't have a vampire's speed, but he managed to get around to the passenger side and put the two of them into that seat, the door closed and locked, pretty damn fast. She straddled him, and he pushed his jeans out of the way as she came down on him, rubbing the silk of her panties against his length. Reaching beneath the short skirt, he tore the panties away, not in the mood to be much more patient than she was. She slammed down on his cock, her pussy already so wet there was no resistance beyond accommodating his thick size. Her internal muscles clenched him, and as she began to rise and fall, he wanted to taste every part of her. He tugged the strap of her dress off her shoulder, revealing her breast cradled high and quivering in a tiny scrap of bra that barely covered her nipple.

He slid an arm over her back, brought her down to him as her hips pistoned. He kissed and licked his way over her generous curves, tugging down the other side of the dress so he could play in the valley between, curl his tongue along one lace-edged curve and find her nipple beneath, lash at it. His cock was in seventh heaven, her slick pussy clamped like a vise over him as she drove them purely for her own pleasure. All he wanted was to give her more.

"Come for me, Quinn," she ordered. He caught the flash of her eye before she lifted her chin, arched back, her own body tightening in climactic response. "I want to feel you."

Damn if the order alone didn't shove him the last few steps up that ladder and launch him off the end. His mind might still fight with the idea of how she could overwhelm his will, but his body had no questions, the issue resolved for all time as far as it was concerned.

He came hard, groaning and grunting like a rutting bull, and she cried out her release in a way that twined with his, resounded through the truck, made the noises reverberate inside the small space, become part of the sensations vibrating through them.

Before he'd barely finished jetting that last hard shot of seed into her, she was moving down his body, mouth and teeth tasting his chest, the ridges of his abdomen. She was such a petite thing, she made it to the floorboards, and when she did, she had hold of the jeans and pulled them down to his knees, leaving him bare-assed on the seat.

"What—"

He saw a flash of her blue eye under a fall of silky blonde hair, and then the gleam of her fangs. He let out an oath as they stabbed into his inner thigh, making him arch up in reaction as she locked onto the femoral there. He felt the rush of blood, a result of his still-racing heart. Yet his reaction wasn't fear. Instead, he put his hand back on her head, fingers twining in her hair as he settled, widened his thighs to make sure she had the room she needed to feed. She had one hand clasped around his thigh above the knee, the other sliding up to hold his cock and balls, knead and stroke. She was right about the second mark, because instead of softening as his cock usually did right after a climax, it stayed semi-hard, as if proving it would take half the time to get ready for her again.

*I could kill you like this, Quinn. Simply keep drinking until you died from loss of blood. It would take longer, with the second mark, but it doesn't protect you from that.*

*Not the way the third mark will, hmm?* He stroked her hair as he breathed deep, slowing his racing heart. She didn't respond, just focused on her meal. When she was done, she licked him as she usually did, which he was beginning to realize was some way of coagulating the blood, because whenever she raised her head, the meal done, the wound wouldn't run like a cut from ranch work would. Unless she wanted to see that flow of blood, that is.

"Enough?" he rumbled, tracing her cheek, her lips. Her gaze was fastened on him in that way that told him nothing of what she was thinking. Could be good, could be bad. He'd wait and see, and deal with whatever came.

"I don't think the problem's going to be me being okay with a stronger vampire taking a taste of me," he said casually. "You seem to get rowdy about it faster than me."

"I expect that had to do with a pretty girl grabbing you instead of a man." She left the floorboards, surprising him when she coiled in his lap, her legs over the console, feet in the driver's seat. He shifted to tuck her head beneath his chin, closed his arms around her. Selene wasn't really the cradling-in-the-lap type, but he didn't mind the change of pace.

"Makes you feel manly, does it?"

"It does at that." He brushed his lips over her forehead. "You okay, honey?"

"Yeah." She sighed, irritable. "Goddamn impulse issues. I never had a problem before. At least not one I noticed."

"Maybe it's the first time since you became a vampire you've found someone you really want to be with. So it's kind of like a teenager with his first love, setting off a whole new set of hormones. All part of 'growing up', vampire style."

She tilted back her head, eying him. "I know I'm not giving you my thoughts, so it's uncanny how you're picking up on them."

"I'm just glad you have a sense of humor about it. It shouldn't upset you, you know. If some guy had grabbed your ass in there, I would have put him through a wall and then followed him out to kick him across the parking lot."

She gave a half-chuckle, an encouraging sound. Though she wasn't letting him in to see what was happening in her head, he had a feeling she was pretty pissed at herself about it. It was still vibrating off her skin. She'd just taken a lot of the mad-with-herself part of it out through violent sex with him. Which worked great as a mutually beneficial solution, all in all.

Another half-chuckle. "Men. So easy. Do you care about nothing else?"

"I'm just glad we drove into the city for dinner. Else the scuttlebutt at the Nightfall post office would go something along the lines of..." He affected a gossipy old woman's tone, exaggerating his Texas drawl. "'Did you know Quinn was getting it on with that hot new bar manager behind the all-night diner, his pants to his knees and everything hanging out for God to see?'"

"And let me tell you, God has blessed that boy," she responded in the same affected voice, reaching down to close her hand over God's blessings, which was getting more proud about it, especially as she started to stroke and squeeze. He closed his eyes, trying to keep it under control, but a little bite of her nails had him meeting her gaze.

"You keep it under control when I say, Quinn. If I want to

make you come in my hand right now, you will. Remember? Who controls your climax?"

He studied her face, the beauty of it, the complicated layers in her eyes, her expression, and suddenly felt his heart twist. What if she didn't give him the third mark? What if she disappeared from his life?

"You, Mistress. Only you. Now and always. All right?" He framed her face, putting his desire, his demand in the touch, his voice. Maybe she'd prefer it to be more of a plea, but he wasn't built that way and he was banking on how she liked that side of him. He hoped so, because he wasn't seeing it changing this century.

"A third mark lives to be three hundred, on average," she said, turning her face to slide her lips over his palm. The tip of her tongue traced the crevice between two fingers, and then she sucked on his middle finger, biting it gently before she straightened. She pulled up the straps of her dress, though she kept him the way he was, jeans down, her bare pussy pressed against his genitals. "The only thing that kills you, other than my death, is some kind of catastrophic dismemberment, like beheading, which basically kills everything, or steel through the heart."

"So for vampires, it's a wooden stake. For a servant, steel? That's peculiar."

She shrugged. *There are many things about the relationship between vampire and servant that defy explanation.* "For instance, when a human is given a third mark, a mark will appear somewhere on your body, usually something symbolic that represents the relationship between the two. We don't direct or impose that. It just happens." Her gaze shadowed. "I expect centuries ago, it would have been called the Devil's mark."

"Or maybe it's another symbol of 'what God has brought together, let no man rend asunder'."

Her gaze lifted to him. "Oh Quinn. What am I going to do with you?"

"Well, what you just did is great. But you know what I want.

And..." He twined his fingers around a lock of her hair, thinking how it always felt softer and silkier than anything she wore, and she wore plenty of soft, pretty things, "I wouldn't be pushing it so hard if I didn't have the feeling you want it too."

"As we've seen, what I want may not always be well thought out. Maybe in a hundred years..."

"In a hundred years, I'll be dead. Maybe it's the same no matter when you meet a human servant. Maybe whether the vampire's sixty or three hundred, the two people involved just know."

Her gaze shuttered again, her mouth tightening, which told him more than he expected she wanted him to know.

"You've been told it's like that, haven't you?" he asked.

"Yes. But that's not the point." She held up a hand. "Enough. Seriously, Quinn. Stop." She took a breath. "You're not to bring up this subject in any way. Subtly, metaphorically, directly, until I'm ready to discuss it again. Understood?"

It was a pretty damn important topic to him, but he could tell by the set of her jaw she meant it. He nodded, then at her look, he added, "Yes ma'am." Though he gave her a bit of that drawl, a glint to his eye, that had her narrowing her gaze in return.

"We're not going to see one another this week," she decided. "I'll come to you then, after I've had time to think about this on my own. No jerking off, no wet dreams, so you better calm yourself before you sleep, cowboy. You won't talk to me unless I reach out to talk to you during that time. Got it?"

Fucking hell. He couldn't imagine going a few hours without her, let alone a full week. "Yeah. Ow, Jesus." He jumped when she reached down between them, pinched his cock hard enough he figured she'd transformed her fingers to pincers. "Dammit, woman..."

"When I come to you Sunday, you better be prepared to take that strap-on we've been talking about." Leaning forward, she spoke against his mouth, her fingers curling around his throat, constricting just enough to let him feel the reduced air flow. "I'll put you through your paces, see if you truly do have what it takes to be my servant. Up until now, I've been holding back with you. You need to think on that."

All he could think about now was that strap-on, and how he was going to get through the week with that running through his head. She cocked a brow. "Perhaps before I decide on giving you a third mark, I'll brand you with one of your irons, give you a mark that's all my creation. Can you stand still while I do that to you, Quinn?"

In her eyes, he could tell putting red-hot metal to sizzling against his flesh was more than a teasing threat. She meant it. The crazy thing was the idea, as unnerving as it was, got a leap of response from his heart and his cock. She must have felt both, for her lips did that tightening thing again, as if she was restraining her own reaction.

"There will be no way to prepare for what I demand of you, Quinn. You must open up your will and be entirely mine. You understand?"

"So far you haven't told me anything I don't already know." He met the challenge with a cocky tone and a direct stare that had her lips curving, her eyes flashing dangerously. "Mistress," he added.

She shook her head at him. This time when she spoke, there was no humor or challenge, just a serious look. "Take the week to think this through, Quinn. From every angle. You can say no. All the way up to the moment you can't."

Leaning close, she brushed her lips over his, grazed him with a fang. Her blue eyes were preternaturally vivid, all vampire. "But whatever you *or* I decide on the third mark," she breathed, "I will take your beautiful, tight virgin ass next Sunday. I won't be denied that."

*Christ.*

# CHAPTER TEN

$\mathscr{J}$t was the longest week of his life. Thanks to the experience of his horse and his ranch hands, he'd kept himself from too many stupid mistakes, but if he'd been thrown on his head, he could have laid the blame square at Selene's feet. Except that was where he wanted to be, on his knees, tasting the creamy skin of her thighs, sliding his tongue over her wet pussy, pleasuring her until she gushed against his lips.

Not jerking off and waking up every hour to make sure he didn't get himself caught up in a wet dream, trying to honor her demands, kept him jumpy. But she'd been right about the second mark letting him do fine with less sleep. She'd said it got even better with the third mark. He'd be able to run the ranch, visit her at the bar, serve her needs and feel refreshed with only several hours of sleep. Pretty fucking amazing.

On Sunday, Quinn leaned against the back porch railing, tension running through his body like a live wire. When he shifted, the muscles of his ass clenched, the slick slide between his buttocks reminding him of how well lubed he was, per her instructions. While he was so hot and hard he'd probably go off when she got out of her car, he wasn't sure about having a huge dildo shoved up his ass. But what really had him antsy was her decision about the third mark.

If she'd tuned in to his head at all this week, he was sure he would have sounded like one of those kids on a trip—"Are we there yet? Are we there yet?" But even if she heard it, she'd said nothing in his mind. He missed having her voice there.

She'd finally called him earlier in the evening, just after she'd risen from sleep.

"What time will you be here?" he asked, trying not to sound like it was a demand.

"Just after dark." Her voice held a hint of humor. "Are you anxious for me?"

"Always." That was no damn lie.

"Did you eat lightly today? Shower thoroughly and lube your ass? Stretch it with your fingers all week as I instructed?" Her voice was so soft and gentle when she said the words he could hardly reconcile it with the knowledge she was talking about him prepping for the strap-on.

He cleared his throat. Yeah, he'd shoved his fingers up his ass, imagining they were hers. "I did, Mistress." He'd come to love calling her that. He didn't give a damn what anyone thought about it.

"Very good. Remember, though, that's only the beginning of the preparation."

His cock had swelled and the muscles of his ass tightened at the sensual threat.

Now he waited for her, the silence of the evening broken by the lowing of cattle in the distance and the friendly nickering of horses in the barn. His life had changed so much in a few short weeks, since the night the petite blonde appeared at the After Hours Saloon. His world had been turned upside down in so many ways.

Thinking it was incongruent with being the ultimate alpha male, he'd denied the submissive side of himself that accepted—

no, embraced—being completely hers. With the third marking, it would be forever. He realized it wasn't just that he wanted it. No, he craved it. Craved her. He was willing to do things he'd never imagined in order to make that happen.

*Selene.*

Just the sound of her name in his head, the image of her in his mind, was enough to send his pheromones on a wild ride. He wanted to possess her, yet at the same time he knew that after tonight he might be hers, her servant to command. The anticipation had him riding the razor-thin rail of both lust and some unnamed emotion.

When he heard the crunching sound of tires on gravel, he strode through the house and out the front door, in time to see her car pull into the parking area. Just the sight of her exiting gracefully from her car made the muscles in his stomach tighten in anticipation of what was ahead and his cock throb painfully. Tonight she was dressed in yet another blue dress, this one with tiny sleeves, a deep neckline and a flirty skirt that came down barely past the tops of her thighs. When she stepped into the halo of the outside lights he could see the outline of her body through the flimsy material. Her hips swayed and the pale gold of her hair rippled over her shoulders as she walked toward him.

He walked down the steps to meet her, lifting an eyebrow at the small satchel she carried in one hand.

"Does this mean you're actually planning to stay the entire night?"

A knowing smile flirted at her lips. "At least until the edge of darkness begins to lift."

He brushed his fingertips along her jaw. "We have to figure out how you can stay here during daylight hours. How do other vampires do it?"

"A topic for another time." She lifted the case. "Let's put this in your room. Then I'd like a tour of the barn."

"The barn?" What the hell?

"Yes. If I'm going to be with a rancher, I need to familiarize myself with—things—on the ranch."

"Are you?" he asked. "Going to be with me?"

She turned her cheek into his palm. "Perhaps. If you're very very good."

Asking for more would be a futile exercise. She'd tell him what she wanted him to know when she wanted him to know it. With his hand at the small of her back, he guided her through the house to his bedroom where they deposited her satchel. Then, taking her hand, he led her out the back across the yard to the barn.

As they entered the building, she stopped and drew in a deep breath. "I never knew horseflesh could smell so good."

Quinn laughed. "Some people would say it stinks, but I've been around it all my life. To me it's better than a lot of perfumes." He stopped just inside the entrance. "So. You want the full tour, or are you looking for something specific?"

"I'd love to see each of the horses, but then I need to visit your tack room."

"Tack room, huh? You really have been doing your research."

"There are horses in New York," she said with dignity.

"I've heard tell. Should I ask what you're looking for?"

"I'll know it when I see it."

A provocative statement if ever there was one. *What did that have to do with tonight? What the hell was running around in her mind?*

He walked her down the broad center aisle, watching her stop to touch the nose of each horse. They came right up to her, even the skittish ones, and rubbed their velvety nostrils against her palm. He hesitated when they came to Midnight's stall. The ebony gelding could be antsy sometimes. Why was he not surprised when the big animal poked his head over the stall door and gave Selene the equivalent of an equine kiss?

"Yours," she said.

"Mine," he affirmed.

"He suits." She rubbed his nose. "Horses are usually skittish around vampires, but the Fae blood draws them to me. Which is nice, because I like big, powerful animals." She gave him a sidelong glance. "Maybe we'll take a nighttime ride sometime."

"Anytime you want."

Nodding, she studied Midnight's intelligent brown eyes. "Not tonight, but I would still like to see your tack room."

He opened the door to the room at the front end of the stalls, a space as big as three stalls together, and ushered her inside. Every bit of tack—all the equipment needed for horses—was kept in disciplined array. Quinn insisted on it. Every man cared for his own and it had to be in tiptop condition. Saddles and bridles filled racks on two walls. On the others were shelves and drawers with a variety of equipment.

Selene wandered from spot to spot, trailing her hands over the supple leather, touching the stirrups. When she lifted a hoof pick and examined it with curiosity, Quinn felt his balls shrivel. No way was that going to be part of their fun and games. But she'd said she was going to put him through his paces, see if he had what it took to really be his servant.

She looked at him and grinned.

"You look terrified, cowboy. My goal is not to injure you, but to bring you pleasure." She turned the pick over in her hands. "This looks more like an instrument of torture."

He relaxed. "It's for cleaning horses' hooves."

"Where are the ropes? Oh there they are." She walked over to a section of the wall where various lengths of rope were coiled on pegs.

He waited in silence while she examined each one, measuring its length, letting the ends slide over her palm. At length, she chose two of them and looped them over one of her arms. She poked in some of the drawers, lifting out a variety of bits, selecting one that had leather thongs trailing from each end. "I need to be sure my stallion is properly tacked," she said.

A tumult of emotions swirled through Quinn. He had no idea

what she had in mind and he wasn't sure he wanted to find out. Maybe this whole thing was a bad idea.

It didn't really matter, did it? Good idea, bad idea, he was hers, he knew it. He wanted her with a need so furious it consumed every bit of him. Whatever she wanted, if he could survive it, he'd do it.

She held his gaze, telling him she was hearing every thought scrolling through his head. Then she tilted her head, an unspoken command to follow her. When she turned, he did, his gaze captured by the round gleam of her bare shoulder, the coquettish tilt of her head as she verified he was following her back to the house. Which she didn't need to do, since he was already bound to her by two marks, but he liked seeing the delicate profile. Selene was all woman, knowing exactly what subtle gestures got a man's blood boiling.

The house was silent, Annette long gone to her own home, the hands settled wherever they were, bunkhouse or other dwelling. She led the way to his bedroom as if she were in charge of the house, and damn all, just maybe she was. The sway of her hips beneath the insubstantial fabric of her dress made him want to reach out and cup the cheeks of her ass. He had to fist his hands to keep from doing that. Selene was in control.

Quinn had left one lamp on in the bedroom, the one beside the bed, turned to its lowest setting. When he moved to turn on the other one, Selene put her hand on his arm.

"Leave it. This gives me more than enough light."

Dropping the ropes onto a chair, she headed for the bathroom with the bit. He heard the sound of running water and wondered what the fuck she was planning to do with that piece of hardware.

*Best not to wonder.* Her voice, in his head.

She came back into the room and placed the bit on one of the nightstands. Quinn stood there, watching her, waiting for instruction from her. When she turned to him, her eyes were hot and hungry.

"Are you ready to do as I order, Quinn? Anything I order?"

He nodded, body tightening in anticipation of what was to come.

She fixed him with her haughty gaze. "I didn't hear you."

He swallowed. "Yes, Mistress."

"Excellent. Remove your clothes for me. Do it slowly. I want to enjoy seeing my package being unwrapped."

He used the bootjack in his closet to remove his boots, an age-old device that allowed him to hook each heel in the notch provided and tug his foot free. Setting the boots aside, he turned back to Selene and unbuttoned his shirt. When he pulled his arms free and tossed the shirt aside, she stepped closer to him and ran the tips of her fingers down the length of his chest. She stopped briefly as she came to each of the old scars not quite hidden by his chest hair.

"I notice these every time you're naked. How did you get them?"

He shrugged. "Hazards of rodeoing and ranching."

A tiny frown creased her brow. "You chose dangerous professions for yourself."

"It is what it is. Nothing was permanently damaged."

He was glad for the discipline he'd learned from rodeoing as she traced every ridge of muscle, brushed the fine mat of hair, drew a line with the tip of a finger from his breastbone down to the buckle on his belt. A shiver skated over his skin as she licked each scar with slow deliberation, as if just her touch could heal him even more. Fingernails flicked at his nipples, sending jolts of heat to his cock and his balls. With her delicate tongue she lapped at his toned pectorals then took a step back.

"Continue," she commanded.

He opened the big silver buckle on his belt and pulled it free from the loops before lowering the zipper of his jeans. She smiled when she saw that he was commando.

"You appreciated it the other night," he reminded her. "I thought you would enjoy it again."

"I'm happy that you choose to please your Mistress."

"Always."

When he was completely naked, he stood immobile while her eyes drank him in. Her slim fingers stroked his cock and she cupped his balls, giving his sac a gentle squeeze. Stepping back, she let her gaze take in every inch of his naked body, from his neck to his feet. One corner of her mouth tipped up in a smile when she came to his shaft, swollen and standing proud and erect.

"I see your body is ready for me."

He gave a hoarse chuckle. "It has been for over a week."

Moving closer again, she wrapped her fingers around it and dropped to her knees to lick the engorged head with sweeps of her tongue. She caught the bead of fluid sitting on the slit and dragged it into her mouth.

Quinn clenched his fists, digging his nails into his palms to maintain some semblance of control. Though she was on her knees, he was the one subjugated here. She would go at this at her own pace and nothing he said or did would hurry her. Indeed, it might only earn him a punishment, although that idea wasn't half bad, either.

Selene drew back and rose to her feet. Bidding him stay in place with just a look, she carried the small satchel she'd brought with her to the nightstand and opened it, removing a tube of gel along with some other unidentifiable bottles. When she lifted out the apparatus that could be nothing but the strap-on, Quinn's heart stopped then stumbled into an erratic beat. He'd certainly seen dildos before. Many of the women he'd enjoyed sex with had their own collection. They'd asked him to put them up their asses while he fucked their pussies, but none of them had ever put one up his.

The dildo for this strap-on appeared larger than any he'd ever seen, although that could possibly just be his imagination. Attached to it was a complicated network of straps and buckles.

Selene held it up. Her eyes possessed a wicked gleam.

"I think this will suit, don't you?"

What was he supposed to say?

*What you know I want to hear.*

"Yes, Mistress. I'm sure it will."

She slipped her dress over her head and kicked her shoes to the side. He didn't think he'd ever get enough of looking at that body, the smooth pussy, the taut nipples, the nicely rounded breasts. He wanted to run his tongue over every inch of her but he knew that wasn't on this particular agenda. Unfortunately. Instead his eyes were glued to her as she fitted the straps around her thighs and hips, adjusting them to fit securely, but he couldn't seem to look away from the enormous penis jutting from her slim body.

Selene stepped closer to him. "Would you like to touch it?" Before he could answer she took one of his hands and molded it around the toy. "I can't wait to see this penetrate you. To impale you with it. I've thought about this a lot, cowboy." She removed his hand and backed away. "Get up on the bed, on your knees. Head down, resting on your forearms."

Swallowing his lingering misgivings, he climbed onto the bed and arranged himself as she ordered. He had never felt so exposed in his life, with his ass, cock and balls unprotected and open to whatever she had in mind.

*Trust her. Completely.*

He wondered who exactly he was trying to convince, but he drew in a deep breath and tried to relax.

She stroked his buttocks, following the curve down to his thighs. He shook at just that light contact. She touched him everywhere, his hips, the inside of his thighs, even down to his ankles, as if memorizing every contour of his body. When she trailed her hand through the hot crevice of his ass he automatically tightened against it.

She gave a low laugh while she fondled his testicle sac. The tip of her finger caressed the tight ring of his anus, circling the muscle before pushing inside. A second finger joined the first, then a third, moving and scissoring inside him, testing the lube.

"You did a good job." She pressed a kiss to the hollow at the base of his spine. "But I'm going to add more lubricant because the strap-on is much larger than my fingers. I have some other adjustments to make."

"Like what?" He couldn't stop himself from asking.

"Not worried, are you? Don't worry. I'll be gentle with you."

*Yeah right.*

She moved away again. From the corner of his eye he saw her at the satchel again.

"I'm going to blindfold you, Quinn. Taking away sight enhances all the other senses and I want you to feel every bit of this. Do you trust your Mistress enough for this?"

*I do. Mistress.*

He realized he was speaking inside her head.

*Thank you. I will take good care of you.*

When she placed the folded cloth across his eyes, he had a heartbeat of panic. Then he centered himself and forced his body to relax again.

Something touched his anus, something cool, and then her fingers were sliding into him, smoothing the fresh gel along his tissues, preparing him for what was to come. He thought he could have stayed that way for a long time, her fingers probing inside him, the feeling was so delicious. A completely unexpected treat. But so much with Selene was turning out to be that way.

She withdrew and he felt something rough around one ankle. The rope she'd carried in from the barn.

"I'm securing your ankles to the short posts at the foot of the bed. I'll be tying your hands as well."

By the time she had finished binding him, his knees were spread far apart, his ankles secured to the corner posts. When she said she'd be tying his hands as well, she hadn't meant to the top posts. Instead she had him go down to his elbows, then even farther, his arms at his sides, hands pointed to the foot of the bed, so she could secure his wrists with the ropes and run them down to tie them to the same posts as his ankles. The position pressed his cheek flat to the mattress, putting a strain on his neck and shoulder.

His Mistress apparently only wanted him uncomfortable in the right ways, however. The mattress dipped as she put a knee onto it. The phallus strapped to her bobbed against his cheek. He could smell her pussy and it eased his tension to know how aroused she was already. As soon as she slid pillows beneath his head he exhaled, the strain on his neck and back muscles easing.

Other things didn't ease, however. If she'd bound his arms above his head, he would have felt less vulnerable, but now here he was. Every muscle in his body was strained from the awkward position, his ass canted up.

One slim finger traced the seam of his mouth, drawing him out of his head. "I gave a lot of thought to how I would do this. I saw pictures of stallions, like your Midnight—"

'Gelding," he corrected in a hoarse voice.

"Excuse me?"

"Midnight is a gelding. That means he's been castrated."

"Well, you can be sure that won't be happening here."

"Damn straight on that."

She chuckled. "As I was explaining, I saw horses restrained for grooming and other things. I thought about putting a halter on you and I may do that one of these days. Stand you up and secure the halter with two ropes. Stretch out your arms and legs. I would have done it tonight, right there in the barn, but I wasn't sure you wanted to put on a show for any of your hands who might be around."

He snorted. "Damn straight about that too."

She kissed his cheek. "My purpose is not to humiliate you, cowboy. Whatever I order you to do is for my pleasure and to ensure you know who is in charge."

"I always know that. Now." He did, tough as it might be sometime. But he had totally lost the ability or desire to argue with her or object to whatever she might want, at least right now.

"Open your mouth, Quinn, and bite down. I've gagged my bed partners before, but I thought you would prefer something more, well, cowboy."

"What bed partners?"

"Casual things, subs for the night in clubs and things like that. No one like you. No one I wanted to keep."

That mollified him, even as other things did a slow flip in his stomach. He felt the cool metal of the bit press against his lips and realized she'd been cleaning it in the bathroom for this. Though he insisted on his men cleaning their tack as thoroughly as if they might eat off it, he appreciated her consideration.

As it stretched his mouth, making his balls tighten and cock leak onto the bed, she tied the leather laces from each end behind his head with the blindfold knot.

She trailed her tongue over his parted lips, first the top then the bottom. "I think we're ready."

The mattress shifted as she slid off and her fingers followed the outline of his extended arm and bent leg as she moved to the foot of the bed. Some kind of rough material slid beneath his wide-spread legs.

"A towel," she explained. "We want to protect these nice bedclothes."

As her fingers slipped between his thighs to capture his cock, stroking it lightly from root to tip, he prayed that he could last as long as she wanted him to.

"What is it you wish to do more than anything, Quinn?" Her voice had a sultry lilt to it. "Speak aloud. I love hearing you try to talk around the bit."

"Give my Mistress pleasure," he managed. "Always my Mistress."

"Very good." Her grip on his cock tightened and her strokes grew bolder. "Perhaps I should make you come like this and wait until later to take your ass. Leave you like this for a while."

*Jesus. Fuck. Damn.*

He ground his teeth.

*I heard that, but I won't punish you. Not this time. Take a deep breath and let it out.*

As he did so, her hands separated the cheeks of his ass and the tip of the strap-on pressed against his opening. With the added lube, it slid smoothly against his flesh.

"More deep breaths," she instructed.

He drew in another one, eased it out and closed his teeth down on the bit as she pushed the dildo into his rectum, one inch at a time. He found the breathing helped him to relax, at least as much as was possible considering the phallus invading his ass. His sphincter muscle clamped against the intrusion but Selene reached beneath him for his balls again and caressed them. The stimulation and the breathing made his body ease its resistance and the strap-on penetrated farther.

With one hand on a buttock cheek and the other still fondling him, she pressed forward. The muscle released and the dildo slid farther into his rectum until at last it was all the way in. *Jesus God.* He'd never felt anything like it. She withdrew and eased back, then pushed forward again. The rhythm she set was driving his body toward a climax yet was barely enough to get him there.

Selene moved her hand to his cock, her touch sending powerful electricity sizzling through him. He knew he was hard enough to drive fence posts and his balls ached with need. Splayed out as he was, he had no power to control the movements of his body and he yanked at the ropes restraining him in frustration.

"Easy," she soothed. "I don't want to rush this."

Yes, rush it, he wanted to tell her. The smooth glide in and out of his ass lit up the nerves in that sensitive skin, especially each time it dragged over that sensitive gland. He had never imagined he'd enjoy something like this but the dark pleasure of it shocked him.

Her thighs slapped against him with each move forward, her fingers tightening around his cock as she increased the pace. His entire body tensed as his climax began to uncoil.

She stopped. Withdrew completely. Removed her hand from his body.

"Mistress," he growled. "Please. I beg you."

"What is it you wish, cowboy? My hand? My mouth? This cock I'm wearing?"

"Yes." He was drooling over the bit. "All of it. Everything."

She eased the phallus back into his body. "At my command."

"Yes. Yes. Whatever you want." Christ, he needed to come in the worst way.

She gave a light laugh. "Really? Anything I want? I think I should do this on a regular basis."

"Please," he begged.

"You only had to ask," she teased.

Now she drove into him rapidly, her hand stroking his cock in cadence with the thrusts of her hips. He clamped down on the bit so hard he was afraid he'd crack the enamel on his teeth. Every muscle in his body tightened.

"Please...Mistress."

"Yes, Quinn. Now."

As his orgasm gripped him with an unfamiliar violence, huge shudders racked him from head to toe. He spewed his release, her small fingers milking him, his come ejaculating with such tremendous force it took away what little breath he had left. He yanked so hard on the ropes binding him he could feel them cutting into his wrists. He was glad for the pillows beneath his head because he was sure he wouldn't be able to hold it up.

She rode him through it, the huge greased dildo sliding in and out of his ass. When the last tremor finally died away he felt as if every bit of energy had been drained from his body. If not for the restraints he would have curled into a fetal position and willed himself into unconsciousness.

*Oh no, cowboy. You don't get to leave my presence without permission. Not even your mind.*

Selene gave his cock one last stroke before withdrawing from his body. The ropes around his ankles were released, her hands caressing the places where they'd bound him. Easing his legs from their painful position, she massaged the muscles with her angel's touch, kneading from ankle to thigh and back again until the strain eased. Then his wrists. More gentle stroking, kneading, rubbing, until the muscles in his arms also relaxed.

*Thank you, Mistress.*

*It's my pleasure. And my responsibility.*

The bed dipped again as she knelt on it beside his head, easing the bit from his mouth. She touched the corners with a tissue, blotting the moisture where he'd drooled uncontrollably. Finally, the blindfold was lifted away.

He blinked at the sudden light, low as it was, jarred back into reality. Selene turned his head and pressed a kiss to his abused lips.

"You did well, cowboy. You pleased me a great deal." She ran two fingers through the folds of her pussy then painted his lips with her liquid. "Taste me. That apparatus has a clitoral stimulator that works very well. I came hard with the effort, although not as hard as you."

He licked his lips. "I always enjoy the taste of my Mistress."

Selene readjusted the pillows and nudged him over to his back. "Because you've served me so well, I'm going to reward you."

His heart stuttered at her words and the look in her eyes.

"You've earned the third mark." She paused. "If that's still what you want."

"I do." His raspy voice didn't half convey his pleasure at finally being made one with her.

"You won't be the same person afterward. Remember that."

"Do it," he said in the same raw voice.

She brushed his tousled hair from his brow and kissed his eyelid, his nose and his cheeks, every touch conveying the feel of a blessing. When she straddled him, her wet pussy imprinted itself on his stomach, her incredible scent filling his nostrils.

"You're mine, cowboy. Remember that."

"Always." His heart stuttered.

She smiled, her drawn lips revealing her fangs, which emerged even farther at his attention. Lifting one of his wrists to her mouth, she pierced the artery. As she did, he felt that lovely sense of suction from her lips, then...something different. Fire. He arched up with a gasp as her mouth suddenly became a branding iron, scorching the place where she impaled him. Not so painful as to be unbearable, but he felt a rush through his veins, an acceleration of his heartbeat, and then lightheadedness, all the physical effects consuming him as the third mark serum released into his blood.

*From here forward, cowboy, every vampire will know you are mine.*

*I am yours, Mistress. Always.*

Visions of the two of them naked and riding Midnight swirled in his mind. He imagined taking her on the horse they rode bareback beneath a bright silver moon. His cock buried deep inside her, the black mane of the horse streaming beneath the stars.

When she lifted her head he missed the loss of contact. The touch of her tongue lapping at the wound was like the feel of velvet. Her lips as they pressed a kiss were warm. But when she smiled at him her fangs were still visible, tinted silver from the third mark serum.

*Is it...done?*

He wasn't sure why he'd asked, but when he did, she seemed surprised he'd realized that there was more to it. "To complete the process, you must also bite me. Drink of my blood." She pointed to a spot on her neck. "Bite me here. Hard. You won't hurt me, I promise."

His body tightened. "I don't want to injure you."

"The pain lasts a millisecond. But you have to do it." She leaned down to give him close access to her neck.

*I never thought I'd be doing such a thing.*

*I never thought I'd make you my full servant. Do it, Quinn.*

He tunneled his fingers in her hair, drawing her head close to him and pressing an open-mouthed kiss to the spot she'd indicated. He sucked the flesh, reddening the skin. Before he could lose his nerve, he bit down hard, puncturing it. He wasn't sure what to expect, but the taste of her blood was rich, sweet...delicious. Somehow he knew it had to do with their bond. Then other things started to happen.

Because of the second mark, he already had a sense of her in his mind, but this was different. It was as if every part of him opened up to her, invited her in. He felt her energy fill him, felt his own flow back into her, as if their souls were weaving together. For a moment it seemed as if she was tugging his heart right out through his chest, a disconcerting experience, but she wound her arms around him, put her cheek against him, made a humming noise.

*I love her.* The desperate words formed in his brain but he knew she could hear him. *I love you.*

*You are mine.* Her mind voice was different, a feral edge to it that said whatever was happening was affecting her as well. He felt her shudder. Gripping her hips with his rough palms, he let the feel of her, naked skin against naked skin, steady him.

*Always and forever.*

*You are mine forever, Quinn. There is no going back. I won't let you go now.*

She'd said it was the last choice he'd ever have the freedom to make, when it came to her. Maybe it was as Sam had implied, that he'd made his choice subconsciously, but the point was, he'd known there was no turning back, even before she declared it now.

"As if I'd want to," he growled.

Her fingers tightened on his wrist. "I was right, what I first thought when I saw you. Magic has touched you."

The odd note to her voice made him struggle to think coherently. "I told you about Sam."

She nodded, sliding her fingers along the length of his bare arm, over his tight biceps, down the skin of his forearm, to his palm, and worked the track back, a soothing yet provocative touch at once. Proprietary.

"Your friend marked you in some way as well. I felt it. A soul protection, Quinn. A blessing, but more than that. He keeps tabs on the state of your soul."

"Like a wire tap?"

Her lips curved. "Less nefarious in purpose. It means you

matter to him. But I find myself resenting it a bit. I prefer my ownership to be exclusive."

The weakness in his body faded, replaced by a surge of strength and a feeling of exhilaration. He brought her head down to him and kissed her hard, fangs and all, absorbing her breath. "It is," he muttered.

She broke the contact. "I don't want to pierce you again," she chuckled.

He didn't care. He wanted to roll her over and bury himself in her. But she tightened her thighs, anticipating him, and licked the skin where she'd marked him instead. "Already you're healing. Look. This is our sign."

The skin on his wrist had already closed. Riding on the flesh was a mark. Somewhat between the raised texture of a brand, and the darker pigment of a birthmark, it was far more detailed than he'd have expected. Narrowing his eyes, he realized it looked like... a bit. The straight bar of metal, the loops at the end for reins, a frayed short rein curling out from each one. Like the one she'd placed in his mouth?

Her smile was a self-satisfied one. "Someone wanted to remind you of this night forever."

*Forever.*

When she moved to lever herself from his body he held her to him another blink before releasing her.

"I feel as if I could round up the cattle by myself." He gave her a lazy grin. "Although I have other things on my mind."

"I want to bathe you. Run my fingers over those rope burns on your wrists before the third mark makes them fade." Her lips curved in a tiny smile. "You were an animal, Quinn. One I'd love to ride again and again."

There was a strange tilting happening inside him, a seesaw between exhaustion and a reservoir of energy, pushing against his insides like a dam about to break. She soothed the odd feeling with another stroke of her fingers. "Easy, Quinn. Let the mark take full effect."

"But my Mistress wants me in the shower."

"She'll have you there. When she says you're ready. For now, she says stay." Her fingers wrapped around his cock, her blue eyes glinting.

"Whatever pleases you, Mistress."

# CHAPTER ELEVEN

*A* couple days later, Selene agreed it was time to go visit Butch. Quinn was glad she didn't argue about him accompanying her. Apparently giving him the third mark had resolved. She'd even had him call Dix, because in the very hierarchical world of vampires, it was etiquette for the servants to make the initial contact, unless a vampire didn't have a servant.

Well, now she did.

*It takes a little while, but when you next wake, the effect will be complete. Your senses will be more acute, your need for sleep reduced. Which means we can make much better use of the nighttime hours.*

She'd told him that as he drifted off that night she'd marked him. Though she'd been right, he was still getting used to the effects. The second mark had been an energy boost, but the third one was even better. His senses—smell, vision, hearing, all of it—were exponentially better. If he had a mere two hours sleep, he was good for a day or more of ranch work, and still had energy to spare even after the other hands were dragging.

They told him his new woman wasn't wearing him out enough, because now it was accepted that he and Selene were an item. Everyone seemed to feel pretty good about it, even Annette, though she fussed about not yet meeting the girl. He figured he'd fortify himself with some alcohol for that meet, but then Selene told him that it took about a keg to get a third mark drunk.

Talking to Dix had been an interesting conversation, for certain. When he called him up, pulling out that business card to ensure he had the right number, the phone had rung about five times. The moment Dix answered the cell, Quinn knew the sounds of a man busy in the daily running of a ranch. It made him feel better about the newness of all this. He proceeded as if it were a call about any other type of ranch business.

"Dix, this is Quinn Pedraza from Last Chance. You remember me? From the cattlemen's meet?"

"Sure do. You were one of the few who didn't want to chew on every agenda point like a cow's cud. Though I still think you're bass-ackward about that groundwater ownership issue."

"Boy, you were just in six beers too many. You'd have seen my point if you were sober."

Dix chuckled at that, but proving Quinn's point about him being up to his ass in alligators, the man got right down to brass tacks. "So what can I do you for?"

"I'd like to request a meet with your boss. I've got someone who needs to talk to him. At night."

Quinn didn't think anyone was listening in on his phone calls, but he figured it wouldn't take Dix long to pick up on what he was seeking. Still it was startling how fast Dix recognized it.

"Someone he's met before?"

The man's tone actually changed to something way more formal, and dead serious as any military man or cop Quinn had ever met. Despite his self-admonition to treat this like any other ranch business, it was a cold-water reminder he was entering a world where he was going to be a babe in the woods. He pushed down his uneasiness about that though. He'd been that way at his first rodeo. He'd figured it out and survived to tell the tale. He knew how to change gears to suit a new environment.

"No sir." Respect, not deference. They were both servants, after all. "She needs help. But she's not coming empty-handed.

She's hoping what she has to offer makes it a mutually beneficial deal."

"Hmm. Didn't know you were involved in that business, Quinn. But when we met, I had a feeling the potential was there."

"That's the way it seems to work. What I'm learning, that is."

"How long have you been working for her?"

Quinn considered how best to put it. "Full salary started about a week ago. Been negotiating terms for several weeks."

"Yeah, usually happens that fast. Butch interviewed and took me on within about a week." Humor laced Dix's tone at the double meanings, but Quinn stayed silent, waiting on the calculations he was sure were happening. Was Dix talking to Butch in his head? Selene was pretty out of it by this time of day, but maybe older vampires were different. The pause stretched out, and then Dix's next words proved it.

"Need her name, Quinn. And where she's from."

"She'd rather wait until she's there. There's a protection issue at stake."

"Wasn't a request."

Quinn bit back an oath, because Dix's voice said Butch meant it, in spades. "If my answer works for you and your boss, we'd like to come tonight. Respectfully." Else they might be running tonight, not knowing if Butch had let the cat out of the bag.

Another pause. "Not a matter of it working for me, Quinn. Only for him." That was obviously Dix's part, the next part coming from the third party to their conversation. "Yeah. Tonight works, if the name passes."

"Selene Torres. Out of New York."

"How long has she been down here without Butch knowing about her?"

"She's been working my bar for about a month now." Selene had made it clear Quinn had to be entirely honest, no fucking with this guy. *An overlord can pick up a lie from a human faster than shit through a goose, Quinn. We tell the truth and see where the chips fall.* Though she'd been pale when she said that. Paler than usual.

Apparently hiding out in a territory without an overlord knowing you were there wasn't a good thing. Which was why Quinn would have preferred the question not be asked. He forced himself not to say anything as the silence drew out, but then he couldn't help it.

"She's tough as nails, but she was running scared. Sir." Now that he knew Dix was the intermediary, he'd act like he was talking to the guy in charge. "She's young. I think she would have reached out sooner otherwise. She didn't intend any offense."

"How young?"

"Sixty-two. Made," he added, probably unnecessarily, since she'd made it clear born vampires were much higher ranked in her world.

"Christ," Dix muttered. "Goddamn baby idiot."

Quinn blinked, not sure from whom that comment had come and too surprised to be affronted or know how to respond. Dix saved him the trouble.

"Be here by midnight tonight. You got access to a plane?"

"Yeah. I fly." He'd get the chance he'd wanted to take her up in his small plane. Further, the flight saved them a long drive that might bleed into daylight hours and give his Mistress significant problems.

"Use it. We have a landing strip. I'll text you the coordinates." Dix paused, and when he spoke this time, his voice had a more informal tone, telling him they might be more "alone" now, just the two of them. "And Quinn?"

"Yeah?"

"Don't ever negotiate or give ultimatums like that stuff about her name when dealing with someone like my boss. He let it pass, because it was a minor point and because you're new to this, but take my advice and don't do it again. You have about as much to learn as she does."

He bit back a lot of retorts to that, but Dix had already cut the connection.

That was that.

Flying was sometimes necessary for the big distances he'd traveled and, since Quinn preferred to be the one at the controls, he'd taken flying lessons once he'd earned enough on the rodeo circuit. Early on, he'd supplemented his rodeo income with ranch work on other spreads and many of the larger ones had private planes. Some had their own hangar and runway, others used private airfields. But however they did it, they were always glad to pay a little extra for a hand who could sit in the pilot's seat.

He'd never been so glad to have the skill as he was for this. Flying his own plane also saved any questions about why he'd be taking off after dark and landing at Butch's private airstrip just before midnight.

He'd contacted Selene to convey Dix's information. She'd made arrangements for the others to run After Dark for the time needed and arrived at his place within an hour after nightfall. She was a little pale and tight-lipped, not wanting to indulge in much chitchat. He'd gotten her stuff stowed and had them in the air as soon as possible.

Respecting her mood, he stayed silent for the first part of the trip, casting sidelong glances at her. She'd stayed pretty much motionless, staring out in the darkness. Eventually, he started to feel a desire to help her relax some. This might go good or bad, but it was his experience being too uptight made a tense situation worse.

"So, can a vampire die if she falls out of a plane?" he asked, a random question just to determine where her mind was at.

"No," she said, without a hitch, as if they'd been having a conversation all along. "But I expect it would still be a tremendously unpleasant experience, because pain is pain. Humans are just fortunate that certain levels of pain kill them. Vampires don't have that luxury."

"How about third mark servants?"

She gave him a glance. "Reconsidering the wisdom of all this?"

"Nope. Just trying to get you to smile." Reaching over, he clasped her hand, found it cold.

"I was insane to pull you into this. I was away from this world for only a few months, but apparently long enough to make me forget how horrible and brutal it is."

"What did Laurent do to you?" He frowned.

She shook her head. "It's not that. He could be a tyrant at times, but it comes with the territory, pun intended." A ghost of a smile, no humor to it, crossed her face. "It's just...it's hard to describe unless you see it. Maybe it's different if you're born into it. When I was turned, the Vampire Council fabricated my mortal death. Made my parents think I died in a car crash on a trip, the body too burned to be identified, closed casket. All while I was locked up, dealing with my blood lust. When I was able to control that, I raged against it, wanted to go to them, see them once more, somehow soften the blow. They forbade that for twenty years, and when you are forbidden to do something, you listen. Or pay the consequences."

Her jaw set. "You learn about the pain thing," she said. "It was Laurent's job to administer that, keep me in line during those first difficult years. Some of it I now understand better, the importance of protecting the existence of vampires, how essential that is, but vampires...we sort of enjoy administering pain. I guess you've noticed that."

Quinn tried to push away any images that came to mind of Selene being punished, harmed. What he heard in her voice, saw in her face, seemed a far cry from the mix of pleasure and agony he'd experienced at her hands. He also tried to push down the rage he felt at anyone inflicting pain upon her.

"When my father died of a heart attack, they let me go see the funeral, from a distance. They buried him next to my grave, which has a body in it that isn't me."

He thought about how his mother would feel if he or one of his brothers was killed in a car accident, then thought about faking it, being alive to know he'd caused her that anguish. He didn't even want to imagine it, which explained the anguish that remained in her voice, all these years later.

She went back to staring out the window. "I've never returned.

I never even go near that town, and I avoid the state if I can. Doesn't matter. I expect Mom is gone now, or close to it, and I haven't seen my siblings in nearly forty years. What will she think when she gets to heaven and finds I'm not there? Finds out the truth?"

They were coming in for a landing. For the next few moments, they were silent again as he brought the plane down, but once it was taxiing down the runway, he reached out, touched her hand.

"I expect she'll realize it was all done to protect her, because her daughter loved her that much."

Her gaze came back to him at that, as if recalling herself and her first responsibility. "Quinn, I need you to listen to me. I know the core of you is about protecting me, but when we're with Butch...it's likely he's going to get rough, to make a point about me being in his territory without his permission, about bringing this kind of problem to his door without any heads-up. If you interfere with however he reacts toward me, he will kill you without even blinking, and it will go even worse for me. You understand?"

He'd brought the plane to a stop at the end of the runway as he'd been instructed. He didn't see any welcome party, but beyond the runway lights, it was full dark. Then he saw the flash of headlights, a signal to draw their attention. With the enhanced night vision the third mark gave him, Quinn could discern an SUV waiting, just as Dix had said. He signaled back and the runway lights were cut, apparently their plane being the only arrival tonight. "What are we talking about? Him hitting you?" No way in hell was he standing by for that.

"Possibly. Very likely, at the least." She gripped his wrist, hard, her nails digging in, and he registered the strain on her face. "This is incredibly important, Quinn. Whatever happens here, I can handle. I can endure. It won't be any worse than what I dealt with under Laurent and during my forced transition. Now that I've third marked you, I can draw strength from you to handle this. I can't do that if you're dead."

Practical, but he could tell from her expression her reason for telling him wasn't for her own benefit. "If I was too weak to stop myself from marking you," she said steadily, "linking your life with mine, please don't destroy me by getting yourself killed as a result of this. Be there for me after. Your job during is simply to be an obedient servant. Don't walk ahead of me, don't speak unless spoken to. I don't know what kind of vampire Butch is, but they can run from really formal and uptight to far more relaxed. It's better to err on the side of the former. Promise me. Please."

He was pretty sure her nails were drawing blood, but he covered her hand with his, met her gaze. "I'll do my very best. I promise. But I can tell you, standing by while some asshole beats on a woman is probably the hardest thing anyone could ask of me."

"Don't think of it that way. This is the vampire world, not the human one. Think of what we are when it's just the two of us, together." She put her hand on his jaw, her thumb touching his lips. "When we're in my world, we have to be something very different, but if we think of that façade as a way to earn those 'together' times, we can get through it, right? Just go somewhere else in your head. Out in the pastures, with a butterfly resting on your hand."

"Where do you go in your head?"

A light smile played on her lips. "I mix new drinks, think of new tricks to amaze the patrons. I love running a bar. Love the customers, love the way it all comes together when it's being done right. I was hoping to open my own place one day before I was turned. I never did that great in school, decided to head for the big city and become a bartender after I graduated high school. It was what I always wanted to do."

"Well, After Dark isn't the bigs, but we're sure glad to have you. Hope you'll consider working there for quite a while."

"Maybe. I've taken a liking to the boss. For all that he hovers sometimes and sticks his nose in where it's not needed."

The lights flashed again.

"Think they're getting impatient." Quinn leaned over to brush his lips over hers. She touched his face again and they held that way for a couple blinks. He took a breath. "Let's do this."

The driver was a tall, steady-eyed ranch hand from Blood Rock. He introduced himself as Jim, and told Selene point blank he was a second mark, making it clear why he didn't seem to think it unusual to retrieve guests in the middle of the night from Butch's private air strip. Other than that, he was as typical as any other hand. He and Quinn made idle chitchat about ranch-related topics on the drive, for which Quinn was grateful, since the normalcy of it helped him ground himself. He did wonder about whether all vampires had an array of servants with second and third marks, but Selene answered that.

*An overlord will often have a variety of staff members with second marks he trusts who are part of his household. It's rare to have more than one third mark at a time, however. Dix is probably Butch's only full servant.*

So it meant third marks were exclusive, special. She gave him a look tinged with exasperation at his fishing, and he squeezed her knee in the shadows.

She didn't join the conversation for the most part, only a short comment here or there when they discussed the bar. Jim mostly talked to Quinn anyway. It might be he had that shyness that most ranch hands had around a pretty female. Quinn bet Selene could get the guy to loosen up if he was bellied up to the bar at After Dark, but that wasn't her focus right now.

It occurred to Quinn then that her aloof behavior and Jim studiously not directing comments to her could be due to the protocol that went along with two vampires getting together. When Quinn put his hand back over hers in the shadows, she let him hold it, give her his warmth, but when they turned up the road leading to Blood Rock, she let him go.

*From here forward, you act as my servant, Quinn.*

*Yes ma'am.* He gave her that smile that usually loosened her up, but she was looking out the window. It was as if she'd suddenly drawn an impenetrable box around her, separating herself from him and the driver, a dividing line between species. He quelled an uneasy feeling about that, holding on to her words. *Think of that façade as a way to earn those 'together' times...*

The Blood Rock made the size of his place look like Annette's tiny herb garden behind the kitchen, but that was okay. He hadn't ever wanted the biggest spread, just a place of his own to run the way he wanted to run it. His dad might never have had his own place, but he had taught Quinn running something well mattered. It became yours, even if it wasn't that way on the deed. Well, now he had both of those things. But it made him think of what Selene had said about running After Hours. Maybe she felt that way too, another thing that connected them.

He liked the looks of Butch's main house. It was a sprawling creation of limestone, granite and flagstone capped with red clay Mexican roofing tiles, the grounds accented with native Texas flora and fauna. As they pulled up the drive, Dix was waiting on the front walkway.

Quinn opened the door for Selene as Jim pulled their two overnight cases from the trunk. They'd packed light, though on the plane they'd worn their more dressy clothes, Selene indicating this was considered a formal audience. As a result, she wore a pair of slacks and a camisole top accented with some silver jewelry. It made her look understated sexy, conservative and in charge. He'd worn dress jeans and a shirt with pearl buttons, as well as his silver-tipped cowboy boots, reasoning he should wear what Butch would consider dressy. Selene had approved, saying a suit on a servant would be too much in these circumstances.

Dix came down the steps to meet them in the drive. "Thanks, Jim. I've got them from here."

"Sure thing, Dix." As the car moved away, Dix gave Selene a short bow. "Ma'am. Welcome to Blood Rock." He sent Quinn a cordial nod and a look, where Quinn got the feeling he was being measured up in a lot of ways. In his business, he was used to the what-kind-of-asshole-is-this look from another man, weighing the value of his professional or personal acquaintance, but he and Dix were already past that. This was a deeper level, a does-this-guy-know-what-he's-in-for look.

Unfortunately, it made him think of what Selene had implied at the bar. He hadn't given it thought before now, other things taking precedence, but if Dix was Butch's servant, and all vampire-servants had the Dom/sub thing happening, did that mean Butch swung toward guys? Quinn thought both of them pretty much oozed the straight-guy thing, but in the Texas cattle world, to do otherwise wouldn't be too smart.

Quinn cleared his throat. He couldn't do anything about that, but he could watch Dix closely, figure out the servant thing by imitation. He hadn't offered to shake Selene's hand as one peer to another, but given her that bow. It told Quinn even if she was the lowest vampire on the totem pole, the highest servant was still beneath her. Selene underscored it by giving Dix a neutral nod back, but his Mistress wasn't overly snooty about it. She was doing what was expected. A façade, just as she said. It reassured Quinn, somewhat.

"If you'll follow me, Butch will see you first thing to discuss your issue." As they stepped into the foyer, Dix handed off their bags to a quiet Mexican woman who didn't even meet their eyes, just disappeared like a shadow. "She'll put your things in your guestroom, Miss Torres. Quinn's in the adjacent bedroom."

Quinn was going to open his mouth and say that they could go in the same room, but a warning flicker from Selene kept him from it. *It's customary for a servant to have smaller quarters adjacent to a vampire. You are invited to my bed according to my desires.*

Even her mind voice sounded more remote, formal. But was it weird his cock tingled at how it echoed her Mistress tone? Other than the dawn, was that why she left him upstairs and went to the cellar most nights? Yeah, some of this might be show, but he was reminded he was also dealing with a woman who was a Mistress, all the other bullshit aside, and it wrapped up nicely with the vampire thing. It bemused him that hearing that tone now could get him a bit revved, but he figured that might be helpful, keep his mind off other less pleasant things.

Dix escorted them down a wide hallway. Quinn noted Butch was a Jim Daly fan, possessing some of his limited-edition prints, as well as those of other artists who captured Texas' wide-open spaces and the type of people it attracted. He also had an unexpected thing for gargoyles, a fair collection of them along the hallway. Small ones, large ones, medium ones, arrayed like a leering, grinning audience that were by turns whimsical, sad or frightening, but highly detailed, as if they'd been living beings frozen there. Strangely, it worked with the art, that mix of Texas western and fantasy legends.

They stepped into a large study, dominated by a massive mahogany desk, several big easy chairs and couch, a wall of books and a foursome of flat-screens, one of which was muted but displaying a basketball game. Butch was sitting in the big chair behind the desk, his booted foot pressed against the frame beneath it, which Quinn saw had been wrapped with an industrial foam to protect it from such treatment.

As Butch rose and came toward them, Quinn noted his expression and body language was not the same as the man he'd seen at the cattlemen's meeting. The aura of command and wealth was still there, but the affable I'm-just-a-cowboy-like-the-rest-of-you vibe was nowhere to be seen. His piercing eyes were far sharper and much older, despite the handsome face. His large body moved without sound, as smooth as a sidewinder across sand. Any veneer that he was human was gone, and it impressed the hell out of Quinn that he could cover it that well on a day-to-day basis. Or nightly basis, as it were. He never would have guessed.

Then Butch stepped in front of Selene, and everything she'd entreated Quinn to remember disappeared. Because Butch hit her in the face with a closed fist the size of a softball, dropping her like a stone.

～

The pain exploded inside her skull, but it wasn't unexpected. Selene knew her next movement was stupid, way too telling, but the alternative was far worse. She threw out a hand in Quinn's direction, speaking in his head so vehemently she was sure it came through to him as a shout.

*Quinn, don't. Hold your ground.*

Butch took advantage of her vulnerable position to give her a healthy kick in the side, one she was sure broke a couple of her ribs, but even worse, tore her silk camisole. Goddamn it, shirts didn't grow on trees for her, unlike him in his big, fancy house.

She didn't attempt to shield herself. He pulled her up by her hair, held her on swaying feet as pain screamed through her side and his eyes pinned her. He was a big man, big as Quinn, but the hand that held her was oddly graceful and long-fingered. It was that way with vampires. Everything about them was beauty and strength together, and though he had a rugged vitality to him, those hands told the story of his physical power. A man who could lift a car in one hand didn't have calluses, no matter how much he rode, worked or busted his ass to make his ranch a success. It was why she was one of the few bartenders without chapped hands. Nothing marked them. Nothing on the outside.

Her gaze flicked briefly to Quinn. Thank God for Dix's insight. He'd blocked Quinn, had an arm over her servant's chest, had him backed to the wall, was speaking to her enraged cowboy, low and fast. Thank God Butch was letting Quinn's reaction pass, though he acknowledged it.

"I'm not going to punish him for you being young and stupid. Not unless he forces the issue."

When he let her go, she fell back to one knee, no choice for it, swallowing a cry at the agony. It would heal. In just a few moments the bones would start to knit and later, unless Butch killed her and it was a moot point, she could take blood from Quinn and regain the strength the healing would take. It didn't ease the pain now, but one got used to that. Laurent had done far worse to her.

Then Butch did something Laurent had never done. Sliding his hands under her elbows, he helped her to her feet and eased her into his guest chair. "All right then. That's done. Here." He put a handkerchief in her hand, closed her shaking fingers over it. "The busted lip bled on your pretty shirt, no help for that, but Yolanda may have some magic she can do with it. She's also a good seam-stress and may be able to work on that rip. Hold that up to your lip. Don't bleed on my floor. She gives me hell about that kind of thing."

His thumb passed over the bleeding lip. Selene raised her gaze to see him take a taste, his gaze kindling at the intimacy. "Might as well get that other part over with, right?"

Bending down, cupping her nape, he sealed his mouth over hers. His fangs speared her cheek as his tongue slid over her bloody lip, stroking her flesh as he took blood from both wounds he'd caused. Though she flinched at the sharp pain, she curled her hand over his, a gesture of acceptance. Hope unfurled inside her. An overlord took blood from a vampire in his territory to mark their whereabouts, as Laurent had. It didn't yet mean Butch would champion her being there, but at least it meant he wasn't going to kill her outright and deliver her body to Laurent to curry favor with the older, more powerful vampire. That had been a real possi-bility, which was why she accepted his analysis of her youthful impulsiveness without argument. She'd as much as said the same to Quinn.

Unfortunately, she also felt Quinn's fury reach new heights. Hitting her had been bad enough. This, an obviously sexual gesture that Butch claimed as his right, his hands sliding down her body, cupping her breasts and exploring while he took his requisite swallow, was enough to push Quinn to suicide-by-vampire-attack.

*It's part of the process, Quinn. Ease back. Please, if you care for me, go to that place in your head. Pretend this is just a bad dream.*

She'd learned to relax during such things, and in truth it wasn't so bad. A vampire could feel pleasure, no matter the source, their carnal instincts far greater than morality or boundaries. So worried about the violence end of things, she'd forgotten to go over that with Quinn. Butch was skilled in his touch, intending to give her pleasure as well as take it, and her breasts peaked under his stimulation, her lips parting beneath his.

But Quinn, for all his acceptance of his role in her life, was still the ultimate alpha male. He'd be riding hard on his desire to pound Butch for what he did.

*Do this for me. Just for me, Quinn.*

"Nice." Butch retracted his fangs and lifted his head, studying her with his intent gray-blue eyes. "Doesn't change the fact you've put me in between a rock and hard place, fledgling."

His gaze shifted to Quinn. "You better take it down about ten notches, son, or I'll have you penned with the stock. Never too early to start learning how to deal with vampire social niceties. I've been around three centuries and believe you me, this is tame. And while you may be wondering what the hell you've signed up for, the sad thing is it's way too fucking late to back out."

Selene's heart lurched as she saw Quinn make a Herculean effort to rein himself back, all while she felt his anger boiling on her behalf, the rage of a good man who had no business being in this world, as Butch had just implied. Though Dix kept a restraining hand on his chest, fingers curled into his shirt in case Quinn made another lunge, Selene could feel her servant reasoning it out in his head. He didn't like any of it, not one bit. Butch hitting her, the way she'd allowed that kiss, but Quinn was a smart man, a brave man. A man who didn't let temper push him past rational thought. He pressed his lips together, inclined his head. Then surprised all of them by speaking in an even, strained voice.

"I'm here for her, sir. However she needs me."

Selene had to exert a pretty fierce effort herself not to show an emotional reaction to that. Butch slanted her a glance. "There may be hope for him yet. Maybe more than for you. Unfortunately, it's a package deal, isn't it?"

"I expect when you were my age, you made some similar missteps," she managed in a steady, cool tone. "Or perhaps not. You gave consent for your turning. You were guided by your sire, not foisted onto an overlord whose main interest in you was your money-making abilities."

"You looking for pity, youngling?"

"Not a bit. Just stating what is. You could have killed me, but I came to you anyway."

"You still haven't left alive," he pointed out dryly, but he returned to his desk and took a seat, bracing his foot once again to rock back the chair. When he glanced at the flat-screen to check the score, the casual pose didn't fool her a bit. Butch was a hundred percent honed on the situation. "So you want to be part of this territory. Why?"

"It's far from Laurent," she said bluntly. "It's run by a made vampire, which means you've had to work harder for the privilege. While I don't expect sympathy or special treatment, it suggests you might give a made vampire a fair shot to carve out a place to call her own, rather than treating her like a slave."

"In our world, many young vampires spend their first hundred years as little more than a vassal for stronger vampires. It is what it is. Why should you be so special at a mere sixty?"

"Because I'm good at what I do. Even better if I'm given incentive to make money for myself as well as you, if I feel like what I'm building and accomplishing is mine."

Butch lifted a shoulder. "Not an unreasonable request, but one that rests solely on my discretion to grant or not to grant. So what if I say no, Selene? What if I send you back to Laurent because I don't want to deal with the trouble you've brought me? And I'd advise you not to prick my ego with insults about letting a Yankee scare me into doing his bidding."

Lacing his fingers, he leaned forward and pinned her with his gaze. "I'm three hundred years old, Selene, and I'm where I am as a made vampire because I've learned not to let my impulses govern me. You have to fight through that shit. If you had done so recently, you wouldn't have tied a human to you when your situation was so uncertain."

"I know that." She bit back the obvious observation that when he was sixty he was probably having the same struggles she was with impulse, but with far more oversight from his sire. As he said, there was no room for self-pity in the vampire world. No Dr. Phils here. She took a breath and shut her mind to Quinn entirely, anticipating the explosive reaction in his head to her next words.

"If you decide I have to go back to Laurent, I'll go. I'll deliver myself to him, no escort required, and the way you know I'll do it is the favor I'll ask of you. You owe me no favors," she added, "but I'm not asking on behalf of myself, but a fellow Texan and a good man. I would ask you to mark Quinn as yours to protect him from other vampires, and let him live out his life on his ranch the way he's living it. He can be relied upon to keep our secret." She met Butch's gaze. "Given your age, your mark would override mine, have a better chance of protecting him if Laurent punishes me with execution."

"No way in hell," Quinn snapped. "Forget it, Selene."

Butch's gaze didn't even flicker in his direction. Selene didn't dare look his way either. Quinn's rejection of the idea was like a blast of heat at her back. She focused on keeping her expression impassive.

"I had Dix do some digging," Butch said, sitting back and drumming his fingertips on the mahogany. "You've put that saloon back on a good path pretty fast. I expect over time you'll branch out, have more than one. Quinn's ranch has good money-making potential, though I'd likely leave that alone for a while. Let him get it on its feet even more."

"Our bonding is recent," she said. "I haven't had a chance to discuss that with Quinn. It's his ranch, his decision. He's not part of this deal."

Butch gave a short, humorless laugh. "You ask me to protect him but offer nothing in return." His expression hardened. "He belongs to you now, which means all his holdings do as well. That wasn't a request, Selene. Not in any way. You know that."

"It's fine," Quinn said. "Selene, it's fine."

No it wasn't. He hadn't signed up for any of this. Of a sudden, she was so weary of it all, so sick of this game. She had embraced who and what she was, didn't wail and moan about it, but then for so long it had been all about getting clear to where she could have some life of her own, run her own bar. She hadn't expected Quinn, but that was no excuse. Butch had brought that into an even harsher light than she herself had, and she'd put a glaring spotlight on it more than once.

When he'd begged her to mark him, the path had been so vivid and clear. But in hindsight, she'd been no better than a teenager having unprotected sex in the heat of passion, just driven by feelings, no thought of consequences.

"I ask you. Beg you." She met Butch's gaze once more, put everything she could into the expression. "I will go back to Laurent without question if you want that. Just please...tell me you'll protect him. Let him live his life, so he doesn't pay for my mistake. I don't expect any mercy for myself, but if you can grant some to him, I'll do whatever you decide."

Butch leaned back in the chair, glanced over at Quinn. Dix had a death grip on his arm, was back to murmuring to him urgently, doing everything he could to keep Quinn from interjecting himself in the conversation in a way that would get him killed for sure. Something crossed Butch's face and he rose abruptly.

"Come with me, Selene. We're going to take a walk."

# CHAPTER TWELVE

*T*he backyard was more of the same flagstone paths, interesting rock sculptures and native plants tufting and spiking out between the stones, a more aesthetically groomed reflection of the wild landscape, showing that its owner identified deeply with his roots here. Wherever his three hundred years had taken him, Butch considered Texas home. Selene knew that hunger for home and permanence as well. Would he understand that? Would it help?

He slid her hand into the crook of his elbow so they walked together in an almost companionable way. Selene leaned, she couldn't help it, because he made it possible for her to do so. She was tired, afraid and damn sick and tired of being afraid.

"When I was fifty-five, I took my first servant." Butch spoke conversationally. "Curtis Rutherford. Champion calf roper. Way too public a personality, so being my servant meant the end of his career. But he was passionate, strong, declaring his willingness to be my servant, no need to discuss all the nitty-gritty details. I quite frankly was a bit besotted, as well as riding high on the idea I was an all-powerful vampire and could do what I wanted, that there was nothing I couldn't make okay. Five years into his marking, he killed himself. Took a piece of rebar, lay down on his bed and hammered it into his chest."

Selene came to a halt. Butch released her, moving off the path to drop to his boot heels and study one of the bushes, brushing his large fingers over a frond. Feathery pieces came free, floated away. "We all hear how it feels to lose a servant," he said, watching them drift, his rugged profile turned to her, the short pieces of his dark hair fluttering over his high brow. "Like having your heart gripped in a fist, all your organs seizing up. Even though we don't need to breathe, we're gasping for air. It's like a glimpse of what death will be like, up close and personal. It's one of the ironies of our world that we own them completely, but nothing else reminds us of our mortality quite so much, or that we can and do love, care, hurt... and grieve."

His gaze lifted to her. "You won't hear a born vampire talk about that. They keep it hammered down, maybe don't feel it at all. Maybe we do because we've been human. Regardless, yes, Selene, I've been where you've been on this. A young vampire makes mistakes just like a young human does, only we seem to have fewer guardian angels watching over us and protecting others from our missteps."

She set her jaw. "I already feel like shit about this. Is it necessary to kick me while I'm down? You already did that. I probably did get blood on your nice rug."

He gave her a fang-baring smile. "A smart vampire finds the balance between spirit and docility. I expect you're a little heavy on the front end, but that's fine. I prefer a vampire to speak her mind, even if I'm going to knock her down for it. Tells me fear doesn't govern you. But shut up. Because I'm not kicking you when you're down." He took her hand, gave it a none-too-gentle squeeze. "What I'm telling you is you didn't necessarily do the wrong thing, even if you did it on impulse."

Surprise filled her. An automatic denial rose to her lips, because obviously she *had* screwed up by marking Quinn when her life was so unsettled, but he wasn't done.

"Only time will tell. Right now you're feeling trapped, and you're trying to figure out how to get him out of it. But he's telling you he's willing to see it through with you. I chose the wrong servant. You could have, but maybe you didn't. Give him the chance to ride this out with you and see where you land afterward. If you're willing to stand up for yourself, accept you made a mistake but live with it, instead of crawling back to Laurent and begging for death like some kind of whipped cur, you might be the kind of vampire I want in my territory. Understand?"

He pursed his lips. "Women tend to decide the best way to handle a problem is accept the blame for everything and make it right for everyone else. In our world, the best way to handle a problem is accept responsibility, say *fuck you* to those who'd take you to task for it and move forward. So?"

He cocked a brow at her. Despite her whirling mind, aching ribs and ruined shirt, she couldn't help a grudging smile at his expectant look. "Fuck you?"

"Are you asking or telling me? Afraid I'll hit you again?"

Her eyes narrowed. "Fuck you."

He nodded. "Better. Good girl. Now we'd best return so you can simmer that cowboy down before Dix has to hogtie him. Which Dix might actually enjoy, 'cause he's got a bit of the Dom in him when it comes to dealing with other servants." His teeth flashed. "Tonight may not be the night to let your boy see that side of things. But he could handle seeing some of what it's about, a testing of the waters, and that would bring me pleasure. Which, given it's my house, is what it's all about."

She blinked at his charming smile that reminded her of a tiger licking his chops, then he tucked her hand into the crook of his elbow again and strolled back toward the house. "So we'll have dinner, bunk you all down. Unless I change my mind, you'll head back to Nightfall tomorrow night. I'll get things going between my Region Master and Laurent's." He slanted her a glance. "Once that's initiated, Laurent can't take you out of my territory until a decision is made, but I have to alert him to the process once it starts, which means he'll know where you are. I'll give you a heads-up right before I call him. But whatever the Region Masters decide, we have to abide by it. Understand?"

She nodded, tension coiling in her lower belly. Facing Laurent again was not something she'd relish. Ever.

"I'll do my best to keep you here though," Butch said, offering her that much. "I can't predict what the Region Masters will decide, but my guess is it will be something along the lines of giving your first ten years of profit to New York to compensate Laurent for his loss. Can you live with meeting your operating costs and handing the rest to him for a decade? It's got to be a fair shake. If you're not making comparable money with what you did for him, he'll call foul and it will get negotiated on much worse terms for you."

It was a sour pill to swallow, but she understood what "much worse" could mean. "Profits on the saloon only?"

"Does he know about Quinn?"

She shook her head, and Butch pursed his lips. "Wishful thinking, probably, but I'll do my best to keep it there. His focus is likely only to be on the vampire side of the equation. By the time he figures out Quinn's your servant, it will be a done deal. Plus the ranch isn't yet making a wide profit margin. The bar's more lucrative."

She nodded, pushing past her desire to howl at all of it. She'd bled for Laurent, literally and financially, and he'd more than earned his money off her. "How about after that? How many years will I owe you?"

"Once you're clear of what you owe Laurent, we'll talk. I'll expect a fairly hefty cut for my trouble for a couple years, then we'll whittle it down so I'm getting the usual tithe I get from other vampires in my territory. That's ten percent after taxes, which is goddamn fair, given the government's cut. I don't really need the money. It's the principle of it, the tradition, the bond it underscores. If it goes the way I think, in fifteen years you'll feel like you're mostly working for yourself. Fair?"

Laurent had taken all her profits, left her barely enough for living expenses and accepted personal credit for the success of her operations. What Butch was proposing worked fine enough for her —in comparison. With one caveat.

She stopped, looked up to meet his gaze. He and Quinn were both tall men. "If they rule to send me back to Laurent?"

He studied her, then nodded. "I'll protect your man."

"Thank you." She meant it. "I know it doesn't bring you much benefit."

"There are debts we all have to pay. I'll consider it my unpaid debt to Curtis." He looked out toward the open land beyond his yard. "I owe him that, no matter what this goddamn world of ours says. It's nice to have someone to whom I can say that, who understands it."

She nodded, feeling a relief in that as well. Then those piercing eyes fixed on her again. "But don't mistake who or what I am, youngling. I may have been human, but I am a vampire, and accepting everything that means and requires is why I'm where I am now. You don't live up to the same, I'll come down on you like a goddamn ton of bricks. Understand?"

"Understood."

"Good. We'll do some dinner now. Give your servant a different education about vampires and what they require of their servants."

She'd been nervous about Butch's decision on Laurent, but now that he'd stated his intentions on that, it left her room to worry about dinner. *Oh shit.*

Quinn had to keep himself from pacing while Selene was gone with Butch. All he could see was her down on the ground and that bastard kicking her. Coupled with the inexplicable contrast of him helping her into a chair, that intolerable kiss and his almost genial behavior afterward. But Quinn wasn't fooled. Those gray eyes and firm mouth had remained unyielding throughout, suggesting Butch could turn on a dime and go right back to beating the shit out of her if he got the wrong response.

Dix stood at the French doors where they'd disappeared out into the backyard, as if he was some kind of centurion at the gate. Though with his denim-clad butt leaned up against the wall, arms crossed, he displayed a cowboy's typically patient slouch. He was a wiry man with sunbaked skin and a lean build, but Quinn had discovered his third marked strength had been more than enough to keep him from lunging to Selene's defense. Quinn was a third mark too, but maybe servants were like vampires. Maybe age brought strength.

"How old are you?"

Dix lifted a brow. "You're lucky I'm not a woman, else I'd be offended. One-sixty two, last I remembered to pay attention. The candles get a little stupid after a while. You start marking decades instead of years."

One hundred and sixty-two years old. Damn if Quinn didn't see it in Dix's sea-green eyes, enhanced by flecks of gold in the irises. His grandfather hadn't had eyes that old. "So Butch's father and grandfather..."

"Him, with different haircut, hair color, different look to him. The childhood years are sometimes tricky, but you make up stories and people tend to accept them. Butch was the estranged son who came home when his father was sick, yada yada. So far it's worked. We've been on this spread about sixty years." He paused. "He had to punish her, you know. There's always a balance of power to be maintained."

"No. He didn't have to hit a woman in the face and kick her while she was curled at his feet. He's obviously a lot stronger than her."

"Yeah, he is. That was part of the point he was making. Reminding her. It's their way. You're dealing with vampires, not humans. Could have been a lot worse. Could have staked her out in the backyard and whipped the flesh from her back, then fucked her up the ass. Waited several hours for it all to heal up and do it all again. It's a favorite way of disciplining made vampires, under the justification that they need the harshness to 'get the lesson straight'."

Quinn stared at him. Dix had spoken as matter-of-factly as if explaining how to saddle a horse. What the hell kind of world was he in? But Sam had warned him, hadn't he? "Sounds like the voice of experience."

"I've seen it done." Dix's jaw tightened, relieving Quinn—a little—with the glimmer of emotion. "It's not Butch's way. But if he has to do it to maintain balance, he will. Vampires only respect strength. If you're weak, you grow stronger. If you're not so clever, you wise up. Else you'll be someone else's whipping boy—or girl—forever. Literally."

As Dix considered him from head to toe once again, Quinn shifted. "I wish you'd stop doing that," he said bluntly. "It makes me fucking uncomfortable."

Dix's lips twitched. "Then you're going to have a real problem with dinner."

He shifted out of the way of the door as it opened, Butch guiding Selene back into the room before Quinn could ask what he meant. He had a feeling he didn't want to know.

"Dix will show you to your rooms," Butch told her. "We'll have dinner at one in the main dining room. More space there." He gave Quinn a considering look, then met his gaze. "Dix will tell you how to dress for dinner."

Dix made a gesture to the archway, and Selene nodded, preceding him.

*Quinn, follow us up.*

As he complied, he was relieved to be out of the presence of the other vampire and all that unsettling innuendo. He'd been focused on the whole Laurent situation, but now the sex issue was right up close and personal in his face and maybe near other parts of his anatomy. Selene had fucked his ass. How different could it be to have a man do it, if he just shut down his brain? Did he really sign up for this?

When Dix pointed her to a door, she went through it, not saying a word. As her door shut, Dix gestured to the one next to it. "Those are your quarters. There's a connecting door in between if your Mistress has need of you. Lock's on her side, not yours."

Further highlighting a servant's status. The house was full of subtle cues about such things and quite frankly Quinn was already tired of it. But then he thought about Selene and realized her position in the vampire world was no different. He pulled his head out of his whiny ass to listen to Dix.

"In the dresser, you'll find what you'll wear to dinner tonight. We don't sit at the table with them. You'll stand behind your Mistress' chair. We eat after they have their dinner and are done with us."

"Christ. Is that the way it always is?"

"For formal dinners." Dix shrugged. "On a normal night, Butch and I might chow down on burgers in front of a game on the widescreen, but vampires have particular rituals when it comes to meets like this."

Quinn set his jaw, nodded. It wouldn't help to ask what would be happening at dinner, would it? He'd just assume the worst and anything better would be a nice surprise.

When he closed his door behind him, he found the room was comfortably furnished but not overly large. Another statement, because they certainly had the space to make it larger.

*Quinn, once you're dressed for dinner, I want you to come see me. But before you do, use the ointment I told you to pack. Lube yourself up well.*

Her tone was as neutral as a robot's as she delivered the ominous instruction.

He quelled the feeling of being cast adrift and all alone, suddenly in a place where the language was foreign and the person he'd come with as much a part of it, separate from him, as the Grand Canyon was wide. But she was his Mistress, right?

Since they'd deigned to give him his own bathroom, he decided to take a quick shower and do a smooth shave. Then he faced what was in the dresser.

The outfit could have been worse. He'd imagined studded leather straps, metal rings to go around his cock and balls. Instead it was just a tight pair of shorts in some sort of sleek material that fit him like a seal's skin from just below his hipbones to high on the thighs. Obviously intended to highlight his ass and every hill and valley of his package. Christ. There was no way he could stand in front of other men in this.

*Are you dressed?*

*Define dressed.* But he moved to take care of the lube. Thanks to her desires, he was now pretty efficient at getting his ass lubricated. As he pushed the shorts to his thighs, braced himself against the bathroom counter to comply, she helped. He felt the sensual hum of her attention, and his cock jumped, responding to it as she made it clear she liked watching him through his eyes, in his mirror, seeing his arm flexing as he fucked himself with his fingers, worked the lube in good to make himself ready for God knew what.

When he replaced the shorts, washed his hands, she spoke in his head again, a little breathless, which just made more of his blood drain to his groin.

*Come here, Quinn.*

He went through that pass-through door, relieved to find it unlocked. He wasn't sure if he could handle the unspoken message if he'd had to knock.

*Everything is about getting back to the bar and the ranch, to what we are normally.*

She spoke the reminder in his head, but when her gaze slid over him, he saw his Mistress wet her lips, eyes widening just a bit. Despite his own discomfiture, his body had no problem responding to her approval. He was starting to find it hard to walk as she crooked a finger at him. "Come here, Quinn," she repeated.

The order actually helped steady him amid this tornado of *what the hell.* She was sitting on the bed in a sexy blue velvet dress that clung to her curves and stopped high on the thigh. She wore black stockings, and he could see the edge of her garters. She also wore some killer heels. She looked edible. For Butch?

No. Because it was expected she'd dress for dinner. For her pleasure and for those looking at her, which, yes, included Butch, but... She lifted her gaze to him.

*Also to make my servant think of the only thing that matters. My pleasure, and how I will make him serve me.*

When he approached at her gesture, she molded her palm over his thigh, slid her hand up over that sleek covering, cupped his cock and testicles, kneaded and played, obviously enjoying the way they felt under her touch. No preamble, just going right for what she wanted, like a man. Her other hand snaked around, gripped his buttock, dug in.

"Nice," she murmured. "I like this look on you. Maybe I'll have you wear these beneath your jeans in the future."

"I think I'd sweat like a son of a bitch doing ranch work. Not exactly breathable cotton." He touched her face, sliding his hand down over her lip. "It's all healed. How're the ribs?"

"All better. I might need some blood later."

"It's yours."

Holding his gaze, she rose to slide her arms around him. As she lifted onto her toes to kiss him, it became a thorough, tongue-tangling gesture that had him tightening his own arms around her, biting back a groan as she rubbed herself against his cock.

*I know that, cowboy. I find a lot of pleasure in the thought you're all mine.*

So did he, even if he was thinking he'd lost his mind. "So tonight?" He knew he'd regret asking.

She sobered, easing back. "I don't know, Quinn. Butch may want pleasure, pain or something in between. What he did to me earlier...he's allowed to punish a vampire in his territory, even push the issue of sex with me if he wishes. I can refuse him on that, though the avenues for recourse if he overrules me and forces it are pretty ineffective. But most of the time vampires exercise their hungers through their servants at formal occasions."

"So Dix is gay?"

"Gay and straight aren't really terms we have in the vampire world. Pleasure is pleasure. Butch has likely enjoyed men and women, and Dix the same."

Quinn tried to wrap his mind around it in some rational way, not panic like a calf let out of a chute. "So...ah...condoms?"

"Not necessary. Vampires nor servants can pass STDs. The only viral disease that affects us is something called the Delilah Virus, and I expect if Butch had that he would let me know before allowing his servant carnal knowledge of mine. We can trust his integrity on that."

She gave him a brief synopsis of the discussion in the garden then. It did loosen things inside him, to hear the specifics about Butch being in their corner, even though the guy still pissed him off.

"This is one fucked-up world," he said bluntly.

She gave him a tight smile. "Is the human one so different?"

"I feel like we've evolved past the whole survival of the fittest, might makes right thing. Or at least we've become enlightened enough to recognize it's not the best way."

"Here you have. How about in Haiti? Russia? Name your dictatorship? What you consider the rule of the land doesn't exist everywhere. Hell, it doesn't exist in nature at all. There is balance between weak and strong, where the strong survive and prosper and the weak adapt or disappear."

He had no answer to that, but fortunately she was distracting him, running her nails lightly up his thighs. She appeared to be fascinated by the way the sleek material outlined his groin and, under her regard, it had to expand its hold. He bit back another groan as she caressed him even more boldly, stroking his length.

"You're going to embarrass me."

"No." Her gaze lifted to him. "I want you to walk down there aroused, Quinn. I want you to show Butch you serve your Mistress, that nothing distracts you from her pleasure. That's all I want you to think about. If Dix is ordered to shove his dick into your ass, make you come, every drop is for me. Every pleasure you feel, however reluctantly wrested from you, from your understanding of what you are or are not, is for me. You understand? Tell me."

"Yes ma'am." He swallowed. Fuck. Damn. Could he do this?

The next moment, it was a moot point. He was following the pendulum curve of her delectable ass down the hall, tracking the length of her legs. The sheen of the stockings and a glimpse of those garters led him like the carrot in front of a stubborn mule's nose. He felt her amusement at the comparison, and it made him feel better. No matter what happened, they were connected. Together.

*Always, Quinn.* Her shoulders straightened, chin lifting as if she'd increased some type of resolve inside herself. When she reached the first floor and turned toward the dining room archway, she sent him one final thought. *No matter what happens, promise me not to doubt that one thing.*

Dix was wearing the same kind of shorts. For a wiry kind of guy, he looked like he had a pretty sizeable package himself. Not that Quinn had any desire to look, but when a man thought something might be used as a weapon against him, he tended to size it up. Dix was standing against the wall behind his Master's chair, just as he'd said. Quinn held the chair for Selene and then, emulating the other servant, he stepped back against the wall behind her. She gave him a flickering glance, apparently not realizing Dix had given him the instruction. She greeted Butch as if the two of them were cordial acquaintances, just sitting down for a friendly dinner. With an edge to it.

The quiet Mexican woman—Yolanda, he assumed—served, once again coming and going like a shadow. At Selene's glance, Butch explained. "She's a second mark. She's been with me quite awhile, a gift from my sire on his last visit, about..." He considered. "Ten years ago. Diego tends to travel and disappear for a few years at a time. She's an incredibly good cook. Dix and the hands get the most benefit from it, but even the small portions I can eat as a vampire are worth it."

He lifted a bottle. "I comfort myself by figuring out the best vintage to go with those bite-size samplers. I've learned to be a wine connoisseur, because alcohol is the one thing we can have to excess without unpleasant effects to our digestive system. You probably have a pretty advanced palate, making up all those drinks in New York."

"Texans have pretty advanced taste buds, all those Tex-Mex flavors. Don't assume I'm a snob."

He chuckled at that. "Here. See what you think, Yankee." He poured her a glass and Dix came forward to bring it to her before he returned to his spot.

"Midwesterner. I'm from Michigan originally." She sipped, nodded. "That's very good."

From there they proceeded into unexpectedly typical dinner topics. Butch spoke of some vampire-related things, but he also asked Selene about the bar and New York, even directing a few questions to Quinn about the ranch. Those discussions sometimes included Dix's input, verifying or differing in approaches. It was an odd setup for dinner conversation, but it seemed to work. Yolanda brought out some small plates with bite-size portions of what Quinn expected would be his and Dix's dinner later.

He hadn't eaten since breakfast, because they hadn't really known what the plan was, and now he knew he should have taken the time, because the rumbling of his damn stomach was going to embarrass Selene. Then again, since he didn't know what the after-dinner entertainment would be, maybe it was best to face that on an empty stomach.

"Quinn." Selene gestured to him. "Come kneel by my chair."

In front of them. Christ. A little awkward and self-conscious, he came to her chair and dropped to one knee, placing a hand on the back of her chair by her shoulder, his bent knee brushing hers. That position felt a little better, a little less servile. Given Butch's speculative look, he maybe should have done it the other way, but she touched his jaw, bringing his attention to her.

*Only me. There's only me in this room. How about you kneel to me the way you would in your bedroom? Or mine?*

As she held his gaze, he found he could do it. He put the other knee down, sat his ass on his heels, though he kept a hand on the chair back. She gave him a forkful of what he had to admit was one of the best enchiladas he'd ever tasted. Yolanda brought more out, as if summoned by Butch, and Selene fed him most of it as she spoke with the master of the house about casual things. Quinn tried not to think of himself as a dog being handed scraps from the table, and it was easier than expected, because in this position, he could see his Mistress' stockinged thigh, the edge of the garter.

*I'd like to feel how nice a shave you did for me. Rub your cheek on the bare part of my leg.*

He bent, did that, and scented her fragrance. Powder and perfume, but unmistakably arousal as well. He'd aroused her by eating from her hand. Suddenly he didn't feel like a pet at all, but a man whose submission turned her on tenfold. Her fingers slid through his hair, tugging, her nails scraping his nape.

*Return to the wall now.*

He pressed a kiss to her leg, earned a more reproving tug to his hair. Dix and Butch were both watching him, and Quinn was uncomfortably aware Butch's regard was laced with sexual fascination. While it was hard to determine what Dix was thinking, it wasn't disinterest, not by a long shot.

"You do much wrestling, Quinn?" Butch asked, tearing off a piece of bread and taking a taste.

"Yeah." At Selene's subtle prompting, he cleared his throat. "Yes sir. I wrestled in high school. On the ranch, there are all sorts of things that have to be wrestled down to the ground."

"True enough. Later on, during after-dinner drinks, we'll tell you how we had to wrestle a bull to the ground bare-handed. Good thing those horns weren't wood or steel," he said wryly, "because he nearly skewered both of us, the bastard."

Dix chuckled at that and Quinn managed a tentative smile in return.

"You and Dix move over there." Butch nodded to the outdoor screened patio available beyond the open double doors of the dining room. The space was clear, no outdoor furniture. "Let's see which one of you can wrestle the other to the ground and hogtie him. Whoever wins, their Master or Mistress gets to decide the prize."

Okay. Not the usual activity one did at dinner, but it wasn't something unknown to him, especially when Dix gave him a grin full of you-are-so-going-to-lose.

The guy was way stronger, more experienced, but Quinn wasn't much for losing a fight either. He'd been the captain of his wrestling team. Dix had moved to a side cabinet, something that might normally hold fancy dishes, and pulled out a coil of rope. As he and Quinn moved onto the patio, he dropped it on the floor in between them. Then he took up a wrestling stance, facing Quinn.

The way Butch was watching them made it clear this wasn't like a football game. Two tough cowboys pitting strength against one another at his command got him off. Quinn distracted himself from that disturbing thought by looking toward his Mistress. When she moistened her lips, her gaze sliding over him as if she could already see his muscles straining and tight, his cock hardened, making it clear he wasn't entirely detached from all the sexual innuendo saturating the air.

Now the reason for the shorts was clear. It was like a gladiator contest, and the audience wanted to see as much of the contestants as possible. Quinn guessed he should be glad they weren't naked, with all sorts of vulnerable parts hanging out. Then he didn't have a lot of time to consider anything, because Dix lunged.

Butch had maybe given him a tip, calling to mind all the reflexes and strength it took to handle stock and rodeo animals. The vampire version of a friendly wrestling match was up there with wresting a bull in truth. Dix gave him about half a second to pick up on the tone and intent, and then he started pushing Quinn's skills hard.

From his tussle with Dix earlier, Quinn knew the other man was holding back some to make the contest more about skill than brute force. Quinn had plenty of the former and embraced the advantage. As they circled, grappled, rolled and broke apart multiple times, Quinn found himself actually getting into the spirit of the competition, trading insults and grunts of effort. They both started building up a sweat, so as they braced weight against each other, tried head locks, different holds and all sorts of efforts to bring one another down, they were handling slick muscle even harder to pin. They traded pins a couple of times, but both managed to wriggle loose. Dix was a damn sinewy bastard for sure, but Quinn was good at getting himself out of tight spots despite his larger size.

Still, time told the real story, and he tired before the other guy, goddamn it. But somewhere along the way, he rebelled against the idea of being trapped against his will, restrained, and the fighting became dirtier, more desperate. That was when Dix's elbow slammed into his mouth, and Quinn punched him in the face, and it became a brawl, with them bouncing off the walls, floor and the low brick border around the patio. A screen tore out of the frame, and then Quinn found himself on his back in the grass, Dix on top, and that rope in his hands.

He bucked, snarled, raged, but in the end he was planted on his belly, rock-hard cock jammed beneath him, his arms pulled back behind him, knees bent so Dix could tie his wrists to his ankles. Quinn cursed him, struggled, but then Dix gave him a slap on the ass and backed off. Quinn's only satisfaction was seeing that Dix was breathing heavy as he was.

"You're a strong son of a bitch," Dix offered. "Good fighter."

"You made your point," Quinn gritted. "Untie me."

"Not my call." Dix's gaze settled on him, his expression spawning a wealth of apprehension in Quinn's belly.

No. No way in hell. His gaze snapped to Selene, and he found her and Butch in chairs they'd pulled over to the opening to the patio, a closer front-row seat to the action.

Selene had that wooden, neutral expression. While he was sure —almost—that she wasn't thrilled to see him in this position with Butch present, it wasn't a position she wouldn't enjoy seeing him in herself, if it was the two of them alone. Hell he might even enjoy it then. But not this. This wasn't the way he was.

He set his teeth, bit his lip perversely to keep him from speaking in his head, pleading with her. If she had anything to say, she'd say it. But her eyes never left him and he held that gaze, his jaw set. Fine. He wouldn't say a damn thing.

He'd think of that butterfly in his hand, trusting him. The blue and yellow delicate colors, so easily crushed, but so strong despite its fragility. Able to endure, hold on through everything...

She rose then. He was braced to feel ashamed as she came closer, that he'd lost, that he was bound like this by someone else in front of her, but then he registered her reaction. Her gaze was skimming over him with pure hunger, lingering on his muscles straining against his bonds. His cock, mashed as it was beneath him, got even thicker, responding to her. When she trailed her fingers over his rigid biceps, down to caress his ass, stroke his calves in their restrained position, he quivered. Catching the hem of the slick shorts, she pulled them away from his ass, exposing the curves as she traced them with sharp nails. Her other hand coiled in his hair, and she tightened her grip on his ass so she could slide a finger into the opening she'd told him to lube up.

He bucked, gasping as she worked him. *Fuck. Mistress...*

*Anything I want, Quinn. Anything that gives me pleasure. Say it.*

*Anything that gives you pleasure.*

*Say it aloud.*

"Anything that gives you pleasure. God...no..." She was going to make him come, his body way more revved up by her watching their wrestling match than he'd expected.

*No. Your orgasm is Butch's call. But only for the moment.*

She rose then, standing over him, and he was staring at her feet in those killer stilettos.

"In a few more years, my servant will kick Dix's ass, my lord."

Butch chuckled. "We'll see in a few years, won't we?"

He moved next to her, and Quinn knew he was staring down at him, could almost feel the heat of the man's gaze on his bare butt. "Go sit down, Selene."

A direct order. Quinn glanced up to see her jaw flex, but she gave a short nod, returned to her chair. Butch's attention was moving over Quinn like he was considering his second meal of the night.

"It's hard, sharing them the first time. On a normal night, I'd go for the straight hard fuck between him and Dix, have Dix take him right here, a prize for getting him hogtied. Nothing as scintillating as watching two men go at it the way they can, all rough and tumble. I'm not so much for the vampire games, all the setup some of the born ones do, like a fucking royal court performance."

His lip curled, showing his disdain for that, but then he dropped to his heels and cupped Quinn's buttock, finger sliding to the seam, through the oil. "But he's a fine piece. I'm thinking I might take the pleasure for myself, then give Dix the leftovers."

*No. Hell no, not happening.* But he didn't have any choice, did he? Still, when Butch shifted, pressing a knee into his shoulder, Quinn didn't think. He just bucked and used every ounce of strength to shove away from the vampire, managing to wrench his shoulder and pull one ankle binding tight enough he could immediately feel the dangerous constriction around the veins. He snarled at Butch like a wild animal and found his throat seized by the vampire, Dix sitting on him somewhere behind, holding him down.

Panic and rage warred together. He'd kill himself and them before he'd let them take choices away from him. Goddamn...the haze of red took everything over and he was bellowing like a bull in truth, wrestling as much as he could, no matter the constriction over wrists, ankles, throat. He might be a third mark, but he was going to render himself unconscious.

No, Selene. Can't do this...Selene...

It was too late to have the thought, lost as it was amid a fierce struggle to resist their efforts to do things to him he couldn't permit, wouldn't permit. No way in hell.

Then suddenly they were off him, standing back, and he was wheezing, everything hurting and throbbing where the rope was cutting off circulation and his breathing.

A knife sliced through the ropes, Dix pulling them free. As soon as Quinn could orient himself, he shoved him away, did it himself. Pulling the shorts back in place, he stumbled to his feet and braced himself for battle, fists clenched, eyes wild.

It took him a few blinks to realize no one was close enough to fight. With his head still whirling, he registered Butch leaning against the patio wall, testing his thumb against the wicked-looking knife he'd used to cut the bonds. Selene sat straight and still in the chair, her gaze not on Quinn at all, but on the distant horizon as if she wished she was somewhere else entirely. It was that which brought Quinn back to himself, made his heart drop.

Fuck, he'd failed. Hadn't he? Proven he couldn't do it. Yet as he tried to imagine a hundred ways to make it better, he couldn't bring himself to think of doing that. She was right. Butch was right. He'd made the wrong choice. Yet he wanted to go to his knees, beg her forgiveness. He couldn't be without her, yet he couldn't...do that.

"It's a learning process. Fortunately, maybe, you're in a position to give him that. In forty, fifty years he'll find the peace with it that Dix did, but he definitely doesn't have it now."

Butch had angled himself to speak directly to Selene, as if Quinn wasn't even there. He didn't seem the least bit perturbed, a small boon all in all. Quinn struggled to get his mind around that, the indicator that maybe he hadn't screwed up as bad as he'd thought. At least overall. He wished Selene would look at him or say something.

"You're right," Butch told her. "If the Region Masters rule against you, it's best for his sake that he stays here. I'll do as you ask. As long as he agrees to the discretion that will keep him alive."

His gaze returned to Quinn, though Butch continued to address his Mistress. "If the ruling is in your favor, it's a good thing this is where you want to stay for some time. Your servant will need the time to wrap his head around his role. Before someone strikes it from his shoulders."

"Perhaps it's just the approach that needs the work, not the servant."

Quinn lifted his head to see Selene's eyes on him. Butch lifted a brow, though he looked amused, not offended. "Do tell."

"You break a horse gradually, introducing the saddle and bit as part of a more rewarding activity. Correct?"

"More or less."

She nodded. "If you will permit me, I think I can offer you a display you'll enjoy, while proving my servant has the wherewithal to manage this. As you said, it's a learning process, and why shouldn't we enjoy the pleasures of watching him learn?"

"Indeed." Butch made a courteous gesture, took a seat again. "What did you have in mind?"

"I will order my servant to make me come with his mouth while your servant brings him to climax with his."

Butch's eyes got a speculative light. "Works for me. I choose the position and restraints."

When she inclined her head, Butch turned to his servant. "Dix, if you'll adjust his position accordingly?"

As Dix approached, Quinn braced himself. Selene held up a hand, bringing Dix to a halt. She rose, moving back toward Quinn.

*I'm sorry, Mistress.*

*Nothing to be sorry for, cowboy. Not a thing.* When she reached him, she put her hand on his face, looked up into his eyes. That petite, lovely thing who inspired such protective feelings from him had tapped into a part of himself that had brought him the most personal and sexual fulfillment in a long time. When he looked into her eyes, despite their surroundings, he felt all those things, as well as more shame. She was right here, standing before him, and he'd failed her.

*Did I tell you that you failed me, Quinn?* She arched a brow, and any vulnerability he'd sensed earlier was gone, replaced by pure, cool Mistress. "Answer me."

"No."

*Then you didn't.* "I'm hot and wet, watching you two big strong men wrestle, and now I'm going to command you down on your back so I can straddle your face and order you to service my pussy. Butch is commanding Dix down onto his knees to take your cock in his mouth, to do his best to make you come before I do. But I know my servant values my pleasure more than his own. Doesn't he?"

He held her gaze. Nodded. *I'm not sure I can let him...do that.*

*That's why he's going to tie your arms and legs, so your only focus, your only choice, is to give me pleasure, Quinn. Now kneel.*

Her hands slid up his chest, up to his shoulders, and began to exert pressure. He tried to block Dix out of his line of sight and, as he sank before her, it was possible. When he was kneeling, staring up at her, at the rise of her breasts, the pursing of her lips, the vibrant blue of her eyes, he could get lost in all those things, in all that she was to him. He barely registered her easing him down to the ground, directing him to his back.

Curling her small hands around his wrists, she eased his arms up and over his head, caressing his throat, his mouth, chest and nipples as his wrists were bound. Dix tied them to one of the three poles embedded into the patio concrete, poles whose purpose Quinn had wondered about and cursed the couple times he'd slammed into them during their match. Selene straddled his abdomen so he couldn't see Dix anymore, though he felt his hands spreading his legs, the ropes tightening around his ankles. Then she started moving forward, gathering up the edges of her short skirt so the garters were fully revealed, and he scented her aroused pussy under the lacy scrap of panties. God, she was beautiful. He was aware of Dix's hands on his shorts, taking them down, and he tensed, but then his Mistress was straddling his shoulders.

"You have one choice, Quinn." She stared down at him, one simple knee bend away from straddling his face, bringing that delectable pussy to his mouth. "What is that choice?"

"To give my Mistress pleasure." His voice was hoarse.

She didn't remove her panties, simply sank down on his face, bringing her pussy up close and personal, but holding it just a lick away. She kept it there as he felt Dix's hands close on his thighs. He bucked a bit, but then Dix's mouth closed over his cock, which didn't give a damn that it was a male mouth on it, though feeling the scratch of his evening shadow against his pelvis was disconcerting. Quinn was just glad he didn't have to see the guy doing it. Selene stayed that tantalizing distance away, her blue eyes focused on his face like a raptor's.

*Please, Mistress.* He swallowed back a groan as Dix wrested a strong spasm out of his cock. Fuck, he was going to come in the guy's mouth before she brought her pussy any closer. Maybe that was what she intended. He licked his lips, stared at it, inhaled. Focused. Not until he gave her pleasure.

Finally, blissfully, she brought it down and covered his face with the light fabric of her dress. He went on the attack, already too revved up to take it slow, but he found her soaked through. His Mistress was highly aroused by all this, and that made something click in his brain. He didn't give a damn if he was being sucked off by man, woman or a Hoover vacuum hose. This was the payoff. Her arousal, her desire.

Her pleasure. That's what she'd said, right? He licked, sucked, bit her through the silky fabric. She ground against his face, cut off his breathing, rubbed herself over his jaw, nose, cheeks, mouth, marking him with her scent while she hummed in her throat and he felt her thighs tighten against his head, clamping and holding him there in an excruciating heaven.

Dix, goddamn him, had brought his hands into it. He'd cupped

Quinn's ass to lever him up deeper and his thumb was pushing into Quinn's anus, playing there. Fuck fuck fuck...

His Mistress was coming first, damn it all. There was no other option he'd entertain. She was arched back, the straps of her dress falling off her shoulders, the curves of her breast quivering, Butch probably watching it all.

That would have distracted and angered him, but his Mistress took care of that as well. Suddenly Quinn could see through her eyes and he found Butch's attention wasn't on Selene at all. Sucking off Quinn had put Dix on all fours. Butch had pulled his servant's shorts out of his way and was slamming into his ass like a jackhammer, was working him hard. Seeing the set of Butch's mouth, the vibrant lust in his gray eyes, feeling the spasmodic clamp of Dix's fingers into Quinn's thighs, trying to hold on to his own orgasm for his Master, shouldn't have turned him on, but the overload of stimulation was too much for Quinn.

*Mistress...*

She started to come then. Though her consent was almost incoherent, it was enough for him. He exploded in Dix's hard-pulling mouth, driven by the force of her climax, gushing against his mouth and lips. He plucked at her clit and swirled his tongue over her labia, making sure he gave her the full measure of it even as his brain fragmented.

He heard Butch come, Dix falling right after. His come splattered against Quinn's thighs, his shins. He didn't care. It was all about Selene, as if this whole thing had been engineered by her, because her mind was open, her unfiltered pleasure swamping him, making it okay. Making it all work. This was a front-row view of what it was supposed to be, what serving a vampire meant. The knowledge he'd seen in Dix's eyes was starting to have a nascent reflection in his own.

She'd been right. It was all in the approach. Earlier, it had been just words, *I'm here to serve her however she needs me.* In this moment, he actually understood what it meant, and he knew some part of him had always wanted to serve a woman this way, this deeply. Those cravings he'd kept shamefully hidden, trying to bury them in an alpha dominant mode, had come to full, vibrant life. There wasn't a single shameful, cringing element to them. He was ready to tear the world apart for her, ready to kneel to her, ready to endure anything for her.

Because it was the two of them together. Always.

She'd said so. She needed him as much as he needed her. No matter what—vanilla, chocolate, kinky, straight or every flavor in between—that was the way it was supposed to work.

# CHAPTER THIRTEEN

*a*t the conclusion of the evening Quinn expected to be exhausted, worn out emotionally as well as physically. But by the time they returned to the bedrooms his strength was already replenishing and it astonished him.

*The benefit of third marking.*

*Thank God for that.*

Her light laughter sounded in his head like melodic chimes. She insisted he shower again before getting into bed.

"I want to wash away everyone else's touch." She stroked his arm. "You did very well tonight, for a first-time situation. You pleased me greatly. But now I want every bit of you to be mine."

Words that could make him suffer and survive anything. That, and her joining him in the shower.

As he watched her create lather with the soap, she told him to put his hands on the sides of the shower and leave them there. Then she coasted her palms over every inch of his body. No area was left untouched. She was meticulous with his arms and his legs, his cock and his testicles, even soaping and rinsing the crack of his ass. She knelt on the tile to cleanse his legs, then stood on the built-in seat to do his upper body. Her touch was as much soothing as it was arousing, and he closed his eyes, enjoying her touch.

When they were both thoroughly rinsed, she shut off the water and dried him with a big fluffy bath towel that she fetched from a towel warmer. Finally she dried herself, took him by the hand and led him into her room. She hadn't allowed him to touch her at all. Not yet.

"I thought vampires slept alone," he said.

"Sometimes we make special exceptions."

A strange but intense emotion came over him. A sense of belonging. His hard-ass father might have loved him. He'd always hoped he did. His mother conveyed the sense of family to him and his brothers. He'd found friendship in the rodeo, even though the faces of those friends changed frequently. There was a certain camaraderie with the hands at the ranch. But never this total sense of belonging. Of being a part of someone else.

Selene's lips curved in a smile. "Because you do belong, Quinn. To me. Forever. What do you do in return?"

He cleared his throat. "I serve you. I give you pleasure. Always."

"Very good. Right now it will give me pleasure for you to lie with me, your arms around me as we sleep." She gestured toward the bed.

What did it say that, even after watching the movements of her slippery, soapy body in the shower, the simple intimacy of holding her in her sleep was as potent a treasure to him as being able to thrust into her, bring her to climax?

Tearing his eyes away from her naked body, he pulled back the covers and arranged the pillows, then stood waiting for her to climb in first. She slid into bed then held out her arms to him. In seconds he had his body wrapped around hers, his arms cradling her. The raw flavor of the night, the brutality, the violent sex, started to recede even further as he held her close, felt her lips brush over his throat. He tilted his chin up and she pierced him with sweet simplicity, taking just a sip or two, her lips moving on him. Her fingers curled and uncurled on his chest, the nails scraping him.

It was a marking more than a snack or meal. While it made his cock stir, it was his heart that did a full somersault, especially as she let out a sleepy little sigh, her fingers drifting across him, her body becoming heavier, melting into his. She trusted him to hold her as she faded into sleep with the dawn.

He found it peaceful as a lullaby, the rock of a cradle. Perhaps the first real peace he'd found in years. Everything as it should be, crazy as that sounded. He followed her, drifting off into a dark velvet sleep.

Occasionally he stirred, but just as easily, finding himself still in her embrace, he'd drop back into sleep again. They slept throughout the day, undisturbed by light, for Butch had given them adjoining rooms on a below-ground level of the house. Butch's master bedroom was on the main floor as well as other guestrooms, but Selene had told Quinn earlier in the evening that the basement accommodations weren't an insult. Younger vampires needed the full darkness that only underground accommodations could provide.

"I can sleep aboveground in a place with the right kind of curtains, but it's not a comfortable sleep. Like being in a convection oven. It shows Butch's courtesy, that he accommodates his younger vampire guests."

Yeah, he was a real sweetheart with that left jab. But despite his sardonic thought, Quinn couldn't remember the last time he'd slept through a full day, and so peacefully, but that was just what he did. It wasn't until just after sunset that he roused, woken by her touch, the light brush of her lips on his cheek, his jaw, his throat before she rose.

They each took their turn in the bathroom, and then shared the space to dress, spruce up. Selene didn't say much, but she had a tender smile on her lips as she passed behind him in the bathroom, curling her arms around him as he paused in his shaving. Taking the razor, she slid in front of him to sit on the counter. She finished the job herself, her eyes monitoring the track of the blade, her hand following it to stroke his smooth skin.

The look in her gaze kindled his lust, tempted him to go right back to bed, but she slipped away when done, giving his ass a pinch before she commanded him to get it moving so they could go meet their host for "breakfast". He was rewarded with an indignant squeal when he popped her ass with his damp towel, and the promise of severe retribution. He looked forward to it.

Fortunately breakfast was exactly that, just a light meal with Butch and Dix. No ceremony or formality this time. No wrestling matches. Just the four of them sitting at the table making small talk. Quinn thought they could have been any four people socializing at a meal and the image made him swallow a smile. Life with Selene had taken an interesting turn.

"I'll set things in motion today," Butch assured Selene as she and Quinn prepared to leave. "I'll be in touch." Then he looked toward Quinn. "She has her work cut out for her with you, but I believe you'll suit."

Quinn had the feeling he'd just received some sort of minor blessing.

Once Jim dropped them off at the air field and they'd boarded the plane, Quinn turned on his cell phone, which Selene had ordered him to leave in the plane. The waiting message from Manuel informed him the bar had had an outstanding night and both Maria and Carol were needed to handle the crowd. Everything went well and the money was locked up. Another message from Kevin said the cattle had all been moved and the pregnant cows separated from the rest of the herd without any problems. And Annette would have coffee waiting for them.

"I wonder if they need me at all," he grumbled to Selene as they took off.

"Feeling a little unnecessary?" she teased. "Don't worry. I'll always need you." She pointed to his wrist bearing the third mark, the one shaped like a horse's bit. "Especially now."

He placed his hand on her thigh and gave it a gentle squeeze. For the flight home she'd worn one of her flirty little sundresses.

He easily slid his hand beneath the light fabric to rest on her warm, satin-smooth skin. Selene hummed satisfaction.

"I didn't think I'd be interested in anything that had to do with sex after last night." He gave a low chuckle. "Apparently you gave me the third mark just in time, Mistress."

"It excites me when you address me that way, cowboy."

"Strange, but it does the same to me." Christ. What a change he'd made in his life. But he couldn't imagine it without her.

Which led to a different topic, one they'd broached before but hadn't pursued. He dug around in his mind for the right words, since he had no idea how Selene would react to it. She might think he was out of his mind.

"I'm in your mind, cowboy, so I know you're there." Her lips quirked. *Your brain is in such turmoil. What's bothering you?*

*An idea. I'm not sure if you'll agree to it.* "I want to prepare a room at the ranch where you could sleep during the day. So you don't always have to hurry back to that cave at After Hours."

She was silent for so long he wondered if he should have brought it up at all.

*Yes, you should have. I'm thinking.*

*I'm not sure if this being in each other's heads is such a good idea after all.*

*Deal with it, cowboy. It's there for eternity.*

He swallowed a laugh. Had he ever in his life thought he'd be discussing things that stretched out timelessly this way?

"There would be problems to deal with," she said at last.

"I'm aware of that. But go ahead. Tell me what occurs to you first?"

"Your housekeeper. What will she think of a woman who sleeps all day while you're out working the ranch?"

He shrugged. "You run After Hours. When else would you sleep?"

"But all day?" she persisted. "You'd be answering a lot of questions."

"Annette doesn't ask many questions," he told her. "I don't get in her business and she only marginally gets in mine. Usually because she has an uncanny way of figuring it out without ever having to ask me."

He reached out, caught her hand. "She has a respect for things that can't be explained, as long as they're not hurting who she loves."

A troubled look crossed her face at that and she looked out the window. "All right. But before we move forward in that direction, we'll wait and see what kind of success Butch has with Laurent."

Laurent. Yeah, the asshole. Quinn wished he could just beat the lousy shit to a pulp.

*If you did you would only cause more trouble for your Mistress. Remember, all the rules have changed.*

He squeezed her thigh again. "Whatever you say. But let's keep it in mind, okay? If Butch can get things straightened out for us, I don't fancy having you spend the rest of eternity sleeping in one place while I'm in another."

"Let's see what happens. Then we can discuss our options."

"I don't like being away from you," he growled, aware of how petulant that might sound.

"I'll take that as a compliment. As long as you remember who's in charge."

"As if I could ever forget." *Or want to.* He knew she liked saying things like that, because it aroused her as much as it did him. "But you didn't hook up with a lapdog, honey." Sliding his hand farther up her thigh, he reached the smooth skin of her pussy. He sucked in a breath. "No panties?"

"A treat for you." She laughed. "If you're up to it."

At her words his cock swelled and pressed against the rough denim of his fly. "Oh, I think every bit of me is up to it."

"I thought of ordering you to keep your jeans open and your fly unzipped, to forget about underwear. Then I remembered we would be thousands of feet above the ground and what I had in mind might be a little dangerous."

"You don't think tempting me with your naked pussy is dangerous?" he snickered.

She was silent. He tried to reach into her head, find what she was mulling over so quietly, but he found he hit a wall.

"I didn't know you could do that. Shut me out of your head." He wasn't so sure he liked it either.

"A third mark isn't a two-way street, Quinn. Only when the vampire desires it. There are times my thoughts must remain my own."

"But I don't have the right to do the same with mine."

"No." She was brutally honest, he gave her that, though she had the grace to flush a little at his look. "I'm still close enough to my human origins that I'll try not to abuse your privacy without good cause. But...you're my first full servant, Quinn. I find I like the freedom to move in and out of your mind. It makes me feel like you're even more mine. In a very primitive way that I know should be offensive." She sighed. "Maybe I'm not so close to those origins as I like to believe."

The pain on her face suggested Selene was no less brutally honest with herself than she was with him. There was an odd sort of *quid pro quo* to that. While he wasn't sure what he felt about her admission that she liked thinking of him as her property, whenever she expressed such thoughts, the emotions she radiated included an intriguing vulnerability, a deep need for him. Maybe he didn't need to be in her mind. Just her heart.

He curled his fingers over hers once again. "Okay, Mistress. But I like it when you let me in. It causes me some problems when you don't as well. It makes me think you don't trust me. Or that I might be failing you."

She shook her head. "I trust you more than I've ever trusted anyone, Quinn. Sometimes the mind blocking is necessary. Please accept that has nothing to do with you and everything with who I have to be. All right?"

He thought it also had to do with her protecting him, and he didn't much care for that. She gave him an even look, didn't respond. But it made him wonder if her next subject change was nevertheless an answer to his thought.

"You did well at Butch's," she said. "In spite of everything, you listened to your Mistress."

His hands tightened on the controls. "I didn't like him hitting you."

"I know." She clasped his wrist, fingers tightening. "But it had to be done. I told you. Violence is a part of this life. It's something we accept. Fortunately, we all heal fast."

"Yes, but I don't have to like it."

"But you do have to control yourself and you did it admirably."

Her praise warmed him, even as the issue clawed at him. He wasn't going to get the image of her going down under Butch's blow out of his mind any time soon. "Well thanks. I guess."

"Since you did so well, I thought you might like a bit of a reward."

His cock flexed again and his mouth went dry. "What might that be?"

"I figured we could make use of what's left of the night after we land, before I have to leave." She tightened her thighs around his hand. "I'm sure we can think of something creative to do with the rest of the night."

Yeah? Quinn wished the damn plane had an accelerator so he could make it go faster.

"That sounds like a plan." Hell yeah, it did.

She ran her fingers the length of his extended arm. "I think we both need a little tenderness, don't you? A respite from last night?"

Fuck yes, he did.

"So," she murmured, "*can* you make this plane go any faster?"

He laughed. "Fortunately we aren't far from home."

Thirty minutes later they were over the Last Chance Ranch. He flipped the switch in the cockpit that turned on the landing lights and brought the plane in on a smooth approach, touching down and taxiing up to the steel hangar. When he pressed another button the wide door slid up and he eased the plane inside.

"Very clever," she commented.

"Pretty basic," he told her. "But it suits my needs for whenever I get to use it. Come on. Let's get up to the house. I see someone left a light on in the kitchen for us."

Quinn reined in his impatience while he did his post-flight check on the plane and locked everything down. He'd ferried them to the hangar in the four-wheel-drive and he used it now to get them back to the house. When he ushered Selene through the mud room and into the kitchen, he saw Annette with a glass of iced tea standing by the counter. It was close to midnight. He lifted his eyebrows in silent question.

"I wanted to make sure you and the young lady got back okay." Her voice, as usual, sounded like gravel rolling around on metal. She held out her hand. "Call me Annette."

A tiny smile played at Selene's lips as she shook Annette's hand. "I'm Selene."

"I figured." Annette looked his Mistress up and down. "You're the one who's got them all chasing their tails at After Hours, right?"

Quinn tensed, but Selene touched his arm in a reassuring gesture. "That's me. I think their tails needed a lot of chasing."

Annette gave a hearty laugh. "You'll do. Yes, you'll do." She inclined her head at Quinn. "You take care of this roughneck too?"

"Hey," Quinn protested.

Selene just ignored him. "And he takes care of me."

Annette nodded. "All right then. I made a chocolate cake, in case you two were hungry. I'll be going down to my place." Pausing at the back door, she raked her gaze over them. Quinn felt his cheeks heating at her regard, as if she could read their intent like they were already stripped naked and ready to go at it like rabbits. "You kids get right on to bed now." She was chuckling as she closed the door, went down the walkway.

Quinn shook his head. "Sorry about that."

"I like her. She's quite a character. How old is she?"

"She always says somewhere between sixty and a hundred and

sixty. I'm not sure I'd know what to do here without her. She gets stuff done that I don't even think of."

"A good person to have."

He looked at the cake tin. "Want a snack before we head off to the bedroom? I mean, I know you can only have a bite, but..."

"You're hungry. I have a better idea." Mischief flashed in her eyes. "Why don't I go to the bedroom and you get yourself a snack?"

"I'm okay. I can wait until—"

"No, you can't." She gave him a look full of heat. "You'll need your energy as my servant, Quinn. If you learned one thing the other night, it's that you never skip meals if you want to be ready to serve your Mistress."

"I don't know." He gave her just as thorough an appraisal head to toe, lingering on her thighs, the thrust of her breasts, the graceful line of arm and throat. The cocky challenge to it made her eyes spark in response. "She seemed to like feeding me herself. Got her nice and wet."

She tossed her hair. "Fine then. Get a snack, lapdog, then bring the cake back into the bedroom to share. We can give new meaning to the phrase eating in bed."

At the thought of all the things he could do with Selene and the sweet treat, his balls tightened and his blood hummed. She pivoted and left him, heading down the hall with a great deal of hip action, the hem of the short skirt flirting just below her ass. She was already slipping the straps off her shoulders, making him want nothing more than to follow. But his Mistress had commanded him to eat, for good purpose. He wanted to fuck her senseless all night long, and no way in hell would he risk running out of steam.

Annette had left a couple turkey sandwiches in the oven as she usually did, and he wolfed them down faster than he'd ever eaten anything. The slice of cake he cut was nice and thick, with lots of frosting. As he hefted the two bags in one hand and strode back to the bedroom with the cake plate, his mouth was already watering, but not necessarily for the cake alone.

At the bedroom door he came to a complete stop, frozen in his tracks, awed by the sight of what awaited him. The covers were folded neatly at the foot of the bed and Selene lay stretched out on the sheet, her entire body tinted gold by the lamplight. She was naked, her knees bent and her legs spread wide so her pussy was temptingly open to him, the pink folds already glistening with arousal.

She grinned at him. "Come here, cowboy, and I'll show you the proper way to eat dessert."

"Yeah? Give me just a minute here. Savoring and all that."

"I don't repeat myself, and I don't like waiting. Get over here."

He'd started to set the plate down on the nightstand, but she stretched out an imperious hand. When he gave her a wry look but nevertheless dropped the bags and came forward, she took the plate from him and rested it on her stomach. "Strip," she said.

Quinn kicked his boots in a corner of the closet and dropped everything else in a pile. Then he was on the bed beside her, his cock dark and throbbing, his heart pounding.

"How are you with frosting?" She gave him an impish grin.

He licked his lips. "That depends on what's involved."

"I think you could do a great job decorating my nipples and my pussy, don't you? I'm sure you've got some very creative ideas."

"Oh yeah," he breathed. "Do I ever."

"Show your Mistress how clever you are. How talented."

Scooping a generous amount of the thick frosting with his fingers, he painted first one nipple then the other, covering each tight bud and the areolas completely. He took his time, enjoying the feel of her and the way her body reacted to his touch. Her breath caught in her throat, blue eyes going to half slits. Her knees quivered. Damn. Those third mark enhanced senses told him her arousal was increasing, the scent perfuming the air more densely around them.

"Last night was very intense," she whispered, her fingers

playing with the hair along his nape, a half-reverent, half-erotic stroke. "Especially for you. You fought Dix so hard. My heart was pounding, just watching you. My pussy was so wet I knew Butch had to be smelling me, but he was just as absorbed in the two of you as I was."

Quinn wasn't that interested in the Butch side of that equation, but fortunately she didn't linger on that. Her touch trailed over his biceps. "Knowing all your strength is mine to command, knowing your dick was just getting harder as you fought..." She watched him, eyes glittering with desire. "I won't ever stop wanting you, Quinn."

Her voice was throaty with desire, but her eyes shone with that overwhelming need that twined with her ownership of him and made him understand at a gut-deep level that it tied them to each other. She was right, about them needing this. Though lust was pulsing in the air, there was a deep tenderness here, a thick wave of emotion that was a big change from what they'd handled the past twenty-four hours.

He bent his head back to his task, continued to swirl the dark confection in wider circles, covering part of her breasts. Breaking off a piece of cake, he crumbled it over the frosting like scattering sprinkles onto an ice cream sundae. She held herself so still, yet he saw her pulse pounding in the delicate hollow of her throat and felt that energy in the air, like a heat spreading over his skin. The more still she got, the more powerful her reaction.

Shifting his position until he knelt between her outspread thighs, he gathered another generous portion of frosting and began to paint her pussy. First the smooth skin at the top, covering it completely, then carefully down the outer lips. Liquid seeped from her, her slit shining with it, and the scent of it teased at his nostrils further, driving him nuts. When she let out a moan, turning her head to press her cheek against the pillow in involuntary aroused response, he was tempted to toss the rest of the cake and put his mouth on her right now.

The thought was so tempting it apparently penetrated the haze of lust he saw reflected in her gleaming eyes. *I don't think so.*

Her mind voice had a breathiness that turned him on even more. He would follow her desires, because no matter what he could think up, whatever she demanded only made him harder.

*It was just an idea, Mistress.*

*You are such a horny bastard, Quinn. I think that's why I enjoy you so much.*

*Actually, the pleasure is all mine.*

She laughed, the plate bouncing lightly on her stomach.

When he painted the inner lips, the frosting mixed with her own juices, shining in the reflected light. By the time he'd covered the entire area, she looked as if she wore a chocolate bikini and he was afraid he'd spill himself right there like an excited teenage boy.

"Time to enjoy dessert," Selene instructed, handing him the plate.

He looked from the cake to her.

"Put the plate on the nightstand and attend to your Mistress, Quinn. Eat."

*Yes ma'am.* He took his time lapping the confection from her nipples and her breasts, first the cake, then swirling his tongue over each ribbon of frosting. He pulled each distended nipple into his mouth in turn, heat washing over him at the eroticism of it. He forced himself to go slowly, giving her every possible minute of pleasure. Reaching over her head, she gripped the spindles on the headboard, arching her body up to his mouth.

Quinn licked until one breast and nipple were free of the chocolate, pausing to take the nipple between his teeth and bite gently.

"I thought I did the biting around here," Selene said, her voice unsteady.

When he looked up he saw the heat in her eyes. "Then you can give me instruction if I do it wrong."

"You're doing just fine." Her words came out on a shaky breath.

By the time he'd cleaned both breasts and nipples he was so

aroused his entire body throbbed. He wanted to say the hell with it and plunge right into her cunt, chocolate and all. But she wanted a special treat and he was going to give it to her or die trying. He was enjoying this way more than having Dix hogtie him or suck his dick.

*I would certainly hope so.* The laughter in her voice made all that seem not as traumatic, yet she was right. This was such a polar opposite of the night before. No brute strength, no pain, no extremes of sensation bruising every nerve in his body. He kept coming back to that word, *tender,* because this moment was laden with it, a tenderness that they hadn't shared until now. He was touched that she would offer this to him and wanted her to know how much he appreciated it.

*I do.*

He would have smiled but his mouth was too busy at her pussy, lapping the frosting from the smooth skin. He drew out the process, gathering every bit of chocolate and every drop of her moisture on his tongue and licking his lips over the deliciousness of it. By the time he thrust his tongue deep inside her she was panting and twisting her hips back and forth. But when he moved his mouth to her clit and thrust two fingers inside her she jerked hard enough to dislodge him. He looked up at her, surprised.

"Not yet. I'm not going over yet." She released her grip on the headboard and pushed herself to a sitting position, lifting the cake plate. Rolling to her side, she patted the sheet next her. "Come lie down, Quinn. It's your turn."

"But—"

"Obey your Mistress."

Christ, she was going to destroy him. But he stretched himself out on his back beside her and waited for whatever came next.

As slowly as he'd decorated her breasts and her pussy, she was even more methodical as she applied the sweet treat to his swollen cock.

"Mmmm. Love chocolate. We must remember to thank Annette for being so thoughtful."

"I'm sure she had no idea the use we'd put it to." Sweat popped out on his forehead as he forced himself to lie still beneath her touch.

"I'm not so sure of that, but do you think she'd like to know exactly how inventive we were?"

"I—No, I don't think—"

"I don't either." Her laugh was soft and low. "But it is an interesting way to enjoy dessert."

Her slender fingers stroked in a steady rhythm, coating his hot shaft, sliding over the skin. Quinn fisted his hands, digging his nails into his palms as he reached for every bit of control. Her touch was bad enough, but when she'd covered his genitals to her satisfaction she knelt beside him and began to swirl the frosting around with her educated tongue. She stroked over his cock and his balls, following the path of her tongue with her fingers until he was sure he was at the absolute limit of his control. He was already so aroused from touching and licking her body. When she probed the slit at the head of his shaft he nearly came off the bed.

"Fuck, Mistress. I can't—I'm—

"Ssh, ssh, shh. It's okay." She drew a line across the hard plane of his stomach with the tip of her tongue before moving the plate to the nightstand. "Lie there for me, Quinn, and let me do the work."

She couldn't eat all that chocolate herself. He knew vampires couldn't digest that much food, but she used a towel they'd brought from the bathroom to clean him off, squeezing and rubbing him, the contrast in friction making his hips jerk, her eyes gleaming with pleasure at his involuntary response. When she was done, she bent and licked off the residual stickiness until he was clean, every trace of the chocolate gone.

Looking up at her, he saw that they now shared a different kind of hunger. She straddled him, opening her pussy with one hand while guiding him to her opening with the other. With an erotically painful slowness she eased herself down until he filled her completely, his passage eased by the moisture lubricating her walls.

"Give me your hands," she demanded.

He held them out to her and she threaded her fingers with his, balancing herself. Her gaze never left his as she began a sensual dance, slide and retreat, up and down, a steady, even rhythm that drove him even wilder.

*Hurry. Please hurry.*

She just smiled at him and licked her lips.

They might have gone on for a long time this way, but he sensed her own orgasm rushing up from inside her. Her pace accelerated and he thrust his hips up to drive himself deeper, the leash breaking. Icy heat spread over his lower back, his balls tightened and strained, the walls of her cunt gripped him hard and they exploded together. Her liquid bathed him as he spurted into her again and again, their juices mingling as much as their blood had.

Despite the intensity of the orgasm, when the spasms subsided and the aftershocks faded, he felt strangely at peace. She had driven the devils of the previous night from his mind, just as she'd promised. Leaning forward, she placed a gentle kiss on his lips. Then she brought his wrist, the one with the mark, to her mouth and kissed it also.

*We are together, cowboy.*

*I am yours, Mistress.*

*Damn straight.*

# CHAPTER FOURTEEN

*Sometimes the mind blocking is necessary.* Those words became Selene's mantra, because for the next three days she had to keep a lot of things locked up inside her mind to maintain a calm countenance. Yet inside that limited space, her nerves screamed with impatience.

But she'd done what she could do. She had pleaded her case with Butch. Suffered through the subjugation of Quinn because that was what was required, once Butch agreed to grant her request. She had been so proud of him, this incredible alpha male who'd put himself in her hands completely in order to belong to her. Serve her.

She now knew why, once having a fully marked servant, a vampire never did without one. Finding that unique combination of submission and service, all of it packaged in an aggressive cowboy who knew his own mind and had a formidable will of his own, was an incomparable gift. It terrified her, another reason to keep a great deal of her thoughts locked away from Quinn. So much could go wrong...

The little interlude with the chocolate cake when they returned to Last Chance Ranch had certainly taken the edge off for both of them. It pleased her that no matter the mood of the situation, the intensity, his entire focus had been to please her.

*You've chosen well, Selene.*

Recalling Butch's words, she certainly hoped so. Since she'd given Quinn the third mark, the atmosphere of their relationship had changed. Without it Quinn never would have submitted to the activities at Butch Dorn's. Nor would their nights together be as erotically intense. As a full servant, he was able to renew his energy more quickly, replenish himself in shorter time periods. He no longer needed more than a couple hours of sleep. While she slumbered through the day, he attended to business at the ranch, fully rested and working alongside his hands. Sometimes she would morph into the butterfly and soar to wherever he was, beating her wings for attention and lighting on his hand to let him know she was still with him, still in control. She loved watching him as he worked, seeing him sit tall and relaxed in the saddle, almost one with Midnight. When she was with him out there on the range, his heart and mind seemed as content as she'd ever felt him.

At night he would come to the bar, usually a couple hours after opening, and stay until she closed. Sometimes he sat in the office, watching the little television in there. Other times he wandered out to the front, sitting at a table chatting with people he knew, or just hanging out by himself. He was more relaxed now, renewing friendships with regulars he'd pushed to arms' length because of his schedule and the stresses of the bar. But always, whenever she was within sight of him, he watched her with eyes that devoured her. Every day only strengthened the bonds of their relationship.

She looked forward to the next three hundred years with her servant. If they could get past Laurent.

Hopefully that situation would be resolved before much more time passed. Quinn had discussed a number of options for moving her into the ranch house. It wasn't just a matter of a dark room where she could sleep undisturbed. They needed to have a logical explanation for Annette as well as Johnny, Kevin and the other hands. Butch had created a positive situation with Dix, so perhaps they could learn from his structure.

Quinn was impatient as well, wanting this to be settled so they didn't have disaster hanging over their heads. If only she'd get some word from Butch. She could just imagine Laurent's reaction when he got the telephone call. The man was given to incredible rages. She'd seen the punishment he had doled out to those who displeased him or violated his rules. Nausea gripped her at the thought. But she'd known a day of reckoning would come when she'd had enough of her virtual indentured servitude and run away.

Had Butch made the damn call already? One didn't nag an overlord. He'd said he'd notify her when he called Laurent, but in the meantime it left her on edge, listening every night for the phone in the bar to ring.

Thankfully, After Hours was busier than ever. Tonight was a prime example. Even though it was a weeknight, the bar was jammed, the activity occupying her physically as well as mentally. For some reason, everyone in town had decided they couldn't wait for Friday or Saturday to kick up their heels. Every seat was full as well as every bar stool. The jukebox was blaring, the tiny dance floor jammed with couples doing a fancy two-step.

She wasn't expecting Quinn. He was interested in a particular breeding bull at a ranch in West Texas, so he'd flown there late afternoon. Dinner was on the agenda tonight with some old friends and tomorrow he'd look at the bull. He'd told her he'd be back about noon or a little after and see her that night. Good. Much as she longed to be with him every minute like a ridiculous teenager, she needed some space to cobble her thoughts together.

As she kept an eye on things while pouring drinks and pulling taps, Manuel hustled in the kitchen. Tonight Maria was scheduled to work, but when the size of the crowd ballooned Selene had called Carol, who was only too happy for the extra money. Selene was pleased at how the two had blossomed under her management, taking pride in their work. Maria was even showing interest in acquiring more bar management skills, talking about taking some business courses at the closest community college.

Selene was in the process of mixing two drinks when the call finally came in. Seeing the Blood Rock Ranch number on the caller ID of the bar phone, she motioned for Carol to take her place and plucked the phone off the wall, hurrying around the corner to the privacy of the hallway.

"Ma'am?" Dix's voice greeted her. Of course. Though Butch treated her as a guest at his home, she was still not officially in his territory and had insinuated herself here without permission. She had no status that would require Butch to be the one who called. It still pricked a bit, but Dix softened that with his next words. "Butch apologizes for not calling himself. He's been in conference with the Region Masters on and off through the day, but he just learned something he knew you'd rather know sooner than later."

Selene gripped the receiver hard, pushing back the bile that suddenly surged into her throat. "That's fine. Do they have a decision?"

"Not yet. Still working on it." Dix paused as if he might say more, then his tone became more neutral. "Butch was going to call New York after he got a little ways into talking to the Region Masters, buy you some more time before Laurent got the heads-up. But the northeast Region Master just mentioned he'd brought Laurent into the loop two nights ago."

She swallowed the disappointment, even as she appreciated Butch's attempt. Apparently the Region Master of Laurent's territory was either his friend—God help her then—or a stickler for protocol.

Dix paused and she heard an exchange of conversation. "Hold on. Actually, Butch has just stepped out of his office and wants to speak to you." Dix's grimmer tone told Selene to brace herself.

"The Region Masters patched Laurent into our conference call," Butch said without preamble. He gave a humorless chuckle. "That wasn't the most pleasant conversation I've ever had, youngling."

"What did he say?"

"As you can imagine, he was less than pleased about moving you into my territory. But it's in the hands of the Region Masters now. However he feels, whatever he wants, he knows he can't remove you until the Council makes its ruling, and then only if it's in his favor."

She rubbed her palm on her thigh. "Did he give you any indication if he plans to head this way?"

"If he does, he's supposed to give me a heads-up first before entering my territory." Butch paused, a silence that made it clear he had dubious expectations at best on that score. "He was extremely angry when I spoke to him, although he did his best to control it on the phone with the three of us. While he knows the Council might frown on him coming here until a decision has been made, it's not prohibited."

"Yes." Every one of her muscles clenched. He'd come. Retribution was part of his personal creed. She tried not to imagine the questions he'd had to answer about her disappearance or the excuses he'd been forced to make. Image was so critical to Laurent, especially in the sophisticated New York environment in which he operated. He'd want to make an example of her.

"Selene?" Butch's voice interrupted her thoughts. "Did I lose you?"

"No." She gave herself a mental shake. "No, I'm here. Sorry."

"Selene, if you wish to come here until the decision is made..."

The offer surprised her, but she steeled her resolve. She knew how this game was played. She couldn't afford to take advantage of this male who she hoped would be her salvation. Hers and Quinn's "That's very kind, my lord. But I knew there would be consequences. I should face Laurent, get it over with."

"I'd have your servant keep his distance if that happens. Even do your best to send him away if he happens to be around. He won't be able to stop it and he might also become a victim."

"I know." The words came out on a sigh. "He's come along very nicely, but—"

"But he still feels the need to defend you," Butch finished. "That was evident when you were here at my place. He controlled himself better than I expected, but I'm not sure he'd get past another bout of vampire-on-vampire discipline."

She bit back a grim snort. Characterizing Laurent's sadism as discipline was like calling a hurricane a spring shower. But she wasn't going to whine. She had to prove to Butch she'd be an asset, not a liability or a "youngling" he had to nursemaid.

"Yes. That's true."

"Vampire discipline can be harsh, but Laurent will likely get in the licks he thinks are fair. If you fight back or object in any way, he might convince the Council not to permit the transfer."

*No. Please, no.*

She swallowed. "I understand. I'll handle it."

"Yeah, I bet you will." Another pause, as if Butch was trying to give her the opportunity to say something else.

She gripped the phone tighter, holding onto her courage. "I hope the Region Masters will allow me to stay, with your permission. You've been more than fair."

Laurent would definitely come here. Selene was positive of it. He would see her leaving as such an act of betrayal, he'd need to punish her so others wouldn't follow in her footsteps. His pride and ego were both his two strongest characteristics and his greatest failings. He could already be on his way. He probably was.

"Thank you for speaking to me yourself, my lord. You do me great honor. I appreciate it." She paused. "Again, if anything should go wrong—"

"You don't have to get all flowery. It's not my thing. I can tell you're a decent female, Selene. Your servant is safe with me. I gave my word as much based on my assessment of your character as his." He gave a rough laugh. "Dix has asked about him. Wants to know if the two of you are coming back this way any time soon."

She wasn't sure how to answer that. "I guess it depends on what the Region Masters decide."

"Of course. But if the decision is in your favor, you might owe me a visit. I'm sure you can convince your servant of the importance of gratitude."

*Oh yeah. But I might have to use the whip to do it.* A smile managed to struggle up from among her tension. "I'm sure we'll arrange something."

"I'll call you as soon as I have word on a decision."

Selene let out a breath as she replaced the receiver. So. Things were in motion. She was glad Quinn was far away tonight. Every instinct told her something bad was imminent and she didn't want her servant involved.

All too vividly, she remembered one night at the bar when a vampire had disrespected Laurent in front of others. The overlord had ordered the man stripped naked and tied to a pole, where he whipped him mercilessly before carving his initials on the man's back. At the end he had ordered two of his minions to use a hammer to break every one of the man's toes and fingers. The satisfaction on his face when he reduced the object of his anger to a bleeding, broken lump was frightening. Laurent didn't just mete out retribution, he thrived on it. The sound of his victims crying out in pain or begging for relief always brought a stark wash of pleasure to his features. The poor bastard had then been dumped in his apartment where he hid during the time it took him to heal. Every time Selene saw him after that, his manner toward Laurent was beyond deferential. Groveling, even.

She couldn't live that way. She couldn't. But if she died...Quinn died. What an impetuous idiot she'd been, marking him before this was resolved.

*Stop it.* She reminded herself of what Butch had said. Fuck it and move on. That was the only way this could work, for her or Quinn. Crying over a decision she'd embraced because of the honest joy it brought to her wasn't going to change anything except steal whatever time she had left to savor it.

Icy fingers skittered over her spine, a foreboding touch signaling that evil was about to invade her life. Maybe she'd be lucky. Maybe the Region Masters would rule for her *and* maybe Laurent would give up without a major confrontation.

*And maybe I'll turn into a human.*

*If he's coming, let it be tonight while Quinn is gone. I've already put him at risk enough.*

Besides, she wanted it over and done with, not hanging over her head. With a sigh she hurried back to the front to take up her chores behind the bar again. The crowd had thinned out a little but it was still busy enough she could tuck her unease in a corner of her mind to pull out later. Still, it was a relief when she finally announced last call and no one gave her a hard time. The last customers made their way to the door, calling good night to everyone. Carol and Maria got busy bussing the tables and sweeping up.

"Good tips tonight." Maria grinned, taking the fold of bills Selene handed her from the tip jar and tucking them into the pocket of her jeans.

"No shit," Carol added, her smile as broad.

"I'll calculate what was added to the credit card receipts," Selene told them, "and have the cash for you this weekend."

"Great," they chorused, then high-fived each other. Selene shook her head at them, but couldn't help smiling at their youthful exuberance. But when she turned to clear the register, Carol drew her attention back to them.

"Um, Selene?"

"Yes?"

"We, uh, just want to thank you." Her lips curved in a shy smile. "For, you know, making this place so great."

The direct compliment warmed her as few other things could. *I was meant to be here. I am going to survive Laurent, damn it.*

"It's my pleasure," she told them. "Now get going. Artie's legacy is over."

"Thank God for that. Will you need us both tomorrow night?" Maria asked. "You think it will be this busy again?"

"It's not my night to work," Carol added, "but I have no plans, so call if you need me."

"Thanks for being on standby. Let's see what happens tomorrow. Go home and rest."

As she waved them off, she zipped the receipts into a cash bag. Locking the door after the two girls, Manuel already having left, she carried the bag into the office to stash in the little safe. Out of habit, her enhanced senses registered their cars starting, the parking lot emptying.

Five minutes later, she felt him.

Laurent had taken her blood, part of an overlord's right and a way of monitoring her specific whereabouts within a certain geographical range. While she didn't have the same ability, never having tasted his blood, a vampire always sensed the proximity of another vampire. There was only one who could be coming to these doors.

Forcing herself to finish putting the money away, she took a deep breath. *Whatever happens, I just have to get through it. That's all.*

She strode back into the main saloon, to the entry doors. He wouldn't knock. He knew she knew he was there. Did he expect her to cower, to try to run? She wouldn't do that. She'd made her choice. It was all public now, in process with the Region Masters.

She made damn sure her hands didn't shake as she unlocked the door, though things quaked deep inside. As she pushed open the double panels, no one appeared to be there, but she left them wide open and went back to the bar. While she waited for him to make his predictably dramatic entrance, she mixed his favorite drink, set it on the bar. Then she came back around and stood before it. She wouldn't hide from him.

He came out of the darkness just like in a horror movie. Not there, then suddenly there. He could have been across the parking lot and moved that fast. He didn't have to pretend to be a nightmare though. He was her worst nightmare, about to come true.

She stood erect, hands at her sides curled into fists to steady herself. Her heart beat erratically and her stomach was a bundle of knots, but she projected a calm she didn't feel.

Laurent looked exactly as she remembered him—tall and lean.

Not Dix's leanness, sunbaked hardness from ranch work. More like a slender, refined knife blade. Appearance didn't matter, however, when it came to vampire strength. Even the weakest vampire could practically tear a building off its foundations, and Laurent was nowhere near the weakest.

His razor-cut black hair just touched the collar of his silk turtleneck, every strand perfectly in place. The jacket of his custom-tailored suit was open, the gray fabric moving with his body. The diamond in the pinky ring he always wore winked in the low light of the bar. If not for the rage so visible on his face and blazing from his black, black eyes, he could have posed for an ad campaign for a successful New Yorker.

One step behind him was Claudio, his servant. Laurent never moved without the exceptionally beautiful male, who had tawny-brown eyes, sensuous lips and black hair that fell in waves from his brow and to his collar. His physique—toned body, tight ass—complemented Laurent's similar vampire perfection. But what made her blood run cold were the two vampires with him, Ernesto and Mike. Both dressed in black, they looked like the personal security force they were. Both men bore a crescent scar on one cheek, marked by Laurent's blood so that when he'd carved it there it would be permanent. Usually, that only worked on servants, but Laurent had done it over and over until it became permanent.

Whatever either male had done to him, it had earned them the sentence of always being under his thumb, following his every order. Perhaps at one time they'd been decent souls, but he'd chosen well. They'd embraced the sociopathic personality of their Master and executed his most brutal wishes without hesitation or emotion.

While ostensibly Laurent used them for general security at the bar with his human patrons, they did his enforcement work with vampires in his territory. That way Laurent could choose a la carte which torments he handled personally and which ones he could watch.

Ernesto turned the deadbolt in the door and took up a stance in front of it, as if they thought she might try to bolt through it. She wouldn't give them the satisfaction. Ernesto had the look of a sleek Hispanic undertaker, his eyes deep set in his smooth brown face, mouth a thin line. Mike, his thick tail of auburn hair a straight line down his broad back, walked to the rear of the bar, disappearing down that hallway to verify that door was locked as well.

Her attention snapped from that to Laurent, who'd stepped forward, bringing him within a foot from her. The hatred in his expression drilled holes in her body.

"Hello, Laurent." She was surprised there wasn't a hint of a tremor in her voice, because inside the shaking was getting worse. Far worse.

"So proud. You'd have done better to let your fear show, Selene. Shown some humility."

His arm moved so swiftly it was a blur, his hand cracking across her face with the force of a wooden board. It spun her around, making her hit the bar, but fortunately she'd left his drink out of range. It shook but didn't spill a drop. Why that made her want to bark out a hysterical laugh, she didn't know.

She pressed her lips together, sealing in any cry of pain. Straightened to face him again.

"You betrayed me, bitch."

*Crack!* He struck her other cheek. He probably thought of this one as more of a love tap since he snapped her head back, rocked her on her heels, but she was still on her feet. The pain sang through her nerve endings, preparing her for more to come.

"What? No argument here?" His lip curled with disdain. "No excuses? No pitiful explanations?"

She didn't have the energy to spare for them. Excesses of pain or fear could shatter the mindshields of a younger vampire. Quinn wasn't far enough away. If he felt her fear or pain, he could be back on his plane and at her door within an hour or two, and she had no idea if Laurent was going to make this an all-night torture session.

Quinn couldn't be allowed to feel her distress. She didn't want him anywhere near this.

Running her tongue over her split bottom lip, she tasted her own blood. She knew it wouldn't matter what she said to Laurent anyway. He'd come here with an agenda and nothing she did or said would make a difference.

"I took care of you. I saw to your welfare. I made sure you had a roof over your head and proper training."

"No." The word was out of her mouth before she could stop it. She felt the sparks snap from her eyes. "You used me, Laurent. I was a hard worker, running that bar for you. You left me with nothing for myself."

God, she was so stupid. This time he used his fist, making contact with her nose. The impact drove her to the floor, her head smacking against the base of the bar. The crunch of cartilage came with a lightning bolt of agonizing pain, more blood. Dizziness washed over her and she swallowed against the nausea surging to her throat.

"Get up." His voice was like the crack of a whip. "Now."

Breathing unevenly, she rose to her feet, clumsy and awkward. She was barely upright before his fist connected with the side of her head, more forceful than the previous blows. Her head hit the rim of the bar this time, the force of it driving her into an awkward heap on the floor again. The blood ran freely from her nose. Forcing her gaze upward, she saw Laurent staring down at her, his hatred and thirst for vengeance blazing even more brightly.

He kicked her, sending a lightning bolt of pain through her kneecap. "You ran away. Ungrateful bitch. After I gave you everything."

She bit back a cry, but not a retort. "You made...me...a slave."

Why couldn't she just keep her mouth shut, take her punishment and crawl away to heal? Why did she have to goad him this way? Butch had warned her to take her punishment and move on, hadn't he?

"Death is often the punishment for runaways." He prodded the damaged kneecap again. "It's an unforgiveable disloyalty. And for what?" He looked around the bar with disdain. "A hole-in-the-wall hangout for the great unwashed? In a lowlife place like Texas? I gave you the sophistication of New York and you threw it back at me."

Death. His words stabbed her with fear, but not for herself. Oh God. If Laurent killed her, Quinn would drop wherever he was, his heart stopping, his life force connected to hers. She'd done that to him.

With every ounce of will she had, she forced herself to stay silent. To do or say anything could seal Quinn's fate. *Keep silent*, she told herself. *He's bluffing. He enjoys torture too much. Death takes all the fun away from him.* He hadn't killed the one he'd tortured in front of her, all that time ago, though she remembered the vampire had begged for death before it was all over. She'd say she'd die before she gave Laurent the satisfaction, but...

"So brave. Not a word out of her." He cast a look at his three minions before shooting his gaze back down at her. "Maybe you want the mercy of death. But you know me far better than that. Death would not be nearly painful enough for you, nor would it give me enough satisfaction. Plus the Region Masters tend to whine if we take choices away from them."

He snapped his fingers at Claudio. The servant, his expression impassive, reached beneath his coat and drew a knife from a scabbard. The long blade reflected the faint light from the ceiling fixtures. Though that should have captured her full attention, Selene found her eyes drawn to Claudio's face instead. Did he and Laurent share the bond she and Quinn did, that emotional closeness? She didn't see how it was possible. Laurent was far too much of a sociopath. She'd have pitied Claudio, except like most servants, his choice to become a vampire's servant was a willing one. Sometimes she'd found his near constant silence even more chilling than Laurent's self-serving monologues.

Laurent drew the flat of the blade across his open palm in a lover's caress, once, twice, three times. From her ungainly position on the floor Selene stared up at him, her heart thumping. Was he planning to carve his initials on her back as he'd done to that other unfortunate vampire? Mark it over and over with his own blood, like he had the scars on Ernesto's and Mike's faces? She'd skin herself before she'd let herself be marked with his name forever.

"Lift that piece of rubbish up," he snapped.

Mike and Ernesto hauled her upright. She tried to plant her feet but her wrecked knee hurt so badly she couldn't put any weight on it. She simply hung there, suspended between the two thugs.

"Strip her," Laurent ordered.

Rough hands tore her dress from her body, tossing the remnants aside before ripping away her flimsy lingerie. Pretty things she'd worn even though Quinn wasn't going to be here tonight. She'd anticipated talking to him before dawn, taunting him with what she was wearing, perhaps bringing herself to climax for him while denying him the right to touch himself on the other side of the phone until she commanded it.

The air scraped over her as she was stripped, making her flesh go cold. Why being raped by Laurent horrified her more deeply than anything else, she didn't know. Maybe because all she could think of was Quinn inside her body, his hands moving with such care over her, even at the point of his most violent need.

"Don't worry, my dear." Laurent's eyes glittered. "I'm not going to fuck you. I wouldn't dirty my cock in the pussy of a turncoat. Someone who betrayed me for all the world to see." He stroked the flat of the blade across her cheek. "What a mess you are, blood and snot all over your face. So disgusting. I can't imagine who would touch you anyway."

So he still didn't know she'd taken a full servant. Thank God. Thank God. If they could just get this done before he found out. Even if she had to go back with Laurent, Butch would protect Quinn. He'd promised.

Laurent traced the column of her neck with the knife tip, pausing at the hollow of her throat to prick the skin.

"Do you have any idea what a mess you left me? I had to come up with a plausible explanation for your absence, then find someone suitable to train as your replacement. I had a problematic few weeks."

*I'm surprised you could find anyone to work for the pittance you gave me. Perhaps if you'd been more generous I'd have stayed.*

Saying that aloud would only antagonize him more. She just wanted to get this over with and crawl into her cave in the basement.

"Nothing to say, Selene?"

The knife dug into one cheek. With a flick of his wrist, Laurent carved a slice to her chin. She smothered a gasp. Whatever she had to do, she wouldn't scream or beg for mercy, and not just for pride's sake. The level of control it took to do that would keep the same outbursts from reaching out and alerting Quinn.

"Nothing yet?" She flinched as he repeated the process with her other cheek before moving the knife lower. He traced her breast, making her heart race. A *no* screamed out in her mind. With obscene grace, he dug the blade into her flesh and opened up an arc over each breast.

"A bit more strength, and I could cut them off entirely. You'd survive, but these lovely tits wouldn't regenerate. How long would you survive without your beauty, Selene? It's one of our most powerful weapons, isn't it? Beg me not to do it. Ask my forgiveness. You know you owe me an apology."

Thank God for his short attention span. Not waiting for an answer, he let the knife drop and scored a line across the top of her cunt.

*I owe you nothing, you bastard.*

"I could take your clit as well. Female castration. You'd never find pleasure again. But if I ordered Mike and Claudio to fuck you instead, make you come despite your revulsion for them, your forced pleasure would be even more terrible to you."

She'd want to die. If she had to, she'd beg as he'd asked. He could do this. Take away everything, even dignity. She wasn't so sure she didn't want to die anyway. The thought of the Region Master making a decision in her favor seemed so far away. But Quinn...Quinn wasn't far away.

*Hold on for Quinn.*

Laurent sighed. "Still no response. Let's put a pin in that idea and move on to your actual punishment."

He nodded at the two men. "Bend her over that bar stool and hold her in place. Claudio, the cat."

She'd thought about skinning herself to avoid a permanent mark from him. Laurent could literally skin her with the cat-o'-nine Claudia gave him now, nine strands of thin plaited rope with pointed steel ends.

The flogger could be used for both pleasure and punishment. Yet as a penance, in the hands of the right person, it caused untold pain, which Laurent well knew. He'd often punished a recalcitrant lover in the back room of the club with this one.

The two men holding her dragged her to the nearest stool and forced her over it face down. Her toes barely brushed the floor, her knee still on fire, and the open wounds on her breasts stung from the pressure. Two pairs of hands tightened down on her, immobilizing her, increasing the helpless sense of horrible inevitability.

She speared a fang through her lower lip, adding one more rivulet of blood to those already on her face. Her cheeks were on fire, she could hardly breathe through her nose and her head felt as if a concrete block had smashed into it. Unable to focus her eyes, she simply closed them and called up Quinn's face. That would be her center, her anchor to help her through this. That and not letting anything through to him. She was an island, cut off from the whole world, Quinn merely a picture in her mind, not connected to the man himself.

The first blow fell on one buttock, the tiny sharp points biting into the skin. She jerked involuntarily but bit down hard again on her damaged lip to keep from crying out. The next blow came, then more, a shower of them in rapid succession, the steel tips like vicious teeth tearing into her skin. The agony spread out from waist to thighs, a continuous blanket of pain smothering her, trapping her. No escape.

Then he moved to the backs of her thighs. He was an expert with the weapon, each steel tip biting into a new spot. When he went to her back, he didn't miss a single square inch, whipping her from neck to waist.

At some point, no one could resist such agony. When she couldn't hold back the screams, Laurent had one of the vampires force a dirty bar rag into her mouth, cramming it in there such that it was in the back of her throat, making her gag, gasp for breath she knew rationally she didn't have to take. Her lungs fought for it anyway, increasing the sense of panic.

Mike and Ernesto increased their grip, pushing her harder into the leather of the stool. The blows came in a measured rhythm, not too fast, not too slow, but timed to elicit maximum suffering. She was sure she was a bloody mess by now but the searing heat that bloomed from every inch of her skin was so intense she couldn't care.

She tried to count the blows, focus on the numbers as a way to get through it, but they came too fast and too viciously. She finally managed to retreat into herself, blocking out the surroundings, Laurent, his men and the vicious blows of the cat. She was so deep in her head, the excruciating agony so unrelenting, she barely realized when the application of the specially designed flogger had ceased.

"Let her go."

She slid backward onto the floor and landed hard. Naked, beaten and bloody. She heard the scrape of Laurent's shoes, then a foot—Laurent's, she was sure—kicked her damaged knee again, following it up with a kick in her ribs. She screamed against the cloth they hadn't pulled free. Her tongue and mouth were dried out, parched.

"This is only a taste of what you'll be getting." His voice was laced with venom. "When the Region Masters send you back to me, I'll chain you in my penthouse, keep you on display like a freak show, until I'm sure my entire territory has seen you and knows the price of betrayal. I'll let you starve for blood for a decade before I kill you."

More sounds of shoes, four sets of feet moving away, followed by the closing of the door.

He was gone. It was done.

Selene lay crumpled in a heap for a long time, not believing it, expecting him to come back and start all over, one of his little mind games to break her completely. But a clock was ticking in her mind, competing with that, telling her she had to somehow find the strength to move. She wasn't going to die from this. She was going to heal. She just needed blood. Quinn would eventually come home, when Laurent was well away from here.

Tears spilled over her bloody face from even the slightest move. She moaned in agony as she made it to her hands and knees, her thigh tightening to hold the one knee up as much as possible, like a dog limping. Though one eye was swollen shut, she could make out where the scraps of her clothing were and crawled to get them. Since she woke up next to them, she realized the effort had made her black out. Panic gripped her until she saw the clock on the wall and realized only twenty minutes had passed. She just hoped in unconsciousness she hadn't let anything get through to Quinn. Unless it was blasted open by something like Laurent's active torture session, opening her mind was usually a voluntary act, like having to pull open a door. So it should be okay.

Trying to push through the excruciating pain, she managed to wrap the tattered dress around her. Gripping her ruined under-wear, she worked her way to her feet by grabbing onto the rail along the bar and maneuvering around it. Behind the bar, she found a pencil and scribbled a note for Manuel on a paper napkin. Her blood smeared it, making her curse, cry with frustration. She hadn't the strength to leave another note, so she hoped he'd simply think it was a wine stain from the bar, even though she was usually meticulously neat.

Manuel had keys. He'd open the door and take care of business.

Quinn was going to lose it when he saw her, but she couldn't control that. She was at the end of what she could control. The most important thing was Laurent was now out of his reach, and Quinn's focus would have to be on caring for her. She needed to feed from him if she were to heal properly and in a timely manner. Every part of her wanted to reach out to him now. For sustenance to heal but also for his arms, his strength, his comfort. Maybe she was still more human woman than vampire after all. That wasn't a good thing in her world, but here by herself, she could allow herself the weakness of wanting the man she loved to comfort her, to make the terrors gripping her inside calm.

Limping so badly she could barely walk, she maneuvered her way to the old storeroom. She got the door pulled closed and locked behind her, but the stairs were beyond her. She fell when she attempted the first one. She woke at the base. Using her last ounce of strength, she pulled herself back past the kegs and supplies to the small back room. Turning the lock on the door, she fell onto the cot mattress and managed to get the blanket over her shaking body, in too much agony to clean herself up.

She couldn't reach out to him, she couldn't. But eventually he would come. She held on to that thought like the promise of salvation, moaned with pain and prayed for oblivion. Eventually it came. When the blackness enfolded her, she sank in to it.

# CHAPTER FIFTEEN

$Q$uinn stepped out of the shower, dried himself off and picked up his razor for a quick shave. The trip had been very successful, the bull all it was advertised to be. Dinner last night had been nice too, with old friends from the rodeo circuit. He had no desire to go back to it, certainly not with the present changes in his life. But he liked the gossip as well as the next man. He only wished Selene could have been with him so he could show her off. Let people know about the magic that had come into Quinn Pedraza's life. During dinner, he'd imagined her sitting next to him, that slim, proprietary hand of hers sliding along his thigh as he kept his arm stretched along the back of her chair. As he turned his head, nuzzled her hair... Christ, he had it bad.

Tomorrow the bull would arrive at the ranch, so as soon as he'd landed on his property, Quinn had radioed Johnny and they'd spent the afternoon preparing for the delivery. The foreman knew exactly how much area to fence off and how big a stall they needed when the brute was inside. The ranch would be breeding a whole new strain of cattle from that big son-of-a-bitch.

A quick bite of dinner after that and he'd headed for the shower, anxious to see Selene.

He studied himself as he shaved, noting the restlessness that plagued him for so long had disappeared from his eyes. Buying the ranch and the bar had only partially assuaged it. It had taken Selene, with her ability to connect with him on so many levels, to help him understand who he really was and feel comfortable in life. The crazy thing was how quick it had happened, but she'd implied sometimes it could be that way for a human meant to be a vampire's servant.

He thought of Sam Red Elk, who'd said he'd find his life intertwined with "the otherworld". He'd guided Quinn out of the troubled, lost teen he'd been in a loud, violent household, yes, but if the old man hadn't opened his mind to the impossible, would Quinn have been able to accept Selene and what she was? He had no idea, but he figured he owed the old shaman, big time. He was glad that the After Hours had been her chosen stop on the highway.

Last night before he dropped off to sleep, he'd tried headtalking with her, but got no response. Twice. It made him a bit uneasy, but the bar had been extremely busy. He assumed she was swamped with work and couldn't take the time to chat. Chat! What a word for it. During the day he knew she was sleeping, but when he tried her again before he jumped into the shower he still got no response. He halfway convinced himself she was punishing him in fun for leaving her overnight. Making him all the more eager to see her. He grinned at the thought. Could be a vampire thing, but that was definitely a woman thing as well. And a Mistress thing. Anticipation coiled in him at the thought.

Okay, he'd see her in person soon enough. That was better.

As he reached for the watch he'd placed on the counter his gaze fell on that bite-shaped mark on his wrist, the brand of the third mark. It was his talisman, his comfort icon. He touched it often during the day while he worked, rubbing his thumb over it or brushing it with the tip of his forefinger. Every contact reinforced his connection with his incredible vampire. His Mistress.

*How did I get so goddamn lucky?*

When he looked at the watch he realized it was after seven o'clock. Selene would have the bar open for the evening and everything humming along with her usual efficiency. His plan had been to get there before she opened and catch a few minutes alone with her, but getting ready for the new bull had taken much longer than he expected. His cock reminded him how long it had been since he'd seen her.

*Oh yeah, a whole twenty-four hours. I'm getting to be a greedy son of a bitch.*

Maybe he'd put on those shiny briefs she insisted on bringing back from Butch's. Haul her upstairs and give her a surprise.

*I can't wait to see you.*

He frowned when there was no answer forthcoming. Fun was fun, but usually she'd respond to something like that. She liked it when he reached out during the early opening hours. She'd said it was her way of keeping tabs on him. Making sure he'd survived his work day and wasn't overdoing, spending all that energy she intended to drain throughout the night. The grin the thought would normally inspire couldn't quite make it to his lips.

*Mistress? Where are you? I miss you.*

Still no answer.

His gut twisted in a double knot. She would never block him unless she thought his being with her would bring him into danger. Had that sick fuck Laurent shown up while he was away and taken out his anger on her? No, Dix had told him Butch would give her a heads-up before he called Laurent. But suddenly Quinn wondered if something had happened, the timetable accelerated. What would she do if that happened? She'd try to protect him. Goddamn it. He was an idiot. What the hell had he been thinking? He'd been so caught up in that fucking bull, pretending his life was like it always was, predictable ups and downs, the only dangers out there those that came with working a ranch...

He wiped his face quickly and had just grabbed the briefs and his jeans when his cell phone rang. The readout said *After Hours.* He stabbed the Talk button.

"Selene?"

"No, boss, it's me." Manuel's voice. "I think you'd better get down here."

Quinn's entire body froze, a terrible foreboding slicing through him. "What's up? Where's Selene?" He could hear voices in the background, the sounds of the early evening crowd.

"Uh, that's it, boss. I was a little late getting here and the place wasn't even open yet. We had folks at the door pounding to get in."

"Not open?" *Bad. Very bad.* "Where's Selene?" Quinn's tone was sharper this time.

"She left me a note on a bar napkin that says she's sick and we should handle the business tonight. Maria's here but I think I should call Carol to come in too. That okay?"

Quinn squeezed the phone so hard he was afraid it might crack. *Sick? Vampires don't get sick. It's that bastard. I just know it.*

"It's just not like her, boss. I thought I should call you. We're kind of worried."

*Not alone in that.* Quinn yanked his jeans on one-handed over his bare skin and reached for a shirt. "You did the right thing. Call Carol and put Maria behind the bar. I'm on my way."

He shoved sockless feet into his boots, grabbed his keys and wallet and was in his truck in less than two minutes. *Whatever's happening, I'm on the way, Mistress. It's okay. I'm coming.*

He hoped she was hearing the message. And that she was where he suspected she'd go if she was in distress. If she wasn't there, he wasn't sure where he'd look. He'd go out of his mind.

He broke every speed limit getting to After Hours, pulling into the parking lot so fast his truck skidded sideways. Yanking out the keys, he ran across the lot and went in through the back entrance. He half hoped to see her in her office, but it was dark. He barreled toward the bar, barely managing to check himself in time to get under control. If this was as bad as he expected, Selene didn't need a maniac tending to her. Or alerting the others to what she was.

Carol spotted him as soon as he walked in and hurried over, carrying a tray full of empties.

"I don't know what's up, Quinn, but I think something's bad wrong with Selene. She never misses a night." She saw it in his face too, he was sure. Still, he put a hand on her arm in reassurance.

"You guys keep the place running. I'll go check on her. I'll take care of it." He hoped to Christ he could.

She wouldn't be in the upstairs apartment. She'd want the darkest place she could find. The converted storeroom at the back of the cellar.

The staff kept the cellar door locked except when pulling out supplies, but he had his keys. As he slipped the key into the lock and pushed it open, he concentrated, seeing if he could feel her in any way. She'd said that was a servant's skill that time would hone, until he'd be able to feel her nearby or in his mind before she said a word. Maybe he didn't have the skill yet, but he didn't feel her in any way. That worried him even more.

As he locked the door behind him, he noticed the bulb mounted to the right of the stairs had been broken, shards of glass on the top stair. The damn thing had always been in too low of a position, easy to hit with an armload of boxes. As he descended, he was thankful for those third mark senses that kept him from having to wait for his eyes to adjust to the darkness. He could make out the outline of the shelving and kegs like they were cast in pre-dawn light, a mostly dark-gray room.

He wasn't grateful for the smell of blood those enhanced senses brought him. At the bottom of the stairs, he found a small lump of clothing. Lifting it in his hands, he discovered bloodstained fabric, torn panties and bra. Her delicate, lacy things, worn to please him and please herself. His gut twisted like a vise. Spattered blood lay beyond them with her shoes, dropped along that chilling path. If such a blood trail was here, it should have been upstairs too, but the aged wood floor had been stained by so many spilled drinks and drunken brawls—before Selene came—it would have blended.

*Selene, fuck...*

He moved swiftly along the wall, already pulling out the right key. Thank God she hadn't pulled a Mistress move and made him give up the key to that little storeroom. He would have broken the damn door down regardless if needed, used that third mark strength to splinter it in its frame.

As he pushed open the door, he saw her immediately. Or rather, he saw the lump beneath the covers and inhaled her scent with his relieved breath. She was here. But that stale-blood scent was way too strong here. Emanating from his Mistress, who was so clean all the time.

He forced himself not to lunge at her. Instead, he approached the cot with soft footfalls and touched that lump, detecting her body beneath the fabric.

Her weak moan sliced into his heart. She had a lamp by the cot, and now he switched it on, seeing she had a scarf over it to keep it dim. She'd placed it there only a few days ago, romantic lighting.

The memory stabbed his gut. It was the first time she'd let him be with her here. Perhaps remembering the pleasure of sleeping with him at Butch's, she hadn't sent him away at the end of the night or left him upstairs. Instead, she'd brought him down here to make love once more, then sleep with her past dawn. Quinn hadn't risen until mid-morning to go back to the ranch, a rare luxury he couldn't resist. He'd brushed his lips over hers, stroked back her hair. Young vampires slept hard, she'd told him, and he'd seen the proof of it, because she barely stirred, but he'd felt a tendril of something inside her mind reach out to him, like a dreamlike caress.

He swallowed hard. Kneeling beside the bed, he drew the blanket back very gently. His stomach heaved at what he saw.

*Fucking shit. That bastard.*

Selene was on her side, facing the wall, and there wasn't an inch of her skin from nape to buttocks that wasn't marked, covered with blood. In the few spots where it had dripped away to the covers before it dried, leaving some skin exposed, he saw a pattern of dots crusted with blood, as if she'd been beaten with a dozen tiny knives. Pushing back the bile flooding his throat, he put his mouth close to her ear.

"I'm here, Mistress. I'll take care of you."

*And then I'll kill that fucker.*

As carefully as possible he lifted her, turned her over so she was facing him on the other side, keeping pressure off her abused back. She made a pitiful noise like a badly wounded animal, which told him she was still out of it. His Mistress had far too much pride to make such a noise. He'd go to the grave before ever telling her she'd made it.

The crusted blood was even thicker on her face, but not thick enough to hide the long cuts from a knife. Her nose was swollen and discharge from it had mingled with her blood. Forcing a calm he didn't feel, he managed to take inventory of her injuries, sickened by the moans she kept trying to stifle.

Then she reached out a weak hand, showing him she was aware of his presence. He took it in his large one, wrapping his fingers around it the way he'd handle anything delicate, breakable and unspeakably precious.

"I'm here, Mistress," he repeated. "I'm going to take care of you."

He'd never in his life had the genuine urge to take a man's life, but now it consumed him. He'd have to tamp it down until he saw to Selene, but then—

*No. Quinn, no. Just help me. That's all I need.*

The one eye was swollen shut, but the other focused on him, pleading. She was afraid, and he'd never seen her show fear. It was fear for him, damn it all.

It took every bit of discipline he had to lock away the thoughts in his head and make his mind a blank except for her needs.

*I* will *help you, Mistress.* He bowed his head and rested his forehead on her hip. *I will help you. Tell me how.*

*Blood...I need your blood. And then...it would be nice to be clean.*

He wanted to weep or snarl. He wanted to get on the bed and

hold her in his lap, let her nurse at his throat like a baby until she drained him dry, took every drop she needed, but he knew that would hurt her torn back. So he drew his pocket knife, flipped it open and cut his wrist, holding the artery under his thumb so every drop would belong to her. Then he set the knife aside and brought his wrist to her mouth, cradling the back of her head. She was so weak he had to shift his hold a bit, tease the corner of her mouth, paint some of the blood on her lips, her tongue. She pressed her lips together, tasting, and then they parted, seeking more.

He brought his wrist close again, tilting her head back so the blood now free flowing from his wrist would obey the laws of gravity and just trickle into her mouth. Some of the tightness in his gut loosened when she finally swallowed. Her lips molded around the wound, and he felt the play of her tongue over his skin as she started to actively feed. A little moan escaped her again, as if the first active taste was so critical it almost added to her pain. He kept his big hand supporting her head, his fingers stroking the strands of blood-stiffened hair from her face.

Those tiny bites that had taken her skin had to be made with a whip. Something with multiple barbed tips. The face was clearly knife work. Her dress was torn down the front, such that it was more of a loose wrap than clothing, one sleeve off her shoulder, the front gaping open to show the curves of her breasts, also stained with blood.

Had Laurent done worse to her? Anguish and rage flooded him at the thought. This was the world she inhabited? Where a fucking overlord was allowed to torture and rape her? His mind worked at a hundred ways they could escape such a life, such a world, but she'd made it clear that wasn't an option. You learned how to survive it, enjoy the times that weren't about this. That's what she'd said. But right now all he could think about was whether it had taken all sixty-two of her years to reach that level of acceptance, because he sure as hell wasn't there with it.

She made a noise as if picking up on his agitation, and he

tamped it down again. He reminded himself of the lesson she'd taught him, over and over. Focus on serving her, caring for her, and let everything else go. For now. He wasn't the type of man who could let it go unanswered forever. Right or wrong, he knew that about himself.

As his gaze roved over her face, it stilled there. The cuts still crusted with blood were less angry-looking than they'd been a few minutes before.

*I will heal completely, cowboy. It will simply take a day's deep sleep after I feed. We're resilient that way.*

*But how did you heal the heart and soul when it was torn apart by such brutality? Did blood help with that?*

*No. You holding me does.*

He met her gaze, her blue eyes beautiful to him even with streaked makeup and one closed by the swollen flesh around it. "I don't want to hurt your back," he rumbled.

She shook her head, a denial of that, and closed her eyes, a silent reinforcement of what she wanted. He didn't want to disrupt her feeding, but she lifted her mouth from his skin herself, licking her lips. She'd closed the wound for him as she always did, a courtesy that made his throat ache. When she opened her eyes this time, he saw the swollen eye was now visible, the tissues less engorged over her cheekbone. Bolstered by the further evidence of her healing, he did what she wanted. Though he lifted her like porcelain, he sat down on the bed, bracing himself against the wall and settling her into the cradle of his lap. She let out a soft noise of relief so strong those unmanly tears came to his eyes again. He fought them back, focused on tending her.

This time she did lift her mouth to his throat, and he was ready for her. Her fangs cut against his flesh, a jagged and painful strike, not her usual precise, quick penetration. When she made a frustrated noise, he figured it out quick. Cupping his hand around the back of her head again, he gave her the pressure strength she needed and the fangs broke through, sinking into the artery, her lips sealing over his flesh.

He banded the other arm around her, holding her, trying not to squeeze when all he wanted was to hold her so tightly and never let her go.

She drank until he was feeling lightheaded, but he wouldn't have said a word if she'd drained him dry. She eventually sensed it and started to withdraw, but he tightened his hold on her head. "Take everything you need, Selene," he said roughly. "I can handle it."

"I know you can," she murmured against his skin. "But that should be enough for now. Just hold me, Quinn. And...forgive me. Don't speak for a bit, all right?"

Hearing her speak aloud was a gift, but his brow creased, uncertain of her meaning or why she was apologizing. Then it became clear. She started to shake, badly. And cry.

She buried her face in his throat, not wanting him to see. She could let him see where that bastard had hit her, but she was ashamed of tears. Even though she'd held fast through all of it, he realized. Not trusting herself to let it go until now, when he held her.

It amazed him, broke his heart. It also told him just how much he loved her. Because of that he let himself trust her and cried a little himself. While holding her, rocking her, murmuring to her in a broken tone, telling her he was there.

At length, the shaking started to recede, and her sobs became more muffled. She let out a deep, shuddering sigh.

"I'd really like a bath, Quinn. And a change of clothes."

He wanted to do that for her too. Damn it, there was no way from the cellar to the upstairs apartment except through the office entrance or that hallway, and that required walking through the bar.

"It's all right," she said. "We'll stay here until they close."

The bar wouldn't close for hours. "Yeah, we will. But we're closing now."

"No. You need the money and the customers..."

"Thought we talked about this long ago." He touched her chin, gave her his best attempt at a stern look. "You may be the boss of me after quitting time, but when this bar's open, I'm the boss. The boss says we're closing early."

He eased her back to the blanket, humbled when her hands tightened on him, an involuntary sign of her not wanting him to leave her. "I'll be right back, Mistress. Promise."

It said a great deal that she didn't argue further, lying limp on the mattress in the way that drunks did, as if they were boneless. The comparison didn't reassure him. Kissing her hand, he folded it back against her. It took an act of will to go, but he strode through the cellar, went upstairs and locked the door firmly behind him. Taking a breath, he squared his shoulders and went to find Manuel.

Thirty minutes later, every customer was out of the bar, with the excuse that it was a family emergency. There was some grumbling from non-regulars, but getting their meal and drinks on the house helped. As did the regulars, bless their rowdy hearts, who helped him shepherd them out. He reassured Manuel, Carol and Maria in low tones that all was well, but that Selene needed quiet tonight. It said a great deal for their regard for Selene that they were far more concerned about her well-being and helping him with anything she needed than a work night cut short.

It didn't matter though. He knew he'd pay them for their time that night as if they'd worked the full shift. Loyalty deserved that. Selene would agree. She'd probably bitch about the revenue they'd lost tonight, but he'd look forward to that spirited argument when she was back on her feet.

Once he had the door locked and the shades pulled, he went back to get her. She hadn't moved, in the kind of somnolent doze she usually only demonstrated right before dawn. But when he lifted her, she wound an arm around his neck, let out that little relieved sigh again, like he was her fucking savior instead of the guy who'd gotten here way too late.

*You couldn't have changed this, Quinn. It's over.* The lopsided smile looked like it pained her. *He had two of his territory vampires with him, and Claudio, his servant. Otherwise I would have taken him.*

*Yeah, you would have kicked his ass all the way back to the Statue of Liberty.* He wanted to howl when he looked at her.

The worst thing was, it was only over if the Region Masters decided in her favor. Right then and there he realized if they didn't, he'd leave everything behind, do everything needed to help her run, hide. If they couldn't run and hide... His jaw tightened. He'd go back with her to New York. No matter what she'd worked out with Butch, Quinn would be at her side through anything she needed, no matter how horrible it got, and they'd figure out how to get away from Laurent again, another way.

So many times, he'd questioned why he felt so strongly for her so quickly, but in the end it didn't really matter, did it? It was the way he felt, and it wasn't changing, even in the face of all this shit.

He carried her up the stairs. Though her petite body had that dense weight thing happening that always surprised him, tonight she weighed nothing to him. He'd have carried her to the ends of the earth. If anything, it was like his feelings had expanded and grown three times since he saw her crumpled on that cot.

Setting her down on a towel on a chair in the bathroom, he started running the bath. Once it was warm enough, he stripped off all her clothes gingerly, steeling himself for what else he might see. There was blood on her thighs, but as he ran the pad of his thumb over her mound, he realized it came from a cut over it.

"He didn't...they didn't..." He was kneeling before her, and she reached out a hand quivering from physical stress, trailed it along his face. "They didn't do any of that."

He let out a breath he didn't realize he'd been holding. On top of everything else, if that bastard had raped her—violated his Mistress—he'd never be able to contain his rage. "I know it's stupid, given what else they did..."

"No it's not. I felt the same way when I was afraid...that he might. One is less...personal, if that makes sense. I didn't want him where...I only want you." Her face creased with a personal pain. "Christ, I'm a terrible vampire. The things I say to you, vampires aren't supposed to say to humans."

"Your secret's safe with me," he managed, his heart clenching.

She nodded, lifting her arms in mute appeal. Rising, he scooped her up, lowered her into the tub. Taking up the softest cloth he could find, he began to sponge her off, finding he had to hold her steady with one hand while he did it, like bathing a baby that couldn't hold itself up. She leaned against him, laid her cheek on his opposite shoulder. As he removed the blood from her back, he revealed that pattern of pinpoints, but also saw they were the first thing healing because of their size, many of them disappearing. He shifted her to do her face with another clean cloth, and found the slices there and on her breasts were closed and diminished as well.

*They'll all be gone by morning. A good nap solves everything...* She let out a snuffled sound, somewhere between a sob and a chuckle. He held her again, bending his head protectively over her, heedless of his sleeves getting soaked with blood-tinted water. She noticed though, her fingers moving to the buttons, fumbling it until he took over, shrugging the shirt off his broad shoulders so her hands could play over his skin, fingertips digging into his flesh as if reassuring herself he was really there. He let the water drain out, refilled it, keeping her warm with his arms around her until the clean water helped with that again.

The tub was just a small thing for the efficiency apartment, not big enough for them both, else he wouldn't have quelled the temptation to get in there with her. But she solved that one as well, lifting long-lashed blue eyes to focus on him, since the one eye had improved enough she could use both again.

"I'm strong enough for a shower now. I want you with me."

He doubted that first part, but if he was in there with her, he could help prop her up if a shower was what she wanted. Nodding, he guided her hands to the tub edge to ensure she had something to hold on to. Rising, he stripped off everything. As she lifted her hands to him, he stepped in, drew her to her feet. She curled her hands around his waist, her cheek on his chest, as he adjusted the water, held the spray away from her until the shower heated. Then he let the water stream down on her.

She tilted her head back, eyes closed, still holding on to him. He framed her face, kissed her cheeks gently, her forehead, her closed eyes, even as the spray made him close his own. His thumbs slid over the knife scars. In some way it seemed obscene that they were disappearing, as if Laurent's brutality could be dismissed so easily.

He ran his hands over her, sluicing off the remaining blood. When she indicated she wanted him to wash her, he lathered up his hands with her fragrant soap, the one with a honey vanilla smell, and washed her thoroughly. He had no intentions of anything sexual at all. She could arouse him with nothing more than a look, but all he wanted to do was care for her. She had other ideas.

As she turned to lean back against him, letting him soap her front, she molded her hands over his as he ran them over her breasts, keeping them there, kneading. She rotated her hips against his cock and the mindless thing immediately responded, starting to harden. "Selene..."

"I need you, Quinn. Make him go away. Drive him from my head. From every part of me."

As she rubbed herself against him, something surged up in him. That rage he'd tamped down to care for her asserted itself in a glorious, territorial haze. He hated that Laurent had hurt her, hated that he'd touched her, torn off her clothes. And more, he felt something deep inside her that matched his rage. Fury of her own. Fury at her helplessness, that she couldn't control that situation or this one, that her fate was out of her hands, his proud Mistress who simply wanted to be free to command her own destiny.

He couldn't be rough with her, but he sensed she wasn't seeking that. He crowded her face forward against the steam-slick shower wall, pulling her hair to the side to kiss her neck, nip at her ear.

Still cradling her breasts, he teased the nipples with his fingers, pressing his cock to her ass. She made a pleasurable sigh, a tremulous thing, her eyes shutting more tightly. He saw her throat move as she swallowed and he wondered if it had a hard ache like what was stuck in his own. Turning her to face him, he put his hands to her waist, lifted her, adjusting his cock so it slid without any resistance into her tight channel, slick and ready for him. She stared at him, the one eye almost fully healed. Her fangs showed, and he kissed them, let her scrape at his mouth as he tangled his fist in her hair, held her, pushed easy inside her as her legs lifted, locked over his waist.

*Yes, Quinn. Fuck me. Make me forget. Let me be who I am with you, even if I can't be that with anyone else. I'm safe inside your heart. They can't change that.*

Everything inside him broke open at that, and he thrust into her, deeper, trying to get all the way to her soul. The clasp of her arms, the clutch of her fingers, her breath on his neck, told him he might already be there. God, she felt so good. Her nails dug in, telling him she needed to feel his demand. But she wasn't guarding her mind so much now, another indication of her weakness that helped him restrain himself, slow down and be even more tender, the kiss drawing out into a nuzzling of lips, causing her to sigh into his mouth. He had the honor of her trusting him to take her all the way home, relying on his strength to move them together, work her up to climax. He held his own back. He hadn't been there for her. He didn't deserve any pleasure. She deserved it all.

The climax was a trembling, near-miss kind of thing that just made it over the pinnacle, hampered by her physical state, but he relished the glazing in her eyes, that immersion in the sensations that took her away for just a moment from what had happened. She was weak and shuddering in his arms afterward, making him wonder if she needed more blood. He'd already recovered from what she'd taken earlier. He'd never been so glad of the rejuvenating power of being a full servant.

"I might need a little more," she agreed. "Let's go back to the downstairs bed."

"Okay." After making sure she was all clean and rinsed, he switched off the shower and carried her out to the chair, wrapping her in a big towel before drying himself and pulling on his jeans. When he sought some clean linens for her cot, she watched him with those mysterious blue eyes. He'd left his shirt off and, as he moved back and forth in the small bathroom, her fingertips trailed over his bare skin.

"You didn't come," she said.

"No, Mistress." He gave her a wry smile. "You didn't say I could."

She studied him as he lifted her again. The fact she didn't say she could walk on her own told him she was still too worn out. The anger was back and a lot of other things too, unleashed by that tender moment. He should be glad for what he could be for her right now, but the alpha male in him couldn't rest with that. Damn it, he had to do something. He couldn't just be here to pick up the pieces.

"Quinn." Her voice was a caress against his throat as her arms slid around his neck again, holding him as he carried her back down the stairs, through the bar and to the cellar once more. Setting her in the chair she had beside the cot, he made up the bed, kicking the blood-soaked covers and blankets aside, probably with more passion than was necessary. Once she was asleep, he'd get a mop and clean up the blood spatter, get rid of those clothes, so she'd wake in an environment that didn't show the violence that had been done to her.

He guessed there was no way he could hide the shift in his emotional tide, but fortunately she seemed to be dozing again, thank God. He tucked her in, but as he began to slide away, her hand latched on to his arm.

"Stay."

"I'm not leaving, Mistress. I just want to get these sheets out of here where you don't have to see them."

Her eyes opened, focused on his face. He sensed her delving even deeper and wished he could block his thoughts the way she could. The way she had. Fuck, she'd been going through this while he was checking out a damn bull, having drinks with his buddies...

"What would you have done if you were here?" she said softly.

It was a harsh kick to the balls, one that made him step back. "Apparently nothing you think would be of use," he said tightly. Bending, he picked up the sheets, balling them up in his arms. He took several steps away from her, fully intending to take them up to the laundry room and stay there until he could get himself under control. He made it five steps before he drop-kicked them against the wall and spun around.

"Damn it, Selene, you should have reached out to me."

"And watch Laurent kill you in front of me?" She pushed herself up with obvious effort, though her eyes had gone cold as polar cap snow. "Is that what your testosterone demands?"

"It's what you need and want that matters."

"No, obviously not. Not if you're more focused on what happened yesterday than what's happening right now." She put her hand on the clean sheets. "This is what I needed from you. You can't control what happens between vampires. I have precious little control of it myself. What I need is a safe port, Quinn."

"Someone who keeps your heart safe. Not your body."

"Yes," she said harshly. "In my world, finding someone who keeps your heart safe is a far more difficult task, believe it or not. I'm sixty-two and you're the first I've found up to the task."

That brought him up short. That and the broken note in her voice, despite her lifted chin and eyes shooting sparks at him. If she wasn't so obviously exhausted, her gaze said she was ready to tie him up and beat him herself. Then he imagined Laurent doing that to her, only with far less pleasurable results than he'd experienced at her hands. His rage descended into a frustration so raw and jagged he felt like he was being torn open from the inside.

He came to her, knelt by the bed, framed her face in his hands.

"How can I be who I'm not, Mistress? How can I care for you if I can't protect you?"

His grandfather had taught him that it was a man's responsibility to protect and defend women. To always treat them with the greatest respect. The absolute opposite of everything he saw when he looked into her battered face.

Her mouth softened and she touched his face in return. "You care for me in the very way you are, Quinn. That's what I need. Trust me to know how to handle certain things until you can figure them out."

He sighed, put his forehead against hers. They stayed that way a bit, then he realized her arm was shaking. With a quiet oath, he eased her back down. "I'm sorry. You don't need to deal with my crap. You need more blood, right?"

"Later. Just lie with me right now. Sleep with me. Do laundry later." A faint, humorless smile touched her lips. "The smell of blood doesn't bother vampires. Promise me you won't leave me until dawn. Stay with me until I'm really asleep."

"I promise." He got into the narrow cot with her, folding her in his arms, her backside nestled up against him. She gave him a playful little rub, reminding him his cock was still unassuaged, but he didn't care about that. Not right now.

*Good. Because I may keep you suffering for a while for yelling at your Mistress.*

He made his lips pull into a stiff smile and brushed a kiss over her temple. Since he could feel that lassitude pulling her down toward slumber again, he rocked them both, humming to her in an off-tune, meandering way, just old campfire songs, things to soothe them both. Her pulse slowed, her breathing changing to an even rhythm.

"Promise..." she breathed.

He didn't know what she was asking him to promise. That he wouldn't leave her until dawn, or something different, but he knew what to answer.

"I promise."

Wasn't that what it boiled down to in the end? An open-ended, blank check between two people meant to be together. *I promise to be whatever you need, love you endlessly, never let you down.*

He knew she'd been trying to tell him he hadn't failed her, but in his world, no one treated a woman like that and got away with it. Laurent wasn't going to be the exception, even if he was a goddamn vampire.

Though Quinn relished holding her, he also chafed at the time. But Laurent had to go to ground as well, right? Every vampire movie Quinn had ever seen said that was when he'd be most vulnerable. That was when Selene was the most vulnerable, after all, and why she holed up here behind a locked door.

When he finally slipped out of her arms, it was a couple hours past dawn, the time when she was in that deep sleep from which only dusk would wake her. Adjusting the blankets over her, he stroked her hair from her face. She was completely out of it, a deep, restorative slumber. Which worked better for his purposes, as insane as they might be. But then a man who put himself on the back of an animal that outweighed him ten times knew a few tricks. He didn't rely on strength as much as smarts and quickness, anticipating what his opponent might do. That's what he'd do here.

First up was getting some intel on this particular bull. Once he was in his truck and well away from the saloon, he pulled off to the side of the road, took a few deep breaths and called up Dix.

"Mornin'," Dix drawled. "Miss us already?"

Under other circumstances, Quinn might have struggled with a response. Figuring out how the typical male razzing worked with a guy who'd had his mouth on your dick like a vacuum hose—all while getting his own brains fucked out by his Master—presented a unique challenge. However, today Quinn had other concerns than managing his own paradigm shifts. "Have the Region Masters come to a decision?"

"They said they'd let Butch know by tonight. Any sign of Laurent?"

"Yeah. Big time." Weighing the pros and cons of it, he nevertheless let Dix know in bald terms how he'd found Selene. Dix let out a curse.

"Son of a fucking bitch. Goddamn, Quinn. I'm sorry. I don't think Butch had any clue he'd be that sadistic of a fuck. Usually they show a little more restraint, especially since she's an asset to his territory."

"Apparently him proving he's not going to be made a fool is way more important to him. So Butch knew he was coming?" He might just have two overlords to kill.

"He suspected Laurent might try to confront her ahead of time, get his licks in before a decision is made. He warned Selene like he promised, offered her sanctuary at the house, which she refused. So he figured if Laurent showed, he might be a bit heavy-handed, but...damn, Quinn. He had no idea. He's not going to be happy about this."

"Well his happiness is at the top of my too little, too damn late list."

"Quinn." Dix's tone of warning was expected, but it was more than that which had Quinn reining back further venom. Dix's genuine regret on his Master's behalf reminded Quinn that Selene still had an ally they couldn't alienate. He let another, even more important worry rise to the top. "Did I do everything she needed? Does she need anything other than blood?" Anything other than someone capable of defending her? He pushed that jagged feeling down viciously.

"No, you did good. It's horrible and miraculous at once, how much of a beating they can take and heal up. The day me and Butch tussled with the bull, that asshole threw me out of the way and took a horn right in his gut, pinned him against the fence. Would have killed a human, but he took a good draught of my blood, about a day's worth of sleeping like the dead, and didn't even have a scar to brag about. That kind of pissed him off."

The fond affection in Dix's voice might have amused Quinn on a good day. Today wasn't that day.

"So she should be fully restored if she gets a good deep sleep." If she was completely oblivious to his doings, all the better.

"Should do."

"Will Laurent stay in the area until a decision is made, or is she expected to go back to him under her own steam if it's ruled in his favor?"

"She could, but I expect if he cared enough to come down and do that, he's somewhere in the area, waiting for the decision so he can take her home if it goes his way. But—" Dix broke off abruptly. "You're not asking on your Mistress's behalf."

"What gave it away?" Quinn bared his teeth.

"Okay, no bullshit now. I need you to listen up, Quinn." Dix's deadly serious tone was sharp enough to catch Quinn's divided attention. "Listen and listen good. You go after a vampire, there is no upside to that. He'll kill you and give your life as much thought as you spitting toothpaste in the sink. Though from what you've told me about him, he'll take particular pleasure in it, because he'll know it's another way to hurt her."

That last part gave Quinn, pause, but then he remembered seeing her bloody face, the torn skin of her back. "What happens if I kill him?"

"You won't. Damn it, Quinn, you're pissed off, I get it. But you're so new to this world. Going up against a vampire isn't like some heroic David and Goliath story. There are a handful of vampire hunters out there, and very few of them have any kind of success. Even those who do don't have long life spans. No need for a retirement plan in that profession."

*Vampire hunters?* So Selene could have human enemies he'd have to watch out for? He'd file that away to deal with another time and focus on the part of that he could use. "But some have managed it."

"Yeah. With exceptional talents for subtlety and surprise, capital ET. No offense, but you sound as if you're in about as subtle a mood as a Sherman tank. A vampire is about ten times stronger than a human and, if you hadn't noticed, they're faster than cars at top speed when they want to be. There are only a couple ways to take them out, a stake or decapitation, and neither of them is easy to pull off. Got it?"

"They experience pain the way we do though. It slows them down."

"Yeah, it can."

"I wasn't asking. I just found my Mistress in a blood-soaked bed, her skin torn to shreds. I saw firsthand."

"You should keep focusing on her care. Stay at her side, Quinn. Trust me. That's the best thing you can do for her." Dix blew out a breath. "I know you're not fucking listening to me. But promise me you'll remember one thing."

"What's that?"

"The most important thing a servant can do for his vampire is serve them. It means a lot more than bringing them a drink or having sex with them. I saw the connection between the two of you. You were starting to get everything that word means. Part of it is sometimes putting away what your gut tells you to do so you can fulfill the most vital part of serving them."

Quinn didn't want to hear it, but he bit out the words. "And that is?"

"Staying alive," Dix said bluntly. Then he cut the connection.

Quinn put the phone down. For a few brief seconds, he sat in the truck, staring at the empty road, the open land around him. In the distance he could see cattle grazing. His hands would already have been up a couple hours, their day well started. He longed to be out working the cattle today, feeling the simple pleasures of sweat and hard work. Anticipating the pleasure of a butterfly landing light on his hat, fluttering around his face so close she sometimes brushed his lashes with her wings.

But today he had other things that had to be done. The hands knew how to manage without him when needed. They knew what was expected of them.

As far as what was expected from a servant, Dix had been pretty damn clear about that. Quinn was supposed to sit on his thumbs and do nothing except clean the blood off his Mistress. But Quinn couldn't do that. He couldn't get past it, couldn't not act. The whole world would be better without this bastard in it. He'd never taken a man's life, never even contemplated such a thing, but there was a code a man lived by, and standing back when some bastard beat the ever-loving shit out of the woman he loved wasn't part of it.

So where would a vampire who believed New York City was the center of the universe decide to stay? He'd compromise his standards big time, staying anywhere in Nightfall, but he'd want to stay close to Selene. Because of his age, he'd be like Butch, not needing to be underground in daylight, but he'd need a place where his privacy was guaranteed, where he could make it full dark during the day. There weren't a great many hotels around Nightfall that would work for that, but Quinn could think of one location that was ideal.

He clicked open his phone again, looked up information. After the operator put the number through, the phone rang several times. Just when Quinn was about to curse, the line picked up, an older man with a smoker's growl answering.

"Morning, Don," he said, with a casualness he didn't feel in the least. "I figured you'd be minding the desk early. Hey, did you rent out one of your cabins to a fellow out of New York? Yeah, I have some business to conduct with him and I thought he mentioned your place, but I dropped his darn card while working yesterday and wanted to make sure I had the right place to look him up..."

It was a long shot, but his instincts had been sound. His fingers tightened on the phone as Don verified that four men meeting that description had checked in under the name Claudio Beringer. They'd rented two of Don's cabins.

After he concluded the call, Quinn put the truck in drive and headed for Last Chance, his mind whirling. There were four of them, but three were vampires. They had to sleep during the day. Ironically, Claudio would be his biggest danger. He remembered how much stronger Dix had been, the benefit of him being a third mark longer, but he also remembered what Dix had said about the vampire hunters who had succeeded.

Skill, subtlety. Cunning.

As dumb as it sounded, since he was connected to a vampire himself, he wished he knew the number for one of those hunters to get more input, but he'd figure this out. Yeah, he preferred the Sherman tank method, but he could do the unexpected. If it increased his chances for success, he'd become the most cunning bastard that ever lived. Laurent had weaknesses. Sunlight. Arrogance.

His mind full of ideas, he accelerated. He had to get some things from the ranch, get off property without Annette giving him the third degree and be onto Don's property as soon as possible. Daylight was burning.

# CHAPTER SIXTEEN

"They rented the ones on the far end of the property, Quinn," Don had said. "You can get there from the service road I use for the landscape maintenance, save you having to take the main drive."

Even with planning, he'd have to think on his feet, adapt to whatever situation he found when he got there. Laurent liked having an entourage, being the head guy. So would he share his space with the other three? Quinn was pretty certain he wouldn't bed down with two vampires he considered his underlings.

Again, Claudio was the wild card. Would Laurent want his servant near while he slept, or would he relegate him to sleeping with the others?

A vampire might keep his servant in the same room to watch his back during daylight, particularly in a new environment. Or would he? He didn't see Laurent having the same relationship with Claudio that Quinn had with Selene. If Laurent figured there was little danger to a vampire here in the middle of Nowhere, Texas, and the door could be bolted to keep out maid service, maybe he'd want to underscore Claudio's underling status by having him stay in the cabin next door. After all, Claudio could just as easily keep a daylight lookout out the window over there.

Quinn remembered how he'd been given a second room at Butch's, connected to Selene's, leaving her the choice to make him sleep elsewhere.

In some ways he'd been sorry to hear about the two-cabin setup, because he'd love to take out the whole bunch. But he wasn't a complete testosterone-driven moron. He'd heard what Dix said. Taking out one wasn't going to be easy, so it needed to be the right one. His specific bloodlust for Laurent aside, everyone knew the head of the snake was the most important part.

Don's info about the service road had given him the idea for his approach, which was good, because in this part of the world there wasn't a lot of thick tree cover for stealth. He'd thrown some tools into the back of the truck, changed into a serviceable T-shirt and jeans. He looked for all the world like a contractor hired to do maintenance.

As he bumped down the dirt and gravel access road, the cabins came into view, the early afternoon sunlight limning the rustic buildings. He stopped about a hundred yards from them. The cabins were spaced about that same distance apart. The two rental vehicles parked between them supported his theory about Laurent's belief in class division. One was a black Suburban, the kind of thing you'd have your hired men drive to look intimidating and official. The other was a luxury Mercedes. He'd probably had Claudio do the driving while he rode in back. What an asshole.

Getting out of his truck, Quinn moved to the open bed and took his time pulling tools out of it before sauntering to the fence line. In a few minutes he'd started work on replacing the predictably rotted section of split railing that formed a dubious aesthetic border between the properties. Don wasn't known for keeping up with grounds maintenance.

Hearing the door to one cabin open, he glanced up. Since the olive-skinned, golden-eyed man stepping out was doing so into full sunlight, he deduced this was Claudio.

"Mornin'," Quinn drawled. "Hope I didn't wake you, sir. Just had to get this fence post replaced before the boss drove me crazy about it."

Claudio had stopped, was studying him closely without saying a word. His tawny-brown eyes were flat as gold coins, as steady as a special ops military vet with a side dose of sociopath. A spear of trepidation shot through Quinn as he abruptly remembered Selene had said both vampires and servants could detect the scent of another vampire. Could Claudio detect the third marking? Or just her scent?

"If you're staying in town long," he added casually, gauging the depth he needed to sink the fence post, "I'd highly recommend the After Hours Saloon. The bar manager and waitresses there are awful pretty to look at, and they serve good food and drinks at reasonable prices. I was just there last night. Damn near had to throw me out at closing, because I never wanted to leave."

Claudio's expression eased, and Quinn bit back a sigh of relief. Giving him the impression he'd brushed up against Selene had helped.

"At the moment, I'm looking for something close by where I can go grab a fast breakfast," the man said.

Right. Claudio had to eat, and Don's fifty acres of rustic cabin retreats didn't offer room service. Don would scoff at the mere idea.

Quinn suppressed a fist pump. Not only was he getting rid of the one person who could handle sunlight, but if Laurent felt comfortable enough to let Claudio go seek his breakfast, that made it even more likely he'd had him bunk down with the other two vampires.

"That would be Elaine's. No more than a couple miles up the road." Quinn nodded in that general direction. "Stay away from the Southwestern omelet. Give you gas for days."

Claudio had no reaction to that. He obviously wasn't much on talking. As Quinn pulled the old post free, he started whistling, ostensibly paying attention to nothing more than the job he'd been hired to do. Thank God he was familiar enough with Don's property to know what might need repair, because when he pulled up the post the base was so rotted it crumbled.

Since he could sense Claudio still watching him, Quinn lifted his head.

"Looks like he let this go way too long, doesn't it?" he said, as if he thought Claudio was just watching him work out of idle curiosity. He took pride in his ability to maintain a casual façade while rage boiled furiously inside him. Claudio had stood by while Laurent tortured Selene, probably even helped. Quinn wanted to wrap his hands around the servant's throat, choke him until his eyes bulged, then force him to drag his Master out into the light that was so damaging to him. But getting him out of the way would better help him accomplish his real purpose.

*When a vampire dies, the servant dies.* Remembering Selene's words, he knew if he took out Laurent, he'd have the satisfaction of killing Claudio at the same time. The most violence Quinn had ever indulged toward another human being had been a barroom brawl. He'd been in a few of those, and most ended with all of them sharing a beer. Killing a man was something a man did only if there was no other choice. But he'd never come home to find someone he loved mangled almost beyond recognition, by men who then checked into a hotel and contemplated breakfast the next day as if it meant nothing. As if she meant nothing.

To his way of thinking, the moment Laurent had raised a hand to Selene, he'd decided to die. Quinn was just going to help him on his way.

Seemingly satisfied, Claudio made a noncommittal noise and moved toward the Mercedes. Quinn returned to his work, not looking up as Claudio got into the full-size luxury rental car, turned the engine over and pulled away on the gravel drive.

Quinn kept working a good five minutes more, even though every part of him was screaming to move, move, *move.*

He studied the two cabins out of the corner of his eye. There was still a chance he could be wrong, but as sharp-witted as Claudio had seemed, there was no way Quinn could have risked asking more pointed questions. Either way, Quinn had the advantage now. The three in those cabins, whatever their distribution, couldn't survive sunlight.

He'd stayed at Don's a couple times when he was with a one-night stand from town he didn't really want to take to his home and risk Annette's disapproving frown in the morning. While he wasn't proud of those lonely couplings, he was glad of it now, because he knew Don hadn't changed the layout of the cabins in years. It was basically a kitchen unit, a sitting area, the bed and a TV. The curtains were thick and could be drawn to keep out the light and heat, but both cabins had east-facing front windows. Big ones, a whole three-set panel.

Quinn went back to his truck, pulled out the items he needed and strode back up the walkway. As he closed in on the cabin Claudio hadn't exited, the slouching saunter of a contractor disappeared from his gait. He tuned out everything, just like when he was about to put his ass on the back of a bull. He focused all his energy on his strength, his wits, his unwavering belief that he could and would make those eight seconds count.

He didn't let himself think about what he was about to do, about how far it was from everything he'd always been. This was for Selene. All he had to do was remember her crumpled form and, even more, remember how she'd asked his forgiveness for getting all shaky and weepy in his arms. He approached the cabin with stealth, keeping an eye out just in case Claudio returned early. His footfalls were nearly silent, like when he approached a crazed cow trapped in wiry bushes. All his senses were on high alert. He tried to blank out everything but the task at hand, but by the time he reached the front of the cabin, all he saw was red, and all he felt was that fury again. He'd ride it like he used to ride those bulls, and hang on for well over eight seconds.

Hefting the hoe he'd brought, he jammed it into the window, breaking the glass, making a wide sweeping motion with the handle to clear a hole with it before he reached in and tore out the blinds and curtains. He moved fast and smooth, like he did when bringing down a calf. No hesitation, no looking until he jumped back and hefted the other thing he'd brought from the truck. A repeating rifle.

He saw the movement inside as the sun blasted through, a shadow that moved fast from the bed, headed for a corner, but he could only go so far. Quinn fired into that corner and, sure enough, luck was with him. The shadow hit the corner at the moment the bullet did, spinning the vampire around. Quinn kept firing, advancing on the window, making that shadow jerk again and again. A snarl of pain reached his ears that sounded more like savage lion than man.

As the male dropped to a knee, Quinn was standing right in front of the window. He swung himself over the sill with one lithe movement, flipping the hoe so he led with the jagged end he'd broken ahead of time. In another two strides, he was upon the bleeding male. He saw the flash of fangs, the crimson light in his eyes as the vampire surged up from the floor, but he was weakened, stumbling. Intending to take advantage of that forward momentum, Quinn seized the back of his neck to shove him right onto the business end of that hoe handle.

Then pain exploded in his head and the world went dark.

"Wake up." The sharp order came with an equally sharp reinforcement. His cock and balls were in agony, his ass on fire.

Quinn lifted his head. The screaming ache in his shoulders told him his feet were off the ground even before the rest of his stretched body did. In the moonlight he could make out several men watching him. His wrists were tied to the top rail of the five-slat fence, his ankles to the lowest rung of it, all of him off the ground, his waist and chest bound to the middle slats rails with no regard for circulation or comfort. Nothing like Selene might have done it, with the intent being restraint for mutual pleasure.

He was stripped naked though, his nether regions out there

dangling in a terrifying way. No, not dangling. All of a sudden, he realized why it felt like his cock and balls were wrapped up in barbed wire. They fucking were. Blood crusted the tender flesh. He couldn't stop twitching because on top of that, his ass felt like acid had been poured down inside of it. He convulsed against the pain just as he felt the hands pulling away from him, finishing whatever they'd just shot into it to wake him up.

Making the nightmare even worse, whatever they'd put in there made his cock start to harden against those sharp edges. He snarled, bit back a cry of pain. Even if he swallowed his tongue, he wouldn't give them the satisfaction. Especially not to the male standing about six feet in front of him eyeing his cock and balls like he was considering having them for dinner.

Fuck. This was Laurent. If the Gucci shoes and expensive haircut hadn't told him that, the air of Prince of Darkness and malevolent satisfaction in his expression would have. But beneath that was a chilling level of rage.

Yeah, Quinn had guessed wrong about the cabins, because this wasn't the vampire he'd nearly staked. But he'd still done damage, gotten closer than a puny human was supposed to. Which meant the Prince of Darkness was majorly pissed.

They'd knocked him out hard. Or maybe they'd kept knocking him out until night fell and they could arrange to display his body like a side of beef in front of their overlord. He was still feeling dizzy and nauseous, and had an odd craving for Selene's blood, as if it would be a tonic for the pain. Maybe her blood restored his health the way his could hers. Something to ponder when he had more time, though he had a feeling his future was very much in doubt.

Christ. That burning in his ass accelerated, and his cock swelled to an even thicker size. He bit down on his tongue to keep from crying out even more, but he couldn't keep himself from writhing, even as his nausea increased at the obvious sexual pleasure his discomfort was causing his enemy. Laurent was sporting an erection under those nicely tailored slacks.

As horrible as the pain was, Quinn found his gut cramping even more at having his sexual responses turned against him. He didn't even want to think what ultimate purpose Laurent would have for that.

"It was a credible plan," Laurent observed, his dark eyes lifting to lock on Quinn's face as it contorted with pain, as his body writhed in the bonds. "When Claudio returned to find how you'd disturbed Mike and Ernesto's rest, he thought you might be a vampire hunter, but once I took a nice long whiff, I could smell her all over you. Little Selene finally took a servant. She sent him to try to assassinate me."

*Oh Christ.* "She didn't. She didn't know." It might be futile, but Quinn coughed the words out on an ash dry throat.

"Hmm. I believe you. It didn't really seem her style. She's more cut and run than stand and fight."

"Maybe she's just live and let live," he rasped. He was going to die of shame and agony together if his cock didn't stop getting bigger and stiffer.

"A creed you and I obviously don't share. Mike was not at all pleased with being shot by you. He wanted to kill you right then, but he wouldn't do so without my say-so, and I need to teach him the pleasures of waiting. Of feeding on fear and pain as much as blood."

Fuck this. Quinn met his gaze, spat again. "Yeah. I get it. You're going to torture me until I beg for mercy, then kill me. Blah blah blah. That's your sick shit deal. Fucking do it, but I'm not going to feed any part of you, you sick fuck."

He'd use rage to fight through the pain. Unfortunately, his response didn't elicit anything from Laurent but a lifted brow. He glanced at Claudio, standing silently just behind him. "He actually thinks he has free will, a choice in all this. That we can't make him dance like our puppet at any time. It's almost charming. Very John Wayne."

Laurent stepped closer. As he did, Quinn saw a deadness in those eyes that made Claudio's lack of emotion seem like Chuckles the clown in comparison. Truth, what he saw teeming in Laurent's eyes reminded him of a writhing bed of hungry snakes. It was the look of a monster, something that fed on despair, pain, a complete lack of hope.

It made his balls want to shrivel back up into his body.

"While you were out, I should have given Mike something to do," he said. "He could have fucked your ass several times. That special ointment Claudio just inserted wouldn't be the only reason you're hurting like a son of a bitch. But perhaps it will be far better to have him do it while you're awake, help you really understand what being a vampire's servant means. It seems Selene has romanticized it a little too much."

At the avaricious light in Laurent's eyes, the frank hatred in Mike's as he stood off to the left, Quinn couldn't stop the image that went through his head. Their bodies pushing him down, grunting over him, his legs spread, a nightmare that wouldn't be a nightmare. No. He couldn't lose it like this. Even though he wanted to recoil in horror, knowing Laurent wasn't issuing idle threats, showing weakness wasn't the best option here. Or at least it was an option Quinn wasn't giving himself. Fuck. His Mistress had stood toe to toe with these three, let them beat her to pieces, knowing she couldn't stop them. She'd blocked her mind to spare him from it. He couldn't do any less than live up to her example.

Laurent cocked his head toward the impassive Claudio. Quinn wondered what was going on behind the gold eyes of Laurent's servant, because he didn't so much as twitch a facial muscle. The wind ruffled his thick mane of hair, taking a few strands across his brow. It was obscene, how handsome he was, how beautiful Laurent was. Except for the scar on his face, Mike was the same. Though his fancy dark clothes had a few bloodstained holes in them still, and that gave Quinn some fierce satisfaction. *Yeah, you can fuck me, but it doesn't change the fact I shot you and nearly staked your ass.*

"For instance," Laurent spoke again, "I guess you expected Claudio was coming from their cabin. But a servant would never feed himself without checking in on his Master to see if he needed anything. Though it was past dawn, Mike and Ernesto don't necessarily sleep as deeply as Selene does at that time of day. You probably didn't realize that, did you? The older we are, the longer past dawn we can stay awake, keep our faculties alert to danger. The advantage to not being a sixty-year-old fledgling.

"I wanted blood and to have my dick sucked off," Laurent continued, "and Claudio took care of both of those things before coming out to find his bacon and eggs. You had a fifty percent chance of choosing the right cabin, and unfortunately the gods didn't favor you. Yes, you cornered Mike, but Ernesto had enough shadows to take you out from behind. You let your temper override your good sense, and now both you and your Mistress will pay for it."

Cold shot through Quinn's vitals as he lifted his head, met those dark eyes. Laurent nodded. "When Ernesto gets back with Selene, we'll see how tough you are. Whatever I do to you, I will do to her three times over. That will really destroy you, won't it? To see your actions taken out on her? I understand human weaknesses. They're the easiest to exploit, your sentiment and care for others."

*There is no upside to going after a vampire.* Dix had tried to warn him. *Oh God, Selene.* Selene, vulnerable in her bed. Ernesto would drag her out, bring her here, and she'd have to go through it all over again. He didn't know enough about this world, Dix was right. He'd acted according to the rules of his world and without enough information about vampires. As a result, he'd fucked up beyond all possible reason.

"No. Don't take this out on her. She wasn't any part of it. It was all me."

Laurent's expression took on a mocking cast of pity. "He still doesn't understand. In our world, you are nothing, human. Less than nothing. If you belong to a vampire, your sins are hers. You attempted to kill a vampire, so once she knows that, she'll know your life is already forfeit. I will torture her for your crimes, I will torture you for them and then she will watch you die. Before we take her back home where she belongs."

He wanted to die right now. If he thought it might ease any of her suffering, he would. But he knew it wouldn't. He would have to face this, face what he'd done. Even though it tore his heart out to think it, he wished she'd never stopped in Nightfall, never had the misfortune to meet him, the idiot who'd brought her to this. She'd told him to trust her, and he hadn't. He'd had to be the big-ass hero who avenged her, rather than doing what Dix had told him he should be doing.

Claudio produced an item Quinn recognized all too well. A single tail, like what Selene had used on him. Laurent threaded it through his fingers. "Until they arrive, I think we'll warm you up with this and then employ the cat, which still has your Mistress' dried blood on it. A person who skins with a knife doesn't know the artistry of doing it with a whip. Before I'm done, you'll understand the lovely nuances." His gaze dropped, lingering hungrily on Quinn's cock. "But first, I think you need that lesson about servants and free will."

He stepped forward. Though Quinn tried everything he could to writhe away, his bonds held him fast. Laurent wrapped his hand around the barbed wire, the flesh beneath. If he'd squeezed, the agony would have been unimaginable, but he did something Quinn considered far worse. His face so close to Quinn's he could have kissed him, Laurent gently stroked, rubbed and manipulated the sensitive area under the glans. Despite the excruciating fire in his ass, whatever it was doing that caused his cock to be hard made it capable of climaxing against the brutal hold of the barbed wire.

No, no, *no.*

"Yes," Laurent said, a sibilant whisper as he bared a fang, stroked it along Quinn's cheek, an obscene caress. They'd bound Quinn's throat to the fence as well, so he had no way to jerk away or bite the bastard, but he couldn't have summoned the mind to do it anyway. In what he was sure was the most terrible moment of his life—after finding Selene broken in her bed—his body bucked and he climaxed under Laurent's hand.

The vampire stepped to the side, staying clear as Quinn snarled in horrified frustration, his hips bucking and come spewing out onto the ground.

Something in his mind broke then. Especially when Laurent leaned in and spoke against his ear again. "Do you want to know why Selene runs, human? Because she knows exactly what we are. Perhaps for the short life you have left, it will sink into your feeble mind. You have no choices. You willingly signed away your fate to this." He drew back, met Quinn's gaze. "I don't blame you. She's quite something. But when you step into our world, you step into Hell. You either decide to accept all of what that means, or you're destroyed by it."

He loosed the single tail so it snaked out to his side as he paced backward. He put the cat in his other hand. "Be thinking about that while I take the skin from your body, one strike at a time. What's good for the Mistress is good for the servant, after all."

The first blow of the single tail sliced down Quinn's chest. Unlike the night Selene had touched him with it, there was no attempt to mitigate pain with the lick of the popper. This was all about dispensing pain. A scream broke from Quinn's lips on the third stroke and Mike shoved a shop rag from his own truck into his mouth, one that stank of oil. It mixed with the scent of his own blood and sweat, the musk of his semen on the ground. His heightened third mark senses brought all those scents together in his nose, made him need to retch.

Laurent switched sides after a dozen lashes. The fresh area he chose on Quinn's back doubled the pain. Ten strikes later, he started to alternate, use the cat. The blood was already flowing, and Quinn felt pieces of his flesh being ripped away with every contact. Everything was pain, inside and out. Only one thought held on in the boiling storm of his brain, and hearing its howl was even more agonizing than what was being done to his body.

*I'm sorry. I'm so, so sorry. God, I'm sorry...*

Did the mantra help? He didn't know. All he knew was he passed the point where he thought he couldn't take any more. Knowing that mattered not at all to Laurent broke his mind even further. He was being destroyed, reduced to nothingness. He could hear the distant scream of his soul, about to be lost to him, but then something changed.

He was moving away, burrowing into himself. Squatting down in some deep place in his mind where he was aware of pain, but somehow removed from it as well. In some weird way, it was like those nights at Sam's campfire as a teenager, aware of the noise and chaos that awaited him at home, but finding a quiet center as long as he stayed within the touch of the fire's light.

Was this what they called a psychotic break? He didn't know, but whatever it was, something inside him started to spin. Slow, like a cap coming unscrewed, lifting him out of that deep place, but still away from what was happening to his body, enough distance to handle it. Maybe it was his soul, staring down at himself, splitting away from the horror of what he'd done.

But what he thought was illusion apparently was affecting Laurent as well, because the vampire came to a stop, staring at Quinn. Moving a couple steps forward, he lifted a hand, as if touching something in the air in front of Quinn. Quinn, in his body but not, blinked at Laurent through sweat, shameful tears. Blood. Laurent had struck his face, maybe a couple times. The guy had good aim, because his eyes were still intact and he was pretty sure if Laurent had intended to blind him, he would have. Would a third mark heal from that?

He heard chanting. Chanting in his mind. Closing his eyes, he immersed himself in the smell of Sam's fire, the sage he threw into it with some other things. That familiar smell, the rhythmic crackling, a soothing center to an unhappy teenager's heart, replaced the stench of oil, blood.

*Feel the quiet, Quinn. Embrace what's there. Just breathe.*

*Sam, I fucked up so bad. I've gone so wrong.*

*No, Quinn. You're learning. Life is all about learning. And love. Hold on to that love. And breathe...*

He was breathing. The pain was easing off, everywhere. When he opened his eyes, wishing it was all a nightmare and he'd wake in the cellar with Selene, he didn't get that wish. He saw Selene, yes, but since he was still in this clearing, all he could think was *no, no, no*. But then he focused on a key fact. Ernesto wasn't with her.

Butch was.

A half dozen SUVs had pulled up to the cabin, the waning moon reflecting off their rooftops. Twenty ranch hands had stepped out of them, every one of them armed. Dix had opened the door of one SUV to hand out Selene, Butch emerging from the passenger front seat, taking position at the head of the phalanx.

Laurent coiled up the whip, handed it to Claudio, though he gave one more searching look at Quinn as if there was something off kilter. Quinn dropped his head back on his shoulders. He felt dizzy, disoriented. Everything hurt, but the pain was this big wave behind a door. He could feel it pushing on him. When it burst open, it would probably just carry him away, but he also still heard that chanting in his head. His throat seemed to be vibrating, and he realized he was humming along with it. But his eyes clung to Selene.

Her blue eyes had gone right to him as well and stayed there. Her face was pale but unmarked now, though her features were strained. All the trouble he'd caused her...

*Yes, Quinn. I'll punish you for it later. For now, hold on, my love. My dear, stubborn, stupid man. Hold fast.*

She'd called him "my love".

"Take care of her, Butch." He could barely speak, but vampires had supersonic hearing, right? Butch's gaze flicked toward him, a possible acknowledgement, but otherwise the vampire looked cold as stone as he and Laurent squared off.

"Butch Dorn." Laurent spoke, his gaze sweeping the Texas overlord. "I only met you at a Gathering once, but you had a somewhat unforgettable presence." His tone made it clear it wasn't a compliment. For his part, Butch gave him a look equally full of contempt.

"That makes one of us. We keep trying to close the borders to riffraff like you, but unfortunately they won't do that unless Texas secedes. A move I completely support."

Laurent ignored that, his gaze moving past him to the small army. "Texans and their guns. They can't harm me."

"I bet your boy feels differently." Butch nodded toward Mike. "From the info Selene gave me, a human just about smoked him using a rifle and the sharp end of a hoe."

Mike looked like he barely suppressed the instinct to show fang. Apparently lesser vampires didn't disrespect overlords, even if they weren't their own.

Quinn's attention hadn't wavered from Selene, but as the words sunk in he realized she'd gotten up to speed about what happened from his mind once she woke.

During that pause, Ernesto was pulled out of another SUV. His clothes were ripped and mussed, and a few bloodstains suggested he hadn't been taken gently. Those wounds must have already healed, but Quinn was satisfied at the evidence of them.

Butch's men from the same vehicle looked happy to be rid of him. When they gestured at him with their rifles, he responded with a curled lip and flash of fang, but he moved back through the clearing to rejoin Mike. Laurent gave him a withering look that didn't bode well. Quinn expected Ernesto would be bleeding again today, but he couldn't summon much sympathy for him, all in all.

Laurent turned his attention back to Butch. "My vampire was taken unawares, a mistake that won't happen twice. Regardless, her human's life is now forfeit to me since he attempted to kill a vampire."

Butch glanced at Ernesto. "He behaved himself in the car with my men. Which is why you're getting him back alive. So I'd say that's tit for tat for Quinn."

"This human tried to kill me," Laurent retorted. "Further

compensation is required than just one subordinate—and inept—vampire's life."

Ernesto tried to remain impassive under Laurent's cutting look, but Quinn saw the swallow. Yeah, today was going to suck for him. But maybe before this was over, Laurent's day would suck far more.

Selene stepped forward. "Fifty percent of what I earn here will go to you, Laurent. For the next twenty-five years."

Butch gave her a severe look, making it clear she hadn't had leave to offer that, but she nodded to him. "That doesn't cut into the amount we agreed I would give you as part of your territory."

"Which is irrelevant if you are coming home with me, as you will be," Laurent snapped.

Butch brought his attention back to Laurent. "My guys and their guns are here to even the playing field. To make it a fair fight. You're all about beating up on a girl when you outnumber her four to one. Or torturing a human, which takes as much effort as kicking a puppy or drowning a newborn."

Quinn would have taken offense, but even in his disoriented mind, he realized Butch must have a purpose for goading the other vampire. It had worked. Laurent flushed red over his pale features. Butch glanced back at his men, his tone becoming conversational.

"One of my favorite entertainments is to draw down with another vampire. Old west roleplaying. See whose fastest and all that. You'd say it was just more of my Texan fascination with firearms, but it's a game, which means I only do it with friends. What I want is to mess up that pretty face of yours with my fists. A bullet wouldn't be anywhere near as satisfying."

Laurent was rallying, his arrogant expression back in place. "I see no point to a fight between us. The nature of our disagreement is more contractual."

"Here's the deal." Butch pressed on as if he hadn't spoken. "You and I do a hand-to-hand bout. If I win, Quinn goes free and clear back to his Mistress. The Region Masters' decision is their decision. That will stand either way."

Laurent's brow creased. "While I'm enjoying the diversion of Selene's servant, I'm not about to get into a barroom brawl over owning him. An unwashed cowboy isn't that appealing to me. I see no benefit."

"I'll draw you a picture then. It's pretty much carte blanche what we want to do to our servants." Butch's gaze swept Quinn indifferently, though he thought he might have detected a minor flinch from the vampire overlord when he noted the state of his cock and testicles, wrapped in the barbed wire. "But Region Masters and the Council feel a little differently when it's happening to the vampires in your own territory. I had my servant do a little checking. There are lines, and you like crossing them. Cross them enough, they become straws on a camel's back. Dix has talked to enough of those straws in the past several hours to make me think that if I registered a few complaints on their behalf, the Council might wonder if you should be an overlord after all."

"The Council won't hear the whining complaints of a back-woods territory overlord. I hold far more weight than you do."

Butch's dark eyes glinted with malice. "It's not where you live, Laurent, but the friends you have. And I have a particular friend. Lady Lyssa."

That gave Laurent pause. Quinn was having trouble focusing on the dialogue, because the pain was rising again, a throb oozing back into the cracks of that wall around his mind. But he realized a new tension had gripped the New York overlord. He was distantly glad for that, but to manage the agony in his body, he looked toward his Mistress, stared at her beloved face. Quinn felt Selene's awareness of him, though like most everyone else, her eyes remained on Laurent and Butch.

"You've heard of her, right?" Butch lifted a brow, his tone deceptively mild. "Not only the last surviving member of our royal clans, she was the former Southern Region Master until she changed jobs. What's she doing now, Dix? I forget." He glanced at Dix, standing just behind him to his right.

"Currently head of the Vampire Council, my lord," Dix said

formally. Butch gave him a wry look, maybe because of Dix's use of his title, but he lifted a shoulder.

"She likes me. At least enough to spend some time on the phone listening to what I have to say. I think you're familiar enough with her reputation to know she's not a big fan of pointless brutality, especially toward the vampires you're supposed to be governing."

Laurent's expression flickered at that, and though he quickly masked it, Butch let out a chuckle. "You just might get busted back down to peon level. That'd be a real shame. You'd have to work for a living instead of enjoying those juicy tithes you extort out of your vampires. So, what do you say to my 'deal' now?"

When Laurent said nothing, Butch added, "If I lose, your secrets are safe with me and you can continue to play your sick little games with Quinn. Though I'm telling you, this kind of shit makes the rest of us think you're compensating for some little boy vampire sense of inadequacy."

Selene made a noise of protest, but Butch shot her a sharp look. She subsided, though the effort obviously cost her. Quinn was on Butch's side. As long as he took care of Selene, his fate didn't matter to him.

With a snarl, Laurent turned away, stripping off his coat. Making a satisfied nod, Butch started unbuttoning his shirt. When he shrugged out of it, he revealed a body as powerful-looking as the fit of the clothes had suggested, roped with hard muscle, but Quinn now knew firsthand that strength for vampires was linked to age. Laurent had a hundred years on Butch. Maybe that was why Laurent didn't look the least worried about the challenge. He appeared mostly annoyed, probably because they'd interrupted his plan and he might have to get his clothes dirty.

As Claudio took the coat Laurent shed, the vampire addressed Butch again. He'd dropped the scorn and arrogance, leaving pure malice in his tone. "When I win, I will kill him here and now, in front of her. In front of you, Dorn. Since a human life bothers you."

Butch shrugged. "The human life doesn't matter to me. What matters is getting the chance to beat the shit out of you. Quinn's a happy means to that end."

As the two vampires prepared and exchanged barbs, Quinn's attention moved to Dorn's men. All of their faces were somber, eyes serious and alert. Dix drew Selene closer to Quinn, but Laurent stabbed a finger in that direction.

"No. She doesn't touch him until the fight is resolved. In fact..." His gaze lighted with pleasure and he tossed the whip to Mike. "He will continue his punishment until the matter is resolved."

"No." Selene stepped forward then, her jaw set. "You bastard."

"Selene." Butch gave her an even look, then shifted his gaze to Quinn. His tone was deceptively mild. "I expect it's going to be a short fight, Quinn."

Quinn shook his head. "Take your time," he rasped. "They can't hurt me. Not as long as my Mistress is safe."

Her features became even tighter, but she reached out to him in his mind. *Hold on, Quinn.*

It was like a simple handclasp, more precious to him right now than even a full embrace.

*We're going to owe this guy our firstborn if he wins, you know that, right?*

*I think he's counting on it.*

The dry note laced with the tension helped him lift his gaze, hold on to hers. Even as he sensed Mike drawing closer, drawing back that whip. Her jaw tightened such that he feared the tension would break it, her blue eyes filled with emotions that destroyed him.

He wouldn't scream. He wouldn't.

The bubble burst, all that pain flooding through him with the first strike. He wrenched his head back as far as his bonds would allow, his body going rigid, fighting the inevitable. He was vaguely aware of Butch and Laurent circling one another, then the ground vibrated as they charged and slammed into one another like a car crash. A blink later the fence shuddered under the impact of their bodies and he saw it splinter, give way three sections down. The whip fell again and his body contorted against his bonds, red fire washing through him.

In the haze of pain he realized the combatants were moving so fast the only way to track them was by the trail they left. Earth furrowed as they rolled down the short hill into the retention pond. The flash of the water against the moonlight showed their movements. He had a brief impression of Laurent landing a blow in Butch's rib cage that should have broken bone like matchsticks, but Butch roared and Laurent was airborne, thudding back onto the bank.

Quinn lost track of them then because agony took over again. The blows were landing one after another, no pause between. Mike was taking his pound of flesh. Maybe a hell of a lot more than that. The pain didn't ebb and flow. It was a crescendo, and Quinn couldn't get above it or around it this time. He'd never experienced such agony in his life. He struggled to get back to that place deep inside, but it was too far to reach. He was being dragged down into another kind of dark place, one way too much like being buried alive to allow him to hold on to his courage.

No, he had to hold on. For her. Selene was watching. He had to prove he was worthy of her, even if he'd been the dumbass shit who'd screwed all this up.

The whip struck his shoulder, but this time it didn't slice and pull back. It fell, rolling along his torn back and catching on the split rail by his bound ankle. He heard what had to be a scuffle behind him, a crack and then a thump. He lifted his head enough to try to find Selene, see if he could figure out what had happened, but she wasn't there.

Instead her hands were on him, her lips on his blood-soaked shoulder. He'd never felt anything so welcome in his life, even as he'd never felt so terrible. She was cutting his bonds free, her and Dix. He was blearily aware of the ranch hand pulling away the ropes, helping Selene ease him to the ground. It was Selene's gentle fingers that removed the barbed wire from around his genitals.

Which still hurt like hell, because the stuff in his ass had brought him back to a full erection in no time, but at least that burning sensation had eased off. Apparently the pain factor of the ointment had a shorter shelf life. One small blessing in the midst of the horror.

Her touch was far more than a small blessing. Even with the discomfort, he embraced that feeling, her hands on him, her concerned face in his field of vision.

"Selene..."

"Sssh." Her head jerked up, then her breasts were pressed against his face, her arms tight around him. She'd thrown herself on him, shielding him. The ground shuddered like an earthquake. From her grunt at the impact, he thought a car had run over them both. Then the pressure was gone. Tilting his head up, he followed the direction of her glance just in time to see the cabin door give way, along with a big chunk of the wall surrounding it. He realized Butch and Laurent had taken their fight back up the little hill, fists pummeling each other as the battle continued, powerful bodies with strength far beyond that of humans destroying everything in their paths. All the males on both sides had moved back to flank the clearing, watching the track of the combat. Then Selene's arms were around him, pulling him up against her again, and that was all that mattered. His Mistress was holding him.

"Quinn, Quinn..." She was whispering his name.

"You should run...now," he said hoarsely. "While they're fighting. Just go. Run."

"I'm done running." She eased him back so he was half-lying on her thighs. "Whatever happens, happens."

"This is my fault. I'm so sorry."

"No. No it's not. It's Laurent's fault. I told you. I want you as who you are, Quinn, and you couldn't have done this differently. Though I certainly wish I'd been awake to stop you." She gave him a mock stern look, though he realized she was also crying. "I would have."

When he'd turned his head to look at her, he'd caught Mike in his field of vision. The vampire was sitting on his ass about fifty yards away. He was holding the side of his head, where an explosion of blood had baptized his face. Quinn blinked, realizing the blunt object that had hit him was one of the two by fours Quinn had brought in the back of his truck. Mike was glaring at Selene, but given that a few of Butch's men were keeping their eyes and weapons trained on him, he'd decided being shot full of holes twice in one day wasn't preferable to revenge.

"When Mike started whipping you again, I told Dix that wasn't happening." Selene's voice was cold, drawing his attention back to her face, the fierce light in her eyes as she stroked his jaw. "He agreed."

Mike probably had a few decades on her, and yeah, she'd had surprise on her side, but it was still frigging impressive, to Quinn's way of thinking. "Remind me not to piss you off."

"It wouldn't help," she said shortly. "You're too stubborn to heed any warnings I give you."

At another time, a far more pleasurable one, she might have suggested using a whip to get him to listen. But he saw how she really felt about that as she traced his wounds. Laurent had striped him down the front mercilessly, and her tears were falling in his blood and torn flesh. He couldn't bear her tears, and managed to raise a shaking hand, cupping her jaw so she drew her eyes from that to his face.

*I'd beg for the touch of a whip from your hands, Mistress.*

That made her cry harder. He wanted to hold her, but he was like a baby in truth, too weak to move. In the corner of his eye, he saw Dix rise from where he'd been squatting within arm's reach. Now that Quinn had been freed, the ranch hand had one focus, and that was the battle going on in the clearing.

With the pain ebbing to a dull roar, Quinn's third mark senses had sharpened, and he could follow the fight better himself, even though there were still moments where Butch and Laurent were moving almost too fast for him to see the details. Then they smashed into a tree so hard he heard a crack. Laurent had Butch against the trunk. Both their faces were bloody, fangs bared. Butch strained against the hold, broke it and landed a punch square on Laurent's nose. Quinn had the pleasure of hearing the cartilage break. But Laurent barely registered it. He hammered Butch's stomach, broke free, and they were off spinning like a dervish again.

Dix's fists clenched as if he could help his Master fight. Watching the hand's body canted toward them, Quinn realized this was more than a pissing match to Dix. And not just to him. *Fuck.*

Dix's tension and the serious looks on the men's faces penetrated Quinn's mind. Gelling with everything he now knew about Laurent, from personal experience as well as seeing the beating his Mistress had taken from him, the full impact of the decision Butch had made registered.

If Butch won, he'd said he'd let Laurent go his way, with the terms of the agreement honored. If Laurent won this fight, Butch wasn't going to be alive. Neither would Dix. A servant died when the Master did.

But Quinn didn't think that was why Dix looked so invested in this. A person didn't become a vampire's servant if their own life was more important to them than the vampire they served.

He realized Selene must know what might happen here as well, because now that her servant was free, she'd gone still and tense, all her attention on the combat. Helped by her strength, Quinn struggled up enough to see more of what was going on.

As Butch and Laurent hit one of the SUVs, and it was clear that Laurent was gaining the upper hand, Selene stiffened, began to rise. "No."

Somewhere, Quinn found the strength to hold on to her. "Mistress, no. If you step in at the wrong time, the distraction could get him killed."

Though he hated being on the sidelines as much as she did, he knew it was true. He took that cue from Dix, the person who most wanted to go to his Master's aid but who was restraining himself. Barely.

If Butch did survive this, Quinn would owe Dix as big a debt as Selene would owe Butch. "Mistress, give me blood."

Startled, she looked down at him. "Yeah, I won't heal as fast, but it will get me on my feet." He was gauging the stance of the silent men watching. Unlike Ernesto and Mike, these men were bound to Butch and Dix by true loyalty. If Butch lost and he and Dix died, this was going to get really bloody. Mike was already back on his feet, standing next to Ernesto, the two of them looking ready to fight if needed.

The good thing about being in each other's heads was there wasn't a lot of explanation needed. In a blink, Selene saw his evaluation of what might happen, understood why he was asking what he was asking. "From the throat," she said. "It's richest there. Do you have the strength?"

He did. Especially when she leaned over him, cupping his head, bringing it to her throat as she raised her chin to give him better access. He didn't like causing her more pain, but he also understood for vampires, the bite of their servant was more of an erotic expression than a functional pain. Though it would be hard to feel anything sexual in the current setting, he wasn't surprised at the flood of intimacy that came from the act. In its way, it was as balancing as that chant that had come into his mind, Sam's wisdom helping him survive such a horrible ordeal.

Her blood flooded his mouth and he swallowed as fast as he could. He'd been right. Because of their connection, the taste of her blood was as welcome as whiskey, and his body recognized its need for it like mother's milk.

It didn't take much. When she broke free with obvious reluctance after he'd taken down about a cup, he could already feel vitality coming back to him. He might not be tiptop for a while, and his skin looked like a bloody patchwork quilt, but he could make it to his feet, especially with her strength aiding him. Turning at a nudge, he found one of Butch's men holding out his jeans and boots, which Laurent's men had apparently left in a heap nearby. Hot damn. He might just feel human again.

He donned the clothes, despite wincing at the pain on his abraded flesh. As he did, he stayed close to Selene's side and kept an equally close eye on the fight. Now it wasn't so hard, either because he was feeling better or because both vampires had slowed down. They were wearing each other out, circling, looking for strategic advantages. A choreographed dance that could end in death for one of them. One of Butch's men called out, brandishing his gun as if he was offering to take a few shots at Laurent.

Butch shook his head. "I said it's a fair fight," he snapped. "No one does a damn thing. I can handle this bastard."

A few feet from Quinn, Dix looked as if he was made of stone. His concentration was so fixed on his Master, Quinn wondered if he was like the coach in a boxer's ring, anticipating Laurent's moves, giving Butch a further advantage. That was something a servant might do, having a wider view of what was around them.

Laurent feinted forward then back. Butch met him, swung and missed. Laurent kicked him in the knee. If it had connected, Quinn suspected it would have broken. Instead Butch launched himself over the strike, a flat-out tackle that banded his arms around Laurent's torso and took them to the ground. Laurent twisted fast as a serpent, but as he slipped out of Butch's grip, Butch got lucky and caught him in a headlock. He flung them both backward, Laurent on top of him, the ground shaking with the force of their fall.

Laurent bucked and thrashed, kicked his legs, clawed at the hold. Butch held on grimly. It reminded Quinn of holding a calf to the ground, trying to stay clear of the kicking hooves, only Laurent was much more lethal and strong. But despite the century differ-ence in their ages, Butch was no pushover. He tightened his hold and flipped them. Quicker even than Quinn could follow, he'd rolled on top of Laurent, seized his shoulders, forced his knee into his back. With a roar, the Texas overlord heaved upward. The crack of the spine resounded through the clearing like a rifle shot.

As if a switch had been thrown, every one of Butch's men had the muzzles of their rifles up and pointed at Claudio, Ernesto and Mike. Claudio had dropped to one knee as if the trauma had resounded through his own body, so he wasn't an immediate threat, but it was clear Mike and Ernesto were on the fence about what to do.

Butch stumbled to his feet, straightened and backed away from his opponent, his broad chest heaving in the aftermath of the exertion. He knuckled blood away from his eye with an impatient gesture and shot a look toward Laurent's two vampires. "A hail of bullets won't kill you, boys," he said hoarsely. "But if you give them a reason to shoot, I'll make damn sure you don't get up. I'll stake you where you lie. The law is on my side, killing vampires outside my territory who threatened my life or those of the vampires I protect."

His gaze shifted to Selene, then moved to Laurent. The New York overlord was still immobilized and in obvious, hideous discomfort, but the eyes he kept trained on Butch were hate-filled. "Is that your plan for me?" he managed with venom.

"It would give me more pleasure than you can imagine." But Butch glanced toward Claudio. "Give your Master blood so he can recover. Then I expect the lot of you to pack up your outfit and get the hell out of here." He returned his attention to Laurent. "The Region Masters made their decision a couple hours ago, which you'd have known if you'd checked your voicemail instead of torturing Quinn here. Selene belongs to me, which means so does Quinn."

Selene's arms tightened around Quinn. Relief flooded him so strongly his knees almost buckled. Thank God. Though it couldn't change the mistakes he'd made, or what the past few hours had cost them, it sure went a hell of a long way to making the future a damn sight more optimistic. Unless Butch decided to kill him for causing all this trouble. Quinn wouldn't blame him a bit.

*Only your Mistress gets to decide if you live or die, Quinn. I'm not quite ready to be rid of you.*

Her voice, gentle in his head but with a core of steel, was almost as capable of making his knees go out from under him as Butch's news. He was so tired. A shower, a few days of sleep where he didn't have to think of anything but holding her—that was all he could ever want again.

Laurent curled his lip at Claudio when his servant approached, but he didn't refuse him when he cut a vein in his wrist, brought it to his Master's lips. While Laurent obviously didn't relish being seen in such a weakened position, he valued survival over appearances. For his part, Butch turned away, moving through his men back to his vehicle. As he leaned his hips against the grill, watching Claudio and Laurent with sharp eyes but a weary expression, Dix brought out a couple towels and a bottle of water.

The moment the fight had concluded, Dix had been inside the circle of men, standing at Butch's back as he spoke to Laurent. Now, though the two males exchanged no words, Quinn wondered how many things were being said regardless. Dix gave Butch a damp towel so he could wipe the blood from his face and chest, but his eyes never left his Master's face.

Quinn suspected if they were alone, Dix would have done the honors with the towel himself, needing to touch Butch. Even though Quinn and Selene were a few yards away, Quinn could feel that need vibrating from Dix. Which meant Butch was feeling it like a palpable force. Proving it, Butch reached out, clasped Dix's shoulder. Then he gave him a light shove, a gesture that said clearly, *"Can't believe you were worried I couldn't take this asshole."*

Quinn had never been much about watching two guys together. No way, no how. But maybe because of the bond he felt with Selene, understanding it better than ever before, Quinn couldn't take his eyes away as he watched Dix take the second towel, run it over Butch's broad shoulder and then linger there, his hand tightening on him. Butch's head lifted, and he murmured to his servant. Gave him a wry smile, then pushed him away again, an obvious reproof not to be such a hen. Quinn's sharpened hearing brought him some the exchange.

"Ye of little faith," the overlord said.

Dix gave him an even look. "I didn't want to show up at the Pearly Gates because you got your ass kicked by a city slicker."

"Neither Heaven nor Hell would want us if that happened. That's why God was on our side." Butch winked at him. Then he turned his attention back to his opponent.

Quinn had kept a sharp eye on Laurent as well, and he wasn't alone. Most of Butch's men had done the same, covering all three vampires and the one servant, rifles still at the ready.

The age of the vampire must help the recovery time once a servant's blood was administered, for Laurent was already sitting up, albeit gingerly. At his curt gesture, Ernesto and Mike came forward, taking over getting him to his feet, since Laurent had pushed Claudio away impatiently after he'd had the necessary nourishment from him. The New York overlord sent Selene a sharp, sneering look.

Interestingly, Butch's men closed ranks around Quinn and Selene in direct response. Apparently Butch had given them pretty specific orders about who to protect in this fight. Quinn saw Selene swallow at the gesture, her gaze going to Butch. She didn't have any precedent for an overlord who thought of her protection as more than a personal benefit for himself. It made Quinn realize there'd been things in his life that she'd rarely had in her own. He hoped she had the chance to experience those better things for a good long time. Maybe he'd get the chance to watch her do so, up close and personal. Things were still too tense in the clearing for him to be entirely sure of anything.

Laurent straightened, his eyes shooting sparks at the men who'd circled them. His expression made it clear that, in different circumstances, he'd dismember every human in the clearing who dared think they could keep him from doing whatever he wanted. But that was another day. Right now, he was paler than usual and having all he could do to stand on his own. The sophisticated New York veneer was gone, stripped away like a custom tailored suit. In a surprising move, Dix brought Claudio another bottle of water and more towels. Claudio gave him a formal nod, then brought the items to his Master, holding them patiently as Laurent cleaned up.

*It's common sense, most of it.* His Mistress sent him the thought. *The full servant is the only one allowed to intimately attend to the vampire, unless the vampire himself invites someone else to do so.*

*It's not that. I was surprised they offered him any courtesy at all.* But maybe in the vampire world, this was a minor disagreement.

Her look suggested, disturbingly enough, he wasn't off track. But then again...

"So you won our fight, fair and square." Laurent conceded that ungraciously, wiping his face and hands before taking his shirt back from Claudio. "But I don't understand why we had to stoop to that level if you already knew the Region Masters' decision. You weren't fighting merely for the well-being of one human servant. Or were you?" Laurent's lip curled. "You were once human yourself, after all. For some of you, the weakness for them never leaves you."

"You didn't think I was weak a moment ago." Butch shrugged back into his own shirt. Leaving it open over his belted jeans, he took a swig of the water Dix offered and spat it out onto the ground, clearing the taste of blood from his mouth. "Yeah, I could have told you the decision, let it lie there. But then you wouldn't have known what you know now."

Handing Dix back the water, he moved back through the circle of men around Laurent, coming close enough there was only a pace between the two vampires. As their gazes locked, Butch's brows drew down, eyes sharpening. He suddenly looked far more dangerous, the way he had right before he and Laurent had clashed. What Quinn saw now was a vampire predator in truth, one whose expression was enough to make the sarcastic cast of Laurent's face falter, the cynical twist to his lips thin.

"You're in my territory," Butch said, every syllable etched with menace. "You entered it without invitation. Pretend all you want, your fate rests squarely in my hands right now. At my order, every man here can fill you and your rabble with holes. I will then personally cut you up into pieces and scatter them on my spread for the jackals to eat. You'll be meat, Laurent, that's all. No more memorable than the tumbleweeds that cross the highways when the winds blow too hard. So let's be civil and call this day's work done. All right?"

Quinn thought every living being in the clearing had stopped breathing, waiting to see what would happen. Then Laurent offered a stiff, dignified nod. He turned to Claudio. "Pack our belongings."

Butch stepped back. Not too far, close enough the pallor of Laurent's face stayed a few shades too light. But Selene's former overlord proved, shaken or not, he hadn't abandoned his own interests.

"Selene was a valuable asset, financially speaking. I assume the Region Masters have ruled on compensation for my loss?"

"They have." Butch gave a short nod. "Twenty-five percent of her profits for the next five years."

It was less than she'd feared. Quinn saw her shoulders ease down even as Laurent's tightened up. He frowned. "Then I wish you good use of her until she turns on you."

As Claudio moved toward the cabin, Laurent turned to follow him, but he paused, finding Selene through the cluster of men protecting her. Lifting her chin, she stepped forward, touching the two in front of her so they stepped aside, though they looked toward Butch, waiting for his nod.

After that brief pause they shifted, and Selene took up a stance in front of them, nothing between her and Laurent but space.

It put her in front of Quinn as well. He might have felt strange about it, but he understood the message she was sending. Laurent had tied her up, beaten her, but she'd won in the end, because she had what he didn't. The type of character that commanded respect from others.

Maybe that wasn't obvious to a lowlife like Laurent, but it was to Quinn, and he saw it reflected in Butch's face as he glanced her way. The overlord confirmed it, shifting his sharp gaze and sharper tone onto Laurent again.

"She turned on you because you weren't the type of overlord who deserved her respect." Butch gave the other male vampire an even look. "I believe in protecting my people more than exploiting them. If they need an ass kicking, I'll give it to them, but to underscore a point, no more, no less. Difference between a parent and a sociopath."

"A parent can be overindulgent. And humans are not our children. They're our slaves. It's something turned vampires never learn." Laurent tilted his head, tossing a look full of sadistic promise toward Dix, standing at Butch's shoulder. "If ever a Gathering provides the opportunity, my lord, I will fuck your servant in front of you to prove the point."

Butch bared his teeth in a feral grin that held no humor, only death. "You're assuming my respect for our rules is why you're alive. You ever come after me or mine again, you're ever in my territory again, you'll disappear, Laurent. One of those vampires that just drifted away, lost to the sun. Count on it. Now get your things." Butch returned to a tone of cool courtesy, the abrupt transition as chilling as the threat. "I'll give you an escort to the airport."

Laurent managed another contemptuous sneer, one more malevolent look toward Selene, but then he turned toward Mike and Ernesto. "Let's get out of this godforsaken part of the world and back to civilization," he snapped.

As they disappeared in the cabin and the men relaxed marginally, Quinn realized it was over. That they'd won, sort of. An elation came with that, a shot of adrenaline, but behind that was the downside. Everything that had happened, what Laurent had done to her, what could have happened...what had happened, all of that was waiting to be faced. On top of that, he hurt, everywhere.

Then there was the fact an overlord had just fought to the death on their behalf. That was a big thought on his Mistress' mind as well, for she squeezed his hand, squared her shoulders. As she moved toward Butch, Quinn followed. No matter that his body screamed all the way to the bone from every twitch he made, he wasn't going to be farther than a cloth yard from her as long as Laurent was in the vicinity. Even if the only thing he was capable of doing was being a whipping boy in her stead. The thought made him wince, but he pushed it away with all those other horrible thoughts waiting to grip him in some post-traumatic bullshit that he was sure was going to drown him and turn him into a weeping baby if he gave in to it.

Butch was leaning against the SUV again, taking a healthy shot straight from a bottle of Jack Daniel's that Dix had produced for him. Giving it to Dix, indicating he should pass it around, Butch looked toward Selene. "Thank God vampires can drink," he said.

Selene stared up at the tall man without responding. When Butch straightened from the grill and faced her, she sank to her knees, startling Quinn. "My lord, there is no way for me to repay you," she said with quiet formality. "Everything you ever ask of me, from this day forward...my blood, my life and my loyalty are yours. I will sign it as an unbreakable oath and give it into your keeping."

Dix had moved to Quinn's side, drawn him back a pace or two, giving the two vampires a circle of space. "That's an oath Laurent would have given his left nut to get from her lips," Dix muttered. "When a vampire comes into their territory, they offer tribute to the overlord as a matter of course, but when they speak those words, it means a hell of a lot more. It means she'll give him anything he demands without complaint or hesitation. Body, blood, life. Every cent she earns. Because of that oath, if he even wants to take her life, he can do so with no penalty from any Region Master."

"What? But—" When Quinn started forward, Dix held him with one hand and a head shake.

"It's important to let them finish."

Butch reached down then, took her hands. Bringing Selene to her feet, he tipped her chin up in his big hand so she met his eyes. "What I demand, youngling, is that you stay in Nightfall and run that bar you love to the best of your ability. You pay your twenty-five percent to that viper for the next five years, then twenty-five percent to me for the five years after that. Then we'll do the standard ten percent." His lip had split and bled during the fight and, perhaps because he'd not yet partaken from his own servant's blood, it still looked raw, but it only added to the rugged appeal of his handsome face when he smiled. "And I expect you and your servant to join us for the weekend at least once a quarter so we can see how he's coming along in your service. Watch him evolve."

*Christ.* Quinn heard Dix's chuckle, got an elbow in his sore ribs. "I sense more wrestling matches in our future," the ranch manager said.

"Bite me."

"You sure about that? Given where my mouth ended up last time we had dinner?"

Jesus. He wasn't sure he was ever going to get used to this.

Butch sobered, touching her face. "You should have informed me what Laurent might do to you. You're brave as hell, and I appreciate that quality, in man or woman. But going forward, I expect you to learn the lesson you're trying to teach your servant. You belong to me and my territory, and I take care of my own."

"I didn't wish to presume." Selene had the grace to flush. "I wasn't yet an accepted member of your territory and I didn't want to take advantage."

"Hmm. Because this worked out so much better, your servant flying off the handle and trying to get himself killed."

Quinn did step forward then, despite the warning note Dix made. "She had no control over that."

Butch's gaze shifted to him. An instant later, he was in front of Quinn, those dark, glittering eyes pinning him with the full force of a three-hundred-year-old vampire. Anything affable in the expression he'd given Selene was entirely absent now. In fact, it was only a notch or two less intimidating than what he'd thrown toward Laurent. "If you learn nothing else today, Quinn, learn this one thing. Your obedience to her will, especially in dealing with vampires, is not about swallowing your pride or being less of a man. It's about serving her. Learn what serving her means, or you're no good to her at all. Do you understand?"

The force of the words alone might have knocked him back on his ass if Dix hadn't shifted, formed a bulwark behind Quinn. Probably to make sure he stayed upright for his Master, but Quinn still appreciated the salve to his dignity. Butch didn't move, holding Quinn in that unbreakable gaze as he waited for what damn sure better be the right response. Quinn didn't back down from any man, but he realized that wasn't what Butch was demanding now. He was demanding what he'd earned from Quinn. Respect.

"Yes sir."

Butch gave him a curt nod. Pivoting on his heel, he strode back to his vehicle. "Jim, you and Moe take Quinn, Selene and the other back home. We'll provide the escort to Laurent and then head for home. I intend to be in my own bed by dawn."

When Dix reached him, Butch caught his servant in a head-lock, one far more affable than what Laurent had experienced. He bumped against the male's body before Dix shoved him away with an annoyed look. But Quinn noticed the servant beat him to the door, opened it for him.

Butch gave him a sardonic look, as if it wasn't something his servant usually did for him or that he demanded, but whatever he saw in Dix's eyes made his mouth ease fractionally. "Asshole," he said affectionately.

"Pigheaded mule," Dix responded. With a snort, Butch climbed in and Dix closed the door. As he turned to circle the front of the car, the servant nodded deferentially to Selene, then met Quinn's gaze. Pausing, Dix offered his hand and Quinn clasped it, a gentlemen's accord.

"Remember, one day at a time, Quinn. Thank God for every one of them you get with her. Don't ask for more. Nobody likes a greedy bastard."

# CHAPTER SEVENTEEN

*T*hose words stuck with Quinn. He didn't think about who Butch meant by "the other", until he climbed into the backseat of the large SUV after giving Selene a hand up into the vehicle. She'd paused as if she'd help him, but he wasn't having any of that. Her narrow look said she didn't have much patience for indulging his need to prove his manhood, but since she allowed it this time, that was fine. He was sure he'd collapse soon so she could tsk all she wanted about misguided testosterone over his unconscious body.

*Don't think I won't, cowboy.*

Though it was an effort to pull himself up after her, the sound of her voice in his head was almost as much help in getting there as the blood she'd given him. Instead of feeling like he'd been run over by a truck multiple times, now he just felt like he'd been dragged behind one for about fifty miles. His skin was still in pretty gruesome shape, but he was thinking a shower that took away the crust of blood and sand would help that, as well as the throbbing all-over ache the brutal experience had inflicted on him.

Being a third mark apparently didn't give him healing powers as rapid as Selene's, but he could already tell the stripes Laurent had placed on him were knitting, which explained why each move felt as if he was ripping them anew, even if he wasn't.

When he fell into the seat, feeling the weight of exhaustion and stress pulling down on him, as well as a hundred things he didn't want to relive in his mind, he discovered a welcome distraction.

Sam.

The SUV was a custom setup, with seats facing one another like a limo, so the shaman was across from him, dressed in his usual faded jeans and a T-shirt with a Starbuck's logo. The guy always had possessed a wicked sense of irony. "Sam."

That one word, and it meant everything.

When Sam met his gaze, Quinn saw a weariness in his face that matched his own. It flooded back to him then—the feeling of being pulled away from the mind-shattering pain, Laurent's hesitation, his puzzled look as he reached out, as if to touch some invisible force around Quinn. The way Quinn had stopped feeling the whip at a certain point, thinking that maybe he'd just gotten so lost in the pain haze that it all felt the same. He remembered Selene, the night she'd third marked him, talking about how he'd already been marked by someone else for his own protection...

How had Sam known? But there was probably no straight answer to that question, any more than there had been to the ones he'd asked in his youth. He just pushed them out of his mind and embraced the tranquility the man infused him with.

"Sam. God." He clasped the man's hand with both his own and Sam's face creased into a tired smile. "What are you doing here? How did you get here?"

"I had a sense you needed me. I was a little late. Sometimes I think the spirits are in the wrong time zone when they give me visions. Perhaps they're on Eastern Standard Time." The shaman frowned, as if he actually intended to take up that grievance with the spirit world. "But fortunately, your lady was just waking when I got to the bar. Your friends intercepted us along the way." He nodded out the window toward Butch and Dix, who were sitting in the other SUV with the windows down, waiting on Laurent and company to be loaded up.

Quinn looked at Selene, who nodded. "He said he could help."

"He did. Christ, he did. I...I was about to lose my mind."

"It was awful." Selene shook her head, the falter in her voice saying that didn't even cover it. Quinn had to agree with that, but all he cared about was her touch as she closed her hands around his arm, a link of love and comradeship. "The pain you were feeling..."

Oh God, he hadn't even thought about it. She would have felt all of it because of their link. Unless she'd blocked it, and he knew she wouldn't have. She'd experienced his every thought, every feeling. Letting go of Sam, he covered her hands with one of his.

"It wasn't the pain that broke me, Mistress. It was knowing I'd betrayed you."

Her head snapped up as if he'd struck her. "What?"

"I didn't trust you, like you said I should." Quinn forced out the words, swallowing a boatload of pride. "I was going to be the typical guy, running off to avenge your honor. Dix tried to tell me, to help me to understand. But I failed you in every way. If it wasn't for Butch and Dix, Sam—hell, your own courage and smarts—you would have ended up back under the thumb of that bastard, thanks to me. The exact opposite of what I intended."

"Oh Quinn." Reaching up, she cupped his jaw. "Yes, you fucked up. But so did I. We're still learning how all this works, you and me. In our world, *our* world," she emphasized, making it clear she considered him part of it too, "things like this happen. It's awful, and terrible, but we learn. You saw it, between Butch and Laurent. Laurent would have killed him if he could, but when Butch won, it was over. Laurent was angry, but he accepted the verdict. The Region Masters have made their decision. I won't ever risk going into Laurent's territory again," she made a face at that, "but he won't be coming after me outside it."

"There goes my lifelong dream to see the Rockettes."

Selene slanted him a glance. Though her eyes softened marginally at his weak attempt at humor, when she spoke, her voice was firm. "The matter is over."

He looked toward Sam. "Just like that."

"You will grieve for what you have lost," the old man said quietly. "Whenever a soul is brutalized, cleansing and healing must happen. But you are strong, Quinn. You learn from the past and the present, but you do not let it dictate your future. You let it guide you, inspire you and instruct you only. You know where to go to find the quiet you need."

Quinn met his gaze. "Yeah. I do. But what about you?"

The man's face creased in a smile. "When we get to the ranch, I will tell Annette to put me up in a guestroom for a couple days and feed me. That you said it must be so."

Quinn snorted, though the chuckle hurt his ribs. "As much as I'd like to be a fly on the wall to see that conversation," his attention turned to Selene, "you're right. There's somewhere else I need to go. Will you come with me, Mistress?"

When he offered her the image in his head, it wasn't a place she'd seen before, but her response was immediate.

"Yes, Quinn."

A gaping hole was in his heart right now, but the gift of her trust spread out over it like a healing balm. He tightened his hand on hers.

"Good."

A hundred years ago, one of the earliest owners of the Last Chance Ranch had built the first structure on it, a little two-room cabin located on the western edge of the property, near a pretty watering hole. It had never been torn down, occasionally used as a line shack for the cowboys working the land. But when Quinn bought the ranch and discovered it, he'd had it restored and upgraded so that he could stay there sometimes. Sam had pointed out it could be his private place to go when he needed a place away from everything. It just so happened to rest on that magical fault line. Maybe that was why it always felt so peaceful there.

Even better for Quinn's current purposes, the cabin had a cool cellar beneath it that he was sure had once been used to store perishable foods or allow working cowboys a place of respite from the summer heat. With the latter idea guiding him, he'd had the cellar turned into an additional living space. The walls were finished and sealed, but the area always smelled pleasantly of cool earth.

He'd put a cot and a reading chair down there, while the upper floor had a more cozy bed and a functioning kitchen with some basic supplies. A generator supplied electricity that fueled the small bathroom and shower.

They'd dropped Sam off at the main house as planned. That was when Quinn realized he didn't have the energy to get out of the vehicle. It was more than the physical toll. He didn't want to see anyone else right now. But he needed to get some basic supplies to ensure his Mistress' comfort at the cabin.

About the time he was about to kick himself in the ass to get it out of the car, Selene placed a quelling hand on his thigh, a nonverbal gesture to stay. As if his Mistress read his mind—and he guessed she'd had—she opened her car door. Before he could protest, she was gone. Jim and Moe fiddled with the radio, talking quietly. Obviously used to displays of vampire speed, they accepted her flash disappearance without comment. Less than a couple minutes later she was back, Quinn's overnight bag from his closet on the floorboards between them.

"Annette will have one of the hands drive a vehicle down to leave for you when you're ready to return. Sam is going to handle filling her in on the things she needs to know."

It was new, her caring for him. Well, maybe not. In a way, she'd been caring for him from the first, helping him with needs he hadn't known how to express. Right now, though, a numbness was settling on him, preferable to feeling or awareness, because whenever he reached for awareness, he saw too many bad things. Selene beaten beyond what anyone should endure... Laurent reaching for Quinn's cock, his breath on Quinn's jaw. Quinn's inability to prevent his own orgasm. Laurent's erection pressed firmly against Quinn's bare thigh, the vampire almost humping his leg while he came.

He shuddered. "Stop the car."

He barely made it out, retching out everything he expected he'd eaten for days. The violence of his convulsions, the agony they shot through him, drove him to his knees. When he surfaced, Selene was there, her hand on his head, stroking his hair. He felt her pain for him, for all of it. When he was all done, his head was down and he was trembling. He was better than this, stronger than this. He needed to get up. He should be able to do it, with the blood she'd given him.

Instead she helped him to his feet, kept a steadying arm around him until he was back in the car. "Keep going," she told the men in the front. "Get us where we need to go."

He closed his eyes, his hand clasped with hers, her free hand tracing circles over his knuckles as the SUV bumped along what was barely a cow path, but Butch's vehicles were outfitted for range driving.

When he realized the vehicle had stopped, he thought he might have spaced out into some weird limbo state. Not a doze, but a trance of not thinking, not doing, just existing. She helped him out again and thanked the drivers, assured them they didn't need anything further. Quinn rallied enough to move forward then, put his hand on the driver's open window. The two men had the kind of tanned, creased faces he'd known all his life, the steady eyes of ranch hands used to dealing with all sorts of unexpected things. Like him, these guys had discovered how big a spectrum that could mean with vampires.

"Thanks," Quinn said. "Thanks for everything."

They both nodded. "Would have been a much better day if that piece of shit had given us an excuse to shoot," Jim said.

"Yeah. Well, can't have everything."

Jim grinned. "Go get a shower." His glance shifted meaning-fully. "If any of us were going home with her, we'd make an effort to not look like shit."

Quinn couldn't pull off a smile, but he did well enough, because the driver gave him an understanding nod, and then they were pulling off.

Quinn turned to see Selene standing a few paces away. She was studying the cabin, the watering hole and the land stretching out behind. Her shoulders adjusted as she took a deep breath, tilted her head back, letting it rest on her shoulders.

He managed to move the few steps necessary to be close to her, standing at her back. He wanted to touch her, hold her, but he felt oddly constrained. "What are you doing?" he asked instead.

"Tasting freedom."

He nodded. He couldn't stand anymore. Literally. Before he could fight it, he'd dropped to his knees behind her. Just stayed that way, head bowed. He couldn't speak or do anything. He just wanted to be near her, like this, making it clear to the whole world what she was to him, even as he needed somehow, desperately, to ask her help to make him feel whole. Which made him ashamed of himself. She'd been through as much and worse, not just today but a lot of days before that, working for Laurent for all those years, dealing with her sire's murder, dealing with so much in sixty-plus years he couldn't comprehend. If he couldn't even survive today, what good was he to her?

"You're trying to make judgments that aren't yours to make." She'd pivoted, and her hand touched his brow, stroking through the strands of hair over it. "Dix was giving you a message, Quinn. Haven't you learned you slow-talking cowboys never say anything carelessly? This world is experienced day by day. Learned, day by day. We have survived this one, enough to have the pleasure of the night. My servant. My love," she added softly, her fingers stilling on his brow.

"I'm sorry, Mistress. Forgive me."

They were almost the same words she'd said to him, back when he'd tended to her at the bar, and he was somewhat horrified to know it was for the same reason. The moment he said them, he started to shake. His throat ached and burned even worse than his ass had earlier, and his heart swelled like it was going to explode.

She dropped down to one knee, her slim arms circling his shoulders, her cheek pressed against the side of his head. Despite her size, she had a firm, strong grip. He didn't care about the pressure against his tender skin. She was the force holding him together as he shuddered, as the images flashed through his head over and over again, overwhelming him.

"I love you, Quinn. I love you. I'm here."

The words spread through him with an encompassing warmth, cradling his heart and soothing his soul. He slid his arms around her awkwardly but with purpose, toppling back so he was sitting on his ass and he'd pulled her into his lap. He held her close as he could, pressing his face in her hair, tasting her skin. It wasn't sexual at all, not exactly. He wanted to rub himself all over her, let her scent and her touch take everything else away. Then he wanted to bury himself to the hilt in her, but not until he was clean. He had to get clean. Wipe away every trace of Laurent's filth.

"Yes, you do," she murmured, though there was a catch in her voice. "Come bathe with me."

There was enough of a moon on the water to give them light, to give him the pleasure of seeing it limn her skin. She undressed first, unpinning her hair so it fell down her back, the blonde strands silver in the moonlight. She wore only a simple dress that clung to her curves. She stripped it off, unhooked her bra, shimmied out of panties, and then came to him wearing only her shoes, some form of heeled slipper that protected her feet. She pushed him back down to the ground with a smile, one that didn't dilute the emotions in her gaze as she studied him. Turning, she gave him a mouthwatering view as she straddled his one leg, removed his boot, then did the other. When she faced him again, standing over him, he lifted a hand toward her, pausing to meet her gaze.

"You may touch me, Quinn," she said, that hitch in her voice again, her reaction to his waiting for the permission. Needing it.

Laying his fingertips on her bare thigh, he caressed her skin, sliding up to trace the crease between thigh and sex. He passed his touch lightly over her mound, again just for the pleasure of touching perfection. Of touching his Mistress.

"Jeans off," she said, her eyes luminous.

He obeyed, though he had to get up to do it and he winced in relief as the waistband's hold eased from his sensitive skin, as he peeled the denim off his ass. He was so tired. Heartsick and tired, but the quiet around them, her presence with him, all of it gave him hope that it would be all right. That Dix's words would be true, that each day was a new beginning, a new slate to do it right. Learn and grow. And love her even better than he had the day before.

"Oh Quinn." She reached up, cupped his jaw. Lifting up on her toes, she pressed her mouth to his, a slow, seeking kiss that had her leaning fully into his naked body. It inspired his formerly numb arms to slide around her, then tighten like a vise, as if he could hold her so close she'd be inside him. The kiss became deeper, needier, and she made a pleasurable sound in her throat. He felt her desire unfurl, felt his abused cock miraculously come to life, and not because of that goddamn ointment. It hardened against the press of her thighs, responding to what she demanded of him. Responding to *her*.

He'd damn well find the strength in the rest of his body to do what he wanted to do for her. For them both. "Take off your shoes," he muttered against her mouth.

"Giving orders," she teased gently, but she slipped out of them. Bending, he lifted her, and found he could do that. He could carry her, and the ability to do that much was a small, precious victory. Praying his knees wouldn't buckle and he didn't step on anything that would spear his foot and make him scream like a girl, he moved down to the watering hole.

The water still held the heat of the day, but was cool enough to be pleasurable. He slid into the depths, letting her legs go so she could twine them around his waist as he moved them toward the middle where it was deep enough it came up to his shoulders. He'd never wanted to immerse himself more.

*Take us both under, Quinn.*

He didn't need to be told twice. Dropping beneath the surface, he groaned with the pleasure of it as she threaded her fingers through his sweaty, bloodstained hair, cleansing it in the flow of the water.

When they surfaced, they floated together, a drifting waltz. She laid her head on his shoulder and he held her as she held him, no words needing to be said.

"Eventually we need to go use the shower," she whispered. "So I can clean my servant thoroughly. Inside and out."

The images she gave him made him flush. "I can do some of that myself."

"If your Mistress commanded you, then you would. But she wants to do it herself." Lifting herself up to kiss him again, she caught her fingers in his hair, pulling enough to elicit a more volatile reaction as she moved insistently against him. His cock nudged between her thighs, but she denied him, adjusting so it was trapped between them, her mound pressed firmly upon it to keep it restrained and stimulated at once.

He couldn't believe he was feeling desire. She'd said a third mark was always ready to rise to the occasion, that that was part of the perks of a vampire having a full servant, but it wasn't the physical capability that startled him. Or gave him warring feelings of shame and desire both, cramping his stomach again.

"Quinn." She had his face in her hands, was pinning him with that steely blue look. "What Laurent did to you, it was no more than a physical reaction. I know that. You know that. Don't give him that power over you. Did you give him your heart?"

"No. God no." He locked his gaze with hers. "My heart belongs only to you, Mistress. Only to you. Now and forever."

"Then don't let him steal your soul." She drew a breath. "There were times...I had to do things at his command. The first time, I felt as you do now. Ashamed, angry, helpless...unclean. But we endure. If we love and live, he has gained nothing from us but a moment of our lives. Butch was not far off on it. Laurent is hated and feared by everyone except perhaps Claudio." She threaded her fingers through his thick hair, wet and slicked back to his skull, then passed her touch over his jaw, his cheekbones, showing him in her mind her pleasure with his features, the beauty of his brown eyes, the strength of his body holding her. "You are a beautiful, brave, amazing man any woman would cherish. I've been fortunate enough to secure your loyalty, enough to bind you to me forever. Do you wish to serve your Mistress?"

"With everything I am," he said hoarsely.

"That was the message Butch was giving you also. Serve me, Quinn, and that service, the bond we share, will be more powerful than anything that comes against us. Before I came to Nightfall, I was running out of hope." Her eyes darkened, showing him the truth of it. "I thought I would be running from Laurent forever, which was just another form of bondage to him. Then I found After Hours and you."

Her lips twisted, at odds with the pain in her eyes, but he saw a fierceness in them as well. "You deserve every good thing, Quinn. But you got me instead. Tonight I realized I truly am all vampire now, because despite everything that happened, I won't give you up."

"I don't want you to," he said back, just as fierce. "You are every good thing to me."

She was right. Understanding that, immersing himself in that, the hold of the past horrible two days lessened. He took them back under again, another baptism, and once under, he put his mouth on hers, guided her legs back around him to roll them in the water, to take advantage of the movement to tease her with his ready cock, win a wiggle and squirm, a pinch that had him smiling against her lips as he brought them back up again. This time the smile felt more real, even if it was still an effort.

"To the shower," she said, and this time there was no doubt she meant right now.

He carried her to the cabin, dipping down to let her snag the overnight bag. Her gaze coursed over the clean, sparse furnishings, but they seemed to meet her approval. When he let her down, she took his hand and the bag and guided him to the shower. The water tank out here wasn't unlimited, but she didn't linger. That didn't mean she wasn't thorough. He found himself pushed up against the wall as she gently removed every bit of crusted blood with washcloth and soap.

"As we both get older, my blood will heal you faster, and your healing abilities will strengthen as well. But most of these are healing nicely."

"I just like hearing how we're going to get older." *Together.* He didn't mind if she used a scrub brush. As long as she was touching him, the discomfort of those wounds didn't matter at all.

Her lips brushed his shoulder. When she was done with all the areas Laurent had whipped, she turned her attention to cleaning other areas, just as thoroughly. Her fingers parted his buttocks, widening the opening between enough to employ the concentrated jet setting from the detachable shower head.

He was embarrassed, but another part of him felt a sense of relief so strong all he could do was dig his fingers into the wall as she washed whatever Laurent had used out of him. It no longer burned, but he was all too aware it made him slick. It had been lubrication for that vampire, not for his Mistress. She was having none of it. She washed him out, using her fingers with devilish intent, not only cleaning him but stimulating him to the point he was practically violating the wooden side of the shower stall.

"Mistress..."

"Yes, Quinn." Her voice was a satisfied purr. "Beg me for mercy."

"God...fuck." He couldn't think. He was going to come if she didn't stop. "Please, Mistress. I want...you."

"Then you better hold out. Hold every drop of that seed for my pussy."

Christ. She could force him over the edge, he knew it, but he fought with every ounce of control he had. When she finally took her fingers and the stimulating flow of the water away, he was hanging on by his fingernails.

"Turn around, reach up and hold the shower nozzle."

He wanted to turn around, hike her up under her arms, slam that petite body against the boards and fuck her like a mindless bull. But when he turned and met her gaze, he was already reaching up, his muscles tight with eagerness and his cock like a pile driver between his legs. She studied it, her tongue touching her lips. Fuck, he was going to come. His thighs trembled with the effort of holding back.

She cupped his ball sac, rolled it around in her palm while she let her other hand play in his chest hair, her nails scraping a nipple. Idly, she rubbed her thumb along the base of his cock.

"I could play with you all night like this, Quinn. Your body pleases me so much. I love all this hard muscle." Her hand drifted down over the ridges of his abdomen, then around to stroke a buttock, her fingers pushing in toward his rim again. He bucked toward her and she avoided the jut of his cock with a merciless chuckle, letting him go to give it a slap. Then she clamped her small fingers around it and squeezed, earning a groan from him. His fingers squeezed the shower nozzle to the point he was afraid he was going to pull it loose.

"Whose cock is this, Quinn?"

"Yours, Mistress."

"So no matter what Laurent made it do, you knew all along it belonged to me."

"Yes."

"So I'll punish you for spilling your seed without my express permission, and then it's over." Her gaze lifted up and met his, and all the things unsaid were there, the truth between them, waiting to scald him clean.

"Yes ma'am."

She nodded. Then she released him, and her fingers slid up his chest again. When she paused, he looked down.

Several of the strikes Laurent had given him with the cat were still prominent. A trio of staccato marks where he'd torn the flesh with those barbed tips, they looked like a blurred constellation on his flesh and seemed less resistant to the blood she'd given him to heal.

"He used the cat on you that he used on me," she said. "He hadn't cleaned it, had he?"

"No." Quinn's brow furrowed at her unreadable tone. "He said...the bastard said it still had your blood dried on it." His jaw clenched. "I wish Butch had killed him."

She kept looking at the marks, her fingers moving over them. "If a vampire wounds her servant, and then marks it with her own blood, it will create a scar. He didn't think of that." Her palm covered the marks, her fingers spreading over them protectively. Territorially. "These are my marks, Quinn. Marks that belong to me, like the man carrying them."

Shifting her attention to his arm, she let her fingers climb upward. She wasn't tall enough to reach her goal, but obeying the implicit command, he let go of the shower so she could clasp his wrist, bring the third mark she'd given him to her lips. As she cradled his hand against her breasts, her head bowed over it, she leaned up against him. He put his other arm around her, held tight.

"I love you, Mistress. Let me serve you. Please. I need to do this."

She lifted her head so they were eye to eye. "All right. Your punishment is to take me to bed, Quinn. Give me three climaxes before you allow your own release."

He'd do her one better than that. "I won't go over until you command it, no matter how many climaxes you want."

He scooped her up in his arms and left the shower. He wasn't waiting for them to dry off. Taking them to the bedroom on this level, no patience to go down to the cellar yet, he laid her wet body on the mattress and covered it with his own. Without any preamble, he spread her legs and thrust into her. He'd deliberately chosen the way it would be most difficult for him not to come, and God, she felt like heaven. He'd seen it in her mind, open to him now, that this was what she wanted first. Him on top of her, surrounding her, holding her, that rutting animal feel that she relished, knowing she was still in control.

She started to come within seconds, telling him how much she needed the feeling as well. He gritted his teeth, her pussy contracting on him. Laurent himself couldn't have devised a worse torment for him, but for her he'd suffer anything. Maybe third marks had better self-control, because he couldn't have imagined being able to hold out like this before that. As it was, it was a near thing, watching her body arch up, her wet breasts quivering, throat arched. He'd nourished himself from that throat to regain strength. She'd cared for him. He'd care for her now.

While she was still shuddering, he withdrew. Her nails raked his flesh, an irritable protest, but one he assuaged when he turned her over. Yes, she was strong enough to put him through walls, but he could also move her around like a pocket Venus. She gave him a narrow glance at the thought, but he promised her in his mind it would be worth it.

He slid some pillows under her to make her comfortable, and then he settled between her spread legs and went to work, mashing his cock hard against the bed to make it mind. In this position, he could not only slide his tongue over and around her flushed clit and swollen labia, but work his way up to her rim. Her cunt was still sensitive from her climax, but he knew how to get it worked up and juicy all over again. He concentrated on the delicate opening of her rectum, dipping his tongue inside as he kneaded her buttocks. Reaching under her, he gripped her breasts, started to massage and manipulate the nipples. He increased the strength of his grip to get rougher as she pushed her ass harder against his face, making little sexy noises that had his cock at painful rigidity.

"Quinn," she gasped, her hands gripping the sheets. He heard her tear the fabric as he moved back down and seized her clit gently in his teeth, rolling his tongue over it, worrying the tight bud. He outlined her labia, sipped, suckled, plunged and nipped endlessly, time having no meaning until the next climax hit her. She screamed out her pleasure, working herself against his face. He had plans for that third climax, but his Mistress overrode them. Still shuddering, she flipped to her back, reached for him, and rolled them right to the floor. He hit on the bottom with a thud that sang through sore muscles, but she was straddling him already, her fangs unsheathing and eyes glittering with preternatural intent. Gripping his cock in her small, strong fingers, she guided it into the blessed heat of her cunt. She was tight, so fucking tight, still slick and spasming from her climax.

She clamped her knees against his sides, put both hands over those marks on his chest and came to a full stop, eyes locked on his face. She began to squeeze him with her muscles inside, not allowing either of them any other type of movement, not until he lifted his hands, cradled her breasts, began to stroke the nipples. Her chin rose, her lips parting, wet as she licked them. She rolled her head back onto her shoulders at the sensation, hummed a litany of pleasurable noises. He kept doing it as she kept milking him inside. It was the most erotic thing he'd ever experienced, seeing her internalizing everything he was doing to her with a bare minimum of movement, as she revved herself up again using his body.

"I will never get enough of using your body, Quinn. I fucking love it." The feral gaze she swept over him told him she meant it. She looked like she wanted to devour him. Confirming it, she caught the wrist that held the third mark and brought it to her mouth, fingers overlapping that brand as she bit, tasting him. He groaned, aroused impossibly further at watching her sink her fangs into that mark of ownership. He was so fucking close, but he kept stroking her breasts with his free hand, loving the jut of her aroused nipples, the wet sucking noise her internal movements were causing between their bodies. He wanted to see her rise and fall, watch her breasts quiver with the movement, watch the flush of climax take her once more. Earn his reward and punishment both.

She could be merciful at times, his Mistress. She began to move like flowing water. Up and down, body undulating. When she released him, he moved his grip to her hips, brought her down harder, loving the expulsion of her sweet breath, the feminine grunt of pleasure.

"Quinn...now..."

She was coming, thrust over that edge once more, and she'd given him permission to fall right along with her. His cock needed no further encouragement. He fairly exploded, shoving up hard inside her, his body convulsing with the violence of it, bucking his ass up off the wooden floor, wanting to drive deeper, harder. He rolled them so he could do that, the male animal in him taking over in truth, wanting to show her he considered her his too, all his.

She allowed it and their cries tangled together, resounding off the walls as the orgasm captured both of them, taking them beyond pleasure into a realm of inexplicable bliss, a place where none of the rest mattered. Not the Laurents of the world or vampires, not domineering fathers or the endless white noise of the world. Nothing mattered but the love between them. Quinn saw heaven in a vampire's blue eyes, wide and glazed, full of him and what they created together.

"I think I have splinters in my ass."

Muffling a laugh against her shoulder, Quinn levered his weight up enough to look down at her. Her tousled blonde hair covered one eye, the other looking like a satisfied blue-eyed cat, amused with them both. Her expression was also soft with even more intent emotions, ones that made him bend, press a kiss to her shoulder. "Let me check."

He lifted her with effort up to the bed, eased her down to her stomach. Made a show of studying her heart-shaped bottom with great thoroughness, eliciting a chuckle from her. She tried to pinch his cock since he was standing by the bed, leaning over her. He evaded her, but bent to press other kisses on the white curves as she let out a little sigh.

"Come lie with me, Quinn."

He did, gathering her into his arms, holding her close, pressing more kisses on her temple, her closed eyes, and then finding her lips for a sweet, prolonged kiss that eased both of them, until he thought they'd melted into the bed. "I need to take us down to the cellar. It will be dawn soon."

"Soon," she murmured. Her arm tightened around him. "I trust you to care for me."

"And I trust you for the same." It was the first time he'd said such a thing to a woman in his life, he realized. Strangely, it didn't frighten him. Instead it felt absolutely right, as if he'd just been waiting for her all of his life.

Her lips curved.

"All right then. Take me downstairs so I can get some sleep. Caring for you is a lot of work, you know."

He snorted at that but complied. When he got them settled again, making sure the door was latched from inside so no one could inadvertently open it to let in daylight, she wanted him right back in the bed with her. He stretched out beside her, cradling her in his arms, marveling at the strength in her slim body. He was sure he'd never get enough of holding her. Of fucking her. Of loving her. Of serving her. Despite the intensity of the past few days, he was infused with a contentment he'd never thought to find. They lay there for a while, saying nothing, his fingers gliding up and down her arm, hers playing over his chest and abdomen.

"I've been thinking," she said at length, sounding half asleep.

"Three words that strike fear in my heart."

"I have faith in your courage." She tugged on his chest hair. He caught her hand, but he loved that he could be so relaxed with her, so at ease. And that she was the same way with him.

"I talked to Alan Jackson's tour manager last week," she continued.

"Of course you did." He grinned in the dark. "Should I be jealous?"

"Only if you misbehave. I want to elevate After Hours to a higher level. Bring in some name acts. Advertise beyond the county."

"Exactly why would any acts of that stature want to come here?"

"Jackson's manager said Alan and others like him look for some down time between the big concert halls where they can play what they like and hang out with their fans in a nonthreatening environment."

"Nonthreatening. Has he ever met you?"

She pinched him, and he yelped, chuckling. "So what did he say?"

"He said Alan might be able to do a one-night appearance at After Hours next month."

"You really are a wonder. Should I ask how you have such a close relationship with the man?"

"I—was able to do him a favor once. In New York." Her voice had a sudden, faraway sound to it that made Quinn think the less he knew about that the better.

"And now he's returning it," he guessed.

"Yes. We'll need to hire some extra help for that one night. Pay for some advertising."

He ran his knuckles down her cheek. "You're the manager. Whatever you decide."

Now it was her turn to laugh. "But I have a very demanding boss."

For the next few moments, they were both silent, then she let out a sigh that had a grumbling note to it. "Oh, and don't worry. I told him there'd be a cap on drinks for the band. You have to watch musicians, or they'll cost you more than they're worth."

He started to laugh.

"God, Mistress, I love you."

*Shut up and let me sleep.*

\*\*\*

**WANT MORE OF THE VAMPIRE QUEEN SERIES?**

Kaela has a secret. She's a strong female vampire—with a burning need to submit. She wants to belong to a Master, and definitely not a vampire Master, who will use the advantage for political or emotional domination.

A vampire's human servant is property, plaything, pawn—and the only living being a vampire can trust. Though she may own him, body, heart and soul, a human servant keeps a vampire from feeling alone in her dangerous, political world.

But what kind of human male will consent to becoming a vampire's servant, a 300-year life of utter servitude, to be her Master behind closed doors? An invitation to the mysterious pleasure island of Eden offers her the chance to discover her elusive hero...and indulge the bliss of surrender.

**CLICK HERE TO READ NOW**
**ELUSIVE HERO**

Reading this in print format?
Look for it at your favorite book vendor!

# ABOUT DESIREE HOLT

Desiree Holt's writing is flavored with the rich experiences of her life, including a long stretch in the music business representing every kind of artist, from country singer to heavy metal rock bands. For several years she also ran her own public relations agency, handling any client who interested her, many of whom might recognize themselves in the pages of her stories.

She is twice a finalist for an EPIC Award, and a nominee for a Romantic Times Reviewers Choice Award. Her release *Rodeo Heat* was the winner of the first 5 Heart Sweetheart of the Year Award at The Romance Studio, as well as a two-time CAPA Award-winner for best BDSM book of the year. She is a winner of the Virginia Romance Writers Holt Medallion. Romance Junkies said of her work: "Desiree Holt is the most amazing erotica author of our time, and each story is more fulfilling than the last."

*NOTE: The incomparable Desiree Holt left us in December 2022. Readers can still discover her wonderful stories at* Amazon *or your preferred book vendor. A list of her fan-favorite books and series follows this bio.*

**f** X

# ALSO BY DESIREE HOLT

# ABOUT JOEY W. HILL

Having penned over fifty acclaimed BDSM contemporary and paranormal titles, which includes six award-winning series, *Joey W. Hill* has been awarded the RT Book Reviews Career Achievement Award for Erotic Romance. A submissive herself, Hill brings authenticity to her intensely emotional love stories.

She is grateful for the support of a wonderful and enthusiastic readership, which allows her to live on her beloved Carolina coast with her even more beloved husband and menagerie of animals.

- On the Web: https://storywitch.com
- Twitter: https://twitter.com/JoeyWHill
- Facebook: https://facebook.com/JoeyWHillAuthor
- Facebook Fan Forum: https://facebook.com/groups/ JWHMembersOnly
- MeWe: https://mewe.com/i/joeywhill
- GoodReads: https://www.goodreads.com/author/show/ 103359.Joey_W_Hill
- BookBub: https://bookbub.com/authors/joey-w-hill
- Amazon: https://amazon.com/Joey-W-Hill/e/ B001JSCIW0

# ALSO BY JOEY W. HILL

Natural Law

Ice Queen

Mirror of My Soul

Mistress of Redemption

Rough Canvas

Branded Sanctuary

Divine Solace

Worth The Wait

Truly Helpless

In His Arms

Ignition Sequence

**Naughty Bits Series**

Naughty Bits

Naughty Wishes

**Vampire Queen Series**

Vampire Queen's Servant

Mark of the Vampire Queen

Vampire's Claim

Beloved Vampire

Vampire Mistress *(VQS: Club Atlantis)*

Vampire Trinity *(VQS: Club Atlantis)*

Vampire Instinct

Bound by the Vampire Queen

Taken by a Vampire

The Scientific Method

Nightfall

Elusive Hero

Night's Templar

Vampire's Soul

Vampire's Embrace

Vampire Master *(VQS: Club Atlantis)*

Vampire Guardian *(VQS: Club Atlantis)*

### ***Non-Series Titles***

Chance of a Lifetime

Choice of Masters

If Wishes Were Horses

Medusa's Heart

Make Her Dreams Come True

Snow Angel (short story)

Submissive Angel

Threads of Faith

Unrestrained

Virtual Reality